WARRIOR'S LINK

Kathleen Garnsey

Paperback-Press
an imprint of A & S Publishing
A & S Holmes, Inc.

ISBN: 1-945669-12-8
ISBN-13: 978-1-945669-12-5

DEDICATION

I would like to dedicate this book to my husband who has put up with all the time I have spent going to critique groups, writer's meetings, conferences, and now my talks and classes. Thank you for always being there for me.

PROLOGUE

O

The Legend

*Find the one who wears the chain
And keep her by your side,
For in her is your counterpart,
From which you cannot hide.*

*Travel into lands unknown,
Will bring your goal to sight,
Trust chosen few along the path,
To fortify your plight.*

*Let your heart forever guide,
In conscience and in deed,
Learn to trust the other one,
To strengthen virtue's lead.*

*Together you will travel far,
To destroy evil's source,
A magic battle to be won,
Will hasten victory's course.*

*Two flames converge as one,
As passion meets the test,
Unleashing nature's mystic power,
Atoning Ora's quest.*

Those who seek life's reward,
Must trace their steps again,
For only those with purest heart,
Perceive the souls of men.

The evil one will build a wall,
And flames must meet the test,
As duty falls before revenge,
Your heart can do no less.

Those in high positions know,
The pain you've had to bear,
Restore peace, end your quest,
For counterpart and heir.

CHAPTER ONE

"Dacton Rovarn," the High Council doyen began. "It has been decided that you *alone* shall investigate the dire situation on Ora. We feel our best warrior can accomplish what an army cannot."

Anticipation surged through every muscle in his body, and Dacton silently thanked the Council for the unequaled challenge. Thirty Protectors had lost their lives trying to stop Zotar Alucard, including his brother, Baleko. Now he had the opportunity to make Zotar pay with his blood for the lives he so callously destroyed.

The doyen's long black robe dusted the polished marmoreus stone floor as he paced behind the other twelve council members seated behind the ornately carved table. He knew the doyen was not finished with his instructions. The easy part was stating the assignment. The hard part would be the rules he was about to hear.

"We did not reach this decision easily." He paused and studied the protector before him. "Some High Council members believe you are too full of vengeance to carry out this mission. What do you say, Chief Rovarn?"

"The Protectorate, as always, has my complete loyalty." Dacton took a deep breath. "If the council wants Zotar Alucard destroyed, I will be happy to carry out that order." His response must have been wrong since the doyen cleared his throat and returned to his seat at the center of the half-moon table, the way he always did when he wanted to exude his powers.

"We need your solemn oath not to turn this mission into a personal vendetta to avenge your brother's death. We want Zotar brought here, before this council, *alive,* to stand trial. We intend to make him an example for anyone who thinks they can defy The Protectorate."

"As Chief Protector, I give my word." Dacton scanned from left to right, analyzing each council member. "Duty to The Protectorate has always been my first priority. The people of Ora are struggling for existence. The loss of my brother's life is inconsequential when compared to the greater picture."

The doyen nodded. "Zotar Alucard is a heinous being and must be captured. We are not ordering his death. *Is that clear?*"

Dacton had to work to hide his displeasure. As much as he wanted Zotar dead, he would accept the terms. At least he would be in control of the despicable man for a time. "I will follow the council's orders."

"You will leave immediately for Ora." The doyen stood and walked toward Dacton. "The Oran government has been infiltrated by Zotar's men, so trust no one. Your only contact will be our Watcher, Kolere. Although he has become High Priest, Kolere remains a trusted member of The Protectorate. You will meet Kolere outside the desert settlement of Destiny. Do *exactly* as Kolere instructs. He knows the planet, the people, and their history."

Dacton maintained his undaunted stance before the leaders of The Protectorate. Since the age of ten he had trained to be a Protector, the most elite force of warriors in the galaxy. Protectors were the ultimate peacekeepers of every planet in the galaxy, but as long as Zotar drew breath, there would never be peace.

"Your mission is two-fold. You must eradicate the reactor in the Peaks of Venda to stop the weather threat. Then you must capture Zotar and bring him here to stand trial. How you accomplish this will be between you and Kolere. Your survival will depend on following Kolere's instructions and your warrior's instinct."

The doyen placed his hand on Dacton's shoulder. "This will be a difficult mission, but The Council has faith you will succeed. May the Powers of the Universe be with you, Chief Rovarn." The doyen pulled his hand back and dug for something in his pocket.

Dacton accepted a briefing chip from the doyen's outstretched hand, saluted, then turned on his heel and marched in proud military form toward the exit. The guards on both sides of the double doors opened them to allow him to pass into the outer hall.

When the doors closed behind him and he was alone, he let out the breath he'd been holding. While he walked toward the supply office he prayed he could fulfill the mission in the manner the High Council demanded. The council was right, he wanted vengeance in the worst way. He did not lie to them, duty was always his first priority, but it would be difficult not to kill Zotar. He had always executed orders to the letter, but accidents did happen.

The walk to the main supply station seemed longer than usual. Maybe it was his desire to leave, maybe it was the challenge to find Zotar, whatever it was he'd never felt this anxious about a mission. He approached the supply office and saw his old friend, Mattra snap to attention behind the tall counter and raise his arm in a salute.

Dacton returned the gesture, then checked the appropriate boxes on the requisition card and handed it to Supply Officer Mattra, who inserted the card into the side slot of the computer. He watched the list appear on the screen.

"Your request promises a most interesting mission."

Dacton nodded, knowing his friend could not ask questions, any more than he could offer answers. It was the code of The Protectorate to maintain strict confidences, and every Protector respected the life and death rule.

When a man became a Protector he accepted demanding schedules, physical pain, and loneliness. Trained to be silent warriors, with duty as their mistress, there was little time for friends or family. Until mandatory retirement at forty annual-cycles, he was bound by the marriage ban. He could pleasure himself at the Protector's Retreat anytime he wanted to, but he hadn't been there since Baleko was killed. Being with a woman that didn't know him was no longer appealing. Dacton smiled at the impish grin on Mattra's round face. "Please have a two man explorer readied and equipped within the time-unit."

"Very well, Chief Rovarn." Mattra saluted, then began to enter codes into the computer.

Dacton noted Mattra's subtle smirk, his way of saying, "Be careful." Mattra and Baleko graduated from the academy together, they had been like brothers. He knew Mattra missed Baleko when they shared an all-knowing look before he turned and walked away.

Zotar's face flashed in Dacton's mind. Their sun-cycles in academy were spent as adversaries, not friends. Zotar's sister died in a fiery crash the same moon-cycle he was expelled for cheating, and Zotar blamed him. When the academy doors closed behind him, Zotar swore he would get even, but how many people would he kill before he accepted blame for his own actions?

When he arrived at his quarters he touched the print identifier and the door whooshed open. The moment he stepped inside, his mother's gentle voice emanated from the call-screen. She was still distraught over Baleko's recent death, and panicked whenever he, or Falcon left on a mission, but he had to tell her before she heard of his departure from the public updates. "Mother."

"From the sound of your voice, son, I fear you have some disturbing news."

"When did I become so transparent?"

"A mother just knows. Please, tell me what it is."

"I'm leaving within the time-unit on a mission."

His announcement immediately deepened the lines on her aging face. Her hair, more silver than an annual-cycle ago, accentuated the dark circles beneath her reddened eyes. He knew if his father were alive she wouldn't be so lonely and depressed. For eight annual-cycles he had assumed his father's responsibilities as head of the family, and he knew how much she counted on him.

"I hope you won't be gone long." Galina wiped a tear from her cheek.

If only he could ease her pain. Her gentle, worried tone said it all. Being the mother of three Protectors had made her worst fear a reality, and he knew in his heart she would be destroyed if she lost another son. "No longer than necessary." Tears rolled unchecked down his mother's ashen face as she nodded her understanding. "Trust in me. I worry about you. Please, take care of yourself, and listen to Falcon." He watched his mother wipe her tears and straighten to her most courageous posture. No words could fill the emptiness they both felt. "I will return. You must believe that."

"I'm sorry, Dacton. I don't mean to burden you with motherly concern. Do your duty, and do it well. Remember, I love you."

"I count on it, Mother." Dacton was grateful for the code of silence. She would fall apart if she knew he would be coming face to face with the man responsible for murdering her son. "Falcon will take good care of you." She tried hard to smile, and he did the same. "You know how he is."

"I certainly do. Your younger brother dotes over me far too much."

Dacton laughed. Falcon was two annual-cycles his junior and already a Captain in the Protectorate. If his free spirit didn't get in the way, he would make Commander before long. Falcon was the youngest, and most practical of the three Rovarn boys, and he knew his mother was in capable hands. "I must go now." He did not want to prolong the inevitable. "Good-bye, Mother."

"Farewell, son."

The screen faded to black. Dacton pulled on the protective silver flight suit and zipped it halfway. He hated the rustling sound the metallic fabric made when he moved, but it was a necessary safety regulation.

Fleet Cruiser IV would orbit close to Ora until he, or Kolere called for help. They would monitor the skies to insure against Zotar's escape, and to monitor all air traffic, but would stay out of Zotar's radar. He had been with his men, mopping up another of Zotar's disasters when the High Council summoned him back. With luck, that would be the last mess by the evil man he'd have to clean, but that depended on what destruction he found on Ora.

For hundreds of annual-cycles The Protectorate had kept only one Watcher on Ora. According to Universal Law, The Protectorate could not interfere with any planet unless peace and human welfare became jeopardized. Why, after all these annuals, had the people of Ora fallen prey to evil influence? The report from Kolere was definite, Zotar had found a way to control the weather, and he had gained a major influence in the government. Four council members were in Zotar's pocket, and that number would soon grow. Zotar would not stop until he gained total control, and with his underhanded, illegal power of persuasion, it would not take long. Greed was a universal language.

The overpowering desire to rip Zotar limb from limb surged through him, but he gave his oath to the council. If he killed Zotar he would dishonor his family, and would be tried, and possibly executed, for treason. He could not put his mother through such an ordeal. The Protectorate had unbending rules to make Protectors obey, and he'd known the rules since before he became a Protector—he'd learned from his father.

He would make his father and The Protectorate proud by completing this mission as ordered. Baleko would understand why he could not kill Zotar with his own hands. His brother had been an excellent Protector himself. To bring Zotar to justice would have to suffice. Hopefully he could follow orders when he came face to face with his sworn enemy. The man who brutally murdered his brother. The sacrifice would be worth it.

CHAPTER TWO

O

Ninety-seven time-units to Ora through black space, sprinkled with the glow of distant stars was a long trip alone in a small transport. He preferred travel on the larger main ship that would follow with his men three sun-cycles after he completed his mission.

It was past time he viewed the briefing chip through the craft's terminal, so he took the tiny chip from his pocket and placed it on the monitor. He watched all the updates Ora had been through, studied the faces of those involved in government. The rest of the vid held very little new information, but he finished watching it, then turned the screen off.

He punched in the course coordinates and reclined the pilot's seat. He thought about everything he'd just seen. Some of the information was sketchy, but he would clarify what was necessary when he met with Kolere. He closed his eyes and prepared to enter the required meditative sleep for the remaining time-units of flight. While he eased into the alpha state, his mind's eye focused on Zotar.

It seemed only a few annual-cycles since they'd both been in avid competition. The instructor at the academy always seemed to pit them against each other because of their equal physical abilities. The main difference between them was evident in Zotar's cold, piercing, yellow-green eyes. Zotar always was, and always would be, a man without a conscience. A man with no regard for life.

Right after Zotar left the academy, he became the most treacherous space pirate ever known to the Protectorate. Zotar had taken too many lives in his pursuit for power, and those lost souls screamed for vengeance. In reality, killing the intergalactic bandit would be too easy. Zotar needed to suffer the same torment he was famous for inflicting on his victims.

If he rested for a few time units he might be able to better concentrate on his mission. He had to rid his mind of revenge and replace those thoughts with duty. That would take work. Possibly sleep was the key.

* * * *

The beeper alarm alerted Dacton to resume manual control of the explorer. He grasped the gyrostabilizer with commanding determination and prepared for the jarring heat blast of Ora's atmosphere. He braced himself, but felt nothing. The chemicals Zotar had released into Ora's atmosphere had erased the entry heat. Anything that effected nature in that way had to be bad. Zotar did not care if he destroyed an entire planet and all its people as long as he got what he wanted.

Dacton directed his craft toward the Yolactra desert and reduced speed. An arid, rocky landscape came into view, barren and deserted, except for the domed city of Destiny on the horizon. A fitting name, he mused, as the computer located a concealed landing spot along the side of the mountain below. He cut to minimum speed, enacted the protective shields, and headed for the designated area.

He eased the craft as deeply as possible into a small cave, the interior walls reverberating while the power system shut down. He grabbed the two packs of supplies Mattra had filled and exited the ship. He tapped on his wrist-com and set the impenetrable safety lock.

Dacton headed out of the cave and braced for the heat. When he emerged into the late afternoon sun, he found the Yolactra desert pleasantly cool. Normally the temperature would have topped one-hundred-fifteen degrees, yet it was barely eighty—further verification of Zotar's diabolical plan. He shook his head and began his descent toward the valley below, careful to avoid the jutting, razor-sharp red rock formations. He hoped the rest of the planet would be more hospitable than the foreboding landscape of the desert.

When he reached the bottom of the peak he looked toward the horizon where the immense, glowing dome mixed with the setting sun and formed such a bright, orange glow, it was hard to look at. The unique oval architecture peaked his warrior's curiosity, but his instructions were to meet Kolere here outside the city.

Time-units passed slowly while he waited for Ora's third moon to rise. Dacton erected the camouflaged survival tent, then opened a ration packet for dinner. He chewed on the dehydrated bits of nourishment and wondered if he would ever find a taste for them. The energy they gave was necessary, but they had the consistency of his pilot's seat. Hearing a footstep, Dacton ducked behind a copious slab of stone, faze-pistol tightly in hand.

"Dacton? It's Kolere. Where are you?"

Dacton waited. Kolere bent to look in the tent. Why didn't the old man use the prearranged password? It could be a trap. Surreptitiously he approached the robed figure from behind. He pressed the fazer against the man's back, and circled the man's neck with his other arm.

"I have come for the Chief!"

Kolere croaked his reply again. Dacton released his hold and allowed the man to breathe again. He meant no harm, but he probably applied too much pressure out of habit. He stepped back and reminded himself to go easy on Kolere. "I'm sorry." He really felt bad for the man who still had not caught his breath. "Why didn't you say that in the beginning?"

"I'm a Priest and haven't practiced my spy techniques for over fifty annual-cycles. Please, forgive my ineptness."

Dacton watched the aged man adjust his brown robe under the braided silk sash. The priest was thin, a bit on the short side, but he had a kind face. "My sincere apologies for any harm to you." He smiled, and Kolere returned the gesture.

"I'm fine." Kolere looked up at Dacton. "I'm tougher than I look." He glanced about the campsite.

"Please, be seated in the tent. You'll find it a bit softer than the rocks." He helped Kolere ease his frail body onto the slightly cushioned floor of the small tent. He heard the man sigh heavily and wondered if the priest had become too soft in his position to be of use as a Watcher. If he could not remember to use a password, what else had he forgotten?

"I am getting too old for this sort of thing."

He sat on a rock just outside the opening and faced Kolere. He noticed something concealed beneath the old man's robe when he shifted uncomfortably. Had the conditions on the planet deteriorated to the point that even a man of the cloth was forced to carry a weapon? It didn't matter, the priest could not physically challenge him in battle. Dacton returned his faze-pistol to its holster and handed the priest a canteen.

After Kolere took a sip, he coughed and rubbed his throat. After another long drink, Kolere handed the container back to him. "Drink all you like, I have more."

"Thank you. The walk from the city was almost too much, not to mention your most apt display of a Protector's abilities." He stared at Dacton. "Even though the annual-cycles have taken their toll on my body, I do remember my training at the academy, and I apologize again for failing to remember proper procedure."

"I should have considered that myself. Now, for business. What has changed since you made the briefing chip?"

"The government has issued an order to kill Protectors on sight, as well as anyone helping a protector."

"Zotar." Hot, fiery anger welled in Dacton's chest, gripped his soul and tightened its hold each time Zotar's name was spoken. Revenge would be his. No one could know of his burning passion to have his hands around Zotar's throat, hearing him beg for his life.

"Cortain's brother, Septra, and his son, Regnar, of the legal faction, Father Makus of the religious faction, and Carron of the trade faction, are all loyal to Zotar." Kolere looked into Dacton's eyes. "Zotar convinced them that The Protectorate caused all of Ora's problems." Kolere shook his head. "Our fields and orchards are dying, the food supply won't last the winter. The people are having respiratory problems, jobs are scarce, and they are angry. The villages and settlements are not equipped for severe weather. The green clouds that form over the Peaks of Venda in the frigid zone dissipate slightly before they reach the desert, but you can feel the drastic effect. This brings me back to Septra and Regnar." Kolere sighed. "They have passed legislation restricting freedoms, making the people more reliant on the government."

"I see." Dacton shook his head in disgust. "Zotar is an advocate of divide and conquer. He has never waged an honorable fight." Kolere's revelations proved The Protectorate's directive to trust no one. Where Zotar was concerned he could have written that directive himself. "Has Cortain fallen prey?"

"No. Cortain is an honorable ruler who serves his people well, but Zotar has severely undermined his power. I've been close to Cortain and the Royal Family from the moment I arrived on this planet. Cortain doesn't trust Zotar, but his daughter does."

"Let me guess, Zotar is courting Cortain's daughter to insure himself a place in the government. Does that sum it up?" Dacton's stomach turned when Kolere nodded his head in miserable resignation.

"Zotar, the clever diplomat that he is, has worked with the council to pass mandates allowing off-worlders to hold government office. He has convinced them their survival depends on him. Zotar insists he's the only one that can save them and lead them into the future."

"Where do I find Zotar?"

"There's time enough to deal with him. First you must destroy the reactor before it's too late. Zotar claims his off-world connections can correct the weather problem, in return he's to be given an immediate council seat. You must remember, only you, I and The Protectorate know about the reactor. Ora does not have the technology at the moment to realize it exists." The priest rubbed his brow. "You must destroy the reactor immediately. That one reactor spews enough chemicals to destroy every plant and animal on ORA in less than a half-annual-cycle. For all we know, it could kill every man, woman and child as well. If the chemicals don't kill them, starvation will." Kolere cleared his throat. "Zotar could evade you for weeks, and we can't afford the time."

"I agree. Ora's welfare comes first." When Zotar created chaos and destruction, he never failed to use the most potent, and punishing methods possible. Confronting Zotar after he foiled his diabolical plan would add another degree of satisfaction to his assignment. He knew his enemy well, and defeat infuriated him. The angrier Zotar became, the more mistakes he would make.

"In less than thirty sun-cycles our winter season begins." Kolere placed his right hand over the emblem that hung from his neck to the center of his chest. "If this chemical release is not stopped, our people will not survive the season, and Ora will be destroyed. It will literally freeze to death."

"I can be in the Peaks of Venda within the time-unit."

The priest shook his head at him wearily. "Why not?"

"You cannot take the explorer. Zotar's ship is docked behind the capitol building in Sobrie. He monitors the sky, and you do not dare draw attention to your presence." Kolere took a deep breath. "You are the warrior in my vision, the chosen one."

"Vision? Chosen one? I..."

Kolere held up his hand. "Please, Dacton, open your mind and accept what I'm about to tell you, and hold judgment until I'm through. This mission will deal more with faith than fact. I realize you're a warrior, trained in logic and calculations, but I'm asking you to stretch the bounds of reality. There are powers necessary to your quest that you know nothing about."

"Explain, holy man." Dacton noted an esoteric change in the priest's countenance. "Explain now."

CHAPTER THREE

O

"Do you believe in the Powers of the Universe?"

"Of course." No matter what planet he had been on, the Powers of the Universe could not be disputed. Every man knew there was a force greater than himself, an all knowing perfection every soul must answer to. Every religion had their own name for the Powers of the Universe, but the most common was God.

"Good. That's a start. Now, are you familiar with our planet's early history?"

"I've done my research."

Kolere smiled. "I'm sure you have. However, what I'm about to tell you goes beyond history books. Hundreds of annual-cycles ago, Ora was in a perpetual state of war. The government overtaxed the people of Sobrie on the food they sold, and in turn, they overcharged to compensate. With such high crop prices, no one could buy them."

Dacton assumed a cross-legged position and listened intently even though he was familiar with the facts of Ora's earlier times.

"The planet slipped into a virtual state of starvation. So many people died that the government forced women into prearranged marriages, and all first born sons had to be relinquished at fourteen annual-cycles to serve in the Military Guard. Something had to be done, so a band of renegade warriors decided to overthrow the Oranian government.

"Aquila, high priest of the land, gave the sacred Delareme amulet to Mandor, Chief of the renegades, to protect him during battle. Mandor fastened the amulet onto his belt before he entered Sobrie. The golden stone, truly a gift from God, was the instrument of destruction for those bent on greed."

The priest had his full attention now that he'd added facts not on the history vids. "What could a stone do?"

"The stone alone did nothing, it took the woman who wore the Crystallinus chain around her wrist to create the magic. The knowledge of how the stone and the chain worked their magic belonged only to the warrior who wore it, and the woman who stood by his side."

"Who was the woman?"

"The king's daughter, Princess Luana. Mandor kidnapped her, thinking he could use her as a bargaining chip. Instead, he won her loyalty, as well as her heart."

Dacton shook his head. "What does an ancient story have to do with my mission?"

"According to legend, history is to be repeated, only this time you will be the warrior wearing the Delareme amulet."

Kolere reached under his robe and Dacton grabbed his arm so fast the old man gasped in surprise.

"Easy, my son. Please, I brought something for you."

When Dacton released his grip, Kolere pulled out a large leather belt with a buckle in the thinner section of the back, but it was the beautiful stone amulet secured in the wide, rounded middle area of the front that caught his eye. Kolere laid the heavy belt across his arms and he stared in amazement. The stone mesmerized him and it was hard to look away.

The rich, yellow stone, surrounded by a gold carved fulcrum, glowed in the moonlight. The artistically cut gem seemed to come alive. What mysterious power could lie within this masterpiece of nature that could cause destruction? There were forces beyond the imagination, with that he agreed, but he preferred to deal in the security of logic.

The Protectorate instructed him to obey all instructions from Kolere, but had the council heard this story? It was possible. The council was chosen for their ability to reason, for their unbiased appraisal, and their capacity to remain open minded. Could this legend just be an old man's delusion? Possibly, but he wasn't in a position to argue.

"Wear it proudly, Dacton." Kolere looked into Dacton's eyes. "I see your doubt and feel your reluctance. But I assure you that you are the chosen one this time. Please, put it on, then tell me how you feel."

What could it hurt? He put the belt around his waist, then secured the buckle behind his back. "The tan leather certainly stands out against my black uniform, and it seems strange to wear anything other than my official uniform.

"I understand that, but I want to know how you feel. Does it give you confidence? Make you feel invincible? Make you afraid? What? Tell me your feelings, Dacton."

"I'm not used to dealing with feelings. I'm Chief Protector. I deal in logic, rules, and laws."

"Dacton, underneath that uniform beats the heart of a man. A man born of flesh and blood, with a heart, and feelings. So, indulge an old man...please?"

"Very well. I was instructed by the High Council to do as you instructed, so I shall endeavor to tell you how I feel" He closed his eyes, took several deep breaths and let himself feel. A mixture of emotions assaulted him, and it seemed like his head was swimming with images.

"Dacton? Are you all right?"

He opened his eyes and found deep concern on Kolere's face. "I'm fine, I just...I...."

"Take your time. This is important."

"I know. It's just that there were so many feelings, but they weren't mine. It's as if the belt has a mind, or memory, of its own." He looked into Kolere's worried face. "I'm fine. The best way I can explain the feelings I had would be to say they were from others who have worn this belt."

"I see. The last time it was worn was before I was born. It has been kept in the secret church vault for longer than anyone knows. The last to wear the belt, as far as anyone knows, was Mandor."

"That could be true, but Kolere, I must know more about this legend you spoke of if I am to have faith in your words" Dacton assumed a cross-legged position, very aware of the stone in the belt. His fingers could not resist feeling the smooth texture of the amulet.

"I have translated the ancient words for you since they were written before the universal language of The Protectorate." Kolere reached in his pocket. "Study it until you feel the words in your heart."

Dacton took the taperal paper from Kolere's outstretched hand. He pulled a small, round light stone from his pocket and held it close to the thin, delicate paper. When he finished reading, he scratched his head and then looked up at Kolere. "What does it mean?"

"I have meditated on the meaning of the obsolescent words many times, but the answer remains unclear, however," Kolere straightened his legs, "I know where your counterpart is, and how to find her."

"You don't actually believe I must find some woman who wears a chain, and drag her with me, do you?"

"Yes, my son. Of that I am *certain*. This woman is an intricate part of your quest."

Dacton shook his head. The Protectorate obviously had no idea of what Kolere wanted him to do, or they never would have sworn him to obey the priest's orders. What Kolere asked was against the warrior's code. Women were never to be put in danger, yet he was being asked to do just that. "Where is this woman you speak of?"

"She is within the confines of the government compound in Sobrie."

"Who is she?"

Kolere shrugged his shoulders. "To know her identity would complicate your mission. Trust and faith, my son, that is the key."

Dacton suspected Kolere knew the identity of this woman, but his smug expression said it would be useless to pursue the issue. The old man was too caught up in this ancient mystery legend. Did it matter? Probably not, but since Kolere said history was to repeat itself, she must be King Cortain's daughter, which added greater risk. "How will I find her?"

"The amulet in your belt will hum softly when you first come near her."

Kolere may be convinced, but it would take more than his word to satisfy a Protector's logic. Visions and legends were the fancy of women and old men, but orders were orders and he was obligated to follow Kolere's instructions.

"Follow orders," were the words repeated over and over on the briefing chip. His proof, and the validity of Kolere's words, would come soon enough. If the amulet did not hum when he came close to this woman, he could disregard everything Kolere said and proceed with his own, more logical plan. He would humor Kolere, and the High Council, a bit longer. "And when I find her?"

"Take her with you and head north from Sobrie."

"Will she cooperate?"

"She has no knowledge of her true destiny."

Dacton shook his head. Kolere was asking him to kidnap a woman! What was all this nonsense about destiny and history repeating itself? History was recorded so mistakes of the past would not be repeated, yet that was exactly what Kolere wanted him to do. Never had he disobeyed a directive from The Protectorate, but at the moment, it was a serious consideration.

"In the morning I will bring you a novice's robe to wear on our journey. Disguised as one of my students you will be admitted into Sobrie without suspicion since they're expecting me tomorrow." Kolere smiled. "You will have to stoop since you're taller than Oranian men. Your identity as a Protector must be kept secret." Kolere laughed. "Besides, stooping will give you the humble look of a priest, rather than the proud arrogance of a warrior."

Dacton mocked a smile. "I will take that as a compliment, Holy Man." Kolere's shaky legs forced him to grab his arm while he tried to rise. He grasped his other arm and lifted him to a standing position.

"I'll return at dawn with what we need for our journey. Get some rest, my son, it may be your last for quite some time."

The elderly man pulled the hood of his robe over long, shaggy white hair, and began his trek back toward the dome that illuminated the desert floor with a subdued amber glow. The meeting with the priest played over in Dacton's mind. There was no logic in what Kolere had told him. Taking a woman along would slow his pace and interfere with capturing Zotar.

When the opportunity came to face Zotar, warrior to warrior, there could be no interference, especially from a woman. Destroying the reactor would be no problem, but traveling with a helpless princess would slow his pace. It was difficult to believe The Protectorate agreed with Kolere's outrageous instructions, but he gave them his word.

CHAPTER FOUR

O

The morning sun peaked the horizon and washed the hills in deep lavender hues that camouflaged inherent, implacable dangers. The unrelenting heat of the Yolactra desert was gone and Dacton zipped his flight jacket higher to ward off the crisp chill. If the scientists were correct, once the reactor was destroyed normal weather would be restored within half an annual-cycle, but some immediate results could be expected.

Hooves scraping against rocks alerted Dacton, and he ducked from sight. Instinctively he pulled his phase-pistol from the holder on his belt, and his finger curled tightly around the trigger. A faint mumbling in the distance slowly became audible, and it was clear the voice belonged to Kolere. He laughed to himself as he listened to Kolere sing, "I've come for the Chief, I've come for the Chief." Kolere was taking no chances this sun-cycle.

Dacton walked toward the priest. "Kolere, I see your training has not escaped your memory after all."

"Self-preservation, my son." He tossed Dacton a hooded robe. "You'd better put that on and start acting like a priest. Both our lives depend on it."

"Is coarse brown the only kind you have?" Kolere glared at him and he had to laugh. Dacton needed no reminding of the mission ahead, but he felt comforted by Kolere's seriousness. The Protectorate had assured him the priest knew his job, but too many annual-cycles on one planet could make a man soft to duty. He removed his flight jacket, stuffed it in the pack, then slid the robe over his head and tied the sash tightly about his waist.

Kolere smiled. "No, no. The sash is not a warrior's belt, it's to be worn loosely." He waited while Dacton fumbled with the rope tie. "That's better. Now, you must ride this mulus. Remember, you're a student priest, and you must always stay behind me."

"Are your novice priests treated like subservient women?"

"How can a student watch and learn if he is in front of his teacher?"

"There is logic in your theory." Dacton smiled. "What about my supplies?"

"Leave the bags behind that rock. I'll have them taken to the mine shack at the edge of the Boranian Mountains. They'll be safe here for now." Kolere watched Dacton hide the packs. "One more thing. As an apprentice, you are not allowed to speak."

Dacton nodded his compliance. As a warrior he had assumed many guises, but never a priest. Involving religion in a mission was taboo since most peace-keeping intervention was necessitated by religious wars. A Protector must follow orders, so until further notice, he was a silent, novice priest.

Dacton took the reins from Kolere then placed the palm of his hand on the mulus' forehead and closed his eyes.

"What are you doing?"

A wry glance sent Kolere into a long belly laugh. Funny indeed. Few knew of his ability to communicate with animals to secure their cooperation. There was much to gain by mutual participation between man and beast, a point he quit explaining early in his youth. Some abilities were best kept secret, especially ones no one else possessed. He swung his right leg over the animal's back and nudged him into a trot. Keeping his knees bent to prevent the toes of his boots from scraping the ground was no easy task. This would be a long ride.

Time-units passed slowly, and the journey turned into pure agony. Why couldn't priests ride taller animals? He could out-walk the mulus, of that he was sure. However, he humbled himself as an apprentice should. He studied Kolere's small, frail form, seated comfortably on the animal in front of him. The man was barely over five feet tall, and looked as though he could use a good meal of roasted porcinia with several hearty side dishes. Priests obviously did not share a warrior's passion for food. His stomach growled loudly.

The briefing chip had mentioned that Oranian men were smaller than his race, except for the Burly people who lived deep in the Boranian Mountains. They were recluses who stayed exclusively in their sector of the planet, fighting anyone who threatened their lifestyle. They had been at odds with the government for so long he doubted they could even remember what they were fighting about.

Sharp rocky landscape gave way to once fertile farmland, dotted with fruit trees, the leaves curled and brown. This agricultural belt was the most temperate on the planet, with a continuous growing season that never suffered freezing temperatures—until Zotar's interference.

Frostbite was evident on every species of plant they passed. More proof of Zotar's lack of concern for all living things. People, animals, plants, everything was expendable to him. Zotar left death and destruction everywhere he went. Dacton closed his eyes. Memories of tortured bodies strewn about a burning city, women half alive, whimpering how they had been savagely raped and beaten ate at his soul. Zotar and his men would never kill a woman after they raped and beat her. They wanted their victims to live so they could remember the vile acts in detail for the rest of their lives.

Why the High Council only wanted to prosecute Zotar rather than execute him still boggled his mind. Of course they hadn't mentioned what the punishment would be when they found him guilty. If death was the sentence, they wouldn't lack for volunteers to act as executioners, but they would have to fight *him* for the honor.

Dacton cursed under his breath. He'd given his word, and he'd stand by it, unless Zotar forced his hand in battle. The High Council would not condemn him for killing in self-defense. The thought brought a smile.

He surveyed the countryside and concentrated on farmers trying to salvage their crops in nearby fields, a sign they were approaching more civilized areas. When the road curved around a wall of trees Sobrie came into sight. He slumped forward, adjusted the hood, and set his mind in the proper mode to carry out the persona of a novice priest. Their arrival could not come soon enough to ease the searing cramps in his legs. Intuition said the short-legged mulus would be as happy as its rider to part company.

* * * *

"Father? Do you have a moment?" Talina entered her father's large, opulent office. When he turned to look at her she saw love light his face.

"For you, my dear, the most beautiful woman on the planet and the greatest joy in my life—always."

Her father was the kindest man she'd ever known, but he did exaggerate about her, yet she loved his attention. "I was worried about you. Samuel tells me you did not sleep at all last moon-cycle, and I doubt you have eaten."

"There's so much to do since the installation ceremony is three sun-cycles away." Cortain took his daughter's hand and led her to the couch where they sat facing each other. "Are you ready to take your place as

Ora's first woman Legatus?"

"I have never been more ready." Talina smiled. "I've never wanted anything more than to serve proudly by your side. Defending our people against The Protectorate, and the barbaric warriors they send, shall be my greatest pleasure."

"Pleasure? Shall we speak of pleasure for a moment?"

Talina felt warmth grow in her cheeks. "Father!"

"There's no need to be shy, my little princess. It's past time to choose a mate for you." Cortain took Talina's hand in his. "I've seen the gleam of excitement in your eyes. There's nothing wrong with wanting to consummate a life mating. I want you to be happy little one."

"I'm sure you'll choose well. I have complete trust in your selection." Talina lowered her gaze, unable to meet his. For some reason, discussing this subject with her father seemed too personal for comfort.

"Your mother and I shared a passion so special, so deep. I want nothing less for you." With the tip of his finger he raised her chin. "Yes, it is my duty as King to choose your life mate. But it would be best if we concurred about the man who will become part of our lives."

"That would be nice, but according to tradition, it's ultimately your choice, Father."

Cortain chuckled. "Tradition, ah yes. We must not break tradition. Therefore," he winked, "I have selected Zotar Alucard to escort you to the ceremony and subsequent banquet."

Talina could not stop the wide smile that Zotar's name created. He was handsome, the most virile off-worlder ever to have set foot on Ora. His company was charming, his wit refreshing, and his body, well, that was another matter entirely.

"I presume you're in agreement?"

"As always, Father, your choice is impeccable, but will our people approve?"

"Changing tradition and policy is always difficult, but you, my dear, have their love and respect. Who better to lead them toward a more enlightened future than you?"

"Nevertheless, being escorted by an off-worlder is truly pushing the limits. Maybe Carron should be my escort?" She had to ask him why he chose Zotar since she knew he did not trust the man. He never said it in words, but she knew him well enough to know what he thought at times. "Father, are you absolutely sure about Zotar?"

"Yes, because I know you care for him. Besides, the Council is enamored with him. You don't want to break tradition and go against my wishes, do you?"

He knew her too well. She did want Zotar by her side. No matter how much she fought the attraction, it was there. He stirred her woman's desires—desires she never dreamed possible. She loved his muscled body pressed against hers whey they kissed. Yes, he was her choice, and she was thankful her father chose him for her escort.

Since Zotar's arrival, tradition had been broken in nearly every aspect of their daily lives. Her people accepted this man willingly, so why shouldn't she? It was her duty to serve the people, and the current movement leaned against tradition. For that reason, the people of Ora would approve of her life-mating an off-worlder. She would simply fulfill her duties with the most attractive man she had ever seen by her side. It sounded perfect.

"Your choice is wise, Father." Talina smiled. She stood, kissed him on the cheek, then headed for the door. "I must work on my inaugural speech. As the first woman Legatus, I owe my people an eloquent acceptance."

"Yes, Princess. And I have a meeting with Kolere as soon as he arrives.

"I would love to see Kolere, it's been weeks since he was here."

"It will be arranged. Now go, write your speech!"

She all but danced out the door. She could not hide her happiness. She'd thought for sure her father's choice would be influenced by his suspicions about Zotar and Septra. Zotar caught her eye the moment he was introduced to her, and everyone in the room knew it. He'd attended the annual Grand Ball that moon-cycle she'd met him, and everyone in attendance whispered about them since Zotar danced every dance with her.

Her father commented to her more than once that she should share Zotar with the other women who seemed to be drooling over him, but thank the heavens, he would only dance with her. Zotar turned down every woman who approached him, which gave her the hope he was only interested in her. That was her deciding factor. Never had she attended such an event where a man only had eyes for her. It felt good, and she was thrilled to think of him next to her at every event. She had always been told if something was too perfect an ugly truth lived underneath.

In Zotar's case that outdated saying did not apply. He was perfect!

CHAPTER FIVE

O

"Kolere! Who have you brought with you?"

Dacton scoped out the guards at the front gate while they approached, but now that they noticed him and Kolere, he diligently kept his head lowered, knees up , and he maintained the humble, hunched over novice position.

"This is Janus, one of my students."

"You must have fed this one meat instead of nuts and berries."

Both guards laughed, and he knew they scrutinized him from head to foot. He'd like to jump off this mule and end their belittling, juvenile jokes, but he could not. This was the most difficult part of using a cover identity. No one quipped about his appearance when he marched up in his Protector's uniform. Although on Ora right now he'd be the main target on their shooting range.

"If it's all right, we must be on our way. Cortain DeAmarant awaits my arrival."

"Proceed. We don't want to keep our ruler waiting."

Kolere nudged his mulus and he did the same, careful to maintain his humble position. The sarcastic tone of the second guard conveyed little respect for Cortain. He knew Zotar had men under his influence on the council, and it appeared some of the guards as well. When it came to duplicity, none were more proficient.

How many men did Zotar control? Did the evil man have a plan to take over the government from the inside out? Or did he have a more diabolical plan in mind? The pleasure of placing Zotar in shackles and marching him before the High Council of The Protectorate might be as appealing as putting him in his grave.

Four guards at the entrance saluted Kolere, their cue to proceed.

Once inside the tall rock fence, he surveyed the area as best he could from beneath the droopy hood. Compared to the sophisticated technology of The Protectorate, the compound was primitive. Simple stone houses trimmed in wood lined the deserted street. The dwellings were built long ago for the employees of the government, but few used them because of their limited size.

Dacton prayed this was not a trap. His mission depended on his ability to remain incognito, which would be impossible if he were forced to defend himself. The empty streets had an eerie feel, but he let it go since the inhabitants were probably busy at work in the capitol building high on the hill.

When they turned the corner he let out the breath he'd unconsciously held. An open-air marketplace with vendors selling every kind of product imaginable, from food to fine jewelry, stretched before him. Sweet incense and perfume tickled his senses while throngs of shoppers crowded the aisles, laughing and talking. Did this go on every sun-cycle, or was it a periodic event? A minor detail not on the history vid.

They passed the last brightly colored awning, and Dacton caught a glimpse of the massive white palace atop the grassy hill that rose from the square to sit aloof in royal splendor. The sharp contrast of opalescent walls surrounded in plush green landscape made the town appear dismal in comparison. The separation of government and the working people had been clearly defined.

They rode so close to the ten-foot wall that his view of the palace was completely obstructed. Escaping over that barrier with a woman in tow would prove an interesting challenge. He'd need a damn good plan, along with a miracle, to elude capture. He probably did not have to worry about a captive, because he doubted the amulet would hum as Kolere predicted. He was a trained operative of The Protectorate, and not just any protector, he was Chief Protector, leader of the very elite warrior squad. His men would disown him if he told them the story about humming amulets and chains. If it did happen, he would then have to acknowledge that a woman would have a key role destroying Zotar. Never.

Mulus hooves clip-clopped on the stone street that led from the marketplace to the palace. The people appeared content with their simple lives, perfect prey for Zotar and his evil. With luck, he would be able to save Ora from the malfeasance of his archenemy.

Dacton lowered his head as they approached the gate. He had to push his warrior's thoughts aside and concentrate on being a humble priest. There would be time enough to plot Zotar's demise, and quiet the screaming unrest of Baleko's soul. The guards snapped to attention, saluted, and waved them through. Keeping his legs drawn high without the aid of stirrups had become a test of endurance. At least the hood concealed the pain of muscle strain he knew was evident on his face while he rode quietly behind Kolere past the open gate.

No one passed them on the road that gradually zigzagged up the incline toward the palace. The Protectorate knew how each administration functioned, but not every rule concerning the people. Their job was to keep peace, not to interfere with government policy, unless war was eminent.

Kolere dismounted and handed the reins to a young guard, Dacton followed suit. They climbed steps that ended before massive metal doors that reflected the setting sun, blinding them until two guards in dress uniform pulled them open. Kolere's sandals were silent on the polished floor, but he had to shuffle his feet so his boots didn't make a sound. The priest was right, he did indeed feel humble stooping and shuffling behind Kolere. At the end of a long hall of executive offices, Kolere stopped before an enormous desk which stood to the left of another, elaborate entrance.

"You're expected, Kolere, but only you."

"Wait over there, my son."

Kolere gestured to a plush, upholstered sofa that rested against the wall to his right. He seated himself and tried to look shorter and smaller than normal. The only way he could fool anyone was if they were not paying attention. If the palace were on alert as they should be, every guard would have a weapon and a protective suit. Ora's security was primitive at best, and they assumed they had no enemies except The Protectorate.

The opulent doors were opened from the inside, and Kolere disappeared into the darkness within. Grateful for the opportunity to rest his cramped leg muscles, he kept his head bowed and made sure the hood covered his hair and as much of his face as possible. The sound of approaching footsteps drew his attention, but he could not look up. From his humble position he ascertained the firm, long strides were male, and he detected a confidence in the loud steps, which indicated the man held some authority.

Gray porcinia skin boots halted at the desk. An eerie foreboding coursed through every vein in his body. Edging the tips of his black, domare hide boots under his robe he silently cursed. Every muscle tightened, and his Protector's instinct sensed what could not be true. The man behind the desk jumped to his feet. "The King will see you momentarily."

A faint grunt was the only response from the ominous visitor, yet there was something all too familiar about the tone. Dacton fought to keep his head lowered, certain that voice belonged to the one man he despised above all.

The door opened and Kolere's voice shattered his angry thoughts— thoughts that would have put him face to face with the enemy that stood an arms-length away.

"Come, my son," Kolere beckoned.

Dacton stood and shuffled as humbly as he could. He took a deep breath, stifled a groan, and followed Kolere out of the building through a back door. They followed a long stone walkway through a central garden, dense with mammoth loto ferns as a centerpiece, surrounded by a variety of flowering plants and perfectly manicured lawns. Tiny purple flowers lined the never-ending path with delicate, velvet-like petals that protected tiny nubs of pink in the center. Even the beauty couldn't dismiss the tension that still grasped every muscle in his body.

Escape over the towering walls would be virtually impossible with a hostage. Kolere had said little about this woman. Her physical condition could create problems. Even if she were fit, she could not scale a ten-foot wall. From Kolere's implication of the legend, she was Princess Talina DeAmarant. With his luck she would be prissy, overly pampered, and full of trouble. Who she was, or was not, mattered little. If the fates were on his side, the amulet would not hum and he could leave the woman here where she belonged.

Kolere turned to his left, walked another fifty yards, then opened a door and ushered Dacton inside, clicking the lock securely behind him.

"You can relax, Dacton." Kolere pulled the window shade down. "No one will bother us here. Cortain knows I am old, and that my journey necessitates a few time-units rest before I perform any duties."

Dacton arched his back, raised his arms above his head and stretched. Once he shook the cramps from his legs he paced the small bungalow. He enjoyed the freedom of his full height and wide stride. Kolere poured two glasses of sweet bacca wine and handed him a glass.

Kolere sank onto the softness of a small pallet in the corner. "Drink it my son, it will help those tense muscles of yours. For me, it eases the pain of old age."

After a small sip Dacton set the goblet on the table. He couldn't risk dulled senses. Entering Sobrie as a priest was the easy part, leaving would be difficult. "Kolere, you must change your mind about me abducting this woman."

"You seem to think it's my idea. The legend clearly states ..."

"Stop. I don't want to hear any more about this legend of yours. My job is to stop Zotar Alucard, not to become an actor in a role some ancient philosopher conjured up out of boredom!" Kolere's disheartened face penetrated deeper than a warrior's cutter. "Kolere, I know you're a man of conviction, and I'd never demean your beliefs, but it's difficult for me to be here when Zotar is..."

"Is setting a trap for you even as we speak. And if you're not prepared for him, he will destroy you. You must take my words as fact. If you don't, it will mean not only your death, but the death of the entire planet."

The priest was a wise man and knew more than he was telling. Was that the reason he had to follow the priest's orders? The Protectorate was always well informed, and only acted in the best interest of the parties involved. Like it or not, he had to listen to the old man.

"Zotar is destroying us by manipulating our weather and our government. He must be stopped. Trust me, Dacton. You *are* the chosen one, the salvation of Ora. I thought you understood this last moon-cycle when you accepted the warrior's belt." Kolere paused for a sip of wine. "You may not believe the Delareme amulet contains the power I spoke of, but guard it with your life, never let it go—and never let the enemy have it. Give it a chance. Isn't that the philosophy of a warrior?"

"Your wisdom is sound, Kolere. But you haven't explained the necessity of taking this woman along, especially if the amulet contains all the power I need."

"The amulet alone does not contain all the power. The prophecy is clear. You must find your counterpart and keep her by your side. This is a matter of trust. I know the Crystallinus chain about her wrist holds the key."

Dacton shook his head. So much depended upon faith in the unknown, a philosophy against his very nature. "What could her chain have to do with the amulet?"

"As I told you, all will be made clear to you in time."

Dacton didn't like the sound of Kolere's relaxed tone. "Don't let the wine go to your head, we have much to discuss." Dacton ran his fingers through his hair. "Do you know the layout of the grounds?"

"What do you want to know?"

"The easiest way to get the woman out of the compound."

"That I can help you with. In the back of the temple, you will find a door that opens to a staircase which leads to the cellarage. In the back corner there is a trap door located in the wall that gives access to a tunnel. Follow the tunnel and you will emerge into a fruit orchard outside the compound."

"Do the guards know of this tunnel?"

"No. Only a few high-priests. It was created to give a ruler his last rights without alerting anyone. If you turn left in the tunnel you will come up in the King's bedchamber, so keep a straight course."

"Good. Now what part of the compound is this woman in?"

"The second building to your right, the one on the far side of the courtyard from the temple."

"Tell me who this woman is, holy man."

Kolere smiled. "Patience seems very difficult for you."

"It has nothing to do with patience. I want the truth. As a member of The Protectorate you are sworn to give it to me."

"Your orders I well know, are to follow mine." Kolere smiled and took another sip of wine. "The council warned me you might fight this, however..."

"The High Council knows of this legend?"

"You seem surprised, my son." Lying down, Kolere inhaled deeply.

Never had Dacton felt betrayed by The Protectorate, but this! Kolere was asking him to break rules every warrior was sworn to uphold with his life, and apparently, The Protectorate concurred. His mind spun as he tried to sort truth from fiction, but it was impossible.

"As you know, and the legend confirms, the truth you seek lies within yourself."

Kolere's words rang true. Everything he had ever been taught came back to the same realization—a warrior should always listen to, and trust his instinct, which was that part, deep within himself, that provided just and honorable answers no matter what those around him might say.

The issue of concern at the moment was the mission, no matter how insane it appeared. Ora struggled for survival, and his duty was to preserve their peaceful way of life, even if it meant his own. Rules were broken at times, a fact no one ever discussed, but was reserved as a last resort. To face that choice when the assignment was barely underway presented a grave future indeed.

"I've arranged for your supplies to be left in an old deserted mine shack just over the last crest of hills before the Boranian Mountain Range. Once you reach that cabin, you should be safe from the Royal Trackers who will pursue you, and the woman, once they realize she is gone."

A loud knock on the door silenced both men.

Dacton stepped quietly into the personal room and closed the door while Kolere went to the front of the bungalow.

"Kolere? Are you all right?" the man called frantically.

Kolere opened the door and stared at the Royal Guard. "Yes, yes I'm fine."

"I heard voices and feared for your safety." The guard entered the building. "Zotar put all guards on alert. He warned of a possible invasion by The Protectorate, and our king agreed. They believe it is eminent."

"As you can see, I'm well. You must have heard me praying. Sorry if I alarmed you."

"Actually, King Cortain awaits your presence. I was sent to escort you to his chambers."

"Very well." Kolere coughed and cleared his throat. "May I have just a moment?" He stepped to the door of the lav, his hand on the knob.

"Of course. I'll wait outside."

"Thank you, my son."

Kolere stepped inside the lav once the door behind him closed.

Dacton leaned against the back wall. "What was that about an invasion by The Protectorate?"

"You're a smart man, so I'm sure you can guess."

"Zotar."

"Exactly. Now, King Cortain is waiting for me. I've told you everything you need to know. Now, go, find the woman. The future of our people rests on your shoulders."

Dacton stared into the depths of Kolere's eyes. His voice sounded desperate, but yet he still had a glimmer of hope in his tired plea. "I swear to do as you've asked. I will find her, and I will keep her safe. You have my word."

"That is all I ask." Kolere turned toward the door. "It will be dark very soon, which will make your escape easier." He opened the door and left the room.

The front door of the bungalow shut with a thud and Dacton quickly moved to the front window. He cautiously pushed at the side of the shade until the courtyard came into view. No guards were in sight, except the one escorting Kolere back to the main building. Darkness rapidly approached and large shadows slowly swallowed the landscape. No matter what he thought of the mission, it was time to move.

He slipped outside and locked the door behind him before he ran to the large tree half-way up the stone path. Dacton paused behind the cerric tree and scanned the grounds. Luckily, the courtyard was full of large plants and dark corners to conceal his movements. He visually located the marmoreus block building where Kolere claimed the woman could be found. He made his way across the walkway, over a section of lawn, and paused behind thick foliage by the glass enshrouded entrance.

While he waited for a pair of strolling guards in the distance to leave the area, he thought about the words uttered by the guard who had come for Kolere. It seemed Zotar had eased his way into control of the guards.

The first step necessary for a military coup against the government.

Two guards exited through the large glass doors, talking and laughing while they sauntered away from the building. With guards like these, he mused, it would indeed be an easy task for Zotar. These men had obviously never seen battle, and would not recognize a threat if they saw one. He waited impatiently for them to move on. Damn they were slow. Kolere's words about his impatience came to mind and he laughed to himself.

Footsteps turned to stomps and he worried the search party would find the passageway. He also heard them knock on walls and chatter to each other. All he could do was hope they did not find their hiding place.

CHAPTER SIX

O

The area was finally clear, so he entered the embellished stone edifice through the clear entry doors. A long hall with many doors of uniform size and color stretched before him, equally spaced, with nothing more than a small engraved gold placard to distinguish one from another. Names meant nothing, so it would be an exercise of trial and error.

Adrenaline pumped through his veins as he pushed open the first door. It appeared to be a conference room, dimly lit, and clearly empty. If this was an office building, why would the woman be here? Maybe she held a position of importance in the government. Or, perhaps she was a servant?

Kolere's information about the woman left much to the imagination. His instinct still said she was Princess Talina DeAmarant, but the mystery would be solved soon, one way or another. Taking a woman on this mission grated against his better judgment, but if she could help destroy Zotar's plan, it would be worth the risk. He shook his head and left the room.

Dacton covertly opened door after door, but found nothing. Could Kolere be wrong about which building this mystery woman was in? At the sound of approaching footsteps he bowed his head beneath the hood and resumed the uncomfortable position he'd maintained most of the sun-cycle.

"Priest! What are you doing in here?"

The guard's voice may have sounded demanding, but judging from the size of boots that stopped in front of him, he knew the struggle would be short. He kept his head low and played the mute priest in hopes the guard would cease his useless questions.

"You're a long way from the temple, Holy Man."

The rough fabric of the wide cuffed sleeve swayed when he pointed down the hall. The moment the guard looked away Dacton applied pressure to the sides of his neck until the man slumped unconscious in his arms. Such easy prey. He pulled the man into the closest empty room and shut the door. He hurried to the end of the hall and quickly turned left. He abruptly stopped when he found an eloquent atrium with a central waterfall that gently splashed a hypnotic rhythm. Lush ferns, mixed with exotic pink flowers, graced the planter that surrounded the colorfully lit display of water.

Behind the circular array of nature, Dacton noticed enormous double doors, plated in gold, with lion's head handles. It was the only place left to look. He walked to the door, but when his hand touched the gold, carved knobs, his amulet began to hum in a low-pitched tone. He released the handle and pulled back his hand. It stopped.

Drops of water danced on the small, round pool and created the only audible sound. Dacton shook his head and reached for the door a second time. A pleasant, melodic hum surrounded him, and gently echoed throughout the atrium. He glanced around to confirm his solitary presence in the foyer. There was no mistake, the amulet hummed.

Slowly he eased the door open and stepped inside. The melodic sounds grew in intensity. By the powers of the universe! The amulet performed as Kolere promised. This was the validation he'd looked for, but never expected to materialize. Kolere's legend may have passed the first test, but there was still much to confirm. With each step he took, the amulet hummed louder. He tried to muffle the sound with his hand, but the stone would not be silenced.

"Who's there?"

The woman had a delicate voice, but she sounded a bit startled. He walked to the fireplace, turned and faced the woman seated in the chair facing him, unprepared for the rapid beat of his heart the moment she looked into his eyes. She was indeed a princess, with regal features from the angelic golden locks around her face, to the tips of her blue-slippers. Her beauty mesmerized him. He'd been with many women in his life, but not one compared to the one who stood in front of him. He let out the breath he'd been holding and inhaled deeply.

The amulet became as quiet as when Kolere presented it to him, but his heart beat so hard in his chest he heard it in his ears. He could not keep his gaze off the blond beauty. It was as if his eyes had a mind of their own and they would not stop looking her up and down. He wished this moment could last forever, but her insistent voice pulled him out of his daze.

"Who are you?"

Her deep cobalt eyes pierced through him, and an all too familiar heat spread through his body. He swore silently, and reminded himself she was not one of the women The Protectorate supplied to warriors whenever they had the need, but his body confirmed what his mind fought to ignore. Words stuck in his throat.

At least he stood before her dressed as a priest, which kept her semi-calm. She would run for her life if she knew how his mind wandered to deeds forbidden to a man in the priesthood. He bowed his head, a mistake since he now had a perfect view of her firm breasts concealed under the pale-blue garment she wore.

Dacton mentally shook himself. The Warrior's Code was clear where female hostages were concerned, and that's exactly what she was. He silently cursed himself for allowing her to distract his thoughts. He swallowed hard, as if the act would push away the images she stirred. He needed to remember who he was, and the mission that lay before him.

When she laid her book on the table beside her, a crystal bracelet slipped below the loose, long sleeve of her gown, and he knew he'd found the woman who wears the chain. By the Gods! He never expected someone so stunningly magnificent. The garment trimmed in gold braid flowed softly about her womanly body. The folds of fabric could not hide the gentle curve of her hips, and he thanked his lucky stars the garment was not more revealing. If it were, he feared the tingling in his groin would grow to a more serious problem, one he could never satisfy with the fair Regia.

"What do you want?" She waited for an answer. "Of course. I forgot, novices aren't permitted to speak. But they are also not permitted in my private chambers."

The firelight danced on her softly-curled hair like the majestic beauty of a setting sun, glowing with life. There was a sovereign tilt to her chin, and her sensuously full, rose colored lips that begged to be kissed, parted slightly. There was no doubt in his mind, she was Princess Talina DeAmarant. She was far more beautiful in person than on the vids he'd watched.

Without taking his focus off her, he pulled up one side of his robe, and removed a small cylinder from the pocket of his uniform and took a step toward the fair-haired woman. When she tried to rise from the chair, he touched the top of the cylinder and a fine spray drifted over her face. She fell back onto the cushions and immediately went limp.

It always amazed him how fast somna worked. If only he could get to his destination as quickly and easily. He shook his head and returned the sprayer to his pocket. He hated to gag and tie her, but he had to follow protocol where an unwilling hostage was concerned. He removed the gag and ties from his pocket and leaned toward her. Slowly he slid the gag between her lips, then tied it behind her head, taking care not to include any of her long, shiny, blonde hair. Then he leaned her forward against him, guided her arms behind her and tied her wrists. It was necessary, he knew, but it did not seem right to tie up such a beautiful princess.

After her arms were secure, he leaned her back against the chair and moved his attention to her ankles. He had to pull her gown up to rest across her knees so he could tie her, but he was not prepared for such smooth, shapely legs. He should not notice, but they were there, right in front of his eyes. She'd probably kill him if she knew.

It had not taken her long to figure out he was not a priest. He wanted to tell her he'd never hurt her, and that he would protect her with his life. Instead, he lowered her gown, slipped his arms around her and lifted her from the chair, then hoisted her over his left shoulder. When he turned his head toward the door, his nose ran into her floral scented gown. Damn, she smelled good. He shook his head, tightened his grip and walked toward the exit.

He eased the door open a bit, and after a quick check of the area entered the foyer, closing the door behind him. The safest route would be the way he came. Half-way down the hall he took a moment to check on the guard he left in the empty office. Satisfied the man was still unconscious, he turned around and made his way to the main doors.

Two guards were headed straight for him. He could not out-run them with the woman on his shoulder, so he ducked into an empty conference room directly behind him. He managed to lock the door and reach the farthest corner of the room before they entered the building. He crouched behind a counter, but it was not tall enough to hide her over his shoulder, so he had to set the woman on the floor. She wiggled a bit when he eased her back against the wall. This was no time for her to wake up and blow their cover. He debated whether to give her another shot of somna. He reached in his pocket and pulled out the canister just when the guards shook the door.

The woman moaned and he wasted no time giving her another spray. He held his breath while she inhaled. Her body instantly fell lifeless, and he grabbed her before she tipped over and hit her head on the floor. He eased her down to a prone position since he may have to fight the guards if they entered. The men were talking just outside the door, but he could not discern their words. Then, as if being chased, they ran down the hall toward the foyer.

Only seconds remained before the guards discovered Talina was gone, and since she was Cortain's daughter, her disappearance would create total havoc. He rushed back to his captive, picked her up, hoisted her over his shoulder again, then hurried to the door. A quick check revealed an empty entryway so he quickly maneuvered out the door and ran through the manicured gardens, trampling the very flowers he'd admired a short time ago. A few yards away the temple entrance stood dark and foreboding, half-hidden beneath vines that hung over the entry covering, clinging to the tall columns on each side.

Lights suddenly flooded the complex, illuminating the area brighter than the height of a sun-cycle. Dacton heard voices behind him.

"Kill the intruder!"

Dacton cradled the woman in his arms in front of him to keep her safe. Ora's weapons were primitive, designed to kill rather than stun. Even if they did not recognize him as a Protector, he knew their orders. Laser shots flew on both sides of him, but all he could do was run for the safety of the temple. He thanked *"the powers that be"* that they were lousy shots, and kept on running in a zigzag formation.

He ran up the temple steps and grabbed the heavy metal door handles with his right hand. When he turned, the woman's legs hit the side of the door when he jerked it open. Damn. "Sorry." She would have at least one battle scar from this moon-cycle. Once inside the darkness blinded him. He coughed when the heavy scent of incense invaded his lungs. Why did they always have to burn that sickly-sweet stuff that always choked him? He focused on a row of candles along the foot of the podium at the front of the chapel, adjusted his captive a bit, then jogged up the aisle.

Face to face with the candles, he worked his way around them and toward the back wall. Behind the elaborate altar he set the woman down, then ran his hands over the wood-covered wall. He pushed here and there, while his fingers explored every niche and crack. Finally he felt a crack and followed it up, over and down. It had to be the secret door Kolere told him about. He pressed against the center and sighed when he heard a click. It was indeed the door, and it popped open.

Once inside the small space he pulled a luna-stone from his pocket and surveyed the area. The ample headroom would allow him to carry her over his shoulder. When he reached for the woman, he heard guards running in their direction. He hid the light-stone and pulled Talina to him, lifted her inside and secured the door. A moment later he heard several men stomping around the podium.

An authoritative voice rang clear above the others, and the man was not happy. He yelled at his men for losing sight of him, and their charge. They were all stunned by his disappearance. Good, that meant they did not know about the door. He waited for them to leave the podium area before he used the luna-stone to get his bearings. He stood, cradled the woman in his arms and turned in the tiny space. A thud echoed in the tunnel.

He had accidently bumped her head on a protruding side beam. "Sorry Regia." He was glad she was still unconscious and did not feel the injury, but he would have to check later to see if it were bleeding. He carefully made his way down the steep and creaky wood steps in front of him and emerged into the cellarage.

The air reeked of damp, moldy soil. He pressed his nose into the fabric of Talina's gown and inhaled deeply of her sweet, flowery fragrance. Her essence drifted into him like a mysterious cloud, a pleasant change to the reality around them. He proceeded to the back corner of the room, all too aware of firm breasts pressed against his back. He cursed himself for allowing his warrior's mind to wander, but any man in his position would have the same thoughts.

Dacton maneuvered around wooden kegs, old pews, broken chairs, and hundreds of annual-cycles worth of dust on top of stored items to reach the stone wall at the far end. He eased the woman's feet to the floor and guided her to a sitting position in the corner of the cellar, then turned his attention to an old wooden door.

Heavy footsteps on the floorboards above caused dust to filter down between the low support beams. He had to wait for the men to move on, but there was no time for finesse. He placed the light stone on top of a stack of boxes then grabbed the covering with both hands and pulled. Nails squeaked and the aged wood gave way to a warrior's strength. He put the door against the wall next to the opening so he could pull it back into place later. He grabbed the luna-stone and reached inside the earthen tunnel. "Thank you Kolere."

The passageway was not tall enough for him to carry the woman, which could prove to be quite a problem. First he had to get her inside and cover his tracks. He visually scanned the area for something to conceal the entrance once they were inside. There were stacks of curtains, chairs, books, and boxes. Then he spotted an old throne a few feet away. It was tall, wide, and even the bottom was boxed in solid. Perfect.

He stepped over to the throne, wrapped his hands around the arms, and lifted it off the floor. After a deep breath, he carried it closer to the opening. It was heavy, but he could lift it from inside the passageway. He picked up an old curtain, returned to the stairway, then laid it on the floor. He gently pulled it across the dirt and dust to smooth any tracks he left. It took effort to make it appear undisturbed, but he was satisfied it would fool anyone who entered the area.

The woman moaned behind him and he turned in time to see her blink a few times, but her eyes remained shut. It would not be long before the somna wore off and his troubles would begin. Since he could not carry her in the tunnel, it might be a good time for her to wake up. He slipped his hands under her armpits and pulled her to her feet, then over to the opening. Carefully, he set her down inside the passageway, far enough away that he'd be able to get back in. Now, to finish the cover-up.

He returned to the entryway, moved the throne as close as he could to the opening, then pulled the door into place. It was the best he could do.

When he turned to pick up the woman, she was gone. He started to raise the light-stone when he heard guards enter the cellar. If she thought she could escape him, she was sorely mistaken.

"Curse her!"

CHAPTER SEVEN

Dacton clasped the light stone firmly in his hand to conceal the light and hurried down the tunnel. Between the darkness and his inability to stand completely upright, his progress slowed. He had no idea where the woman had gone, but in the small space he'd surely trip over her. He felt his way along the earthen wall that seemed to go on forever. Then his hand found an opening to his left and he knew exactly where she had gone.

He entered the tunnel to his left and allowed the light-stone to shine down the short corridor. There she was, huddled at the end, sitting on the dirt floor, still tied and gagged. He could not believe she had managed to hop this far away so fast, or that the somna did not work well on her.

One glimpse of her vivid blue eyes told him everything he needed to know. Hatred burned in her fixed gaze, and if looks could kill, he'd be dead. That made him smile, which was a definite mistake. This was one Regia he could never turn his back on, yet he admired the spirit she proudly displayed.

"I will not hurt you." She stared in disbelief, and he had no way at this point to put her at ease. She remained in a frozen position, only her eyes darted around the small space. At least they were safe in the side tunnel for the moment. "I've never hurt a woman. Now, if you promise to cooperate, I'll remove the gag." He moved closer to her, reached behind her head, untied the scarf, then stuffed it in his pocket for possible later use.

"I'm supposed to believe you? A man who takes me from my home into the bowels of the earth?"

"Aah, she talks. And yes, you should believe me." She turned her head away from him, so he inched closer to her and turned her chin toward him with his finger. At first she fought him, then gave in and faced him. Tears streaked her face and guilt ripped through him. What had he done? How could he even begin to explain to her what he did not understand himself? "Please, just come with me and I won't hurt one pretty little hair on your head."

"I will stay right where I am, thank you."

"Don't make this difficult."

"Do you even know who I am?"

"Not exactly, but..."

"Then why must I go with you? What use can I be?"

"Excellent questions, and I understand your concerns. All I know is you're supposed to come with me. And we must go now."

"If I refuse, what will you do?"

"Smart woman. I will put you back to sleep."

"Fine. But you must un-tie my hands or I'll lose my balance."

"Your logic is good. Turn around." Dacton pulled the small, concealed cutter from his pocket, cut the nylon tie, then put the tool back.

"Thank you. Lead the way."

"Ladies first. Always." He gestured for her to walk back the way she'd come, and she followed his direction. When they reached the main tunnel, he pointed left and she walked in that direction. This was too easy—she was up to something, of that he was sure. Even the woman had to hunch forward to move along the path, and he enjoyed the sight of her nicely rounded derriere that swayed from side to side. Without notice she stopped, and he ran into the target of his admiration. "What's wrong?"

"The cobwebs are too thick here. I need something to move them."

"Fine." He inched past her, pulled a long cutter from his belt and used it to knock down the pesky, sticky webs. He reached behind him when he sensed her moving backwards and grabbed her hand. Her hand shook, and he knew she was scared. He slashed down a few thorn bushes which had made their home in the abandoned space.

The woman would run when she emerged, but she was no match for a Protector. If she was indeed Princess DeAmarant, she would not be in shape to run, since her main function was to look pretty and entertain diplomats at parties. According to the legend Kolere quoted, it didn't matter who she was, only that he keep her safe by his side.

The end of the underground passageway was finally before them, completely obstructed by dense brush. He pushed against the overgrowth, but it did not budge. All he got for his efforts were several large thorns stuck in his palm. He glanced at the woman behind him. "Can you hold this for a moment?" They both crouched down, but when he handed her the luna-stone their hands touched and he felt her fingers shake.

Dacton picked several thorns from his hand, yet he could not stop looking up at the beautiful face that watched his every move. He also kept glancing at the crystallinus chain around her wrist. What magical powers could live in something so delicate?

"You're bleeding."

Her voice pulled him back to reality. "I'm fine." He wiped the blood on his pants, drew his cutter and began to hack away at the miserable thorn bush. Nature had obviously kept this the most well guarded secret of all time. Based on the growth of the vines, no one had been through here in hundreds of annual-cycles. He glanced at the woman while she slowly sank down the stone wall to a sitting position. At least she could not escape without alerting him. He slipped the luna-stone in his pocket and began to hack away at the vegetation.

Thorns pressed into his palms and Dacton sucked in his lower lip, grateful the small thorns didn't stick to his calluses, cursing the larger ones that penetrated his skin while he continued to battle the lethal plant. Finally he cleared a space large enough for them to pass and he reached for her hand, not surprised at her evasive movement. He slipped his hands under her arms and pulled her to a standing position.

Moonlight filled the opening and highlighted her face. A loathing fire burned in her beautiful blue eyes, and contempt distorted her perfect face. He took the luna-stone from her and slipped it in his pocket. "Do not try to escape. I do not wish to harm you. Just follow my lead." He took her hand and led her out of the tunnel.

Dacton stopped in front of the opening and replaced the brush he'd hacked off so it would appear undisturbed. He took her hand and helped her through the thorny thicket. She cried out and he turned. When he glanced down he saw a large thorn in her ankle. He bent down and pulled it out. Her gown had been torn in several places. This was not working. He slipped one arm behind her, and another under her legs and lifted her up against his chest. She looked shocked. "You are not dressed properly for this." He could say more, but he left it at that.

The thicket seemed to go on forever, but he finally found himself outside the quagmire in a fruit orchard. He eased her down to a standing position, then bent and removed thorns that stuck him through his pants. While he was bent over, his captive made her move. When he stood he watched the filmy blue fabric of her gown dance on the moon-lit wind while she darted in and out of the trees. He smiled. She would have to run a might faster to escape, but it always took a little time for a hostage to learn the rules.

Her shimmery gown glowed, and she looked magical—and so very tempting. Dacton broke into a dead run and a few moments later he had her pinned to the ground. She struggled beneath his body and gasped for breath. "I'm sorry." He rolled her over, but he was not prepared for the hateful stare he found. She pursed her lips and squinted her eyes, and he knew she held back a bitter reply.

No woman, especially one as beautiful and innocent as this fair-haired maiden, should be treated like a captured animal. The tie he'd cut off had already left red marks on her wrists where she struggled against it. Another tie would cut through her skin. He stripped off the priest's robe he still had on and slipped the garment over her head. She pushed her arms through the armholes as if she were glad he put it on her. Maybe it would stop her shaking.

The distant howling of fanged semitas meant the first search party was leaving the compound. The semitas' large feline bodies were fast, but the Trackers had to keep them on distance-leashes or they would not only risk the woman's life, but theirs as well. Once a semita tasted blood they consumed their prey until every last piece of flesh was devoured and only bones remained.

When Dacton reached for her, she lifted a leg to kick him, but instead of making contact, the robe restricted her movement and she fell to the ground. He tried to hide his smile, but he could tell by her expression he'd been unsuccessful. He admired her pride and spirit. Unfortunately there was no time for such antics. "That was entertaining. Now let's go."

He pulled the woman to a standing position then hoisted her over his shoulder. There was little time before the vicious tracking beasts would close on their trail and he could make better time carrying her than fighting with her. He wanted to curse Kolere and his damned legend.

Grunts and groans from his captive, along with his boots striking the ground were all he heard in the still night. There was an occasional semita scream, but that was to be expected. He ducked low branches of frost-bitten fruit trees while he ran, his left arm tightly over the woman's thighs. Compared to a warrior she weighed next to nothing, but her endless squirming and muffled squeals wore thin on what little patience he had left. If he put her to sleep she would not be able to help keep balance.

They were now in neatly furrowed fields of vegetables, but he had to jump one irrigation ditch after another. There were dense scrub-trees in the distant foothills, and he pushed harder to reach their protection. The mission must succeed, but his main concern was the woman. She was his responsibility now. He would keep her safe, even though she would never forgive him for kidnapping her. An echoing semita howl set his mind back on course.

There had to be a river he could follow to conceal their tracks from the unrelenting animals. The rapid pace of his jog slowed her kicking, and she had become quiet, almost resigned. He knew her ribs and stomach would be sore for several sun-cycles, but he was running for his life, and the lives of everyone on the planet.

Field after field of wilted leaves crumbled beneath his feet. The extra weight of his captive slowed his pace and Dacton concentrated on controlling his breathing. Thundering hooves, mingled with haunting shrieks of the hungry semitas, spurred his pace and tested the limits of his endurance. Soft fields gave way to low branches and jutting rocks. Navigation was difficult, a good omen for him on foot, and a deterrent for his pursuers. The hoofed esroths the guards rode could not maneuver over rocks with a rider, but it would not slow the semitas. He had to find a river because the only thing that would stop them was losing their scent. He had to find water.

Through tightened shoulder muscles Dacton felt the woman go limp. As long as she fought he knew she was all right; now doubt crept into his mind. His own strength was taxed, surely she passed out from exhaustion, not injury. He pressed on over rough rocks and boulders. They both needed to rest, but not until he made sure his tracks would be lost by the search party.

When Dacton peaked the hill and slid down the back side of the steep, rocky slope, he found the answer to his prayers. With renewed strength he jumped into the nearly waist deep creek and followed the flow through the narrow canyon. When he reached a fork in the icy waters logic said go right where the way was clear, instead he waded deeper into the thick overhang of foliage to the left.

By the Gods! More of those damn sticker bushes. Did this planet have any friendly foliage? Thank the Powers of the Universe the woman wasn't awake for this new round of battering, and he could only hope the priest's robe kept the thorns off her. The creek narrowed and hungry thorns grabbed at their bodies, ripped clothes, and sought flesh. Dacton eased the woman from his shoulder and cradled her in his arms.

The brisk moon-cycle breeze and icy water couldn't mask the heat he felt from the woman in his arms. He had to be crazy. Part of him was freezing, and part was tingling with a warmth he couldn't deny. This was absurd. He didn't know her, yet his body responded to her in a way he could not explain. Her angelic face, so serene in the faint moonlight begged to be kissed. Dacton shook his head and wondered where that stray thought had come from. He was Chief Protector on a mission of dire importance, and how this woman looked was of no consequence. He sank deeper into the chilling flow that swiftly carried them down stream.

Long blonde hair clung to his arm when he slowly emerged from the water at a small clearing, the woman's body, still limp in his arms. Her skin had turned nearly as blue as her gown. He glanced around. With no map to follow, all he had was his warrior's intuition, and he could not afford to be wrong. Talina's survival depended on him.

The wailing of semitas had ceased some time ago, and Dacton desperately needed to catch his breath and check on Talina, if that was indeed her name. She lay still in his arms, her life in his hands. He glanced down at her unconscious form and cursed himself for her situation. She had been safe and warm in her own home, then he came along and put her in harm's way. Kolere had better be right about all this nonsense, because if he were wrong, he would answer to the Chief Protector, and he would show the priest no sympathy if Talina came to any harm.

He spotted the perfect alcove low in the side of the rocky cliff and made his way to it, then gently laid his captive on a large, flat, smooth rock and began to look for injuries beneath the tears in the priest's robe.

Her still form had an aura of childlike innocence, yet her womanly appeal was ever present beneath the wet thickness of the robe that had molded to her. The curve of her hips and the swell of her full breasts did nothing to quiet his already heavy breathing. Her face escaped the ordeal unscathed, a face that had burned itself into his memory from the instant he laid eyes on her.

When he picked up her hand to check her pulse, moonlight gleamed off the crystal links that encircled her delicate wrist. She was cold, but otherwise she appeared to be fine. What mysterious powers were hidden in that bracelet? He fingered the Delareme amulet at his waist. It was cold to the touch, yet he remembered the warmth that radiated from it when it hummed. Ancient legends and mystical secrets boggled his logical mind.

He leaned against the wall of the tiny concave hiding place and closed his eyes. His arms ached, but he wasn't sure if it were simply sore muscles, or from the feel of her body. Curse it all! Why did she stir such emotion? This was not the proper reaction for a Protector toward his captive, yet he couldn't deny the sensations she evoked each time he touched her. Did Kolere and The Protectorate know what they asked of him? He reminded himself he was a warrior, strong of mind and body, trained to handle any situation. After countless battles and dangerous missions he could certainly handle one small woman.

CHAPTER EIGHT

Talina DeAmarant blinked heavily several times before reality consumed her in its ugly grasp. Every rib in her body felt crushed, her stomach hurt unmercifully, and the pounding in her head made it difficult to focus. When she rested her hand on her stomach it met with rough, wet fabric. Where had this strange covering come from?

She sat up, her eyes darting from side to side, her mind reeling with every imaginable question. Where was she? How did she get here? Her memory was sketchy, but she remembered a very large man had taken her from her residence. She'd always been afraid of the dark, but here she was, in the dark, without supplies, and miles from any kind of trail.

The man who abducted her terrified her, but if he wanted her dead he could have killed her long ago and saved them both the aggravation of tromping through the wilderness. Since he obviously wanted her alive, he was her only hope for survival. Slowly she turned to look behind her.

Two black boots confirmed her fears. Talina closed her eyes and pondered the advisability of looking further. She sighed, opened her eyes and found tight black pants that did little to conceal strong muscular legs. Her perusal elevated to his thighs and lingered a bit too long on the unmistakable bulge of his manhood. Dear stars! She was reacting to the sight of him. Her heart beat faster and a blush crept from her cheeks to warm her entire body.

This stranger was her enemy and she needed to size him up as an opponent. That was all she was doing, or at least she tried to convince herself. A wide leather belt cinched his trim waist, and the unusual stone in the center beckoned for her touch. The amulet was as tempting as the man wearing it, but he was dangerous.

Her examination continued up a well-toned, contoured stomach to rest on wide, muscular shoulders. Curse him! He had carried her from her home on those shoulders, and she would make him pay. He was too big to be an Oranian, and too handsome to be one of the men who arrived with Zotar.

Dark stubble covered his firm, square jaw and cheeks. The bridge of his nose held a small battle scar which added to his masculine allure. Black hair, short around the front and sides fell wildly about his shoulders in back. She remembered how the firelight made his dark gray eyes seem warm and friendly, with a devilish twinkle. He hadn't scared her then, in fact she found herself curiously interested. Of course at first sight he masqueraded as a priest, but from all appearances, he was a warrior.

Dear stars, he was a Protector! The description fit perfectly; large muscular build, a commanding presence and always in control. But Zotar was wrong. Protectors weren't ugly monsters, at least not this Protector. In fact, she found him extremely attractive, more so than any man she'd seen. Such a thought was ridiculous. He was a ruthless killer, out to destroy her people. Or so she'd been told.

The Protectors had obviously begun their invasion, and she had to get back to the government compound to warn her father. As supreme ruler of Ora, he'd put a stop to this warrior's intrusion. A twinge of remorse shook her cold, shivering body at the thought of this man's execution. But all Protectors had to be killed if Ora were to survive.

Talina inched her aching body to the edge of the rock and searched for an avenue of escape. When she eased one leg over the side a loose rock fell and landed with an echoing thud upon the barren mountainside below. It was the only way, and she'd have to hurry if she wanted to escape, so she maneuvered her other leg over the side.

When she tried to push away she was grasped tightly about the waist from behind. "Let me go, you animal!"

"I've been called many things, woman, but never an animal."

"Only an animal would kidnap a woman from her home."

"I prefer to say I have borrowed you for a time."

His warm breath against her neck sent a shiver down her spine. "Borrowed me? What in the galaxy does that mean?"

"You are necessary to my quest." He pulled her toward the back of the shelter.

Talina inhaled, but the thin air did not fill her lungs and she struggled for breath. "What use could I possibly be to you?"

"You ask too many questions, woman."

"Quit calling me woman." She felt his gaze penetrate through her even in the darkness, and the heat of his hands on her waist only added to her need to flee. "And quit touching me." The corners of his lips turned slightly upward in a mocking smile that made her hate him even more.

"What shall I call you then?"

Dear stars, he didn't know who she was. Perhaps she could convince him he made a mistake and he would free her. "Just let me go, you fool. I can be of no use to you. I'm a mere servant in the royal quarters."

"I think not."

"How would you know?" The stubborn man picked up her hand and studied her palm.

"You show no signs of physical labor, Regia."

Talina swore under her breath when he smiled at her. Of course he had perfect teeth, and an air of arrogance she wanted to slap, even though his expression sent shivers through her body. She dismissed the reaction to the cold, but the part of her that was woman verified it was his touch, his piercing gaze and his raw masculine appeal. "Let go of me, you monster!" She jerked her hand from his.

"Monster, am I?"

"Yes. And if you don't release me this minute, I'll..."

"I admire your fight, Regia, but I suggest you cooperate."

"And if I don't?" She had to show him she would not give in to his intimidation.

"I will do what is necessary."

She did not want to know what he meant by that, nor did she plan to remain in his company long enough to find out. He might be bigger, but if Zotar was right, he was not more intelligent. Surely a woman with her education could outsmart this massive bulk of a man."You don't scare me." She prayed he would not view her defiance as a bluff, which was all she had. "My people will find me and destroy you in the process." He glared at her and she immediately realized her mistake. "What kind of a warrior are you anyway, hiding behind a woman?" Silence hung heavy between them."Let me go!"

The distant wail of semitas snapped the beast to attention. He grabbed the tie and reached for her arm. "You will not tie me again." Talina stood defiantly.

Rage coursed through her veins while he bound her wrists in front of her. He grabbed the end of the lengthy cord and pulled her to the edge of the rocky shelf. He grasped her waist, lifted her down off the rocky shelf until her feet hit the ground, but she found herself pressed against his body.

A strange sensation of longing and desire poured through her. That could not possibly be, she despised him, yet his embrace excited her, and she sensed he was holding her closer and longer than necessary. She reprimanded herself for reacting to him then thrust her knee into his groin to prove her words, happy to hear a muffled, painful groan.

"We can do this the easy way, or I will be forced to place you over my shoulder."

She answered his statement with a scowl.

"I presume you prefer to walk?"

Talina nodded. It was degrading to be carried around like a sack of holus being taken to market, not to mention painful. Her stomach and ribs could not take any more abuse, and she did not want to be touched by the dangerous Protector. No man treated the only daughter of Cortain DeAmarant like this. He pretended not to know who she was, but she sensed he knew.

He grasped the rope firmly and led the way up the rocky slope toward the summit. Talina held up the front of the priest's robe with both her bound hands, but she continued to stumble in order to keep up with his longer stride. She refused to show weakness, even though the sharp, jagged rocks cut like razors through her slippers. Damn him! She vowed revenge. Zotar was right, Protectors should be killed on sight. And upon her return, she would take great delight watching his punishment carried out.

The air chilled rapidly with each step toward the summit. Her body shivered uncontrollably. The man had no feelings, he just kept climbing and pulling harder on the rope that cut deeper into her wrists with each tug. Talina stumbled. Numb from the cold, her wet feet had lost the ability to function and signal pain.

If she suffered frostbite and couldn't walk he might decide to leave her behind, but alone she would surely die from exposure. She was trained for government service and eloquent social functions, not wilderness survival. Either way she was doomed. Her battered body could not take one more step. "Please stop!" The Protector turned and closed the space between them.

He was a breath away, glaring at her with dark, angry eyes. Talina shuddered when he lifted her off the ground and cradled her in his arms, arms with a superior strength that made her feel safe. She must be desperate, or delirious, to even have such a thought.

"J...J....ust leave me." Talina felt warm tears roll down her cheek.

"No Regia."

"P...P...Put me down wa...wa...warrior." Her teeth chattered so badly she could barely form words. For a brief moment she sensed a flame of compassion buried in his stern gaze.

"P...Please." Talina's aching head suddenly felt lighter. She took several fast breaths. The warriors face began to blur, then swirl. No longer able to fight, she gave in to the buzzing in her head and the blackness that swirled around her offering solace.

CHAPTER NINE

O

The woman went limp in his arms and her contorted expression of pain give way to the same angelic glow he'd seen before her capture. Damn it all! Being responsible for her agony touched a cord deep within his soul.

Inflicting pain on the enemy was second nature to a warrior. He'd killed many men in combat, and forced truth from others, but never on a woman. What the Protectorate forced him to do to this woman was unspeakable. Kolere and The Protectorate were responsible, he only followed orders, but for some reason, that excuse wasn't enough.

Guilt, a most unfamiliar feeling, tore through him. He knew he should have followed his warrior's instinct and refused to abduct her, even if severe consequences awaited. However, Kolere had been so sincere and convincing, and he was under orders. He focused on her long lashes, noticing her small, straight nose and high cheekbones. She was royalty, of that he had no doubt. Kolere knew who she was, and so did he. But right now all he could do was continue on, so he continued his climb up the mountain with Talina in his arms.

The rocky crest finally came into sight and the glow of Ora's three moons brightened the closer he came to the top. The raucous cries of semitas had once again disappeared, leaving only the wind and a faint cry from a venditare circling high above to breach the silence of the seemingly endless moon-cycle.

When he readjusted his hold on Talina the moonlight glistened off her slippers, but his attention was drawn to blood stains that had soaked through the thin, torn fabric. "Why didn't you tell me?" It did no good to scold the sleeping beauty in his arms.

The stubborn woman just complicated the mission even further. He would have to wait for her feet to heal, or continue to carry her. She was most pleasant to look at, a fact he enjoyed more than he should, but that would put them both under greater strain. Her body could not withstand further travel over his shoulder, but travel they must.

With a little luck he could secure an esroth or two. Riding would expedite travel time, especially since Kolere vetoed use of his ship, and he was right since Zotar had the skies of Ora well covered. However, he had a hunch Kolere had a hidden agenda with motives he had yet to discover.

When he scanned the side of the mountain he caught a glimmer of something about halfway down. It must be the metal roof of the mine shack Kolere promised, and none too soon. He tightened his grip on the woman in his arms and hurried down the rocky incline. The building was close enough now to see details, from the smokestack in the roof, to a cracked window and a small entry door.

At the door, he gently lowered Talina's legs to the ground, keeping one arm tightly around her. He opened the latch and nudged the door with his shoulder. It was stuck. He took a step back, lifted one leg and thrust his boot against the wooden obstruction. It flew open with a bang and dust played on faint beams of moonlight that penetrated the opening.

Dacton pulled the light-stone from his pocket, picked up the woman and entered the cabin. The sparse furnishings were crude, but included a cot, a small table, one chair, and a stone hearth in the center of the back wall. It would do. He carried his hostage to the cot, laid her down, then went back and closed the door.

When he turned the woman lay bathed in moonlight from the window above. Her perfect skin appeared to glow, and her shiny blond hair caressed her neck and shoulders. He stepped over to a small table and placed the light-stone in the center, then began to make a fire. Kolere had provided a good supply of wood, a flame clicker and paper. A blessing to be sure since there were no trees in sight.

It seemed the priest had thought of everything, or had he? He was sure the priest never considered what being alone with this beautiful woman meant. He wasn't worried about his reputation, but he knew what this could mean to hers. Somehow he doubted a high priest would consider temptations of the flesh, yet since he'd laid eyes on his delicate hostage, that's all he'd been able to think about.

Flames sprang to life, but he knew it would take a while to warm the room. He stood and turned, but found himself frozen in place. His gaze fell on the delicate rise and fall of Talina's breasts. She looked so peaceful, so tempting, and so off limits, but her wet clothes had to come off, and her feet needed tending.

Dacton cautiously approached the cot and grasped the bottom of the wet, tattered robe and gown. It all had to come off if her body were to warm to normal temperature. "This is for your own good." He knew she would not agree with him, but he did not want her to freeze to death, so he pulled the garments above her knees. The sound of a gasp made him look at her face, surprised to find her eyes wide open. She blinked hard several times, then let out a terrified scream that pierced the thin, metal walls.

"Get away from me, you monster!"

* * * *

Dacton took a step back. "Screaming is hard on the ears, Regia. Yours as well as mine."

"Since when are you concerned about me?" She pushed the wet cloth down to cover her legs from his probing scrutiny. He made her skin crawl, standing there all smug and superior, secure with his warrior's ability to keep her under his thumb.

She wiped dust particles from her lashes and focused on vague memories of the past few time-units. While her eyes were closed she mentally searched for something familiar to dispel the agonizing reality of the moment. Surely she'd wake up from this horrible dream and find herself in the comfort of her personal quarters, but that hope quickly vanished when the warrior touched her ankles and sent a most disquieting wave of sensation through her body.

She forced her eyes open and glared at the man who had not taken his gaze off her. He was tall, very muscular, and far too egotistical. The black uniform outlined his powerful physique which, under different circumstances, she might like to explore further. What drew her attention was the unusual stone in the center of a wide belt that cinched his trim waist. Why would he wear such an ornate belt on such a plain uniform? Protectors were rumored to be tenacious, but intuitively she knew the belt served a greater purpose than simple adornment.

First one shoe, then the other slipped from her foot. "What do you think you're doing?"

"I intend to care for you, whether you like it or not."

"Well, it's your fault I need medical attention." She raised to a sitting position. Her head spun and she thought her temples would explode, but she desperately fought to remain conscious. "I suppose you should tend my wounds since you're responsible for them."

"Your arrogance is showing, my lady."

"I am not *your* lady!"

Dacton smiled. "And I thank my lucky stars for that."

"You, you son of a..."

He shook his head and touched her lips with his index finger. "You try my patience, woman."

"I didn't ask to be here, nor do I want to be. So if I offend you, feel free to leave. And stop calling me *woman*. My name is Talina, and I'm..." She stopped short, realizing she had his full attention. Damn him! He'd invoked her temper and she'd let him. Even worse, she'd let her anger betray her. She had to fight him and be successful, which meant she had to stay one step ahead of him.

Now that he knew her name, he knew exactly who she was. How could she have let him enrage such a reaction? The very thought of him expanded the incessant pain in her head. She was a DeAmarant, and she would die to protect her royal heritage.

She swung her legs off the cot and stood, but the agony her feet inflicted forced her back down on the pallet. The man rushed to her side and helped her lie down, his touch gentle and caring. She cringed at her weakness. He was the enemy, a fact she could never forget.

"Enough of this foolishness, Regia."

Talina stared into the depths of steel gray eyes and searched for the concern she could have sworn he showed just a moment ago. He masked his feelings well.

"Stay there."

He pulled a polished cutter from his boot and held it up in the air. He did have a convincing way about him. Her body trembled, and her heart raced. Fear turned to panic when he lifted the priest's robe to her waist. "Stop!" she screamed, pushing the robe back down. Dear stars, he was going to rape her!

"Cooperate woman, or I'll tie your hands to this pallet."

"No!" The warrior dropped his knife, picked up the rope-sash and tied her wrists to the rough frame of the cot above her head.

"That's better. Now I can take care of you."

"May the Powers of the Universe damn you to Diabolus!"

"I'll be right back."

Tears of anger and helplessness formed as she fought the ties, but it was useless. If she lived through this, she vowed to make him pay with his life. Talina glared belligerently at him when he returned and sat on the pallet. She would not show weakness to her violator.

Silent screams raged within. Her virginity could only be lost on the marriage pallet, according to custom. If he took it from her, she prayed he would kill her so her father would not be shamed. It was possible her people would forgive her if she were raped, but she would never be able to face them again.

He turned and walked to the far corner by the door. What was he doing? Her head lifted to catch a glimpse of the warrior's firm buttocks and sinewy muscles when he squatted to retrieve something from the floor. Was this a strange preamble to rape, or had she been wrong? He reminded her of Zotar, whose body she avidly admired, yet there was an overpowering potency about this warrior that Zotar did not possess. How could that be? No. He was her enemy, and that's all there was to it. She was a fool to even give his seductive male body a second look. For all she knew he still intended to rape her— or worse.

A towel in one hand and bandages in the other, he stood at the end of the pallet. He wiped the blood from her feet with a gentle, comforting touch. Not at all what she'd expected. Was there more to the man than rugged brutality? Did he have a compassionate heart beneath that harsh exterior?

"Untie my hands." She met his eyes once again, this time without hate or fear. If he did possess any human qualities she must find a way to appeal to that side of him. "Please?"

"If you promise not to fight."

"I have no fight left."

Talina anxiously waited while he untied her, then rubbed her freed wrists, exhaustion slowing her movements. She watched him pick up the cutter and resume his position by her feet. He used the shiny blade to cut measured lengths of bandage, his delicate touch a sharp contrast to his crass attitude. Was he helping her out of kindness, or was he under orders of some kind? Either way she was grateful. The warmth from the fire and his stimulating caresses returned the feeling to her feet.

The royal daughter of Cortain DeAmarant wasn't allowed to socialize with men who showed an interest in her, unless her father appointed an escort for a public function. Life-mating for the future ruler of Ora was a political arrangement. It had been drilled into her from childhood that the proper mate was a necessity, and that when the time came, her father would select the perfect man for her needs. A man who had the respect of the people, and who fit well into government affairs.

There were no warriors on Ora, only palace guards. The guards were trained to fight, but none could match the powerful Protector at her feet. Being in his potent presence was frightening, but as the future leader of Ora, Talina knew she must think of her people above her own safety.

The Protectorate was a threat to her planet, and this Protector had to be a key part of their plan to destroy Ora. Why else would he have kidnapped her? She had to learn his secrets. The time had come to reevaluate the situation. She stood a better chance to gain valuable information if she pretended to be on his side. Then she could escape and tell her father what she'd learned. Yes. That was her best option, since fighting against his superior strength was useless. Besides, she could not run in bandaged feet.

She studied his strong face while he concentrated on her wounds. His square, firmly set jaw indicated stubborn power. Were Protectors the mindless fighters the war council proclaimed? Looking at the complex man at the foot of her pallet, she doubted the assessment.

It would take all the inner strength she possessed to convince him she was sympathetic to his plight—whatever it was. Possibly, his task was to deliver her to his superiors, making her a pawn to control her father. She'd never allow herself to be used to manipulate the government. First, she had to earn his trust to learn his intent.

"Thank you." For the first time she noticed a softness in his eyes that caught her off guard. "My feet feel better."

He nodded, then walked to the only chair and sat down. Talina scooted higher on the pallet, and used the wall as a backrest. She wished he'd stop staring and say something. "Are you going to kill me?"

"Only if you force me to. Now remove the robe so it can dry by the fire."

A chill stabbed her heart. His voice sounded cold and aloof. It seemed he had a wall around him to insulate any and all feelings. Was he truly a cold, uncaring, emotionless and controlled man? She bit back a heated reply. "You know, I'm only going to slow you down." She pulled the robe up over her head, careful not to take the thin gown with it, then handed it to him. "Why don't you leave me here and be on your way."

He stood, walked to Talina, grabbed the garment then hung it over the end of the makeshift mantle. "I wish I could."

Talina detected a glimmer of hesitation that said he wished he could. Was it possible duty weighed heavily on him? He shook his head with an infuriating arrogance. Nothing in her training had prepared her to deal with a warrior, but she needed to learn fast. It was doubtful he came alone, and any knowledge gained from him now would be invaluable later. If there was a later.

"What is your name warrior?"

"Dacton."

His name fit him, strong, masculine and powerful. "Why are you here?"

"Enough questions." He shook his head. "Rest. We'll be leaving soon."

Dacton wiggled his large form down in the chair until his head rested against the high back. She knew he couldn't be comfortable, but she wasn't about to suggest they share a pallet.

Her battered body screamed for relief so she scooted back down and rolled to her side, but she made sure she could keep her gaze on him at all times. She knew it would prove fatal to trust this man. Zotar warned her that Protectors were programmed to destroy, without feelings of remorse. Yet if he were void of emotion, would he have tended to her wounds? There might be a glimmer of hope for Dacton.

He crossed his large, muscular arms across the wide expanse of his chest and closed his steel gray eyes. Even relaxed he appeared threatening. His powerful torso strained against the form fitting shirt with each measured breath. A twinge of shame coursed through her. Her body reacted to his. Enemy or not, she could not deny the tremors of desire he inspired.

Such thoughts could not be allowed, but the memory of being cradled so protectively in his arms was inescapable. Admitting she enjoyed being held against his potent body seemed sinful, but she couldn't deny the intense magnetism she felt, even if it violated everything she stood for.

She blinked several times, but the weight of her eyelids made sleep impossible to fight. The lustful feelings that invaded her mind were a result of exhaustion. That had to be the reason. She should rest for a moment and regain her senses, but how could she? It was her responsibility to watch the enemy and report back. Ora was more important than sleep. More important than anything.

CHAPTER TEN

O

Dacton jerked upright in a cold sweat. Another moon-cycle without precious sleep. Only embers remained in the hearth, but Talina slept peacefully in the dim light of the luna-stone, and for that, he was grateful. The reprieve from cobalt eyes, filled with fear at the sight of him, would soon end.

The woman thought he was a rapist and a killer. She was only half-right. Until they were farther away from Protocol, he had to use fear to insure her compliance, even if she viewed him as a despicable monster. Fear was a far better alternative than physical restraints.

Kolere's insistence of Talina's importance was the cause of her abduction, yet The Protectorate's code of silence made answering her questions difficult. But some explanation would be necessary to elicit her help. He stood, stretched, then quietly slipped outside.

The cold chill of early morning always cleared his head. He gazed across the wide valley at the foot of the mountain. What lay waiting for them in the lush expanse of green grass and trees below? Could he protect her from all the hidden dangers they were sure to encounter? He knew he'd give his life to save hers.

The brush covered foothills below eased into distant forested mountains where destiny awaited them. Dacton envisioned the map he'd studied so many times and mentally set his course. He'd traveled north as instructed, so the tree covered peaks on the far horizon must be the mysterious Boranian Mountains. The stories pertaining to this sector of the planet did not paint a pretty picture, and the statisticians on Bronic could not dispute the hostility the inhabitants would provide.

The briefing chip also warned of large animals, but little was known about them since The Protectorate hadn't explored the planet in over a centrum. The challenge of facing unknown enemies fueled his warrior's spirit and tapped into his very essence.

The dangers ahead may have charged his senses, but it was no place to take Talina. She was his responsibility, and he'd guard her with his life. Not because he needed her for his quest, but because he had inadvertently placed this cultured, delicate Regia in harm's way.

The door creaked behind him, but he didn't turn. She would be full of questions he had no answers for.

"Where are we?"

Talina's sleepy voice made him smile. "Near the Boranian Mountains." Dacton turned, surprised by his body's reaction to the sweet face that searched his, even if she was dressed in that ugly priest's robe again. "Have you ever been here before?"

Talina shook her head slowly. "It's forbidden."

"If there's something I should know, you might want to tell me now." He watched her gaze across the valley, but a worried expression marred her delicate features. Deep in thought, her lips parted slightly, as if she wanted to warn him of some unknown danger. It had to be her choice, he wouldn't force a response, but he wished she'd close her mouth so the urge to kiss her would stop. "We'll be leaving soon." She shivered and shook her head.

"No. We can't go into those mountains."

Dacton fought his desire to pull her into his arms and warm her with the heat of his body, a heat she fueled with her presence. A foolish thought for a warrior. He had yet to gain her trust, which was all he could allow himself to take from her. A professional distance was necessary, and involvement with a captive went against all rules. To Talina, he was the enemy, and it was best he kept it that way.

"Can you walk?" She nodded, but he was not convinced. "We shall see about that."

Dacton returned to the cabin and retrieved the luna-stone and backpacks. A few moments later, he stepped outside to find Talina walking on the rocky slope. She was quite a sight with wild blond hair blowing in the breeze, and the sash tied tightly around a small waist. She paused and bloused the robe higher to avoid tripping over the tattered bottom, but still she stumbled several times before steadying herself against a rock.

When she took her next step, he noticed fresh blood seeping through her slippers. He threw a backpack over each shoulder and headed for Talina. She was about to hate him all over again, but it was for her own good. He scooped her into his arms, which immediately caused her to fight.

"Put me down!"

Her soft, feminine body curved nicely against his chest, and the sweet aroma of flowers still teased his nose each time her hair blew in the breeze. The golden locks that had glistened so silky and shiny before the fire when he first laid eyes on her were now tangled, which only added an exotic allure to her all too sensuous appearance.

"Do not persist in foolishness. Your feet are bleeding, and the terrain is rough. If you wish to walk you must wait till we reach the grass." She pursed her lips at him. It was all he could do to hide the smile that tugged at the corners of his lips. "My decision is final, Regia."

Dacton began his descent down the steep, rocky mountainside toward the valley below, Talina tightly in his grasp, her arms around his neck. Firm breasts rubbed his chest and caused fiery thoughts a seasoned warrior should never have.

Blood pumped hard through his veins and settled with a vengeance in his groin. Curse it all! He had always been in control when in the presence of a woman, even when they were sent for his pleasure. *He* decided when to be aroused, and when to take his satisfaction. Even if Talina wanted to make love, it would seriously jeopardize the mission.

To succeed in this endeavor he had to concentrate on the reason he was here, and push all romantic notions from his mind. Lives were at stake and he had given his solemn oath to The Protectorate to put an end to Zotar's reign of terror.

Zotar.

Only a clear mind and able body could defeat such an enemy, and defeat him he would. The Protectorate sent the right man. Nothing would stop his pursuit, and that included the most beautiful woman in the galaxy, the woman in his arms. The woman he could never let into his heart.

* * * *

Talina sighed in relief when Dacton set her down on the grassy riverbank. She removed what was left of her slippers, unwound the bandages, then eased her feet into the clear stream water. She wiggled her toes in the soothing flow, and thanked her lucky stars they were off the unrelenting mountain. The warming rays of the bright orange sun spread through her body, and she leaned her head back to ease the stiffness in her neck. She was on the ground now, but she still felt Dacton's rock hard body against hers, his arms wrapped tightly around her, and the sound of his heartbeat against her ear.

Dacton paced behind her. If the man were human, he would collapse in the grass and relax. Carrying her had to be a strain on him, but it hadn't slowed his pace, or his resolve to take her into the forbidden mountains. His physical performance seemed like the humanoid robots Zotar wanted the council to purchase.

Zotar had so many innovative ideas of how to increase Ora's technology. The council trusted him, but remained reluctant to accept all his ideas. She'd pleaded with her father many times to purchase interstellar ships so Ora could increase their trade and productivity. Now that Zotar was working with the council, they might be able to join the twenty-seventh centrum instead of maintaining the old ways.

The elders fought progress, refusing to join the Galaxy Commerce Board. They weren't even receptive to the few neighboring planets who had approached them with offers of trade. Computers and ships intimidated them, but they all knew change was in the wind.

Every new seat on the council would eventually be filled by people who agreed with progressive thinking. The arrival of Zotar several moon-cycles ago had evoked heated arguments among the council members. Zotar was a slick talker, and persuasive enough to help her implement the ground-breaking changes necessary for a better life on Ora.

Zotar was a dynamic speaker, self-assured, and extremely knowledgeable about the technology Ora so desperately needed. His interest in her people's progress was what drew her attention, and she'd thought him a most handsome man—until she laid eyes on Dacton. Zotar asked to be her escort for her installation banquet. Dear Gods, that event is next sun-cycle!

Talina fought back tears that burned at her lids. There was no way she could get back in time even if Dacton released her. She was to be the first woman Legatus Ora had ever had. She was proud to have such an honor. Now her cousin Regnar would be installed in her place and there would be nothing she could do to stop it.

"Let's make use of the water while we can."

Dacton rushed past her and walked toward the wide expanse of river to her left. She followed him, shocked to see him at the water's edge, shedding his clothes! He was already naked to his waist, and made short work of his boots, then pants and whatever he wore under them. He now stood with his backside toward her, completely naked, and he was quite a sight. In a flash he was in the water, but her mind could not erase the sight of him wearing nothing but his own skin. He was magnificent, his muscles well toned, ready for war, or any physical endeavor.

She used her hand to shield her eyes from the sun's reflection on the water so she could see beneath the surface. Of course she only wanted to see if he was all right since he'd disappeared under the surface; at least that's what she told herself. Then Dacton burst into view from under the sparkling water. Talina's eyes widened when he stood, exposing his naked body to just below his navel. Propriety required she turn her head, but his outstanding muscular frame magnetized her gaze.

His biceps flexed when he pushed back the thick mass of dark, wet hair from his face. Dear stars, he was exquisite. He turned and dove under again briefly exposing the tight, well-rounded buttocks she admired. Her heart pounded wildly, and she struggled to catch her breath. She could not let him know the effect his bronzed bare skin had on her. He was a dangerous man, her enemy, yet she ached for his touch.

Seeing his muscles glisten in the sunlight was proof positive he was the most impressive warrior she'd ever seen. No man on Ora could defeat him in battle, of that she was certain, although the beasts that inhabited the Boranian Mountains were another story. No one could survive an encounter with the gruesome pengore.

He swam closer, and her pulse raced faster than his strokes. An uninvited tingle assaulted her empty stomach when he beckoned for her. His outstretched arm bore the marks of her fingernails, along with thorn pricks and scratches too numerous to count.

"Join me." Dacton wiped water from his face with his hands. "You never know when another opportunity for a bath may come along."

Heat prickled her cheeks. How dare he suggest she get in the water with a naked warrior. The moral standards on his planet might allow such behavior, but she could never ignore her royal mandates. She shook her head.

"Suit yourself. It may be your only chance to bathe."

He swam out of sight, and she let out the breath she'd been holding. She remembered the hot, scented baths that were drawn for her each morning by her personal servant. But there were no luxuries here, only bitter reality. He could be right. Once they reached the mountains it would be too cold. If he didn't see her it couldn't be considered improper. Besides, who would see them out here in the middle of nowhere? Without delay she shed her clothing and dove in.

Cold water grabbed her body, nearly taking her breath away. She raked her fingers through tangled hair to remove the dirt, wishing Dacton could be removed as easily. She tipped her head back and relaxed in the slow, swirling current.

"Glad to see you changed your mind."

The deep voice sent shudders through her body. She jerked her head straight up and covered her breasts with her arms. He was behind her! Dear stars. She hadn't heard him sneak up, but she should have known he would never let her out of his sight. She swallowed hard and turned to face him, making sure only her head was above water, fearing he'd already seen too much.

"Feel better?"

"Yes." Devastated would be the appropriate answer, but she didn't dare let him know. Dacton had a knack for destroying every moral fiber in her body, which left her feeling defenseless in the process. He swam in a tight circle around her, which did not help.

"You're cold."

He wasn't touching her, yet every move he made disturbed her body which shook nervously. She wanted to distance herself, but he offered no escape. "Have you no decency?"

Dacton halted in front of her and looked to his left, then right. "I see no one to worry about."

"Leave me!"

"You give orders like royalty." He ducked below the surface and back up again. "What is your job in the palace?"

Talina turned her back in defense of his piercing gaze. "My job is of no import."

"I think it is."

"You assume too much."

Dacton moved close enough to trace the crystal bracelet with his finger. "I believe this makes you special."

Sparks flew up Talina's arm, and she eased herself away from his touch to stop the unwanted response. "That is a mere piece of jewelry." She turned in time to see a disbelieving expression melt into an amused grin that creased the corners of his mouth.

"I will learn your secrets, Talina. You cannot hide them from me forever."

His words struck terror in her heart. Her father's life, and the lives of her people, rested in her ability to fool this man. Kolere had placed the Crystallinus chain permanently around her wrist on her sixteenth birth-cycle. He said never to remove it, for magical powers lie within the translucent links. Kolere insisted the future would reveal a use for it, along with an honorable soul, pure of heart, someone she would work intimately with to protect her people.

Since the threat of invasion by the Protectorate, she had often wondered when this kindhearted person would appear. It had to be soon if she were to be of any use to her people. One warrior from the Protectorate had already landed, and possibly more. But what action could she take while in this Protector's custody?

Patience, she reminded herself. Kolere had never been wrong

concerning prophecy. If he said she would be an important factor in Ora's salvation, then she had faith it would come to pass as predicted. This strange quest Dacton was on might serve to put her in contact with the person Kolere assured her would come. Yes. She must maintain her faith, it was all she had left.

Dacton touched blond hair that floated above Talina's shoulders. "When will you realize I am not your enemy?"

"Never."

"You will in time."

The man was consumed with misplaced confidence. No amount of time would cause her to betray her father, or her people. Dacton would never hear from her lips more than she wanted him to know. She backed away and desperately swam toward shore.

CHAPTER ELEVEN

O

The bright sun on the water obstructed Dacton's view of the supple body that cut through the water and awakened his masculine desire to a fevered hardness he strained to suppress. She stopped and glanced back at him with a murderous look. It was his cue to leave, of that he was certain. By the Powers That Be, how he wanted to watch. He'd caught a brief glimpse of her firm breasts when she floated on her back, now he hungered to see her long legs, and that cute little derriere that teased him during their escape.

No woman had ever affected him this way, and he didn't like the invisible spell she seemed to weave over him. It was a sensation he had to ignore if this mission were to succeed. He was just keeping an eye on his captive, like any good warrior would. A self-imposed mind block was in order, but he needed enough quiet time alone to enact such a mental barrier.

He laughed. His logical mind could conjure up any excuse it wanted to for staring at a beautiful woman, but there was no denial of the physical effect she elicited. The thought of making love became so vivid it shocked him back to reality and he quickly swam to the hidden cove where he'd left his clothes.

As Chief Protector he considered himself above such infatuations. Many women had tried to seduce him to better their professional rank, and he'd always maintained complete control. Control was a warrior's most important tool, and he intended to recapture his. He took several deep breaths to regain his composure while he dressed.

Dacton fastened the warrior's belt in place and strode back to Talina, who was sitting on a fallen tree trunk, dressed in her blue and gold gown. Her stunning appearance tested his new resolve. He straddled the log and sat facing her, his emotions tucked neatly away.

"We must talk, Dacton."

"I'm listening."

"You need to know what's in those mountains you're so determined to climb." She raised her eyes to meet his. "The Boranians...Burly People as we call them, they kill intruders."

"How do you know this?"

"It doesn't matter how I know." She shook her head. " They aren't your only threat. There are pengores that will tear you limb from limb before eating your flesh down to your bones! I suggest you heed my warning if you value your life."

He tried to hide his skepticism from her stare, but how could he explain to her that he had to succeed no matter what dangers lay ahead? The future of Ora depended on him, The Protectorate depended on him, and whether Talina knew it or not, she depended on him. Excuses were not accepted, only results. "I stand warned." Dacton rubbed his sleeve across the face of the amulet, brushing off a bit of grass that marred its appearance. "Now, tell me where I may find these Burly People."

"You're a stubborn man, and a bit stupid I fear."

If Talina were a man there would be a fistfight right now, instead he took a deep breath. If she believed him incompetent he might be able to trick her into revealing the significance of the Crystallinus chain. Time was short and he was growing tired of the game. If any progress were to be made and confidences won, a bit of honesty was in order.

"Regia, I..."

"Stop calling me that you fool," she sniped.

"Ah, a stupid, stubborn fool, am I?" He swung his leg over the log, stood and paced in front of the insolent woman. Damn the rules. He had to explain. She could not betray him out here in the middle of nowhere. Besides, she seemed fearful of the Burly People, as she called them, so he doubted she would talk to them. He studied her inquisitive gaze.

"Where shall I start?" Dacton crossed his arms and continued, "You are Talina DeAmarant, daughter of King Cortain." He watched her complacent expression fade.

"You knew that when you kidnapped me. All I want to know is why? What use can I be to a Protector?"

So she knew his identity as well. It mattered not. She had nowhere to run, or the ability to get far even if she did slip away. At least his first guess about her identity proved correct. "What do you know about Protectors?"

"All I need to."

"Well then, how do you propose to save your planet from freezing?

Everything will be permanently destroyed if we do nothing."

"The weather is from God. There is little anyone can do."

"Natural weather, yes. But I'm speaking of the chemical alteration of the upper atmosphere to block the sun's warmth enough to create an ice age."

Talina stood and began to pace. "We will all be dead of old age before an ice-age grips the planet." Her back and forth movements picked up speed. "Why would you care what happens to our planet? Protectors only want to create war and destruction."

"Who told you this?" Dacton demanded.

"My father...and Zotar."

"Zotar? By the Gods woman, have you lost your mind! You can believe nothing that despicable fugitive says."

"I suppose I'm to believe you? A man who kidnapped me and put me through endless torture? I think not!"

When she walked beside him he stopped her by placing his hands on her shoulder, then pulled her tight to his body. "Torture?" Dacton laughed. "I am very capable of torture, and you would know if I'd used my techniques on you." He shook his head. "Believe what you must, but hear me well. You will accompany me on this quest and do as you're told."

He released her, donned the backpacks then scooped Talina up in his arms and began to walk. "If I waste steps you will spend much longer in my arms. Now, where do I find the Burly People?"

"East!"

* * * *

"Talina must be installed as Legatus. We must wait for her return." Cortain bowed his head.

"We believe," Septra gestured to the rest of the seated Council members, "the best interest of the Council will be served by Regnar's immediate appointment and installation. There is no need to upset the populace any further."

Zotar laughed to himself. It was always gratifying to see two brothers at odds. The only thing better would be if they had swords and physically battled it out. That he'd pay to watch. Instead they each wanted their child to be second in command. He hated to tell them it would not matter in the long run since he would ultimately be in charge, and there would be no Legatus.

Cortain shook his head. "You may be my brother, Septra, but I cannot allow your son to take a position he is not ready for." He turned his attention to the entire council. "Just allow me a little more time to find Talina. My Royal Guard assures me they're close to finding her."

Septra stood. "I fear emotion has dulled our King's judgment." Septra took a step back. "I ask the council's permission to include Zotar in this discussion."

Zotar tried not to let his smile show. He needed to proceed with caution, but the council, and their so-called leader, were falling right into his hands. Cortain knew if he denied Septra's request it would make matters worse. "Permission granted."

His diabolical plan to take over the government of Ora just received a push. It was great to see Cortain's authority being questioned daily, and even better when the votes taken by the council went against him time after time. The real fun was that no one realized *he* was pulling the strings. Zotar cleared his throat. "I am honored to be of service to the council."

"As you know," Septra began, "Talina has been abducted. We would like your input since you're familiar with The Protectorate and their warriors."

Zotar repressed his pleased demeanor. Fools! Talina's kidnapping changed a few things, but nothing he couldn't use to his advantage. She was a spoiled bitch. A bitch he planned to life-mate in order to cement the Ora takeover. When she was found, he would still use her for power, and it would be pleasurable. Her beauty would make her a most appealing sex slave, and he would revel in her enslavement. But for now, he would further his advancements politically by manipulating the members already loyal to him.

"The Protectorate obviously wants to use Princess Talina as a pawn." Zotar stood. "I believe she will be safe for a time. They will send specific demands for her release, and we must be ready for them. We must also prepare a plan of our own."

Cortain cleared his throat. "What do you suggest, Zotar?"

The concern in the King's voice was touching indeed, but everyone on Ora knew he'd do anything for his daughter. This had actually turned into the perfect plan. He could further turn the council against The Protectorate and milk them for everything they had. He would find Talina and keep all the ransom for himself.

"You have already sent your Royal Guard to find her, but they are not battle trained in the same manner as Protectors. I suggest the council put me in charge of creating a fighting force, using the existing guards, as well as volunteers from the general public. I will begin with the remaining Royal Guards so they can teach the others. I fear Talina's disappearance is just the beginning. We must be prepared for an invasion."

Everyone in the room gave him a nod of approval. It appeared the Council members would accept a war against The Protectorate. The only holdout was Cortain. He'd spoken with the old King before and he despised the very thought of wasting lives and destroying land for power. But right now he knew his precious daughter's life depended on his decision, and he was smart enough to know it might take an army to get her back.

Cortain held up his right hand. "Agreed."

"When do you expect this invasion to take place?" Septra asked.

Zotar walked around the table so he could face the entire council. "It is most likely underway. We don't know how many warriors were involved in taking Princess Talina, but be assured, more Protectors are on their way."

Septra nodded. "Your advice is sound."

"Ruler Cortain, do I have your permission to do anything necessary to stop The Protectorate and bring your daughter home?" Zotar watched Cortain shake his head. Cortain knew he'd lose power, but he had no choice under the circumstances."

"We will take your suggestion under advisement, Zotar, but The Council must take a vote and pass an addendum. You will be informed of our decision."

"Thank you," Zotar politely bowed, turned on his heel and marched out of the chamber to allow The Council to deliberate. They'd give him an army, they had no choice. Three of the highest ranking members were in his pocket, and they held substantial influence over the others. Ora would soon be his.

Best of all, he would get his opportunity to finish off the Rovarns, and Dacton would be the next to die. Killing Baleko had been child's play, but what better way to enrage Dacton. The bastard would soon learn how he'd felt when Julya, his only sister died. Revenge would be sweet, and he planned to make Dacton wish he'd never been born!

* * * *

The time-units wore on and dark shadows now shrouded the path. The sun-cycle was near completion and they had yet to find signs of life. Dacton was right, supplies and transportation was a must if they were to survive in the cold, upper regions. If the Boranians were uncooperative he'd probably steal what they needed. She did not know Dacton well, but she suspected he would let nothing stand in his way.

Dacton stopped abruptly, grabbed her hand, and pulled her into a stand of short willowy trees. He forced her down by placing his hands on her shoulders. His "warrior's instinct" was on full alert. "What's wrong?"

He covered her mouth with his hand. "Say nothing and stay here. It's imperative you stay right here."

Talina nodded her compliance. Dacton was her only protection against the Burly people. She watched Dacton disappear from sight and silently prayed for his safety. Her kidnapper might be an enemy of the government, but the Boranian people viewed them both as trespassers.

The Burly people recognized no law, and took no prisoners. The silence around her was deafening. Where had he disappeared to? Was he lying helpless in a trap, never to return? The thought sent a shiver up her spine. It felt strange to worry about the warrior she wanted to kill, but her life now rested in his hands.

Her pulse raced when the brush in the distance rustled. Three men carrying bows and spears leaped into the clearing. They stood taller than Dacton, but it was hard to tell due to their wild hair. They were visibly strong, and would prove a true test of Dacton's strength. Talina knew little of the Protector's ability or bravery when it came to a confrontation, but she was about to watch the ultimate test.

Blood throbbed uncontrolled in her veins. Dear stars! She hugged the tree when the men glanced briefly in her direction. Where was Dacton? The sound of whooshing arrows cut through the air, stilling her rapidly beating heart. She peeked around the tree trunk in time to see Dacton dive behind a hollow log an instant before three arrows buried themselves into the hard wood, the vibration of their impact echoing on the placid air.

She held her breath and visually searched the edge of dark green foliage for any sign of Dacton. The men rushed into the woods after their prey, and Talina feared for Dacton's life. She rubbed sweat from her palms against the rough fabric of the priest's robe and waited. She might never see Dacton again, a thought that brought terror to her heart.

For some unexplainable reason she felt a mystic bond with the warrior. Deep within her soul she sensed he held the key to her planet's existence. That thought made no sense, yet it was real, overwhelming her other thoughts. Dacton had to survive, there was too much she needed to learn about the enigmatic intruder.

One of the Burly men suddenly flew backwards from the thick brush that surrounded a small, open area, groaning as he hit the ground. The sound of fists connecting with flesh resounded in the otherwise quiet forest before a second man fell on top of his comrade.

Dacton rolled from the brush into the clearing, tangled fiercely in battle with the last opponent. They struggled, each blow harder than the last. The two men, both intent on victory, were now on their feet. Talina gasped when one of the Burly men pulled a cutter from his boot and lunged for Dacton's throat.

Dacton took a few steps back, then spun twice and inflicted an overpowering blow with his foot to the head of his attacker. The man fell on his back. Dacton grabbed the cutter, put one knee on the man's chest and held the weapon against his throat. Dacton glanced in her direction as if insuring her safety.

Talina clutched at her heart. Dacton raised the blade above his. She was about to see a killer in action, a sight she couldn't bear. Closing her eyes she reminded herself that he was only protecting her. The suspense was too much, she had to know. The moment she opened her eyes she watched Dacton thrust the cutter down.

From her vantage point it was impossible to see how much damage the blade had done to the man on the ground, but she knew he was dead. While she watched Dacton rise slowly to his full height, the grunts and groans of the battle still echoed in her ears.

An eternity passed as she stared at the warriors. Three on the ground, one standing straight, undaunted staring at his last victim. Dacton had emerged the victor. Talina never dreamed Dacton's life would be important to her for any reason. All she'd thought about was revenge against the audacious warrior, never giving serious thought to his mortality. For some inexplicable reason his life mattered to her.

"Finish it!" she heard the bearded man yell, his eye on the blade buried in the ground next to his head.

"No!" Dacton stepped back. "I will not be the cause of your death."

Talina's eyes widened. Here was the man she'd believed to be a vicious killer, granting another man his life! A Protector with compassion? It couldn't be, yet she just witnessed his act of clemency.

CHAPTER TWELVE

O

The Burly man rose to his feet. "You have defeated me in battle. I relinquish my right to rule. It is yours, according to law."

"Who are you?" Dacton asked.

"I am Krow, leader of the Boranian people."

"I am Dacton."

Talina watched Dacton hand Krow the cutter in a gesture of good will. The men silently sized each other up and glared in true warrior fashion. Men. It was always a battle for supremacy, especially between these two. She had to admit that Krow looked intimidating with his dark ruby eyes, and a build that was close to Dacton's.

"I respect your position and your ability in battle, but I do not wish to rule your people. I am on a mission of grave importance. My only intent is to secure a few provisions from your people for my journey."

Dacton stood his ground and waited while Krow sized up the situation. She knew both men were in the process of deciding whether to trust each other, which made her very nervous. She did not want to witness another fight between them. Dacton extended his arm in friendship, which made Krow smile and extend his forearm. They grasped each other's arms in what she decided must be some kind of a traditional warrior's greeting.

"Anything we have is yours."

"Thank you."

She was relieved to see both men smile at each other since they were both obviously proud men. Krow appeared to be a fair and capable ruler which was to their advantage, and nothing like she'd been told her entire life. Krow walked to where his two men lay semi-conscious and nudged them to rise.

"Put your weapons away. Dacton is a friend."

"My companion and I have come in peace."

"Where is this companion you speak of?" Krow asked.

"Talina," Dacton called across the clearing, "please come here."

Talina slowly stepped into view and walked toward the four men. When one of the men looked her up and down her skin crawled. Right now she wanted to run as far and as fast as she could. Instead she continued toward Dacton.

"Nice woman!" one man blurted.

"She is *my* woman, and I will kill any man who lays a hand on her."

"We understand. Please forgive Pado and Delon. They're young and have much to learn."

"No harm done."

Dacton looked ready to kill all three of the Boranians, and Krow gave his men a stern, authoritative glance. Dacton nodded his compliance, but she knew he was not happy.

"I will take you both to my home where you can rest. This way."

Krow turned and headed toward the hills in the distance. Talina was surprised when Dacton offered her his hand. She accepted willingly, and the warmth of his fingers around hers provided the unspoken message that she was safe with him. Yet every time he touched her she felt the same excitement spread through her body. His unmitigated strength and animal magnetism formed a combination she found irresistible.

Watching Dacton in battle confirmed what she'd thought from the moment she laid eyes on him. Dangerous, strong, capable, arrogant, self-assured, and devastatingly handsome, from the top of his dark hair to the bottom of his black boots.

For Talina, the future ruler, these thoughts were taboo. But for Talina, the woman, they were very real, no matter how hard she tried to deny the realization. She should be terrified of her kidnapper, but at the moment, she owed him her life.

When he claimed her as *his* woman to Krow, a curious twinge of pride pervaded her thoughts. She should be furious, but the thought of being his woman stirred unbridled fantasies. What would it feel like to taste his kiss and stir his masculine desires? A warm tingle assailed her womanhood and she knew she was treading in dangerous territory.

In order to push the disquieting thoughts of Dacton from her mind, she concentrated on the landscape. The moon-cycle blooming pyra flowers were beginning to open, and their sweet scent drifted on the cool, faint breeze. Scrub trees gave way to tall, majestic evergreens as the steep path led them higher up the mountain.

Stepping carefully over rocks to guard against reopening the wounds on her feet became more difficult as the rough fabric of her robe snagged small twigs, dragging them behind her. She stumbled, but Dacton's strong grasp held her firm. Talina glanced up to find his dark gray eyes fixed on her feet.

"I will carry you." Dacton scooped her into his arms.

Resting her head against his chest, Talina threaded her arms around his neck. She listened to the rapid beat of his heart through the thin, black fabric of his shirt and brushed off a lone salix leaf, the last remnant of his battle.

Talina closed her eyes and remembered last moon-cycle. She should hate him for ripping her from her life and preventing her installation as Legatus, but it was impossible to fear him while she was cradled protectively in his arms, surrounded by the masculine power that was his alone.

Dacton could have killed the Burly men, yet he let them live. It was thought that Protectors did not have a benevolent bone in their body. When he said he would kill any man that touched her, he was very convincing. However, she was his hostage, and he was not defending her honor. He simply had to keep her safe so she could serve his objective, whatever it was.

She glanced at his large hands wrapped around her knees and they were cut and bruised. He had proved himself to be the brave and competent warrior she had believed him to be, but she still was not sure about his decision to join the Burly people in their settlement. A soft pallet and a warm meal would be celestial, and there appeared to be no danger. Even though they were enemies, she knew the Burly people would never harm her as long as she was with Dacton.

A bonfire glowed eerily across the face of a sheer rock cliff that rose majestically before them. They paused behind the fire and several Burly men came out of hiding to join them. A glance at Dacton's square jaw planted in determination gave her reassurance. The men moved a large, fairly flat and round rock that revealed an opening into the stone edifice. Her heart beat faster. Were they both being taken prisoner, never to see the light of a sun-cycle again? Dear stars, she hoped Dacton knew what he was doing.

The heavy stone slid to stop with a resounding thud. Talina stared in amazement as Dacton eased her to the ground. They stepped inside the opening and found themselves on a large flat, rock balcony that looked down into a immense cavern. Hundreds of people had assembled below them, their gazes riveted up toward them, and their collective voices reverberated off the interior stone walls.

Krow held his hand up and silence fell over the crowd. "I have brought friends. Make them welcome."

A woman, dressed in long red pants and tunic, that had stood far to the side on the platform, stepped forward toward her. She was beautiful, with long, dark, curly hair, and exotic round, dark brown eyes. Her features were flawless and she appeared very friendly. Could all the stories she'd been told about the Burly People be false? She would soon find out.

"This is my wife, Leana. She will take care of your woman."

Leana took Talina's hand and started to lead her away.

"Stop!" Dacton moved to Talina's side and took her hand in his. "*My wom*an stays with me." He pulled her to his side.

Talina stared up at Dacton. What was this *my woman* stuff? She'd hoped for a chance to talk with Leana alone and possibly persuade the woman to help her. Leana had such a kind face, and she appeared to be about her age.

When Leana looked into Krow's eyes, Talina envied the love that sparked between them in a brief, but endearing glance. Leana's loyalty to her man was blatantly evident, which meant she would do nothing to displease him. Talina was glad she'd seen that open display before she revealed herself. Krow and Dacton had bonded on the battlefield, and she understood what that bonding meant. For now, she would have to play the part of the warrior's dedicated woman.

"Follow us." Krow took Leana's hand while they descended the long, curved steps that led to the main floor of the gathering area. He glanced back at Dacton. "We have much to discuss."

Dacton slipped his arm around Talina's waist and half carried her down the stone steps. The curious families had formed a clear aisle through the center of the main area where they stood. When they reached the back area, Krow opened a door, and they entered what appeared to be a large conference chamber.

The room was furnished only with a long, massive table and chairs made from a type of wood she'd never seen before, polished to a high sheen. Krow sat at the head of the table in a carved, wooden chair and indicated Dacton take the seat next to him on the right, while Leana guided her to the seat across from him. A young girl, no more than sixteen annual-cycles, walked into the room and set a pitcher of wine and four stemmed, clear glasses in front of Krow who ceremoniously filled each glass. He then handed one to her, then Dacton and Lean.

Krow raised his glass in the air. "I would like to make a toast to new friends."

They all touched glasses over the center of the table and in unison said, "New friends," before taking a drink.

Dacton licked his lips." This is good, my friend."

"I would serve you nothing less than our best. It's made from the rubus berry which only grows on our mountain." Krow studied Dacton. "You are a Protector?"

Talina nearly choked on her wine. Terror struck her heart. Everyone on Ora viewed Protectors as their enemy. Although she had no idea what the Burly People thought, it was possible she and Dacton had just walked into a trap they could never escape from. Dacton may be a talented warrior, but no man could take on the entire tribe outside the wall.

She took a deep breath, praying it was not her last.

* * * *

The Protector's code of silence just became a useless rule. He circled the rim of the glass with his finger and nodded. "I am a Protector, but I am not your enemy, nor am I an enemy to the government of Ora. I mean no harm to your people." He glanced down into the mirror-like finish of the table. No wonder Talina thought he was an animal. He stroked three sun-cycle's growth of beard and ran his fingers through disheveled hair. He rubbed his arms to ease the tension of carrying Talina for so long.

"You would not be at my table, sharing my wine, if I had no trust for you."

Dacton studied Krow, who was a good foot taller than he, every bit as strong, and approximately the same age, though it was hard to tell. He had a full beard that covered most of his face and long, shaggy brown hair that concealed the rest of his features. "I am honored you consider me a friend."

"You could have killed me, and my men, but you spared our lives. In our society, that makes us life-bonded friends." Krow stared into his wine. "You are the only man ever to best me in battle."

"It is not you I have come to battle with. I'm looking for a man named Zotar Alucard. Do you know of him?"

"There is a man we call *The Evil One* who has built a stronghold high in the ice-lands, which we refer to as the death zone."

"Why do you call him *The Evil One*?" Dacton wondered what Zotar had done to these people. He couldn't help notice the surprised look on Talina's face that indicated she and Zotar were intimate friends, possibly lovers, but he would get to the bottom of that later, when they were alone.

"When we first saw enormous ships in the sky, we watched from a safe distance. When they began building a fortress beneath the ice I sent scouting parties closer to investigate, but each time I lost many men. I was told gruesome stories of how Zotar captured my best warriors, and tortured them beyond human endurance. This I call evil."

"Do you know what is going on in the stronghold he built?"

Krow shook his head. "We haven't been able to penetrate the ring of heavily armed guards that patrol the outlying areas."

"What types of weapons do the guards carry?"

"They are a hand carried pistol that emits a blue beam. Upon contact it severely burns its target. Some of my men have survived such attacks, but their wounds never heal."

"What you describe is a cremare-ray weapon, which has been outlawed throughout the galaxy because of its mutating effects on the body."

Krow rubbed the back of his neck. "You know much."

Dacton nodded, sharing a silent pain with Krow. They had both lost valuable warriors to Zotar, and he sensed the same driving need for revenge within Krow that burned in his soul. The same need he swore to the council not to pursue. Zotar fed his ego by killing. Baleko's death was a thrill kill for Zotar, purposely orchestrated to spur their longtime personal feud. If Zotar never existed he would still have his older brother by his side. And the peace of the galaxy would remain intact.

"I offer you my scouts, and as many men as you require for your journey."

"I appreciate that my friend."

Krow took a long drink then set his glass down. "Your woman will be safe here while we are gone."

He glanced at Talina who scowled at Krow's suggestion, proof she feared the Burly people more than one Protector. Ironic indeed that he brought her face to face with another enemy. The planet was in need of peace, and before he left he would investigate the problems that existed between the Burly people and the government.

"You are a generous man, but I cannot take you, or any of your men with me." Confusion was evident in Krow's eyes. Dacton had heard the pride in Krow's voice when he'd offered his warrior's services. He had to be careful not to insult these people in any way. "I appreciate your brave offer of assistance, but it is imperative the woman and I go alone." Dacton downed the remaining wine then met Krow's gaze. "I wish I could explain, but the safety of everyone on the planet rests in the secrecy of my mission. As a warrior, I'm sure you understand."

"What can we do to help?"

Dacton watched Krow raise his chin and nod, grateful the Burly leader honored his request. "We need supplies for our journey."

"Have you come this far on foot?"

"Unfortunately we have." Dacton watched Talina chug down her fourth glass of wine, her eyes had become glazed, and she looked more relaxed than he'd ever seen her. She looked even more seductive than the first moment he'd laid eyes on her. That thought set off his mental alarm to keep his distance. He turned his attention back to Krow.

"I will give you two of my best esroths."

Dacton recalled his many experiences with the four legged beasts Krow mentioned. They could travel fast, the only catch was keeping them happy so they would serve their rider. Starting out with esroths unfamiliar with them could be difficult, since the rapport between an esroth and its master required a delicate balance.

Krow smiled. "Don't worry, my friend. I shall give you two of my most cooperative esroths." He refilled all four glasses.

"The wine is good." The sweet taste of the rubus berries could be addictive, but Dacton finished off the last of the deep, purplish-red liquid. He started to feel a bit light-headed and decided that would be his last glass.

He focused intently on Talina. Her eyes looked heavy and she swayed slightly in the chair. He'd lost count of the number of glasses she'd consumed, but judging from her euphoric appearance, she no longer had a care. She caught his gaze and smiled. It wasn't just a simple smile, it was exotic, promising, and explicitly sexual.

"We take pride in our winery, but best of all it contains aphrodisiac qualities." Krow smiled first at Dacton, then Talina. "You and your woman shall spend a most memorable moon-cycle."

Dacton swallowed hard and pushed his empty glass to the center of the table, his gaze fixed on Talina. She didn't blink at Krow's announcement, in fact, he doubted she was even aware of her surroundings. She parted her lips and licked them slowly while she studied him far too intently. He was doomed! With a little luck she'd fall asleep and he'd have nothing to worry about, yet the thought of her touch and the taste of her mouth stirred a most pleasing desire in the pit of his stomach.

"You look tired. A hot bath has been prepared in your quarters. Leana," Krow called, "please, escort our guests."

Leana bowed slightly at Krow and gestured toward the door.

The moment Dacton stood, the rubus berries took their toll on his exhausted body. He should have known better than to drink on an empty stomach, but he couldn't be rude and refuse Krow's hospitality. His head spun when he walked around the table, and when he touched Talina's arm to help her to her feet a most disturbing desire burned in his groin. It would be a long moon-cycle indeed.

"Dacton," Krow called when his guests reached the door. "Get plenty of rest. Tomorrow we will discuss the dangers that lay ahead."

CHAPTER THIRTEEN

Leana escorted Dacton and Talina down several halls and into one of the many guest quarters. "I believe you'll find everything you need." She walked to the bedside table and pointed to a terracotta bowl. "I requested dilek leaves to be soaked so they will be ready to use after her bath. Wrap her feet in them. Their healing powers are strong. I'm quite sure you want your partner to walk again."

"That would be wonderful. Thank you, Leana." Dacton struggled to keep Talina upright. Leana gave him the kind of smile that said she knew what would happen once she shut the door behind her and they were alone. Alone. The thought of spending another moon-cycle with the beautiful, alluring princess made him shudder.

Talina wiggled free and staggered toward the large copper tub in the back corner of the room. He followed close behind her, quite sure she would not make that walk on her own power. Sure enough, he grabbed her waist to steady her when she nearly fell face first to the floor.

Sweet herbs and floral essences mixed with steam and filled the room with an intoxicating fragrance that reminded him of how tempting Talina was to him. She struck a very enticing posture, whether she knew it or not, and he had to distance himself before he became a victim of her charms. He had never before faced a hostage situation like this before. It was difficult since he wanted to make love to her, to feel her skin against his, to....

His mind yelled, "Stop!" Those thoughts were dangerous and ill advised. If he wanted to succeed on this mission, he had to keep his mind and body in line with The Protector's Creed, the set of rules every Protector swore to follow. His position as Chief Protector was no excuse to disobey the strict rules. If he did not follow the Creed, how could he expect the men under him to comply?

Krow had supplied everything for a moon-cycle of passion. A hot tub, large enough for two, more wine, an inviting fur covered pallet, torchlight, and scented candles to enhance the mood. There was also a large bowl of fruit, which Krow probably thought they might feed to each other. He was grateful to his host, but how could he control the need that already consumed him?

The wine wreaked havoc with his good intentions, and he wished he hadn't let his guard down and consumed so much. How could Krow and his people function drinking it all the time? He released his hold on Talina and placed her hands on the edge of the tub.

"Look at the bubbles!" Talina giggled.

She scooped a cloud of suds into her hands, then playfully blew them into his face. "Take your bath before the water grows cold." She blinked at him lazily, with a seductive look on her face, then threw her arms around his neck and pressed her firm breasts against his chest. "You can manage by yourself." Dacton removed her arms then wiped bubbles from his face.

Talina pulled off the priest's robe and smiled. "I think not."

Her beguiling eyes held a most alluring invitation. He had to walk away, but before he could, Talina removed her long blue gown. She stood before him in a silky-pink undergarment that made his mouth water. He took a deep breath and studied her face, then his gaze moved over bare shoulders, then slid down over her breasts, and waist to linger on her legs. He bit his lower lip and cursed.

"What's the matter, warrior? Have you not seen a woman before?"

Dacton cleared the lump in his throat. "None as lovely as you, Regia." He hadn't meant to say that, but she probably wouldn't remember a thing in the morning, which worked to his advantage. If she knew how tempted he was to make love to her, she could use that power against him, and he wasn't sure he could resist such temptation.

Talina swayed then fell against his chest. Her arms threaded around his neck once again and she gazed into his eyes. The taut peaks of her nipples burned through the thin, pink fabric that covered them and penetrated their impression into his skin as if he were bare-chested.

Instinctively Dacton closed his arms around her and brushed her lips with his. The overpowering need to join with her screamed in every pore of his body. How could wanting her be wrong when it felt so right? Blood pooled heavily in his groin. He fought the impulse to kiss her, knowing once would never be enough.

His male essence was awakened by the exotic Regia, and for the Chief Protector, that was dangerous. She'd tested his will from the moment he'd laid eyes on her, and the wine he'd had dissolved the last of his control. He had to fight these carnal desires he could never satisfy with Talina, desires that could destroy them both. "Get in the tub, woman."

"I need help."

"Fine." He lifted her off the floor and lowered her into the tub, underwear and all before she bared her entire body, an act that would send him over the edge. He watched her sink below the bubbles. Seductive cobalt eyes invited passion, and pouty lips begged to be kissed. He groaned, then turned and walked away before his body betrayed his warrior's better sense.

Dacton took a seat at the nearby table. He held his head between his hands and stared at the food before him and the decanter of wine. "Curse that drink!" One more glass would put him in the tub with Talina, and he could not afford to throw caution to the stars. His career could be ruined and the mission jeopardized, all for a moment of bliss. No. He was stronger than temptation. Food might neutralize the wine's effects. He ate a slice of meat and tried to ignore the sounds coming from the tub.

"Dacton?"

Talina's voice was seductive. Damn that woman!

"Help me, please."

Water sloshed and he turned his gaze on her, slightly afraid she might drown in her condition. By the Gods! She stood naked in the tub, wet hair clinging to her breasts, clumps of bubbles sliding down her slick body. His heart beat wildly, every muscle froze, his arousal aching to explore her secrets.

"Come help me, Dacton." She swayed back and forth.

Long blond hair nestled against smooth, pinkish-white skin, that emphasized places his fingers ached to explore. His heart pounded heavier than when he'd battled Krow and his men. She was more exquisite than he'd imagined, so perfect, and so forbidden.

"What's wrong, warrior?" She held her hands up. "As you can see, I'm not armed."

"My sweet Regia, you have the one weapon a warrior fears most."

"Let me prove you have nothing to fear." She smiled. "Bring that handsome body over here."

Dacton pushed back from the table, grabbed the white robe from the pallet and stomped over to the tub. He covered her for his sake.

"Have you no sense of adventure?" She pouted. "Or is there something wrong with me?"

"There is nothing wrong with you."

Talina pressed her lips to his ear. "Then make love to me. Now. I want you."

When he scooped her into his arms, his hands grasped slick, bare skin. This was definitely a mistake. The inviting words she spoke were wine induced, and so was her forward behavior. He wanted her, all of her, more than anything he'd ever wanted, but Talina was off limits. Even if he were free to take the sweetness she offered, it had to come from Talina, not the wine. He pulled back the covers and laid her on the pallet. "Talina, you must let me tend to your feet."

"It's not my feet that need attention." Talina laughed. "Are all Protectors this slow?" She grabbed the robe and threw it off. "You told Krow I was your woman. Prove it!"

Dacton retrieved the garment and placed it across her. "Please, keep this on while I take care of your feet."

"Then will you mate with me, handsome Protector?"

Through her incessant flirting he saw her innocence. If she were experienced he could not have stopped their joining. She would have been all over him, and his resolve would have failed. This fair princess was a virgin, and so she must remain.

One by one he took the large, wet dilek leaves from the bowl and wrapped them around her battered feet, gently massaging the herbs against her tender soles with long, smooth strokes. When he glanced up she was asleep. He pulled up the heavy fur then brushed stray wet hairs from her face. A light kiss on her forehead was all he could afford to give if he intended to leave her untouched.

Dacton undressed, grabbed the other robe and headed for the tub. He eased his tired body into the consoling suds, the warmth nurturing his aching muscles. The sweet scent in the air reminded him of what he could not have. It would have been so easy to love her, to teach her how to give and receive passion. But that was not his job, just a pleasant dream.

The tranquilizing water soothed his body, but his mind raced. He had mentally mapped out every move, but his plans had not included the wants and needs of a woman. This mission had taken a strange turn indeed. It was supposed to be simple. Eradicate the reactor, locate Zotar, and return him to the Protectorate. Yet he was here, with Talina, while Ora fell deeper into Zotar's clutches.

He would stop Zotar, of that he was certain, but could he allow him to live? His oath to the Protectorate was valid, but so was his solemn promise to avenge Baleko's death. He would have to chose between duty and honor. Zotar tortured Baleko unmercifully then sent a vid-chip to The Protectorate that showed Baleko from his moment of capture to his last, agonizing breath.

Zotar had despised him since their sun-cycles in the academy, but murdering Baleko to force a confrontation between them was senseless. They shared a mutual hatred that could destroy them both. The battle he faced was a double-edged sword that ripped him to his very soul.

He stood, dried off and slipped on the other robe. Based on the way it fit, it belonged to Krow. He tied the soft, cloth belt then walked to the pallet. Did he dare lay next to Talina? She was asleep, and after his bath, that's all he wanted. What could it hurt?

* * * *

Talina blinked several times in an effort to focus. The dull throb in her temples cruelly reminded her that she overindulged in rubus berry wine. Her last memory was sitting across from Dacton in Krow's reception room.

A deep breath revealed something heavy across her stomach, and she slowly turned her head. Dacton slept next to her, his arm curled possessively around her. Terror struck. Dear stars, what had he done?

When she moved slightly under the heavy, furry pelt she realized she was naked. Where were her clothes? She eased slowly and carefully from beneath Dacton's arm so she could roll out of pallet without disturbing the sleeping warrior.

On the floor at the head of the tub lay her blue gown and undergarment in a wet heap. Did she take them off, or had Dacton? A shiver coursed through her. If he undressed her, he'd also seen her naked. No. She refused to think of that now, all that mattered was escape.

On a small chest at the foot of the pallet were two sets of clean, neatly folded clothes. Without hesitation she donned a deep red tunic and pants Leana left. She eyed a pair of women's brown leather boots on the floor, but she doubted she could get them on her sore feet.

Consumed with thoughts of Dacton she had not realized that her walk had been painless. A quick glance down revealed a leaf still stuck to her foot. She steadied herself against the wooden trunk, pulled off the leaf and stared in amazement. Only tiny white lines indicated where deep cuts had been.

How could that be? Had Leana helped her with her bath and medicated her feet? She wished she could remember so she'd know who to thank. Now she could escape, return to her father and warn him of the Protectorate's invasion. She would no longer have to be carried and dragged about by the ruthless warrior.

A shiver ran down her spine. The thought of Dacton's strong arms around her brought a smile. He had protected her in battle, and carried her when she could not walk. She suspected his kindness had been more for him than her. He had a crazy agenda she knew nothing about. Her goal was to get back to the capitol and her father.

Only the Gods knew what Dacton had done last moon-cycle! That man ripped her away from her family. He was the cause of her pain, and the reason she missed her installation as Legatus. Damn him to Diabolus! He was her enemy, a fact she could not forget, no matter how she felt about him. Once she returned to Sobrie, her father would send the Royal Guard to capture Dacton, and he would pay the price for his crime.

Talina laced up the boots and headed for the door. She turned and looked at the tub. Warm water and bubbles tickled her memory, and Dacton holding her in his arms. Or was it a dream? She ran her hands through her hair. It was tangled, but clean. The bath was real, the sleeping warrior was real, so whatever happened between them during the moon-cycle was real as well. She glanced at Dacton one last time before her hand lifted the latch slowly, without a sound.

"Leaving so soon, Regia?"

Curse it all. Why did he have to have such sensitive ears? She hadn't even gotten the door open. He may have stopped her this time, but the sun-cycle was young. "I wanted to find Leana so I could thank her." That was a believable lie.

Dacton smiled. "Good idea, but you will not leave without your man."

"You are not *my man*, warrior."

"After last moon-cycle there should be no question." Dacton rose from the pallet and walked toward Talina. "Don't you remember?"

Before Talina could even ponder the possibilities of Dacton's insinuation there was a knock on the door. She pulled it open, relieved to find Leana's radiant smile. "Krow and I would like you to join us for breakfast."

"It would be an honor," Dacton replied, putting his arm around Talina's shoulders.

She cringed inside at the gesture, but her heart beat faster under his touch. He squeezed her arm and she glanced up. She wanted to slap his face and kiss him at the same time. Her mind must still be clouded by the wine. "Yes." She forced herself to focus on Leana. "We would be honored."

"Good. We'll expect you shortly."

Leana walked away, and she let out the breath she'd been holding. How could she face Dacton? He indicated they mated last moon-cycle, and she had no memory of anything inside their room until she woke this sun-cycle. If she did lose her virginity she should feel different, but it seemed nothing had changed. Somehow she'd expected far more from the experience than this. Besides feeling embarrassed, she felt relatively normal, if there were such a feeling.

She shut the door and turned slowly to look at Dacton, who had yet to remove his arm from her shoulders, so she did it for him. "I'd like some space, if that's possible." He said nothing, he just stared at her like a catamoose who had just swallowed a bird.

CHAPTER FOURTEEN

"I'm glad to see you enjoyed your breakfast." Krow studied his guests while the dishes were removed. "Leana's clothes fit Talina well."

"I must agree with you." Actually the fit was excellent since it showed her every curve and asset. Her blonde hair spilled recklessly across her shoulders, but she kept her head bowed and concentrated a little too hard on her food, which she mostly pushed around on the plate.

Dacton sipped the hot herbal tea. He should not have let her think they'd made love last moon-cycle. He'd thought it a joke, but instead he'd turned into a bigger monster to her than she already thought him to be. He should tell her the truth, but they had a long, hard journey ahead, and it might be easier if she hated him.

Krow looked Dacton in the eye. "I implore you to change your mind about going to the frigid zone."

"I cannot. I must go there. It's my duty." Dacton met Krow's gaze. "You understand duty."

"Then be warned, my friend. Pengores roam freely in the snow region, and no warrior has ever survived an attack."

"Have you seen one?"

"Yes, but only from a distance. You will know when one is close because of its rancid odor. The Pengore walks on two legs like a human, is covered with long white fur, and has one large horn in the center of its forehead. It's said the only way to kill one is to cut off his horn."

"So no one has ever killed a Pengore?"

"Many men have died trying." Krow poured more tea. "They're fast on their feet, and very agile for their immense size. Your only hope to survive an attack is to climb a tree. Because of their weight, they cannot follow, but they will wait close by until you fall from exhaustion or starvation. Escaping the Pengore is impossible."

"What do their tracks look like?"

"It is circular, with three protruding toes. You'll have no trouble recognizing them. I know of no other animal with such prints."

Dacton rubbed the back of his neck. "Can you provide me with weapons?"

"I will give you the best sword and cutter our craftsmen make."

"Thank you, Krow." Their weapons would be primitive, but if what Krow said was true, he might need the sword. Krow stood and motioned toward the door. When they stood next to each other, Krow gave Dacton a firm slap on the back.

"Remember, you and your life-mate are always welcome in our settlement. If you ever need help, just ask."

"Talina and I appreciate your hospitality." Dacton grasped the warrior's arm in a show of thanks. "I also know where to find good warriors if the need arises." He watched Krow smile proudly.

"Come, I will take you to the esroths."

As they walked, Krow's words, *your life-mate,* played in his mind. Talina would make some man very proud, but it would never be him. As long as he was Chief Protector, his heart could belong to no woman.

* * * *

Leana embraced Talina in front of the main entrance. "We enjoyed your visit, and hope you will stop on your way back." She squeezed Talina's hand. "I tied extra parkas to the back of your saddle, the rest of the clothes and supplies are on the pack esroth. You will need them where you're going." Leana smiled. "Please, be careful."

"Thank you for your kindness." Talina leaned her head toward Leana's ear. "I'll never forget you, Leana."

"Nor I you. Take good care of your warrior. He is a good man."

Talina glanced at Dacton. Could Leana be right? He seemed nice and honorable, but he was her captor and it could all be a trick to gain her cooperation. She could trust no one. If Krow and his people knew who she was, their warm welcome would turn to hatred. As Dacton's woman she was accepted, as the Princess DeAmarant, she was their enemy.

The Burly people and the government had fought an embittered war over a centrum ago, but there had never been an agreeable end to their disputes. What few survivors were left fled to the Boranian Mountains to rebuild their society, and as long as they stayed here, the government allowed it. But if they set foot in Sobrie, they would be killed. Now that she'd met Krow, and Leana, and put faces on the Burly people, she could no longer think of them as the unknown enemy. If she ever returned to Sobrie, and took her rightful place, she would do everything she could to negotiate peace between their peoples and end the Burly people's forced isolation.

Talina's gaze focused on the mystical golden stone cinched firmly around Dacton's trim waist. He looked dangerously appealing in Krow's natural tan leather pants and dark blue tunic. He'd shaved and appeared younger than the thirty-plus annual-cycles she'd guessed him to be. He possessed a charisma that pulled her toward him, a force to be reckoned with and avoided.

Krow removed his furry vest and gave it to Dacton, who put it on with a stately smile. Then Krow handed him a sword and scabbard along with a cutter. He pulled the sword from the scabbard and the early morning sun gleamed on the polished metal. He held it out in front of him and eyed the length. He must have seen something he liked because his smile grew larger and there was a childlike gleam in his eyes.

Krow stepped closer to Dacton. "I see you approve?"

"It's perfection." He turned the sword in a circle. "You have a master craftsman. Please give him my compliments, and my thanks." He sheathed the sword and affixed it to his belt, then slipped the cutter into his boot.

Talina allowed Dacton to help her mount the shorter esroth with the smaller saddle. It felt strange to be astride such a large animal. Many annual-cycles had passed since she'd ridden, and the thought of sore muscles brought a grimace. But riding was faster than walking, and offered her a new opportunity for the freedom she so desperately needed.

She watched Dacton place his hand on her esroth's forehead and close his eyes. What in the galaxy was he doing? The large animal stood perfectly still for the longest time, then nuzzled Dacton's chest. His actions were strange, but what did she know about Protectors?

Krow and Dacton grasped arms in warrior tradition and said their farewells. Watching two of her enemies form a bond only reinforced her need to return to Sobrie. From what she'd seen in Krow's camp, they would join forces with the Protectors against the government. She couldn't blame Krow if his loyalty fell to The Protectorate. He had just cause considering the heartache the government had inflicted. She had sympathy for the Burly people, but her place was in Sobrie with the government. They were her people, and she had to get back. This sun-cycle.

Dacton mounted like an expert, then prodded his esroth into a trot, the pack esroth's reins firmly in his grasp. Talina's beast followed, and she bounced on the leather saddle until she found the rhythm of his gait. She reached down and patted the animal's thick, hairy neck. They had to become friends, especially if she wanted the esroth's cooperation in her escape plan. When two esroths traveled together, they would throw a fit when separated. It would take her a while to bond enough to attempt such a maneuver.

In Sobrie, esroths were shaved to make them more beautiful to the eye, and to aid their comfort in the warmer climate, but the increasing cold would prohibit that practice. So much had changed, and it was only the beginning. Zotar claimed he could stop The Protectorate from freezing the planet, and she prayed he could. Thank the stars he had landed on Ora, and wanted to help. Dacton insisted Zotar was responsible for their weather problems. One of them was wrong. Which man intended to destroy her world?

If eyes were the window to a man's soul, Dacton held the upper hand. Zotar's eyes were frightening at times, even when he'd looked at her as a woman, she saw a cold, distant and calculating demeanor. Dacton's steel grey eyes had run the spectrum from undiluted anger, to deep compassion. True, he'd scared her with his stern glances, but even in the mine shack, she'd seen a hint of softness that Zotar had never shown.

To decide which man held the truth could be the most important decision of her life, and the lives of every man, woman, and child depended on her. But how could she decide alone, without consulting her father and Kolere? They had more experience, and would reach a conclusion without emotion, which her involvement with both men might prevent. Or would her heart know what her mind could not accept? She'd considered herself ready to become Legatus, but doubt now reared its ugly head.

Time. She needed more time to decide. She'd put too much faith in Zotar, a mistake she did not plan make with Dacton. Who was Zotar? No one had questioned his visit, they had all been taken by surprise since he was the first off-worlder to land on Ora in recent history. Zotar was a problem, but so was the man ahead of her, leading her deeper into forbidden territory.

Dacton's riding skills were nothing short of expert. Expert indeed, she hoped his esroth would take a dislike to him and dump him on the ground. That would be a sight, and a perfect lesson in humility. The man had to have a flaw, everyone did, and she'd take great pleasure when she found it. He glanced at her over his shoulder from time to time, but he'd not spoken a word.

Tall straight pinus trees with needle-like leaves covered the steep hillside, and she could barely see since the sun could not penetrate through the dense forest. She had to make her break before the terrain,and light grew even worse. "Easy boy." She slowed the esroth's pace to distance herself from Dacton. She'd made her decision, it was now or never.

The esroth nervously danced in circles, but Talina pulled back on the reins firmly, turned him around, and spurred him into a run. Cold wind on her face promised freedom, a way back to the life she loved. A life Dacton had taken from her. Hooves pounded on the hard ground even louder than her heart. She talked to the esroth while he dodged trees and rocks. Why couldn't the blasted animal run any faster? She no sooner finished that thought when the esroth slid to an abrupt halt and she flew over the animal's head and landed hard on the ground.

* * * *

Dacton pulled his mount to a stop and listened. He'd lost sight of her, but from the sounds echoing in the canyon, she was still on the move. He silently cursed. Her attempt to escape was no surprise, just a waste of time, time that was running out. When he caught up with her they needed to talk. She had to cooperate. When would the woman realize they had a job to do, that he was on her side, and it was senseless to fight?

He stroked the esroth's neck and continued up a small slope, knowing this exercise in futility was his fault for not confiding in her. Although, telling her about the mission would not necessarily elicit her cooperation, but at least she'd understand his motives.

When he crested the hill he laughed at the sight below. Talina lay sprawled on the ground, picking pinus needles from her hair. She stood, rubbed her backside, then stomped over to her esroth who had found a bit of grass to nibble on. She grabbed her mount's reins with a determined look on her face, then lifted her leg.

When Talina's foot pushed on the stirrup and she hopped off the ground to swing her leg over the esroth's back he hopped away from her and she landed firmly on her rear. Dacton inwardly smiled when she stood and rubbed the seat of her pants, oblivious to his presence.

"Enough entertainment, woman." She turned so fast she nearly fell again. He nudged his mount to walk down the slope and pulled to a stop in front of her.

"I am not a woman!"

"Indeed. I've seen proof." He laughed. "You *are* a woman." He watched Talina's face turn red and her dark blue eyes burned with fire.

"You know what I meant." Talina clenched her fists and rested them on her hips. "You're the poorest excuse of a man I've ever seen!"

Dacton jumped from his mount and grabbed her shoulders. "Those were not your words last moon-cycle." He tried to stop the smile that tugged at the corners of his mouth. He shouldn't play with her innocence, but the temptation was too great, especially since she insulted him "I trusted you this sun-cycle, and you violated that trust. Must I beat some sense into you?"

"You might as well beat me after what you did!" Talina gritted her teeth.

"And what did I do?"

"You...you...raped me!"

Dacton pretended anger. "And you flatter yourself, Regia. I have never taken a woman against her will!"

"You're nothing but an arrogant Protector who takes what he wants, and the rest of the world can go to Diabolus! You're nothing but a liar! You took me by force from the palace. I suppose you deny that as well?"

He grabbed her wrist before her hand made contact with his face. "Yes I took you from the palace, but that is all I took. Your maidenhood is intact." Dacton shook his head. "I have not lied to you. Stretched the truth maybe, but I saw enough of you to know you are definitely a woman. That was not your imagination. I helped you out of the tub so you didn't fall. I put the robe around you, doctored your feet, and *slept* next to you. Slept being the only operative word. Nothing else."

"*Nothing* else?"

Dacton released her wrist, unable to erase the disbelief he heard in her voice. "I only require your cooperation, not your favors." She stared at him long and hard and he knew she looked for the truth. It was up to her if she believed him. He kept his expression determined and stoic. "I will explain everything when we camp for the moon-cycle. Agreed?"

Talina met his gaze. "And why should I trust you? I doubt you know the truth."

"You may be right. Kolere left much unsaid, but he assured me you would learn to trust me. He said to have faith, and I am trying." Dacton kept his body rigid and still.

"And how do you know Kolere?" She shook her head. "You just threw his name at me because you know I am close to him and you want to gain my trust."

"Have I?"

"No."

"As I said, I will explain everything later. For now, we must go."

"I suppose I am at your mercy, for now. But I have no reason to cooperate with you, or trust you." She kicked a rock and it rolled down the hill. "Do you swear to tell me everything? I have a right to know."

"Yes Regia, I promise. It is past time you knew."

CHAPTER FIFTEEN

O

Thunder shook the ground and lightning cut a jagged path through the dark evening sky. Dacton hammered the last stake into the ground and secured the tie downs. Under normal conditions the small tent would not require such security, but the impending storm promised trouble. He stood and walked back to the esroths to make sure their tie lines would free themselves if the animals bolted in the storm. He'd rather lose an esroth to the wilderness than to have him break a leg or a neck.

Krow had chosen well, he thought while he patted their rumps and received a small whinny in return. Not once had the sturdy animals faltered on the rough terrain. They were good mounts, but his explorer would have saved time and been a damn sight warmer. If they'd flown he would never have met Krow, and he suspected their meeting was not by chance. Kolere's secret agenda had begun to reveal itself, and he wondered what the legend would divulge next.

The sky growled loudly and the large animals danced nervously. The approaching storm upset them, which was odd since esroths did not usually react to weather. Dacton touched each of their foreheads and sent a calming message that included their loyalty to remain close to him. He thanked Talina's mount for stopping her escape as he'd asked before they began their journey.

"What are you doing?"

He hated to be disturbed while communicating with animals, but he was glad Talina had no idea what he was doing. He doubted she'd understand, most people did not. "I was checking our esroths. They should be fine."

Dacton picked up the supplies he'd removed from the pack esroth and headed for the tent. He piled everything along the far back, then returned for the saddles that lay on the ground next to Talina. The closer he walked toward her, the deeper her scowl grew and the more her muscles tensed. "If you need a moment alone, you'd best take it before the sky opens up." Talina nodded then headed toward a clump of thick brush at the edge of their camp site.

A deep groan in the sky followed by a flash of light reminded him it was going to be a long moon-cycle. Being cooped up in a little tent with Talina could prove to be a more difficult challenge than the unknown wilderness and bad weather.

He promised to explain everything to her, and that meant another, more complete breach of The Protectorate's rigid code of silence. Revealing the details of his mission would be difficult, especially Kolere's instructions. Would Talina believe the legend? He knew nothing of her religious beliefs, or her knowledge of the past. In fact, he knew little about the woman. He picked up both saddles and hurried to the tent.

* * * *

Talina sat quietly, secure in the dense brush. What did Dacton have planned for this moon-cycle? He denied taking her virginity, and she believed him. Her body felt no signs of being violated, but her mind did. *Something* happened in that cave. Faint memories played in the recesses of her mind. Soon she would remember.

He'd said he only helped her from the tub and tended her feet. A shiver worked its way down her spine when she thought about Dacton seeing her naked. She should be ashamed he'd seen her, but she wasn't, and that bothered her the most. He stirred emotions contrary to the beliefs and traditions of her people, emotions buried in her heart. Emotions that scared her.

Dacton had turned her life upside-down. She'd learned nothing so far, but this moon-cycle she planned to coax every truth from his lips and learn his secrets before she made her decision. Her people's lives might well depend on her ability to be civil to the Protector. First she had to decide if he were friend or foe.

Treetops glowed in the constant flashes of light, the sky rumbled loudly, large drops of water began to tap the ground, and. the wind kicked up violently. She jumped to her feet and ran to the tent. Curse it all. The downpour hit moments before she pushed through the front opening of the tent.

"Have we not enough water outside?" Dacton smiled and handed her a cloth. "You're getting everything wet, woman."

Dacton's voice was teasing, and the irresistible grin on his face made her smile. Was he finally going to show his human side? His weakness? Possibly, but she must not forget who she was, and why she was here. She forced herself to play along. "Please forgive me, mighty warrior. I would hate to see you melt before my eyes."

"I shall grant you forgiveness. Just this once."

Talina laughed when he tried to bow in the cramped space and bumped his head on a saddle horn. "One should never bow while sitting."

"I must agree." He rubbed his forehead.

By the light of the luna-stone his dark eyes took on a soft, caring, mysterious hue. If he had come in peace, she would place him at the top of her list for a life-mate. Tall, muscular, strong, ruggedly handsome. Yes, he was the finest candidate she had ever seen—equaled by none.

Examining his physical attributes made her fingers itch to roam the well defined expanse of his chest and down his flat abdomen to... What was she thinking! She hadn't had such intimate thoughts about Zotar, and he was the man she'd imagined life-mating with. Zotar was handsome, cunning and persuasive, but he didn't excite her like Dacton.

Was she attracted to Dacton because he was dark and dangerous? She didn't know him well enough for it to be anything else. The idea of any relationship with the man was ludicrous. He was a man to fear. Sure, he claimed to be on her side, working to save her people, but he could still be her enemy.

Rain pelted the tent and the sky grumbled angrily overhead. She watched Dacton rummage through a supply bag and pull out several sticks of dried meat along with bread and cheese. He handed some to her.

"We need to discuss the mission."

"Your mission, not mine." Talina took a bite without taking her eyes off Dacton.

"Kolere says it is up to both of us." Dacton took a bite of bread.

"By the stars, what does Kolere have to do with my abduction?" Talina watched Dacton's expression turn serious and a bit angry. She refused to believe for a moment that her life-long mentor had any hand in this ridiculous outing.

"I've seen your interest in this amulet." He tucked a thumb into the belt behind the stone. "Kolere gave it to me, along with an ancient legend that says, 'Find the woman who wears the chain, and keep her by your side.'"

Talina gasped and covered her mouth with her hand. Her body shook, unable to comprehend the shock of Dacton's words. Kolere was the only person on the planet, besides herself, who knew those words. She dropped her hand. "You must have tortured him to obtain such information."

"I believe it was the other way around, to be sure." Dacton ran his fingers through his hair. "I pleaded with him to leave you out of this. I never wanted to put you in danger. You must believe me."

A brilliant bolt of lightning flashed so close Talina covered her ears and closed her eyes. A moment passed before two strong hands closed over hers and gently eased them down. A warm secure feeling pushed aside one fear, but ignited another. She opened her eyes, his steady gaze focused on her. Her hands burned from his touch. She pulled back, but his grasp held firm. She knew from the set of his jaw, and tense neck muscles that he waited for her reply. "A part of me believes you."

Dacton released her hands. "You've been told Protectors are your enemy, so I understand your reluctance to trust me."

"You are correct in both assumptions. I will never forgive you for what you've done to me, and what you plan to do to my people."

The horrifying sound of a large branch falling from a nearby tree and crashing to the ground alarmed them both. The tent shook violently due to the increase of the wind's velocity. It was a wonder the tent still stood. At that thought, one of the tent's support ropes broke and the front left corner flopped helplessly in the assault.

"We have no time for games. I've come to save your planet from certain destruction, and to return Zotar Alucard to The Protectorate to pay for his crimes."

Talina shifted up on her knees. Anger welled like a tidal wave heading for shore. He would say anything to trick her, to shake her calm. "What has this man done?"

"Do not pretend he's a stranger."

Talina lowered her gaze, but she saw his body tense and knew he grimaced. He even let out a frustrated groan. Obviously she could not fool him, which frustrated her, so at least they had the same attitude.

"Zotar is wanted for treason on three planets, piracy throughout the galaxy, and numerous murders—too many to list. Just know the man is evil."

"Why should I believe you?"

"The Protectorate has proof. Zotar's actions are well witnessed and documented."

"You hate this man, don't you?"

"He stole something from me I can never replace."

"You must be mistaken, I've known him for almost an annual-cycle, and he has never..."

"Enough!"

Dacton's voice was way louder than the raging storm. She knew by his demeanor that he was dead serious. Zotar had indeed done something terrible to Dacton.

"You have no comprehension of his capabilities. If you did, you would share my desire to see him die!"

Talina pushed herself back until the side of the tent pressed against her, the driving rain pounding her body through the thin fabric. Zotar a murderer? Dacton was a deluded liar, and for a moment she thought he'd strike her in his uncontrolled anger. He seemed obsessed with Zotar, and the tone of his voice said he'd stop at nothing to see the man dead. Nature raged around her as fast and hard as the beat of her heart. "You're wrong."

Dacton leaned closer. "Do not act stupid and naïve. You're a princess, about to be installed as Legatus, so act appropriately. What I speak is the truth, and if you want to save your planet, you'd better listen to reason." He unzipped the door of the tent then pulled Talina toward the opening. "What do you see?"

"Rain, wind and..." A bright bolt of lightning pierced the hillside immediately followed by a long roar of thunder. "Lightning."

"What color is the lightning?"

Talina pushed herself back into the safety of the tent and wiped the water from her face. She stared blankly at the impatient warrior.

"It's green, woman. Are you blind?" Dacton secured the door flap. "Lightning on your planet has always been orange. It suddenly turns green and you don't question why?"

"The change is more visible here. We noticed some color difference in Sobrie, but Zotar said..."

"You try my patience!"

"I cannot try something you do not have!"

Dacton laughed under his breath. "You may be right. I'm just trying to make you see what's going on."

"If you'd quit treating me as a dumb woman and explain yourself better, maybe I would."

"Fair enough."

"Now, tell me why Kolere insisted you bring me along, against my will." Talina took a deep breath in an effort to remain calm, but the bristly warrior before her did not make it easy.

"Because of your bracelet." He picked up her left hand to examine the clear links around her wrist. "Kolere insisted it contains magical powers, along with the amulet, to destroy Zotar's plan."

"You keep talking about Zotar's plan, but you never explained it."

Dacton took a deep breath and exhaled slowly. "Zotar wants your planet. Right now he's using the weather threat as a means to gain recognition from the council. Once they agree, or should I say reward him, for stopping this threat, he will convince them to give him a seat on the council. If that doesn't work, he'll create another problem he can solve."

"Zotar said The Protectorate was behind our weather changes," Talina added. "He said it would be costly, but he could stop it."

"Exactly. You may not believe all of this, but think, Talina. Why, after a centrum, would The Protectorate suddenly intrude in your lives? And if you remember, Zotar arrived on Ora shortly after the weather became a problem."

Talina noted the sincerity in his voice, and his eyes verified the passion he had for his mission. Dacton and Zotar were both convincing in their stories, but she had to decide for herself who was right. It was easy to believe Dacton's version since Zotar wasn't here to defend himself. "Why does Zotar want control of Ora?"

"He wants power, wealth, and revenge. In his own twisted mind, the only way he can be respected is to control the galaxy."

Talina watched Dacton's eyes narrow. "The council already holds him in high esteem, and he has mentioned a council seat." She eased forward to stop the rain from pelting her back. "I don't understand how he could be so different than he appears."

"Zotar is a master of disguise as far as his real self is concerned. He was publicly disgraced and humiliated when the Imperial Academy expelled him for cheating. On Bronic, my home planet, such dishonor is punished by exile. When Zotar left Bronic he vowed revenge against The Protectorate, and he intends to carry out that threat. He plans to build an army, and conquer one planet at a time."

"How many has he taken over?" Talina asked, trying to absorb the shocking story.

"Only one. We defeated him on Gravis, but he succeeded on Dolor, a small, sparsely populated planet outside of this galaxy and The Protectorate's jurisdiction."

"Why would Zotar choose Ora?" Talina shifted nervously, the feverish wrath of the storm adding to her apprehension. "We don't have large quantities of precious gems, or other resources, our people aren't highly educated, compared to other cultures, our men are small, not the best candidates for warriors. So why, Dacton? Why us?"

"Because you're easy prey, with no army, no weapons, and no technology for him to battle." Dacton shifted closer to Talina. "Ora is only ninety-seven space-units from The Protectorate, and a planet that can grow enough food to supply an army. It would make a perfect staging area for an attack on The Protectorate."

"This is too much to comprehend." It would take time for Dacton's story to settle in her consciousness, time he insisted they did not have. Had Dacton been honest? Or was he part of The Protectorate's plan to control Ora?

"Would I be correct to assume that Zotar has expressed an interest in becoming your life-mate?"

"How could you know?"

"I know Zotar better than he knows himself. He's attracted to power, and beautiful women. You can provide him with both."

Should she believe Zotar, a man she knew longer, who she'd come to trust with her dreams and her heart? Or Dacton, the man who abducted her, robbed her of her rightful position, and placed her life in danger? But if his claims were true, he had just cause for his actions.

Talina swallowed hard, not sure if she wanted an answer to the question she had to ask, a question that could be the deciding factor of Dacton's honesty. "How did you join alliance with Kolere?"

"He is a very perceptive man who has your best interest at heart, as well as peace. Long ago Kolere came to Ora as a Watcher for The Protectorate. When he took on the priesthood he relinquished his position as a Watcher. However, he loves this planet, and those who live here, and only wants the best outcome for everyone."

Dacton paused as if he did not plan to continue. "Go on. Please."

"He contacted The Protectorate about Zotar and the moves he was making. The High Council met, and sent me to stop Zotar. I met Kolere in the desert outside Destiny. We talked, and that's when he told me about the legend and gave me this belt." Dacton fingered the amulet. "I'm not sure if this matters to you, but Kolere only instructed me to find the woman who wears the chain, he never revealed your identity."

"Kolere knows me well, and knew I would not leave the palace willingly."

"That, plus your life would be in danger if your people thought you sided with a Protector."

"I've trusted Kolere from the sun-cycle I was born." Talina looked into the depths of his eyes. "Kolere placed this bracelet on my wrist for my sixteenth birth-cycle. He said I would need it to help my people, and that it was never to be removed. He recited a legend to me, but I'm afraid I've forgotten the words."

A heavy crack of thunder made Talina jump and she landed flush against Dacton's chest, his warm breath heavy against her ear. Her heart raced faster than she ever thought possible. He leaned his forehead against hers, his arms circled around her back. As his lips inched closer she parted her mouth. She wanted to taste the forbidden pleasure she knew he'd give, even though she shouldn't. For every reason her mind conjured to push temptation away, her body disputed with increasing need.

Lightning struck beside the tent with a blinding intensity. The immense snap of power violently shook the ground, and the sound of wood cracking and splintering overtook their senses.

"No!"

Dacton rolled over with her in his embrace and shielded her with his body. Then it happened, something fell from above and crushed the tent. Only Dacton's back saved her from injury. She prayed he had not been hurt. What would she do without him?

CHAPTER SIXTEEN

"Roll away from me!" Dacton's arm muscles shook from strain.

Talina rolled free of his body. She watched in horror when he succumbed under the weight and was crushed to the ground. "Dacton!" She scooted closer and pushed against the collapsed, rain-soaked tent to see his face. "Answer me, Warrior!"

Panic engulfed every pore of her body. Her hand trembled when she touched his cold forehead. Her fingers found something warm and sticky. Blood. She grabbed his hand, placed her fingers on the inside of his wrist, and desperately searched for signs of life. He lay unconscious, but he had a pulse, even though it beat weak and slow, and his breathing was so shallow she could barely detect movement. But, he was alive.

She reached behind her, grabbed the luna-stone and held it up to his face. His steel-gray eyes were hidden behind still lids, blood oozed from his hair, down his forehead and onto his cheek. "Dear God!"

"Okay, I can do this." Talina took a deep breath and exhaled quickly in an effort to calm the overwhelming fright that threatened to consume her. First she would have to remove what had fallen on him. She put the luna-stone between her teeth, pulled the hood of her parka over her head and struggled to unzip the front opening which now lay flat and heavy with water. Success came slow, but not the rain. Water poured through the opening and gushed toward Dacton's face.

Talina grabbed the rag she'd used earlier and wedged it between his face and the tent floor so he wouldn't inhale liquid into his lungs. He couldn't die on her, not now. She inched her way out of the flattened shelter.

Wind-driven rain pelted her face as she confronted the savage storm. She turned her back to the wind and held the round light over the tent. As she feared, he had been crushed by a tree, and it was up to her to remove it without injuring him further. She did not have a warrior's strength, and there was no one to help. Defeat consumed her with more intensity than the storm.

Something pushed on her back and her heart jumped in her chest, but the weather muffled her scream. She turned to find Dacton's esroth's nose in her face. "Thank The Powers of The Universe you're still here." She patted the neck of the drenched animal. A rope hung from the esroth's halter and instantly she formed a plan.

She lifted the now tattered tent flap and wiggled her way back inside till she was next to Dacton. Her hand found his leg and she moved it down his muscled leg until she reached his boot. Her fingers threaded around a cold shaft of metal. She carefully pulled the cutter free, then wiggled up to the edge of where the tent wall and floor connected. The sharp blade easily sliced through the fabric and opened the side of the tent for easy access.

Before she could remove her saddle she had to replace it with something to keep the full weight of the tree off of Dacton. She peeked outside. The one thing these mountains were full of was rocks. She scooted outside through the slit she'd made and began to pick up the largest, flattest rocks she could carry. Soon she had a pile tall enough to stack. First she shoved them all inside, then crawled in herself and stacked them along Dacton's side next to her saddle.

Gently she pulled and tugged to ease her shorter saddle free, relieved the tree's weight shifted to the pile of rocks instead of crushing Dacton to death. She prayed the remaining saddle could sustain its position until she removed the tree. Thank the Gods her saddle had been smaller. The leather had sucked up a lot of water and had gained several pounds. She half drug it to the esroth's side.

After a deep breath, she lifted the saddle waist high, then with commanding determination she managed to hoist it head high. With one last push she managed to drop it on the esroth's back. She reached under his belly, grabbed the soggy, leather billet strap, and threaded it through the ring on the saddle skirt. When she tried to tighten the cinch it was like rubber, and stretched more than she thought possible.

Adrenaline pumped harder, and she found a strength she never knew she possessed. She wiped her eyes, not sure if it was rain or tears, grabbed the rope tied to the esroth's halter and walked him around the tent and carefully positioned him so the tree would move in the right direction. She untied the rope from the halter and moved it to the saddle horn. Once she tied it to the saddle she grabbed the free end, secured it around the tree trunk that held Dacton prisoner, and thanked her lucky stars it was long enough.

"Okay baby, nice and easy. That's it." The esroth groaned. Talina pulled on the bottom strap of the halter. "Come on, you can do it. We have to save Dacton. Come on." She pulled with all her strength, but she slid in the mud and landed on her backside in the rushing water that flowed around her from the surrounding hills.

The esroth was now next to her, pulling with all his strength. He danced and jerked against the line until he lost his footing. The esroth's legs gave , and she watched in horror when his hindquarters hit the ground. "Whoa boy. Easy." She managed to stand and grab the frightened animal's halter. She pulled and the animal snorted. With all her strength she pulled again, this time the esroth managed to reposition his back legs and rise to stand on all four. Talina hugged the esroth's neck and patted his rain-soaked hair. Her hand eased its way up to the animal's forehead. "I don't know what Dacton was doing with his hand on you, but I'll try anything." She spit water from her mouth.

Sheet lightning flashed so brightly it blinded her. The esroth bolted forward in one tremendous leap and pulled the uprooted tree with him. "Thank you!" Talina rushed to untie the rope and free the esroth. She patted his rump. "Good boy." She untied the rope and freed the animal. "You did a great job, and I thank you. More than you know." She must have lost her mind to talk to an animal in a severe storm, as if he could understand! The lightning may have prompted the burst of energy, but somehow she felt the esroth wanted to help.

Now she needed to check on Dacton. He no longer seemed like her enemy. When he'd battled Krow and his men, she'd had the sick feeling of his mortality. The same feeling pervaded her thoughts again. She could not let him die. She knew then, as she knew now, their destiny was linked, joined in some inexplicable way to the future.

Fighting wind, heavy rain, and blowing debris, she struggled back to Dacton's side. Karma, destiny, or fate...it didn't matter as long as he survived. She removed the wet rag beneath his cheek and slipped her arm under his head. The bleeding had stopped and she wiped his face with the cloth while he lay cold and unmoving.

There was nothing dry to be found, and water poured in where she'd cut the tent. She doubted there was much of the tent intact, but at least the rain did not fall directly on them. She pulled the light stone from her pocket and placed it by their heads, then wrapped her arm around him. He had to wake up. The silly fool had forced her to be here, and he *would* see her home!

In her heart she knew it was more than that. He was dangerous, he was a Protector, and the most exciting man she'd ever met. He made her body ache for his touch. Even through her anger, when he claimed her as "his woman", she'd felt proud. Dacton was invincible, he had to be. He was now "her Protector", and she needed him.

She pressed her body tighter against him and hoped her body heat might help, even if she was wet and half frozen. Damn the weather, and whoever caused it!

Their conversation played in her mind. Dacton said Kolere insisted he take her. Kolere? The man who had been like a second father, a man she trusted and respected? It was a hard concept to grasp, but Dacton knew of the legend, and only Kolere could have told him. She'd always wondered if Kolere had confided in her father, but even if he had, her father had not seen Dacton.

She stroked the side of his face and traced the hard line of his jaw. The stubble of his beard teased her fingers, but the fire that erupted with his every touch was gone. He felt cold, the way she'd once believed him to be.

How ironic to lay beside the man she'd wanted to kill not long ago, and to worry he might die. He'd shown her he wasn't the uncaring monster he pretended to be. She would even put up with his arrogant remarks and rude behavior just to see him well again.

They would survive this, and she'd help him. No more fighting, or planning escape. She would work with him, for the planet, and for her people. She'd heard dedication and concern in his voice, not the rumored brutality of a killer. It didn't matter who was responsible for the weather threat, she'd deal with the guilty party later. If Dacton could find and destroy the source, she would gladly go with him. The welfare of her people came first, and the best way she could ensure their safety was to be at his side, to see for herself.

Dacton's theory could be true, and if Zotar was the culprit, she'd find proof. It was hard to admit, but she believed Dacton's claim that The Protectorate was innocent in this conspiracy. So many theories, so many lies, yet truth always surfaced to prove itself.

The only thing that mattered this moon-cycle was Dacton. If she were meant to be Legatus, it would happen when she returned. As far as life-mating Zotar, that would never happen. He'd showed signs of selfish ambition, which she'd ignored. When she'd been near Zotar, she'd thought he stirred her womanly desires, but after being with Dacton, there was no comparison.

She pressed her lips to Dacton's and wished he could return her kiss. From the moment she'd seen him, her thoughts were of little else. She wanted his arms around her, his chest pressed tight to her breasts. What would his powerful physique feel like naked against her? Their arms and legs entwined, their mouths joined passionately? Her womanhood throbbed. She should feel guilty for wanting him, but it felt right. May the Gods help her.

She closed her eyes. If only they were at Krow's cave now, in the room they'd shared, under the warm fur cover. It would be heaven. Dacton would make love to her. Not the rape she had accused him of, but slow and deliberate. They would explore each other, taste sweetness and ecstasy.

The morning may bring a change of heart, but the thought of him gave warmth to the bone-chilling darkness. Had she seen the same need in his eyes? Or was she imagining the attraction between them? Thunder cracked loudly and Talina clung to her Protector even tighter. She couldn't tell him how she felt, and he might not care if she did, but he was hers now—and now was all she had.

CHAPTER SEVENTEEN

O

Talina opened her eyes, and stared at him as if he were a complete stranger to her. Then her lips parted and she let out a shriek that pierced his ears. "Regia, not so loud. For some reason I have a headache." Without warning, Talina pushed his shoulder so he went with it and rolled onto his back. She quickly straddled his abdomen, grasped both of his cheeks in her hands and planted a short, hard kiss on his lips. She pulled back and smiled. What had he done to cause such a response?

Without a word Dacton placed his hand behind her head and guided her back for more. His tongue slipped into her willing mouth and searched every sweet corner while she returned his kiss with a fever that drove him wild. His manhood pressed tight against his very waterlogged pants, but nothing could suppress the fire she ignited. Reluctantly he ended the kiss and freed her head from his grasp. "Does this mean you're glad I didn't die?"

Talina pulled back and laughed. "It does, but don't get any ideas."

"Never." The blush on her cheeks said she was vulnerable, scared, yet curious. She'd caught him off guard with her show of affection, but he had to admit, it was the nicest morning greeting he'd ever had. Protectors never woke with a woman at their side. They slept alone, to guard against attachments, and if Talina offered such a wake-up call every morning, he could become instantly attached.

Talina wrung out the bottom of her tunic. "How do you feel?"

"I've been better, but I'll live." He loved the smile she gave him. Who knew she could become even more beautiful when she was happy. "We need to get out of this soggy tent." She climbed off him, lifted the fabric of the side wall and stepped out. "Now I know why we're so wet."

Talina laughed. "I made an adjustment last night."

"I see that." Inch by inch he struggled out of the tent, but when he tried to stand, he was not quite ready for the struggle. He finally managed to stand straight once again. Thankfully his back had not been broken, but he wished the damn headache would quit. He peeled off his vest and shirt and hung them over a limb of the fallen tree to dry.

"You're badly bruised." Talina steeped closer and ran her fingertips over Dacton's dark purple ribs. "Are they broken?"

Dacton raised his arms above his head, twisted and bent in all directions. "No, just bruised. A condition I'm more than familiar with." When he turned to face Talina her gaze became fixed on his chest. Was she admiring him, or plotting her next retaliatory move?

"Thank the stars."

The concern in her voice sounded sincere. "What has come over you, Regia? Did the storm dampen your spirit?"

"No." Talina took a step back. "I thought about what you said last moon-cycle, and I've decided to help you."

Her change of opinion seemed sudden, so caution was still in order "Has this realization come from fear, or understanding?" She couldn't have altered her opinions this much over the moon-cycle, but he'd give her the benefit of the doubt.

"When I thought you were going to die, I realized that if what you said was true, my planet, and my people will not survive unless *we* save them. And I know Kolere would not send me into the wilderness with a Protector unless he had a very good reason."

"Fair enough." It was too early to celebrate, but he was grateful her struggle had temporarily subsided. "We have to get out of these wet clothes." Dacton watched Talina walk off with a smile on her face. She was acting strange, or was he just seeing her relaxed for the first time? There was more to the woman than he knew, but it would be dangerous to learn more.

Dacton pulled two backpacks from the tent and searched for dry garments, but found none.

"Dacton!"

He heard Talina call him in a happy voice, and wished she could stay that way forever. Only a few time-units ago she'd tried to escape, ready to kill him if necessary. How could a woman change her mind that quickly and seem so sincere? What puzzled him most was her kiss. There had been no pretension, or hesitation. Not even the best actress could convince him if he hadn't felt it for himself. Knowing she needed him could explain part of her light mood, but not all of it. If she still viewed him as her enemy she would have left him to die last moon-cycle. Instead she'd saved his life.

Talina looked less and less like a hostage and more like a woman—a very desirable woman. He had to forget their kiss and the feel of her tempting body pressed against his. He was a Protector, sworn to duty, and obligated to keep her safe. If Zotar even suspected he had a soft spot for her, he'd use her without thinking twice; a perfect example of why The Protectorate initiated the marriage ban.

Emotional blackmail was the easiest way for any enemy to invoke cooperation, even in a warrior. As a Protector he was prepared to die for the cause, but he knew of no man that would sacrifice his family, especially his life-mate. Talina was important to her people and Ora's future. He had to focus on his mission, and there was no room for personal feelings.

He found her behind a bush, her back to him. Her golden hair glistened in the sun, and caressed her naked body. The sight of fair skin, and soft curves caused blood to settle in his groin. He retreated quietly before he forgot every rule he'd been taught. She'd feel violated if she knew he'd seen her, and things were going too well at the moment to risk a setback.

"Where are you?" he called from a safe distance.

"Over here. I found some clothes Leana wrapped in waterproof cloth, so stay where you are, I'm changing."

A little late on that announcement since her bare skin was now etched in his memory forever, and the effect she had on him was quite visible. "Did you find anything for me to wear?"

A pair of pants and a tunic flew over the top of the bush. "Thanks." He removed the wide belt, pulled off his boots and made quick work of removing his rain-soaked pants. He actually felt warmer naked in the cold morning air. When he reached for the dry pants he caught a glimpse of Talina out the corner of his eye. He fought a smiled. She might be innocent, but her hungry gaze certainly was not. He laughed to himself when he heard her walk away.

"Are you dressed?" she called.

"I'm decent." Dacton finished fastening the pants and pulled on his boots. He turned to find her deep blue eyes glued to his chest.

"Dear stars, look at you." Talina stepped closer.

Her delicate hand reached out for him and her fingers traced a scar on the left side of his chest. He'd just regained his control and here she was, running her hands across his body. By the Gods! How could he ignore her as a woman when she tempted him at every turn?

His arm slid around her waist and he pulled her to his chest, trapping her arms in front of her. He lowered his mouth and tasted her again. She was sweet and warm. Her tongue danced with his, and he felt a repressed passion within her he longed to free. He wanted to love her slowly, to savor all she had to offer, to teach her the ways between a man and a woman. However, he knew that as a princess, Talina could only release her passion with her life-mate. He ended the kiss, but held her shivering body tight. Her eyes locked with his, and he saw a trust he could not violate.

"Regia, I must warn you. To play games with me will endanger your life."

Talina caught her breath. "I didn't consider that a game."

Dacton smiled. "You should." She was so naive, and it was best to leave her that way.

"What if I said I don't care?"

"Then I would have to make love to you right here, right now. Is that what you want?" He felt her supple body go rigid in his arms. She lowered her gaze and he released her. "As I thought." He pulled on the dry tunic then picked up the warrior's belt and fastened it in place. He knew she'd be angry and he braced himself, but he'd meant every word he'd said. Making love to her would be magic. He wanted to hold the beautiful Regia in his arms, feel her respond to him, and hear her voice whisper his name. It would be heaven, but they would both have Diabolous to pay.

* * * *

Talina watched Dacton walk toward the tattered tent. Her fingers touched her lips where his lips had been. She'd never forget the feel of him. He had challenged her, and she failed. She was no match for the seductive warrior. Besides being a fearless Protector, he was obviously experienced with women, and that put her at a disadvantage. She didn't know how to play coy flirtatious games like other maidens. She found his kiss exciting, tempting, but most of all, intoxicating. He made her want more. Dacton had a no-nonsense way of looking at everything, but she'd seen it in his eyes—he wanted her.

The storm must have dampened her thinking. She'd as much as offered herself to him! Talina DeAmarant, willing to give her virginity to a Protector? She must be crazy to throw caution to the wind simply because a man pressed his burning need against her, promising fulfillment and passion. Only lust could make her so careless. Raw animal attraction had that effect on men, and obviously women could suffer from it as well. He wanted her the same as she wanted him, no matter how ludicrous it seemed. Now that she acknowledged what it was that sparked between them, she could control herself.

This mission would end, and Dacton would return to The Protectorate without question, or regret, and she would be a branded woman, facing life alone. Her people would never accept a Protector as her escort, and definitely not as her life-mate. She'd be lucky to keep them from killing him. If they were destined to complete this mission together, so be it, but she'd keep her distance, and her virginity. Because they had spent time alone together, she was already considered a branded woman, but that did not mean she had to give in to temptation and make matters worse.

The bush behind her rustled. She held her breath while fear pounded in her chest and her heart raced. The sound moved closer and closer. She slowly turned and headed toward Dacton, afraid she might provoke an attack if were a.... No, it was not be a Pengore. It was probably a snake. Halfway to the warrior she broke into a run and did not stop until her arms were around his waist, her face buried in his chest.

"What's wrong Regia?"

"There's a...a..." Her voice failed and all she could do was point.

Dacton squeezed her tight then released her. He picked up his sword from the pile of supplies and pulled it from its scabbard. "Stay here."

She watched him disappear into the brush. Her pulse throbbed through every inch of her body and she began to shake. It would not be Krow's men, so it had to be.... Dear Gods, no! Her blood pumped faster. Was there anything the man feared? She prayed he was safe and not under attack by a Pengore.

Laughter rang through the trees and she knew her fears had been unfounded. First she saw the top of Dacton's head, then the rest of his body came into view as he made his way up the hill. What in the stars did he have in his arms?

Dacton closed the distance between them, a wide grin on his face. He stopped in front of Talina and held the small furry creature in one hand for her to inspect. "This, my fair Regia, is an Atew. Very harmless I assure you. He tells me he only wanted to make your acquaintance."

"He talks?" She stared at the furry little animal.

"To me he does." Dacton touched the animal's forehead. "He wishes to be our companion, and he would like you to hold him."

Talina took the furry red Atew from Dacton, but needed both of her hands to support him. He was the size of a one annual-cycle-old baby, with big round black eyes that stared up at her while he squeaked happily. She stroked his back and he began to make sounds like a feline purring. She glanced at Dacton's handsome face to find a devilish smile and a twinkle in his dark eyes.

"He wants you to give him a name, Regia."

Talina smiled and turned her gaze back to the creature in her arms. She'd never had a normal childhood, or a pet. When she scratched behind his ear the thought came to her. "Kiko. Your name is Kiko."

Dacton smiled. "He is very pleased."

Kiko snuggled against her breast and his satisfied purr grew louder. "How does he talk to you?"

"We make a mental connection." Dacton petted Kiko's back. "We read each other's mind."

"Is that what you do with the esroths when you put your hand on their foreheads?" Talina noticed his reluctance to answer and wondered why he seemed shy about such a remarkable ability.

"Yes. Each animal has their own vibrational level, and when I touch them, I tap into that unseen current, and the lines of communication open."

"I've never heard of such an ability, but it sounds intriguing." Talina placed Kiko on the ground where he clung to her leg with his short little arms, and his long fingers tightly grasped the fabric of her pants. "Do all of your people have this talent?"

"In general, no. Only a few psychics share the ability."

"How did you gain such powers?" Talina laughed when Kiko formed himself into a ball and rolled around in circles.

"My aunt is a psychic, she taught me. There is much to learn from animals."

She watched Kiko roll away from her and close the distance between her and Dacton. He landed against his leg and the furry guy fell backwards, kicked his stumpy legs and squealed wildly. She had to laugh at his silly antics, and even Dacton chuckled at him.

"I fear we have gained a mischievous helper for our quest."

Kiko jumped to his feet, scampered to the tent and dove inside.

"It appears you're right." Talina laughed when Kiko bounced around inside the tent and pushed the walls out in a different place every time he jumped. "You're the reason the esroths did not run away in the storm. If hadn't been for the esroth you'd still be pinned under that tree."

"You saved my life."

Talina turned her back on him before he could she her cheeks turn red. She felt the heat nearly burn her face, and she could not let he see her as weak.

"Don't be embarrassed. I know what you did for me, Regia, and I offer my thanks."

"I had to keep you alive since you dragged me out here in the wilderness to do, God knows what."

"It's comforting to know you'd miss me." Dacton stepped closer. "I won't forget what you did." He picked up her hand and raised it to his lips. "Please accept my sincere thanks." He kissed her fingers.

A shiver ran down her spine. His sincerity pierced through her, and his light masculine touch awakened feelings she'd vowed to ignore. "You're welcome, but..."

"No buts, no excuses." Dacton brought her fingers back to his lips and gently rubbed them back and forth before leaving a kiss on the back of her hand. "Don't make light of what you did. You could have left me to die, but you did not. That's all that matters."

"I wish that was all that mattered." Talina glanced at the torn tent then back at Dacton. "Where are we going?"

Dacton crossed his arms over his chest. "The Peaks of Venda."

Shock shot through her and her eyes widened. She felt her smile turn to a frown. "Why? Nothing lives there. It's a frozen wasteland!"

"You don't know about my conversation with Krow, but he confirmed what The Protectorate knew. Zotar built a reactor there, and it's our job to destroy it."

"*Our* job? What in the stars can I do?"

CHAPTER EIGHTEEN

"Kolere said you hold the key, and I trust his wisdom." That was a difficult statement, but if he wanted her help, he could not show doubt. If Kolere were here, he could explain all the magical nonsense he claimed they possessed. The amulet had been quiet since he'd found Talina, and her chain had done nothing more than adorn her wrist. If they possessed tools of destruction he'd be surprised.

Talina stared. "I have no key, if that's what you're thinking."

"Do you doubt Kolere?"

"I never have before, but this is hard to understand."

"Let me show you." He walked to the tent. When Dacton raised the cut side of the tent Kiko jumped up in the air and landed in the middle of his chest. When the creature grabbed his tunic and clung tightly he heard Talina laugh behind him. If Kiko had the power to make her happy he'd put up with the little fur-ball and his mischievous ways.

"I shall find you a place to sleep." Dacton grabbed a supply pack and emptied the contents on top of the tent. He gently helped Kiko inside one of the two pouches, then carried the pack to a nearby tree and hung it over a low branch. "He'll be happy there for a little while."

Dacton returned to the collapsed shelter and found what he'd been looking for before he'd scared Kiko to death. He shook water off of the scroll then held it out toward Talina. "It's a bit soggy I fear, but still legible." She took it from him and he patiently waited while she read every word.

Talina finished, rolled the ancient scroll then clutched it tightly against her heart. What he was not ready for were the tears that ran down her cheeks. "Why do those words upset you, Regia?"

"Kolere read this to me on my sixteenth birth-cycle."

Dacton decided to busy himself, since the look she gave him seemed to beg for a bit of space right now. When all the wet items were situated in the sunshine, he turned and found Talina perched on a nearby rock. She held the scroll in front of her, head down, and her hands were shaking so badly he was surprised she had not dropped it in the mud below. He had to wonder if those words held a deeper meaning.

He walked over to her and sat next to her on the large, flat rock. "Please, tell me why you're crying. I want to help." She looked at him, her face full of emotion, but he doubted she actually saw him.

"I don't believe you understand what is written on this paper." Talina raised the scroll, then lowered it. More tears fell. "Two flames converge as one, refers to lovers consummating their life-mating, or their love. "Everyone on Ora knows that phrase since it has been a part of our life-mating ceremony for over a centrum. In fact, rumor held that those very words were added at the wedding of Princess Luana to her warrior, Mandor.

"Kolere read this to me, but he actually gave it to you, therefore it must be very important." She shook her head. "I suppose Kolere tried to prepare me for this moment, but...." She sighed. "I did not understand much of anything back then. He also said time would make all things clear. The legend is clearer now, yet I have no idea what to do."

"I know what my assignment is, but I am also unclear about what Kolere wants from both of us." He reached out and tucked several locks of loose hair behind her ear so he could better see her beautiful face. "I suppose we will learn together what it all means."

"Right now everything sounds ambiguous. What do you think?"

"Don't get angry, but we cannot afford to dance around the issue, Regia. It indicates we are to make love, to bond as only lovers can."

She squared her shoulders and took a deep breath. "I agree. The only question is, do we?"

Dacton turned toward Talina, picked up a thick lock of hair and let it sift through his fingers. "I will never do anything to hurt you, and I will not force you to do anything you do not want to do." He pulled her into his embrace and held her shaking body. "I'm here to save you, your people, and your planet."

He felt Talina's heart race against his chest. She was in his arms, a man she barely knew. Did her body scream for his touch the way his screamed for hers? Was fate asking a sacrifice, or had it offered a blessing? She pulled away from him and sat up straight next to him.

Talina clasped her hands in her lap. "How do you feel? I mean do you want to... ah..." Talina took a deep breath. "Do you think we should, aah, consummate our relationship?"

"I'm a warrior, Regia, not a philosopher...and certainly not a monk. As a man, I cannot deny my desire for you. As a warrior, I don't see what purpose would be served by our joining."

"Purpose?" Talina stood up.

"Regia, do not be angry. It's important to discuss our feelings and ideas." Her lips were tightly pursed, eyes squinted, and he could swear he saw anger boil in her veins. "I don't know what I said that made you so angry, but..."

"If you think for one moment that I cannot resist you, and that I willingly want to join with you, you're a fool!"

Dacton stood and rested his hands on her shoulders. He felt her shake, a sure sign of nerves and fear. "Regia, I meant no insult. It is your reputation I'm considering."

"It's too late for that. We've already spent two moon-cycles together, alone, and it only takes one to become branded!"

"Branding a woman is an archaic rule that should be abolished. If I leave you untouched your future life-mate will know you aren't truly a branded woman."

"You're deluded! Since you're here on a mission, I'm sure you've done your homework. You know exactly what I'm talking about. But what do you care? You're not a public personality, and you're certainly *not* a woman!"

"I'm glad you noticed." He smiled, but it seemed only he thought it amusing. "Sorry. I never meant any harm to come to you, and that includes your reputation." Dacton loosened his hold. "I will lay down my life to save yours. You must believe that."

"I must?" She sighed. "You have no right to tell me what I *must* do, or not do. Your words are empty."

"You're right." He shook his head. It seemed he'd made a real mess of things. To say he had not used diplomacy would be an understatement. This was his last chance to gain her cooperation. A warrior always knew when it was now or never. "I am very sorry, Princess Talina. I realize I ripped you from your home, and due to time limitations, I have pushed you to this point. If there had been a nicer way, I would have used it. Under the circumstances I had no other options, and for that I apologize."

She looked at him as if he'd become someone else. What was going on in that beautiful mind of hers? He faced the aged old problem of how to deal with women, something he had yet to master. He took her hand and led her to sit on a large, fallen tree. Her stare made him nervous. She was sizing him up and thinking about her next move, and he had no idea what that might be.

"Talina," he paused and searched for the right words. "I know I've done nothing to earn your trust, but my objective is to save your planet from destruction. The legend has complicated my mission and created obstacles I never planned on."

"You mean me, don't you?"

"Honestly?" She nodded in a no-nonsense manner. "Yes, but only from the standpoint of being slowed down. I'm trained to move quickly and alone, or with other men who move at my pace." He hoped her silence meant she understood. "I'm sure I'm not telling you anything new."

"Why didn't you ignore Kolere and the legend?"

"My orders from The Protectorate were specific. To follow Kolere's directions to the letter."

"Well, I'm not under any orders, and..."

Dacton toyed with the blond curls that hung down her back. "And you will do what's right for your people. You know you will serve them best if you follow your heart."

"You think you know me, warrior, but you don't."

Dacton let the locks fall from his hand. "You're loyal to your father and your people. A bit stubborn, but the kind of woman that will do what is asked of her. You've been tutored your entire life to fulfill this very role. You'll do what's right, no matter the sacrifice." Dacton picked up her hand and pressed her fingers to his lips and tenderly kissed them. "Tell me if I'm wrong, Regia."

"You want me to admit that I'll sleep with you for my people's sake? You insist I help you, but won't say how. You claim you're here to apprehend Zotar for The Protectorate, then you slip and say you intend to kill him. You don't deserve my honesty, or trust." She jerked her hand back. "You're no better than the man you hunt!"

Talina all but flew off the log and wasted no time putting him as far behind her as possible. They were finally talking, which was good, but he'd obviously insulted her again. She looked like she wanted to kill him if she could.

She was a complicated woman, and far too beautiful. When he talked to her he'd seen more emotion mirrored in her dark blue eyes than he'd ever seen in another human being. She hid a deep passion she knew nothing about. He'd told her the truth, however, there was more to it. He had to finish this conversation once and for all.

He stood and walked to where she leaned against a tree, her arms crossed over her breasts. She glared at him, the need to strike evident in every fiber of her being. He had to get her to listen even if he infuriated her. He suspected she would prefer the direct approach. "Well, princess, are you going to listen to me, or are you going to continue with your misplaced anger?" He kicked a rock with the toe of his boot.

"It's more like your misplaced arrogance, warrior!"

"I deserved that."

"And a lot more. You said you didn't like games, well, neither do I, so stop playing with me."

Dacton lowered his arms to his side, his hands fisted. "Fine. You deserve the whole story. Let's sit." He escorted her to a nearby rock and helped her sit, then he knelt on the ground and faced her in an effort of humility.

"Zotar captured my brother's ship and killed his entire crew. He held my brother, Baleko prisoner for twelve sun-cycles, and tortured him endlessly, until his battered body could stand no more and death relieved his pain. Zotar recorded every detail on a vid-chip and sent it to me." Dacton lowered his head and stared at the ground. "Yes. I want to kill Zotar. For Baleko, his men, and all his other innocent victims." Dacton looked up and saw Talina blink back tears.

"I'm sorry about your brother. No man deserves such treatment." She reached out and touched Dacton's cheek with her hand. "If Zotar did that to a member of my family, I, too, would want him dead." She pulled her hand back. "I understand your need to kill Zotar, but you're letting revenge consume your soul."

He took a long, deep breath and focused on Talina's expression. She seemed to have genuine sympathy. He was not sure she believed what he told her about Zotar, but she was right about revenge consuming his soul. "Zotar murdered my brother in cold blood, and I intend to make him pay."

Talina shook her head and sighed. "You don't fear death and that's what makes you dangerous to everyone, including yourself. Your driving passion to kill Zotar will leave you with no future once you deliver your revenge. You can't live solely for retribution."

"I will have my vengeance, and you will have your planet." He noted a reluctance in her demeanor. "If you're worried about Zotar's miserable life, don't. He'd kill you in a heartbeat if he even suspected you did not believe in him." She pursed her lips and stared at him in disbelief. "You like the man, don't you?"

"What I know about him is not bad, so you cannot blame me for my opinion of him."

He turned and walked away from her in an effort to cool off before he exploded. How anyone could like that horrific man he would never know. Of course Talina did not know about everything the man had done, or how evil he truly was, so he could not blame her for her feelings. She would never share his deep-seated need for revenge, and that was fine, as long as she cooperated.

The crunch of dry leaves beneath his feet brought him back to reality. He had to calm himself and gain her trust and cooperation—not an easy task. This entire mission seemed next to impossible, but he had accepted it on The Protectorate's terms and given his word. Now he had to make it work, whatever it took.

He began to walk back toward her and heat spread through his body. Every time he looked at the woman his mind flew to forbidden places. He must be losing his mind to allow any woman to affect him in such a primal manner. He'd always taken pride in his control where women were concerned, but Talina stripped away every one of his honorable intentions and replaced proper thoughts with desire, lust, and the promise of forbidden pleasures.

"What is it, warrior?"

He could not tell her what had been running through his mind, so he quickly changed mental gears. "By taking you from Sobrie I realize I created as many problems for you as I did for myself."

"You prevented me from being installed as Legatus, my rightful place by birth. A position I've prepared for all my life—a position I fear has already been filled in my absence by my cousin, Regnar, who is a close ally of Zotar. By taking me, you allowed it to happen."

"That may be, but you're talking about a job, I'm talking about keeping your planet from complete annihilation. There is nothing happening in the government that cannot be changed."

"A job? Really? I was about to be the *first woman Legatus*! Do you have any idea what that means?" Talina let out a scream. "Of course you don't! You couldn't possibly know. It's not exactly like you gave me a choice. I might have gone with you if you'd bothered to explain yourself."

"You'd willingly have come with *me*, a Protector?" Dacton shook his head. "Lying does not become you, Princess."

"You're right. I need to be in Sobrie to keep my father from being forced from the throne, and possibly worse."

"Even a Protector can stop only one disaster at a time." Dacton stepped closer and laid a hand on her shoulder. "I'll see to your father and the government when we return."

"That may not be soon enough. He could be dead by then."

"He's being looked after."

"By who?"

"A trusted friend."

"Yours, or mine?"

Dacton slowly pulled his hand from her shoulder. He should be ashamed of himself, but he wanted to kiss her. Would his kiss make a difference to her, or would she still hate him? It did not matter since he would keep his distance. "A mutual friend."

Talina laughed. "We have no mutual friends. In fact, I doubt you have any friends!"

He smiled. It was all he could do at the moment. He understood her frustration all too well since he shared the same emotion. "You may be right about me, but your father has friends—friends who care, and The Protectorate cares."

"Really? The Protectorate?"

Dacton grinned. "I was hoping we could work together to keep your father in power and save your planet. If that is your desire, you can help me get this stuff dried out. We can't leave with wet supplies. Not where we're going."

CHAPTER NINETEEN

"Progress is excellent. Your army should be battle ready in a few sun-cycles." Zotar studied the cowardly leader. Ruler Cortain, indeed. He would be ruler soon, and Cortain would be—dead. As for his pretty little daughter, he might let her live as long as she was faithful to him, and did as she was told.

"Very good." Cortain rubbed his forehead. "Is there any word from the search party?"

"I'm afraid not." He wanted to put Cortain out of his misery right now, and he would, but he still served a purpose. The time was not yet right. He had to be patient to bring his plan to completion. Cortain looked like he was going to cry. Of course he missed his precious little bitch of a daughter, but he should act like a man. He told the old man he wanted to life-mate Talina, but he never would.

Everything had changed since Talina's departure from Sobrie. The people grew restless. Septra and Regnar were about ready to dislodge Cortain from his throne. Little did they know he was about to create a war and turn this peaceful planet upside-down.

As Ruler of Ora, Cortain was useless. The fool sent his private Royal Guard, his best and most loyal men to search for his daughter, but they had yet to return. "Cortain, I feel a need to search for Talina myself." Zotar carefully studied Cortain's reaction. "With your permission, of course."

"I think your services would be better utilized here, Zotar."

"With all due respect. My training program is in capable hands, unlike Talina. I have the skills necessary to find her. I will succeed where others have failed. If you value her life, you will not deny my request." He knew his words struck a sensitive cord.

"How many guards will you require?"

"Twelve men are at the ready. We only await your word."

"Sir! Sir!"

Zotar turned to see one of his men running toward him with something in his hand.

"This just arrived on the ship's com."

He took the sealed envelope from the man and ripped it open. He quickly read it, then handed the ransom request to Cortain. He watched the ruler read, and based on the expression on Cortain's face he knew, beyond a doubt the stupid father would pay every credit he had to get his precious little girl back. He was weak, and Talina made him weaker, which also made the job of unseating him from power even easier. But first he would become richer. The Protector may have Talina, but Cortain thought the note was from them. His plan was finally coming together.

"Zotar." Cortain shook his head. "Go find Talina. According to this demand, we have ten sun-cycles. If you cannot find her, return on the ninth sun-cycle and arrangements will be made to pay their demands."

"I will do my best, sir." Zotar bowed, then turned on his heel and left the room. He could almost smell the millions of credits coming his way, not to mention the power. Ora would be his, and his alone.

* * * *

Dacton could not believe they had wasted the entire sun-cycle waiting for their supplies to dry. The saddles were still damp, and so were their fur parkas. The rain soaked mountain faded behind them the higher they went into the forbidden territory of the Boranian Mountains. Patches of ice dotted the hillside where puddles had frozen. The air had become thinner and his lungs burned with each breath he took. Large green-tinted clouds obscured what little sun remained, but at least they had made some progress.

Talina may have greeted him with a kiss, but now she seemed angry. She had not spoken a word since she mounted her esroth. Was it something he'd told her? He'd probably made a mistake to confide in her about Baleko, and his desire to kill Zotar. Why had he been so careless?

He'd let his emotions rule his mind. Even a young cadet knew better. Rules. He'd broken every one. He silently cursed Kolere. No, his own actions were unforgivable. There was no excuse. He'd exposed himself to her, and he couldn't do a damn thing about it now.

It wasn't Baleko, or Zotar that stirred her anger. She'd bristled when he said their joining would serve no purpose. It may have been callous to say, but it was for her own good. He could only bring her pain, and she deserved so much better. He did wonder if she had a desire to mate with him because she was attracted to him. Or was that his ego talking?

Whatever the reason, their joining would not be a good idea. He may have wanted her from the moment he first held her in his arms, and she now consumed his every thought, but that did not give him permission for anything. Her every touch sparked a need and increased the temptation, but he dare not give in to lust which could lead to self-destruction.

Nothing in his life had ever been simple, and this mission was proving no different. He was well prepared to destroy the reactor and battle Zotar, but he was not ready to deal with a relationship with Talina. When she hated him he could be the ruthless warrior she expected, but he could not revert to the heartless, unknown Protector after she saved his life. What surprised him most was that he enjoyed her company.

Kolere had presented him with quite a dilemma, but there was only one solution. If she came to him it would be of her own free will. He wanted her to want him for himself, yet he sensed she might seduce him out of some misplaced sense of duty. When he glanced back at her, he realized he wanted her under any terms. He wished he had a logical explanation for his feelings.

Dacton raised his hand to warn Talina, then pulled his mount to a halt and dismounted. He watched Talina stop her esroth beside him. She looked weary, her body shivered, her lips quivered and were nearly blue. The expression on her flawless face tore at his heart. He extended his arms and lifted her off the dark hairy beast and eased her to the ground. They all needed a rest.

"Tha...tha...thank you."

Dacton nodded then moved to the pack esroth to remove the large fur pelt that covered the supplies. He took the pelt to Talina and draped it around her shoulders. When he snuggled the cover under her chin his cold hands brushed against her icy skin.

"I never kn...knew it could be so co...cold." Talina stared for a moment then smiled. "Even the whiskers on your face are covered in ice."

"I'm afraid it will get worse, Regia. Are you up to it?"

Talina nodded. "Wh...when will we reach the Peaks of Ve...Ve...Venda?"

"Late tomorrow."

"Why didn't The Protectorate se...se...send an army to solve the problem a long time ago?"

"They did Regia. Zotar intercepted their ship and killed them all." Baleko's face formed in his mind, contorted with pain, bloody from

Zotar's abuse. One look into Talina's eyes and he knew she understood. All that statement did was stir his need for revenge. If he killed Zotar, it had to look like an unpreventable accident. The council trusted him to complete the mission as assigned, and until now, he had never disobeyed an order. As much as he hated to let The Protectorate down, family loyalty came first. No man murdered a Rovarn without paying the ultimate price.

"I still don't un...un...understand why The Protectorate sent you alone. By the stars, you need an army. How are we going to destroy the reactor by ourselves? Do you really think Zotar would be foolish enough to leave it unguarded?"

"Of course not. But an army draws attention, as well as a ship large enough to transport them. Surprise is our best weapon."

"Fine, but they still should have given you a few men." Talina coughed. "Don't say it. I know. Tr...tr...trust you, you're the biggest and meanest warrior in the galaxy. But frankly, that does little to ease my mind. And it sure in Diabolus doesn't make me feel wa...wa...warmer!"

Dacton glanced at the sky. "We'll make camp here."

"This looks like as good a place as any to become an ice cube, furrrr...ozen for eternity."

Dacton pulled Talina to him and wrapped his arms around her. "I will not let you freeze, Regia."

"I think we should go back. Krow and his men are only two sun-cycle's back. You know he wants to help. Please, Dacton."

"We can't. You know that." She laid her head on his chest as if she had just resigned. It felt good to hold her, even if she was shivering. He laid one hand on the back of her half-frozen hair. She needed warmth, and fast.

"I think you have a death wish, warrior."

"No, but I do have a wish to start a fire." Dacton turned, but kept his arm around her back and eased her over to a rock not far away and helped her to sit. "Wait here while I gather some firewood." She nodded so he turned away from her and hurried up the nearby hill. He gathered branches while walked up the pineus needle covered slope, careful to avoid the hidden rocks. Talina had no idea how fast she could freeze to death in this wilderness. The temp was lower than he'd anticipated at this altitude, which meant they were getting closer to the source.

If Talina died, it would be his fault, and he refused to have her death haunt him for the rest of his life.

* * * *

Talina sat and shivered while she waited for Dacton. It seemed as if he had been gone forever. He was one stubborn man, with an agenda all his own, and she did not like being part of it. The weather had taken a turn for the worse and tiny ice pellets bounced off the extra fur pelt Dacton had thoughtfully wrapped around her, but it no longer kept her warm. She pulled the hood of her parka down lower over her face to protect her eyes. There was no place to hide.

He said he would not let her freeze and she had no choice but to believe him. At least when Dacton was near, her body felt warm and tingly. She should not feel that way around him, yet she could not help herself. In all honesty, she wanted his touch, his kiss, his arms around her, to be held tight against the hard length of his body. May the Gods forgive her, but she wanted him with her, and not just as a Protector. No. She wanted him to be the one to teach her about love.

She looked up and saw Dacton headed toward her with an armful of wood. He dropped it in a pile then picked up his personal backpack. He pulled out a thin sheet of foil looking fabric and carefully piled rocks in the center, then proceeded to build a fire over the stones. He seemed to adapt to everything with ease and always knew the right thing to do.

The scowl on his face chilled her to the bone more fiercely than the cold. He was determined to have everything his way. Was he concerned for her people as he claimed, or was his motive to destroy Zotar at all costs?

Fear for her father's life settled over her like an ominous cloud. She had no doubt that while the defiant Protector dragged her into the unknown wilderness, her father's rule could fall into the hands of Regnar and Septra. They had made futile attempts in the past, but now that she had missed her installation as Legatus, Regnar would take her place. She knew without being told the deed would be done, and that they were more than happy she was missing.

Deep in her soul she sensed a huge betrayal had been put into motion. She sensed her father was in danger, and the feeling grew stronger with each sun-cycle. Dacton would not take her back until he destroyed the reactor, so she might as well cooperate. She would do anything to hasten her return. Yes, anything, and that included giving her virginity to the Protector.

There, she admitted it. She would sacrifice her body to save her people. To spare her father shame, she would leave Sobrie for a distant land and start a new life where no one knew she was a branded woman. Ora was a large planet, surely she could find a place where no one would recognize her.

The thought of bonding with Dacton was most appealing. He was handsome, his body magnificent in every way. Any woman would be honored to have his affections, but that was not what he offered. If they mated, it would not be a matter of the heart, only necessity. Dacton did not care about her. His only concern was revenge and he had made that more than clear. She would be a fool to think he was here to court her, or become her life-mate. It was irrational to long for a piece of his heart, but the need pulled at her more fiercely with each sun-cycle she was with him.

A scurrying sound behind her made her turn just as Kiko jumped at her in a big, flying leap. She caught him in her arms, drew him close, and wrapped the fur around them both. He began to purr and Talina wished all problems could be solved as easily.

CHAPTER TWENTY

Dacton finished the last few tasks, all too aware of Talina's penetrating gaze on his back while he worked. Her silent scrutiny was worse than her accusations. He had to keep her by his side and insure her safety, but could he? Talina was the first woman to even get close to his heart, and he feared she was a woman he could fall in love with.

That was a problem. All Protectors knew the rules and swore an oath to uphold them. As Chief Protector he'd enforced the rule many times, and had lost good men in the process. The non-commitment rule stood firm, and included the Chief Protector as well as anyone he commanded.

Dacton erected the tent, and double-checked every repair he'd made. Talina still remained silent. She was either mad again, or too cold to talk. He laughed to himself. Talina had every right to be upset with him. He'd failed miserably in developing any kind of a relationship with her, not that one was necessary. He'd never shared experiences with a woman, nor spent so much time with one. Kolere would probably scold him for his behavior.

Any thoughts running through that pretty little head of hers were none of his business. She was entitled to her privacy, but he didn't like the tension that had grown between them. He concentrated on the tent. The sooner it was up, the sooner they could avoid the wind that cut through them, and let the hot stones bring feeling back to their numbed bodies. To survive the frigid moon-cycle they would have to share body heat, whether she liked it, or not.

"I didn't think I'd ever see the tent in one piece. That sealer thing you used really did a good job. We don't have anything like that here."

Dacton hammered the last stake into the ground and stood. He watched Talina hug Kiko and rest her chin on his head. "You have no faith." He was happy to hear her voice again. He picked up the supplies and tossed them into the tent. "Move inside Regia, it will be warmer." He almost laughed when Kiko jumped on her back to hitch a ride when she crawled on her hands and knees. But in that position, his gaze did not stay on Kiko. He was in dire need of a distraction, so he turned and walked toward the fire.

As much as he hated to disturb the warm flames, he kicked the burning wood aside and wrapped the glowing rocks in the fireproof tarp. He dragged it to the entrance of the tent then headed back toward the esroths.

Steam rolled off the animal's backs, and he wished humans could stay as warm as these beautiful animals. He gave each of them thanks, along with their freedom for the moon-cycle. The esroths needed to romp, play and graze, which they could only do back down the mountain. Animals could not put into language their thoughts, but they conveyed their loyalty and cooperation in a way he understood. He picked up the saddles and headed for the tent.

When he opened the flap he found Talina arranging the small area, setting out what was left of the fresh food Leana had sent. He lifted the saddles over her spread and settled them in the back, then took off his gloves and rubbed his hands together to warm frostbitten fingers. Talina reached behind him to zip the flap, but he stayed her hand, then pulled the rock-filled tarp inside. "Close it now."

"That's warm!" Talina leaned over the silvery fabric.

Dacton folded the covering back and showed her the pile of heated rocks inside. "It's an old trick."

"You are clever, I'll give you that. But I wouldn't think on a planet like yours, you'd learn primitive survival techniques."

"Protectors spend most of their time in primitive terrain on other worlds, doing what's necessary to survive."

"Do you protect women often?"

"Are you asking how many women I've spent moon-cycles alone with?"

"Not exactly, I was just curious about..."

Dacton caught Talina's hand when she reached for a piece of bread. She was trembling, and her eyes held a strange mixture of emotions. "You're wondering how many women I've made love to?" He watched her gaze fall from him to Kiko. "I will not take advantage of you Regia, you have my word. Nothing will happen between us that you don't want to happen." Her gaze moved back to him, but she had no reply.

The woman was a mystery, unlike any woman he'd met. Slowly he released her, but she did not pull away. A spark of fire blazed in her blue eyes and he wished it were desire, but he suspected a very different feeling. "We will need to share body heat this moon-cycle."

She took a deep breath, tilted her chin higher, and sighed. "I understand."

They ate their modest meal in relative silence, except to reprimand Kiko for taking their food. The furry little Atew kept the atmosphere light, but Talina seemed unusually nervous. When they finished their meal she quickly gathered the food supplies and returned them to the sack. Kiko scratched at the tent flap, so Talina unzipped it and he scurried out.

The moment the area was clear, Dacton reached for the pack he'd never shown her. He emptied the contents on the fur cover. "Each and every item is a vital survival tool."

"Some of those things look dangerous." started here

"That's a navigational device, that's a utility tool." Dacton noticed the uncertainty in Talina's eyes. "Yes, some of these weapons are dangerous."

"Why the sudden urge to share them with me?" She stared at Dacton. "Is this a test?" Talina shook her head and smiled. "I could easily turn them against you to escape."

"You could, but I wouldn't recommend it." He nearly laughed at the defeated look on her face. She was a smart woman and knew she could not survive in the wilderness alone, and he was sure that angered her royal pride. It was best to continue with the lesson. "This is a fusura. You can repair almost anything with it, as you've already noticed. It fuses objects together, either with heat, or if you press this button," he pointed to a small indentation under the short handle, "with chemicals. For material you only need heat."

"I see." Talina cleared her throat. "What about the rest of your unique little toys?

"Toys?" Dacton groaned. He took a deep breath, determined not to let her distract him. "Now this," he pulled a small round object from his pocket, "Is an EG, electronic guard. It's always on, but you can adjust the warning volume. It will alert you to anyone that approaches."

"What if it's non-human?"

He laughed. "Yeah, been there. It detects by heat and motion, nothing is missed." He picked up the largest object and carefully offered it to Talina. "This Regia, is a faze-pistol. It will stun your target, or you can adjust the setting here." He pointed to a round dial on the side of the handle. "By increasing the number, you can instantly kill whatever you aim at. The larger the object, the higher the setting needs to be. Even the lowest setting will force a man to the ground, but not for long."

"Why are you telling me all this?"

"For your safety...and mine." He slid the weapon into the palm of her hand and closed his fingers around hers. "I don't know what we'll encounter, so I want you to be prepared. You may have to use this." He guided her finger around the trigger. "If that time comes, do not hesitate."

Talina shook her head. "I will not kill for you." She pushed the faze-pistol into his lap.

"I am not asking you to kill for me. I'm more than capable. I just want to know that you will at least stun your target long enough to escape." He held the pistol in his hand and studied her scared expression. "You must understand, Regia, I will not be able to stay at you side all the time. If you hesitate you could die. How will you help your people then?"

"Do you really think you can turn me into a warrior? I've never hurt anyone in my life, and I will not start now. Killing is second nature to you. You hold that weapon as if it were an inseparable part of your hand, but I can't."

This was not going well. His intention of teaching her how to protect herself had only managed to ruffle her feathers. Her defenses were tightly drawn, and all he could do was pray she'd use that same anger against an enemy if necessary.

"Talina, I am only suggesting you use a weapon in self- defense. Regard me a killer if you like, but you must focus on survival, no matter the consequences. When someone wants to kill you, you cannot begin a moral debate. You must react."

The only warriors he'd ever trained were willing participants that could not wait to kill on command. Even with time and repetition, he could never do the same with Talina. Time was a luxury he did not have, yet he had to prepare her to take a life if necessary. "You're right, I'm trained to kill. And it is second nature to me. I will kill to protect you, but I must know you will protect yourself."

"I can't say what I'll do if I'm in that situation. You expect too much from me!"

"No, Princess, I do not. You are heir to the throne of Ora. Your people and this planet mean everything to you. All I ask is that you do what you have to do." He thought he saw a spark of understanding in her cobalt eyes. "I have killed, but never for the thrill as you may believe. Only in the line of duty, and in defense of powerless victims."

Had he penetrated that stubborn demeanor of hers enough for her to see the logic of his words? He watched her squirm and play with a golden lock of hair that had escaped the hood of her parka. If anything happened to her he would never forgive himself. His patience wore thin. "Do you understand, *woman?*"

"I understand perfectly, *warrior.*"

Every time he called her *woman,* he could count on an angry response, but he wasn't here to woo her, or gain her friendship. This was a mission of grave importance, nothing more. Yet, if that were true, why did he have to fight the urge to pull her into his arms? He wanted to taste her sweet lips, and feel her body against his. He fought the need to convince her, as only a man could, that everything would be all right.

"How high can you set that thing before you kill a man?"

Dacton smelled success in her timid question. "Six. After that there are no guarantees."

"What are these?" Talina held up several oval shaped objects.

"Those are not for you." He said, gently sliding them from her grasp. "They are very potent explosives and must be handled with care." He picked up another weapon, "You will not need this either."

"You plan to use explosives on the reactor?"

"Exactly. If they don't destroy it, nothing will."

"You missed one."

She handed him a cylinder of similar size, but it was round and no bigger than her thumb. "No, Regia. This is somna. It will render a man unconscious for over a time-unit. Just push the top down one click and point at your target's face. It is only effective within a ten foot radius, but the chemical is very potent. Exact aim is not critical, but you must take care not to inhale any of it yourself, or you will wake up on the ground next to your victim. A two click dose, and the recipient may never wake up."

"Then this will be my weapon of choice."

Her hesitant smile told him he'd made progress. "Somehow I expected you'd like this." He put the cylinder in her hand. "Just remember, somna has no effect against humanoids, or any variety of robots."

"Do you expect any?"

"Zotar has many of them, but I don't expect to see any." He did not want to upset her further, she had enough to worry about. "I want to be sure you will defend yourself if necessary."

The EG expelled a constant beep that continually grew louder. Dacton's hand flew to his cutter. High-tech weapons served their purposes, but nothing felt as secure in a warrior's hand as a well balanced blade.

"What do you think it is?" Talina shivered. "Be careful."

When he unzipped the flap Kiko somersaulted inside and landed in a heap atop the pile of weapons. Talina picked him up and settled him in her lap, his contented purring brought a smile to her face. "At least you had a demonstration of the EG."

"You're right. It works very well."

When she looked at him he saw a new calm in her eyes, and a glow to her skin. It could be the muted light inside the tent, but she looked more beautiful this moon-cycle than he'd ever seen her. He secured the tent flap to distract himself. "Kiko is very devoted to you." He resumed his cross legged position, but when he looked at Talina, he was still mesmerized by her fair features.

"I'm honored." Talina bent and kissed Kiko on the top of his head. "Don't forget to thank Kiko for testing the equipment. You know how he likes to help. Don't you baby?" She scratched Kiko behind his ears. "I've never had a pet."

"I thought every child had at least one."

"Ordinary children, but not the daughter of the king. The palace is not suited for animals."

"Or children." Dacton watched her nod. "You've sacrificed much to be a princess."

Talina looked into Dacton's eyes. "Not really. The rewards are many. I've been denied little."

"Only a normal life."

"What do you mean?"

"Well, did you have school chums? Friends to play with? Did you hang out at the swimming hole and roll in the grass with the sun on your face? And don't forget having a puppy."

"I see what you mean." Talina lowered her lashes. "I had a private tutor, and was not allowed to play. My life has been spent in study and preparation."

"As I thought."

"Dacton, are you sure my father is safe? Who is looking after him? Please tell me. You know I can't betray you out here, and I'll know as soon as I return."

She was right, and he hoped knowing would put her at ease. "I asked Kolere to watch over him." Dacton noticed a hint of a smile. "I told you it was a mutual friend."

"I didn't think we had any mutual friends."

"It seems we have one." Kiko squeaked loudly. "Make that two." Dacton reached out and ruffled Kiko's fur, and in return, the animal's short, stubby fingers grabbed his index finger and held on tight. Dacton sat back and watched Talina reach toward him, disappointed she only wanted to touch Kiko. He'd made a wise choice telling her Kolere cared for her father because she now appeared relaxed.

Kolere would notify The Protectorate if he needed help. A command ship left the sun-cycle after his departure to maintain a distant orbit around Ora, and Kolere possessed a transmitter to alert them. There was an army on board that could deploy on a moment's notice. Neither he nor Kolere wanted to involve them. He hadn't told Talina he could summon help with one of his *toys* should the occasion arise.

A full invasion would not fulfill Kolere's Legend, or offer the opportunity to surprise Zotar. He refused to be denied the long overdue confrontation with his nemesis. Besides, he enjoyed Talina's company. As far as missions went, this was by far the most interesting, and challenging one in quite some time.

"Dacton?"

"I'm sorry. What did you say?"

"I was explaining how devious and manipulative Septra and Regnar can be. They've remained in the background, waiting for the opportunity to seize power. Now that I'm missing, they'll take what they want."

If Septra and Regnar were anything like Zotar, he understood all too well. "You said they're close to Zotar?" He hated to say the despicable man's name.

"Very close. In fact, they introduced Zotar to the council. Septra and Regnar are Zotar's biggest promoters. There's no telling what they'll do if my cousin becomes Legatus in my absence. They could gain total control of the council before we can stop them."

"I see." Everywhere Zotar went, duplicity followed. Zotar had an uncanny ability to sniff out traitors. The adage of like gravitating to like certainly held true where this cunning operator was concerned. The thirst for power, and the capacity to exact the same response in others remained Zotar's prime objective. Dacton shook his head. "Exactly how much power does the position of Legatus hold?"

"Second in command, and should anything happen to the king, the Legatus takes his place." Talina sighed. "Do you see my concern?"

"Your concerns are just, but they wouldn't be fool enough to kill your father. Not this soon." Dacton combed his hair with his fingers. "If they did, it could cause an uprising."

"How can you be sure? They could say he had a heart attack from the stress of my disappearance. Everyone knows how close my father and I are. A stroke at his age would not cause suspicion. We have to get back, I have to..."

"Calm down, Regia. One thing at a time." Dacton took her hand in his. "Zotar will move slowly until he meets resistance, and that won't happen until we return. He needs the people for his army, and wants their support. If he, or anyone else, killed Cortain it would cause unrest among your people. Zotar tried the quick way to power on Strata-II not long ago, and barely escaped with his life. No, even Zotar isn't fool enough to kill your father right now."

"That sounds a bit dramatic, don't you think?"

"Nothing is too dramatic where Zotar is concerned. There's still time. We *will* stop him, Regia."

"You don't paint a very pretty picture." Talina picked up Kiko and placed him in her lap. "I hope you're right about my father's safety."

"I'm a Protector, we're always right." Dacton smiled, then stroked the now sleeping Kiko. The animal was fortunate to have the warmth of her lap to snuggle in.

"You're a bit too arrogant for your own good, warrior."

Dacton grinned. "I've been called that, and worse." A high position required confidence, and a belief in one's abilities, which was easy to misconstrue. For a Protector, there was no other way. To accomplish the mission at hand, he would have to draw upon every strength he possessed.

The velocity of the bone-chilling wind increased, and the temperature had dropped faster than normal. He picked up the heavy fur pelt and handed it to Talina. The tent could protect them from the wind, but the glacial air had already grown crisp to the lungs.

"We will need to share the pelt." Dacton's heart beat a bit faster at the thought of sleeping close to Talina. He thought about his flight suit in the other backpack. He hated the damned metallic fabric, but it was designed to adapt to the wearer's body requirements. No, he would save it for more extreme conditions, this moon-cycle they would share.

"I don't know why Leana only gave us one cover." Talina pushed part of the fur his way.

"Because in her eyes we're life-mated. She expects us to share one pallet. Does that bother you, Regia?"

"Of course not. Your little charade was essential to our safety. I may not be a warrior, but I'm well trained in diplomacy. You knew how the Burly people would feel about me if they knew my identity. And how else could you explain traveling alone with a woman?"

"Actually, I was afraid the men would fight for your womanly favors and decided to spare them the trouble." Talina's lips tightened and she stared at him in a peculiar way, as if she wanted to slap him.

"Spare them the trouble?"

"Yes. Didn't you see how Krow's men ogled you that sun-cycle in the meadow?" He couldn't very well tell her how the thought of another man's hands on her sent rage boiling through his veins, and ignited the urge to fight any man who tried to lay a claim on her. She thought he meant she was not worth fighting for. She could not be more wrong.

For now he would let her believe whatever she wanted because she kept her distance when she stayed angry. The last thing he needed was for her to lie next to him all warm and willing, and look at him with eyes that made him melt. She caused him to ache with desire, yet he gave his word not to touch her—unless she wanted him to. Damn the rules, and damn his honor. It would be a long moon-cycle indeed.

CHAPTER TWENTY ONE

O

Talina laid down as far away from the virile warrior as possible under the circumstances and faced the side of the tent. He scooted closer to her and pulled the heavy fur up to her neck. Kiko curled against her stomach and she was grateful for his warm, cuddly body. Here she was, in the middle of nowhere, with a man she did not know, and a furry creature that had been all too happy to adopt her. This was a first, especially since it was the most un-princess-like thing she had ever done.

How did The Protector view her? It didn't matter what he thought, she was still Talina DeAmarant, future Legatus, and one day, ruler of Ora. Once Ora was safe, Dacton would leave as abruptly as he had arrived. Zotar would be captured or dead, and she would no longer have a potential life-mate. She would also be through with The Protector.

It seemed like they were getting along better. He had not even thrown a chide remark her way in quite some time, which was good since she'd had enough of his male superiority for this sun-cycle. Although he was quite appealing when he took charge with an unequaled confidence not seen in most men.

Enough thinking, it was time for sleep. She closed her eyes, but never felt more awake. How would she ever sleep with such a virile, handsome man lying next to her? Granted, he had no more choice in the matter than she did, but it put them both in an awkward position. This was the most disconcerting situation she had ever been in, yet part of her had begun to enjoy the adventure, and the unequaled challenge.

A bubo hooted in the distance, then shrieked loudly before the sound of his wings flapped in flight. She'd seen the magnificent birds do just that many times in the royal gardens. She missed Sobrie. Would she would ever see her beloved city again? Even more important, could she help solve the extreme weather problem that threatened to completely destroy the entire planet?

The weather was too cold for the methodic buzzing and humming of insects, which also meant it was too cold for crops. So many things needed for survival depended on good weather. Dacton claimed Zotar was behind *all* of their problems, an idea she tried to understand, but could not process. Zotar had lulled her into a state of admiration and she thought she had fallen in love with him. He even mentioned life-mating her, but she had yet to answer him because in her heart she knew the truth—she did not truly love the man.

Dacton rustled around behind her, then she felt him press his body against her back, and his arm moved over her waist. She pretended to sleep, but was far too aware of the rise and fall of his chest, his groin to her derriere, his knees against her legs, and his arm curled dangerously close to her breasts.

If she protested it would make things worse, if she rolled away she would lose the warmth that penetrated through her. Curse him! She had agreed to share body heat, she just had not planned on the physical effects, or the thoughts that flew through her mind.

Ice pellets tapped on the tent with a steady rhythm. She reminded herself that this closeness was for survival, but why did he have to feel so good? His manly scent mixed with the natural essence of nature, and she had never been this aware of any man. So why did this make her angry? Because she cared what he thought about her, and she wanted him. Damn her to Diabolus, she wanted him!

From the first moment their eyes met that fateful moon-cycle, she felt the pull of his potent masculinity. She was not proud of the feeling, yet she could not deny the impact his presence had on her. She hated him, loved him, despised him, craved him. Too many emotions too quickly. Would she ever be able to sleep?

* * * *

Dacton's eyes flew open when he felt something soft and warm press against his arm. By the Gods! His arm was under her parka and Talina had wiggled beneath his grasp and inched down so her breasts rested on his forearm. He had slept without his parka, which until now, had provided a safety net from direct physical contact.

His blood pumped harder and joined forces in his groin. He was becoming aroused again, and every effort to fight his body's reaction had slipped away long ago. He had laid his parka on top of the fur for added warmth, and he did not dare move or the accumulated heat would escape.

When he had carried her, tended her injuries and fought for her, he knew it was more than duty. He had nearly lost his mind in Krow's cave when he saw her naked in the tub. Never had his desire been so strong. Now this. Would it never end? Did he want it to end? Talina whet his sexual appetite and pushed him to precarious levels of restraint. He could control his advances, but nature's drive would not be quieted as easily.

Rules ceased to exist from the moment he met Kolere. If the legend proved true, he was destined to make love to the beautiful princess. So why fight the inevitable? If she were willing, what harm could there be in two people pleasuring each other?

Dacton found his hand cupping her breast. He remembered all too well how luscious her rosy nipples looked, and how they had begged his mouth to caress their peaks. Then he covered her with the robe just in time, but there was nothing to save him now.

Talina rolled over and Dacton's hand immediately suffered the loss. Thank the Gods her heavy parka eased back into place to protect him from further torture. She now faced him, her arm slipped over his waist, and one of her legs pushed between his.

He hoped she rested comfortably because he had never been more miserable in his life. To have the woman he desired touching him so intimately, and not being able to mate with her, made his predicament quite painful.

There was not enough room in the tight leather pants he wore to be so ready for joining with her. Sleeping with this woman was no easy task. He could just picture her waking up in this intimate position. She would be furious and give him a tongue lashing, even though it was her arm around him, and her thigh nestled against his swollen manhood. That thought made it difficult to surrender to the exhaustion that held him motionless.

* * * *

A bird squawked loudly and Talina opened her eyes. The new sun-cycle found her entwined with Dacton. It was hard to tell where her body stopped and his began. He looked so docile and content she was afraid to move. They should both savor the serenity of the moment, and the comfort of each other's arms, for only the Gods knew what dangers waited.

How had they become so intimately tangled? Did Dacton desire her as she suspected? She wasn't sure because it was she who clung tightly to him. His arm rested in the only position it could, around her back. He definitely aroused her mating urges, and she reveled in the sensual assault. If it were so wrong to want his love, why did she feel such a burning need?

His body responded as ardently as hers. She felt his arousal against her now, the same as she had last moon-cycle. Only now she couldn't see the fire in his eyes since they were closed. He gave her strength when she had none, and offered hope for her future. Whether he knew it or not, he had earned her trust. The battle of propriety was the last barrier, and even that seemed fruitless.

Since childhood Kolere had spoken of her unique destiny, and of the man who would win her heart. He warned love would take her by surprise, but to trust her inner voice to guide her. Was Dacton her predestined lover?

She had been wrong to think Zotar might be that man. Very wrong. Zotar had come into her life unexpectedly and stirred womanly feelings she had never had. But then Dacton arrived and unleashed an insatiable hunger she could not deny. By society's standards she would no longer be considered a virgin. She'd already spent four moon-cycles with Dacton, when only one was necessary to become *branded*.

No princess in history had ever been branded. Branding a woman was common in the populace, but never for royalty. She was doomed to be the first in many areas. There was no way to know how her people, and her family would react. Even if she were allowed to become the first woman Legatus and subsequent ruler, she would most likely be the first single ruler. No man would want her now.

She could almost picture Dacton, standing before the council, shouting orders and demanding she be given her rightful position. He might scare half of them, but the other half would kill him.

There were still a few men her father could force to life-mate her, men who would take a branded woman, men who wanted a position of power and credits but not a mate. They would never respect her, and certainly not love her. What did the future hold? Would she be hailed as the princess who saved the planet, or the one who slept with the enemy?

* * * *

Zotar handed his reins to the closest man then brushed dust off his pants with his hands. "Are the others in position?"

"Yes sir, just as you requested. Three up ahead in those bushes, three on each side of the road behind us, three in the back, and the rest of us are here in the middle."

He stared at Mylar, his new right-hand man. Killing Mylar's predecessor was unfortunate, but he never tolerated mistakes. "They know to take *one* prisoner?" Zotar pulled a cremare-ray weapon from the saddlebag and examined the dull metal.

"Yes sir, you made it clear, but I worry the men will hesitate to kill."

"Tell them if they disobey my orders, I'll kill them instead. Is that clear enough to inspire the cowards?" He laughed when Mylar nodded, mounted his esroth and swiftly headed to pass the word. These men were no more ready for battle than a group of little girls, but he was not worried. He could annihilate the whole lot with one sweep of his weapon. No wonder The Protectorate banned its use, but he had enough cremare-ray guns for an entire army safely locked in a chamber behind the reactor.

It was too soon to give these fools such power. He would wait until he had total control of the government, which should only be a lunar-cycle away. Regnar was the perfect puppet, and Septra, the overly doting father, played his part perfectly. While he was gone, those two idiots would depose Cortain and no one could blame him for the coup.

It would only be a matter of time before he seized complete control of Ora. He still had to find Talina and The Protector if he were to profit from the ransom demand. It had been a stroke of genius to send the demand himself, and the credits would further his cause. Dacton and Talina were both a threat to his plan, so the least they could do is line his pockets.

Once he laid his hands on the pathetic warrior, he'd put him on public display in the marketplace courtyard. A little humility would serve Dacton well, and show the people they no longer needed The Protectorate, as long as he was in charge—and the bitch would pay dearly as well. First he'd take his pleasure with her in front of Dacton. The sympathetic Protector undoubtedly had a soft spot for the whore by now. He couldn't wait to see the enraged look on Dacton's face when he watched Talina spread her legs wantonly, begging to be satisfied.

Playing with both of them would be amusing. He wanted Dacton to die inside before he took his miserable life. No torment would be enough to repay Dacton, the man responsible for Jana's death. His sister would be proud to know her death would soon be avenged.

If it wasn't for Dacton he wouldn't have been court-martialed and expelled from The Academy. The Protectorate may have exiled him from Bronic, but Dacton would pay for the humiliation and pain he caused. Baleko Rovarn had only been an appetizer, now his appetite longed for the main course—Dacton Rovarn, Chief Protector.

Once this was over, he would erase the youngest Rovarn as well, He certainly did not need Falcon to become a thorn in his side. Not one

Rovarn deserved to live, and it was up to him to finish the job of removing them from existence.

"They're coming!" Mylar panted.

Mylar was out of breath, but at least he was trying to earn his new position. "Good." Zotar took cover in the thick brush by the side of the path and waited. Six men on foot, armed with bows and cutters approached, unaware of the ambush. Nothing was better than a fight, especially a one-sided battle.

Zotar gave the signal to attack and all twelve men converged on their prey. Blades flashed in the sun, while grunts and groans breached the once peaceful countryside. He watched three of his men fall to the ground in pools of blood. He smiled. They would never make soldiers anyway.

The six Burly men were accomplished fighters, and made short order of killing two more of his men. Enough, he thought while his finger itched on the trigger of his cremere-ray weapon. He chose one Burly man to remain alive then fired exacting blasts of fiery rays at the others, burning large holes through each of them.

Satisfied, he strolled toward his remaining men who held one survivor immobile on the ground. He tucked his favorite weapon under his belt. "Tie his hands and throw the rope over that branch."

His men did as they were told while the bearded man uselessly struggled to free himself. Zotar grasped the end of the rope and pulled until the man's toes barely scraped the ground. Now that the man was supported solely by his wrists, the knot tore deeper into his skin each time he writhed.

Blood stained the rope and slowly trickled down the man's arms, always a pleasant sight. If he did not suffer, he would never talk. Every man had a breaking point, it was just a matter of finding it before the bastard succumbed to the torture. "Where is the woman and the warrior that passed this way?

"I've seen no woman!"

The man's voice was already strained, but Zotar pulled the rope until the man's feet were well off the ground. He loved the way the man kicked at the air and made his wrists bleed more profusely. "Don't lie to me!"

"I have seen no woman!"

The Burly man had the audacity to spit at him. Luckily he missed or he'd put his cutter in his throat this very moment. "Tell me or I'll kill you!" He pulled a cutter from his boot and raised it to press tightly against the man's throat.

"You'll kill me either way, evil one."

"If you give me the information I seek, you will live. Now where did they go?" He applied more pressure to the blade and blood trickled down the center of his captive's neck. "I'm waiting."

"All right! I'll tell you after you lower my feet to the ground."

Zotar abruptly let out the rope and laughed when the man struggled to stay upright. "Talk!"

"We found the man and woman you speak of..."

The man's voice was ragged and sounded as if he were gargling. He wanted him to talk before he choked on his own blood. "Go on."

"They were intruders. We killed them!"

"I don't believe you!" Zotar hoisted the man off the ground to hang from his wrists once again. "I want the truth!"

"They're dead." He coughed. "They're dead."

"You senseless fool!" Zotar tied the rope around the base of the tree to secure the hanging man's position. "I will give you one last chance to confess, or I will slit your miserable throat!"

"You will anyway, so be done with it!"

The helpless young prisoner was quite assertive under the circumstance. He did admire the fool's courage, but he would never tell him that. Too bad the idiot did not work for him, he could always use a brave man willing to die for a cause.

"It's hard to believe you wasted your last breath. As you wish." Zotar held the cutter behind the man's right ear and pressed until the blade pierced his skin, then slowly and deliberately raked the cutter under his jaw line until he reached the left ear. He smiled when a torrent of blood spilled from the gaping wound.

"Any last words?" Zotar laughed when the man tried to utter one last curse, but all he could manage was a death gurgle. He watched with pleasure while the young man choked on his own blood. Whether the warrior had told the truth or not, his reward would have been the same.

"He's dead," Mylar uttered.

His men stared at the pathetic sight, and he knew they were useless to his cause. He would have to toughen his training program before engaging in further physical confrontations. These men had no stomach for war, they were weak.

Zotar pulled the cremare-ray weapon from its resting place at his waist and pointed it at his men. "You have failed miserably, and I cannot tolerate failure!" He took a few steps closer and glared into each man's eyes. "You can either die where you stand, or run for your worthless lives. Which shall it be?" He roared while they all turned tail and ran for the tree line. "Gutless bastards!"

He took aim, pulled the trigger, and watched the infra-blue heat beam sear the closest runner in half. "This is too easy." He cut down the remaining men, leaving gaping holes in each of their backs.

How he looked forward to Dacton. At least the proud Chief Protector would go down fighting, unlike the inadequate mortals that lay smoldering on the ground.

Zotar laughed loudly. "And next will be my favorite nemesis, and the princess whore he will die to protect."

CHAPTER TWENTY TWO

Dacton opened his eyes after a restless sleep to find Talina's beautiful face right in front of his. Judging from the way she lay draped over him she enjoyed the closeness of his body as much as he enjoyed hers. The intimate position was above and beyond what was necessary to share body heat.

He remembered every move, every touch, snuggle and caress she had lavished on him during the moon-cycle. It had been a struggle to play the part of a sleeping barbarian, too deep in slumber to notice her, or the desire that burned to escape. Her womanly appeal was strong, but his warrior's resolve held true. Now he had to free himself of her embrace before she felt his arousal pressed against her, or had she felt it all along? He sat up and she reluctantly rolled to her back.

"Wake up Regia. We have much to do." He inwardly smiled while she rubbed her eyes in a feigned effort to wake. She had no more been asleep than he had, and from the languid expression on her regal face, did not care if he knew. What was she up to? Women! He would never understand them, and had no reason to. He had ten more annual-cycles before he would be forced to retire from his position as Chief Protector. Only then could he consider a life-mate, and delve into the complexities of the female mind.

He sat up, grabbed his parka, put it on and pulled the hood over his head. He crawled out of the tent to be free from Talina's allure. The cold air pierced every ounce of clothing and chilled him to the bone. The farther north they traveled, the more their physical endurance would be tested. As if the uncertainties of the mission itself were not enough, their lives precariously rested in the hands of nature that had been manipulated by man.

The wind immediately bit his fingers to the bone and he wasted no time ducking back inside the tent for his gloves. Talina let out a small scream. "I didn't mean to scare you."

"I...I...know."

Dacton assembled the supplies on top of the pelt that no longer kept Talina warm. "Put on every piece of clothing Leana sent. Our only hope against the cold will be layers." He removed his parka, slipped on another leather tunic, the furry vest from Krow, then replaced his coat. He pulled his flight suit from the bag and handed it to Talina. "Wear this over everything else."

Talina stared at the silvery garment. "What is it?"

"My flight suit. It's a special fabric that retains body heat."

"Why didn't you give this to me last moon-cycle?"

"Because there is only one, and I needed your body to warm me."

"Needed, or wanted?"

The truth hung heavily between them and he chose not to answer. She smiled at him and he knew she had felt his need. "Keep this pair of socks in your pocket. You'll need them when we reach the ice."

Layer after layer, the beautiful curves of her body disappeared before his eyes. It was just as well, he had far more important matters to consider. "Are you warmer now?"

"Not as warm as last moon-cycle."

The blush on her cheeks pulled him like a magnet and he leaned closer. "Did you enjoy last moon-cycle, Regia?"

"We shared body heat, that's all."

"We shared far more than that. Don't pretend, Talina. There's nothing to be ashamed about. We shared a pallet. We slept close, and that excited you." He traced the fine line of her jaw with his finger. "I know you want me."

Before she could protest he pressed his lips to hers. Rigid reluctance eased into compliance, then sizzled to fiery desire and he tasted her voracity. He pushed deeper to enjoy the taste of her and to take all she could give. He wanted to rip off every piece of clothing she labored to put on, to feel her skin, and caress her soft curves. He could show her pleasure, and prove he was not the barbarian she believed him to be.

To be Talina's first lover would be a privilege. By Oranian law it had to be her gift to her future life-mate. His desire to be her first nearly took him over, so he had to end the kiss. Gently he pulled back and stroked her long golden hair. The sweet taste of her had to sustain him through the inevitable battle.

Talina lowered her eyes. "We should not have done that."

"I told you not play games with me."

"There have never been games between us, Dacton."

He laughed. "Do you think I believed you every time you tried to be nice to me? No. I knew that first moon-cycle in the cabin you would rather see me dead than continue in my company."

"Much has changed since then." Talina took his hand and stared into the warrior's eyes.

"I agree. That's why I knew you wanted me to kiss you." He squeezed her hand reassuringly, and wished he was better at conveying his feelings. How could he tell her he wanted to make love to her, but could never life-mate her? If he resigned his position with The Protectorate for love he would learn to hate the woman responsible, as well as himself. That could never happen. He knew Talina could not wait ten annual-cycles for his career to end, nor would he ask her to make that sacrifice.

"Change can be good, Dacton. We're about to change the fate of this planet. Our missions have merged, and we're close to fulfilling the legend. Don't you see?"

"I see all too well. You're confused by emotions and feelings you've never experienced, and you believe I can satisfy your curiosity. Trust me, Regia, I can pleasure you more than you dreamed possible, and take delight in doing so. But if I do, there is a price to pay. Are you willing to make the sacrifice?"

Dacton waited for her answer, yet how could she answer when he had not told her the price of loving him? Her eyes pooled with emotion, and his heart raced faster with the thought of making love to the sensuous princess. "When we make camp for the moon-cycle, you will give me your answer." He kissed her forehead. "In the meantime, I'll saddle the esroths."

He felt her gaze on his back while he walked away. If she wanted a show he could give her one, instead he simply saddled the esroths while she watched his every move. This was not the first time a woman studied him, but it was the first time for a woman he cared about. He tossed the saddles on the animals' backs, then tightened the cinches.

When he turned to look at Talina he instantly regretted the move. She had desire in her eyes, and he knew she shared his need. The thought of holding her naked body in his arms tempted him, yet how could he hurt her? She might tell him it did not matter, but he had seen women like her devastated by lovers who took what they wanted, then left them alone to cry out their misery. Could he break Talina's heart, and devastate her future? He did not want to be that man, yet to share a pallet with her would make him guilty. Could he live with himself if he shared his love with the princess?

He quickly moved around the campsite and gathered all the supplies and packed them for the trip. Once everything was packed he took down the tent and secured it on the pack esroth. Once the site was clean and secured, he helped Talina mount. Words were no longer necessary between them since they both understood the next steps they had to take. He mounted his esroth and nudged him forward into the barren landscape ahead.

The farther they traveled, the colder it became, although it was difficult to tell since he already felt completely frozen. The forest slowly began to thin and he saw a flat, treeless area ahead. He halted his esroth at the edge of the barren sea of ice that stretched before him then turned his gaze to Talina. "We'll have to leave the esroths, it's too dangerous to ride."

She wrinkled her forehead and sighed deeply. He could not blame her, he felt the same way. "The walk will not be easy, but we cannot risk the esroths' lives. We need them for the return trip. Plus, we would be more visible on their backs than on foot."

"Your reasoning is sound, but it does not mean I want to walk across a frozen lake." She sighed. "However, I see no other options." She looked into Dacton's eyes. "Do you?"

"I'm afraid not." She nodded and swung her leg over the esroth's neck. He reached up, placed his hands on her waist and helped her to the ground. "Take a break, walk around, or sit, whatever you like. I'll unsaddle our mounts and grab the necessary supplies." He watched her nod and walk away from him. Every cell in his body screamed against taking her into a dangerous situation. He also realized why Protectors were forbidden to get close to a woman, or life-mate. Decisions became complicated when feelings got in the way, and he had no time for that now.

He made short work of removing the saddles, supplies, and bridals., then gently laid his hand on his esroth's forehead. He sent his mount the message to remain behind, but to return to this very spot each afternoon to wait for them. Included in his instructions was a huge thank you for their loyalty and cooperation. He sensed they understood a moment before they turned and headed off into the forest behind them. When he turned he found Talina with Kiko in her arms. "I'm afraid he will have to remain behind as well."

"I told him that, but he doesn't like the idea."

"You understand animals now? Or is it you who doesn't like the idea?"

Talina smiled. "A little of both I suppose."

"Kiko, my little friend," Dacton said, ruffling the fur between his ears. "We will return for you. What? Yes, I will take care of Talina." He listened quietly, then replied, "You already know the answer to that."

"The answer to what?"

"Nothing," Dacton grumbled while he moved the saddles and extra gear behind the nearest rock. He placed a thin tarp over everything and made a small shelter for Kiko. Just when he laid a small fur pelt on the ground for a carpet, Kiko bounded inside and curled up. He touched the animal's forehead, sent a thank you message and told Kiko to wait here for their return. Then he returned to where Talina stood, staring at the walk ahead. "Put your socks on over your boots." He pulled two pairs from his pocket and handed one to Talina.

Talina pulled the socks from her pocket and slid them over her boots."I doubt this will keep my feet any warmer.

He could not help but chuckle at the look on her face while she stared at her feet. "No, but it may keep you from breaking that pretty little neck of yours on the ice."

"Oh." Talina stepped onto the slick flat plane of ice. "You're right, it does help—a bit."

"Everything slides on ice. Any help is good." He finished putting the last of the supplies into the one larger backpack, then slipped it on over his heavy coat. She glanced back at him while he adjusted the straps over his shoulders.

"Are you coming warrior? It's fr...fr...freezing out here, hurry up."

Dacton stood and walked toward Talina, who seemed to gain confidence with every step she took. Then she hastened her pace and ended up flat on her back. He shuffled over to her as quickly as he could. Relief spread through him when he found her uninjured. He chuckled. "You're not much of a skater, Regia."

"Stop laughing at me! The only ice I've ever seen has been in my drink. It's not meant to walk on."

"Maybe not, but that's what we must do." He bent down, slipped his arm around her and pulled her to her feet. "The trick is to take small steps and shuffle your feet so you stay in contact with the ice. Whenever you lift a foot you risk..."

"I know, I already did that." Talina glanced back over her shoulder. "I wish we could ride."

"Four legs are better than two, but even they fall. If your esroth went down, he would not be able to get up, and he'd freeze to death. Not to mention crushing you in the process."

"You're right, of course, but we'll never get there at this rate."

"Patience." Talina nodded, then took a step forward only to fall back into his arms. He could barely feel her through all the clothes.

"I'm freezing to death and want to finish this mission as quickly as possible." She shook her head and groaned. "I have another problem…"

"Can I help?"

"It's my legs, they're sore from riding and don't want to do what I tell them to do."

Dacton adjusted the hood of her parka which she wore over his silver flight suit, then stroked her cheek with his gloved hand. "I've felt that before." He tightened the hood's tie under her chin and tied it in a bow. "We both want this over with, but we must also insure our safety." He bent his head level with hers and pressed his lips against hers.

Talina grabbed the sleeves of his coat and pulled him closer. She returned his kiss and matched each of his probing tastes with thrusts of her own. He wanted her badly, but this was not the time or place. He pulled back and placed his gloved hands on her cheeks. "We are making no progress this way, Princess."

"I disagree warrior, that kiss was progress."

A bright blush filled her cheeks, but she quickly looked down at the frozen ground to hide her embarrassment. "We have a long way to go, and it isn't getting any warmer."

"Your flight suit is good, but I really cannot feel my feet or hands."

"You are not alone in that feeling, Regia." He helped her to her feet but kept his arm around her. "We must continue. Lean on me." For the first time he felt comfortable with her by his side. He was not good at expressing feelings, so he could only hope she knew what he meant. "Keep your head down, and don't talk, Regia. We're facing the wind and it will burn your lungs."

He felt her head nod against his side. This would be a long walk indeed, and he could only pray they would arrive at their destination before the cold overtook them.

CHAPTER TWENTY THREE

O

The frosty wind howled like the call of death, and their breath billowed on the frigid air and froze in front of their face. Nothing broke the bleak, glacial emptiness that lay before them. White ground blended into a gray horizon that flowed up into the dismal, hazy green sky.

"I'll lead. Just hang onto my coat so you don't fall."

Talina grabbed the back of his parka and he began to walk. She knew he wanted to protect her from the wind as much as possible and keep her on her feet. Contentment flooded over her and she found the solace only *her Protector* could offer. The kiss they shared opened her eyes. She felt she had finally met the real Dacton, instead of his alter ego, *The Protector.*

They were on a mission to save her people from a horrible end, and she knew she had the most capable man in the universe to assist her. Dacton no longer seemed like the dark, sinister enemy she once perceived. He was now the only man she wanted by her side, or in her heart.

The wind howled and blew sleet into her face and it stung. She could only imagine how Dacton felt in the lead. He sheltered most of the weather from her face, but it stuck to her parka. It was difficult to remember not to lick her lips, but the biting wind cruelly reminded her. She wanted to stop and taste Dacton again, feel his warm breath on her cold face, and confirm once more that he desired her.

Dacton skillfully supported her every step on the treacherous ice. Every now and then he would turn and give her a look of confirmation and support as they trekked further into the endless wasteland. A sick feeling pervaded her thoughts with an ominous warning. Dacton seemed oblivious to the impending danger that awaited them. She was glad he was confident, but it would take more than that to save Ora and their lives.

They traveled in silence time-unit after time-unit with no place to rest in the land Krow called "the death zone". Heavy fog began to form and the gloomy sky grew black. Green striations slashed the horizon on their gradual assent to mingle with the clouds above.

Talina kept her head down with one gloved hand holding the edge of the hood over her eyes. The journey seemed endless, but with Dacton leading the way she could endure anything.

* * * *

Through the sleet and the mist Dacton caught his first glimpse of the Peaks of Venda. They were majestic, rugged, ice-enshrouded and ominous, jetting several thousand feet toward the sky. It would take at least three more time-units before they arrived. He prayed Talina was ready to face her real enemy, and that she would protect herself if the need arose.

Everything on the briefing chip was embedded in his memory, but The Protectorate had no idea what lay inside the dangerous mountain. He felt Talina's steps weaken and she put more weight on his back. She was too short to put her arms around his neck, and it was too dangerous to carry her on the ice.

"Please tell me we're almost th...th...there."

Talina's sleet encrusted hood cracked when she looked up at him. "Yes, Regia. Look." Dacton turned her chin with his finger until she faced the jagged outcroppings in the ice. "That is our mission. Are you ready?"

"I'm scared Dacton, I'm afraid you'll be..."

He put his hands on her cheeks to still her words and to try to stop her teeth from chattering. "Did I hear you right? Scared?" Dacton laughed and gave her a reassuring hug, ice cracking and falling from both of their glazed fur parkas. "The woman who fought and kicked like an animal? Who wanted to escape at any cost? Who thought she could match strength and wits with a Protector? That woman is scared?"

"This is no time to make f...f...fun of me, Dacton, I have good reason. You may not fear wh...wh...what awaits, but you're not invincible." Talina stared into his eyes. "I don't wa...wa...want to lose you."

"Indeed. Does that mean you've changed your mind about me?"

"I have." She stared at his face. "Don't look at me like that, I'm serious. As much as I hate to admit it, I was wrong about what kind of ma...ma...man you are."

"And what kind of man am I, Regia?"

"You hide your emotions well, warrior, but your heart is good, and I know you'd never hurt me. I may not agree with the methods you used to get me here, but you were justified."

Dacton lowered his head and pressed his lips to hers. Warmth spread through his body the more his tongue dueled with hers and the closer he pulled her to his body. She tasted wonderful, but it was the tender message of desire he found hard to resist.

He groaned deeply then slowly pulled back. "That is one way to warm up." She gave him a half smile. "Don't be afraid, Regia. I will protect you with my life."

"That's exactly what I...I'm afraid of. If anything happens to you the mission will fail. Our responsibility is great, and the only backup you have is mmm...mmm...me."

"I've come to believe you're all I need."

Talina opened her mouth to speak but he silenced her with an urgent kiss. A kiss could say more than words. He was terrified for her. If anything did happen to him she would be alone out here in the middle of nowhere, surrounded by the enemy. He would not let that happen—ever.

For the moment all they had was this kiss, but if the fates were with them, this moon-cycle could prove most interesting. He ended the kiss and looked into her eyes. "We still have more ground to cover, and we do not want to freeze out here. So hang on to me and let's move. The sooner we arrive, the sooner we will warm ourselves. But if you need to rest at any time, just say so."

She silently nodded so he turned his back on her and waited for her to grasp his heavy parka. Her touch was barely perceptible through all the clothes and his near frozen body, but she did as he asked and he started walking toward the peaks.

The trek was not easy and the time-units passed slowly. It seemed to turn colder by the step, but it was hard to tell when your feet and hands were numb. He looked up and realized they had finally arrived at their destination.

He helped Talina to sit behind rocks close to the entrance of the stronghold. After he removed his backpack and sat next to her he searched through the bag and pulled out a stunner. He handed the weapon to Talina. "Remember everything I told you. Don't think...react. I have no way of knowing how many men guard this complex, so stay behind me, and don't let your guard down. I'm counting on you to watch my back."

Talina stared wide-eyed and nodded.

"The moment we're inside, remove your gloves so you can handle the weapons better. Do not talk, use sign language." Her glassy stare disturbed him. He wasn't sure where her mind had wandered, but he had to find it fast. He grabbed her shoulders. "Talina?" He waited, but she didn't respond. "Answer me, Woman!"

Talina shivered. "I'm sorry, I just..."

"You said you believed in me, and now is the time to prove your words. Trust me, Regia." His heart ached when he saw a lone tear roll down her cheek.

"I do."

Dacton wiped the drop from her face before it froze and hugged her more protectively than he ever had. He feared what would happen if he lost her. He would never allow such a tragedy. He pressed his lips to hers. He needed one last sweet taste of the woman he loved.

By The Powers of the Universe, it was true. He could no longer deny what was in his heart even if he was afraid to admit the fact that he loved Talina. On Bronic it was against the law for a Protector to make a life commitment, but no one could stop him from loving this woman.

They would survive this, and if her decision was what he expected, they would make love. It had been over an annual-cycle since he'd taken physical satisfaction with a woman, but Talina would be the first woman he ever made *love* to. The thought scared him as no enemy ever had. His career as a Protector could be over in a heartbeat if The Protectorate knew how he felt about Talina, but his decision was made and he would pay the price.

He never questioned his instincts and did not plan to start now. If he died in battle with Zotar, he would die a happy man, but he had no intentions of meeting his end at the Peaks of Venda. He would have his Regia, the woman who had taken her place in his very soul.

Laughing to himself, he thought how right Kolere and his legend had proven to be. He wanted Talina for the woman she was, not the enigma history eluded to.

He knew how frightened Talina was and her safety gnawed at his consciousness. He did not give a damn about himself, or the enemy, only Talina. She had penetrated the armor of his heart despite his efforts to keep her out.

The reality of The Protectorates' life-mating ban sank in with a clarity never before possible. He had become more vulnerable because of his feelings. He also knew Zotar would use her as a weapon against him if he even suspected his love for her. He had to be careful, but he knew he could not prevent the inevitable. Their love was written in the stars.

CHAPTER TWENTY FOUR

Talina crouched behind Dacton before the entrance of a tunnel that led into the mountainside. The last time she'd seen him this alert and determined was when he encountered Krow's men. He held their lives in his hands once again, but this time she would help. This time she trusted him completely.

Dacton gave her a sign to remain where she was while he entered the darkness within. She'd given her word to follow his instructions, but it was hard to let him out of her sight.

A high-pitched hissing sound reverberated in the tunnel. She assumed it was the sound his weapon made when fired. He needed her help, she could feel it.

Slowly she entered the semi-darkness and felt her way against the frozen wall. She removed her gloves and shoved them into a pocket as Dacton had told her to do, and reminded herself to react instead of panic.

A terrible hiss cut the silence and the tunnel glowed bright blue. She ran toward the flashes of light, rounded a corner and found Dacton battling three guards. Lazer beams bounced off the walls while she hurried toward him, careful to stay covered. When she looked around the rock beside her she saw him fall.

"Dacton!" Without further thought she ran to him and slid to a horrifying stop. Her heart stilled, and she prayed Dacton was still alive. Her scream had alerted one of the enemy guards who turned, his weapon pointed it directly at her.

"Get down!" Dacton yelled.

She watched in awe when he sprang to his feet, lunged at the attacker and knocked him to the ground. Talina dove to the rocky floor. She glanced back and saw a gaping hole where she'd stood. These men had weapons that could melt ice and burn through stone!

Dacton fired a red beam of light from a weapon he had not explained. When the rays penetrated the man's head, sparks flew and smoke billowed. He fired once again and hit a second man in the chest, and an explosion turned the body to flames. Talina turned her head, unable to bear the killings she knew were necessary. Tears burned at her lids. She had to believe they had done the right thing.

Strong arms pulled her to her feet and over the two smoldering bodies in their path. They followed icy walls that gradually returned to stone without further resistance. Dacton gave her one last sign to insure silence as they approached a heavy metal door. She watched from behind as he pushed the door ajar and eased his head inside. He quickly retreated and pulled her close.

Dacton removed the faze-pistol from his belt, set it to the highest number, then lowered his head to her ear.

"Stay here and use this if anyone comes. When the area is secure, I'll be back. React, Regia."

She heard his whisper loud and clear. He was gone in a flash, closing the door behind him. She focused on a dim light perched high on the stone wall a few feet in front of her. She eased her body down the rough stone wall until she sat on the ground. Her legs shook so bad it was difficult to stand.

Her mind reeled with the remorse of murder. Those men were dead. Had Dacton killed them, or was Zotar ultimately to blame? She'd learned from Kolere annual-cycles ago that there was no such thing as an innocent victim, but it was a hard theory to grasp. Dacton did what he had to do. She concentrated on why they were here. They had to succeed.

A loud explosion rocked the door, and she heard shot after shot being fired. Dacton was entrenched in a fierce battle, and she did not care what orders he'd given. The last thing she needed was for his egotistical pride to get him killed. He'd told her to react and not panic, which was exactly her plan.

Talina crawled through the door on her hands and knees. The moment she was inside, rock fragments rained across her back as a blue ray etched a deep, jagged scar in the stone. She dropped to her belly on the metal landing and thanked her maker.

Echoing footsteps stilled her thoughts. "React, Talina, just react," she mumbled as the footsteps neared. Her finger tightened around the trigger as she took aim when the man cleared the last metal step.

The guard spotted her and pointed his weapon. Before he could fire, she pulled the trigger, and he fell from the steps to the cavern floor below. Dear God, she'd killed a man! Dacton had turned her into a murderer! She low-crawled to the edge of the steps to verify her victim's fate. Talina swung her legs around, her feet finding the third step. The moment she stood, the guard jumped to his feet and she blasted him twice on her way down the stairs. Giving the fallen man one last glance, she ducked behind a storage cabinet.

Why hadn't he died the first time? Dacton said the highest setting would kill a man instantly, but he'd only been stunned. It didn't matter now. She checked for more guards then ran. The overpowering need to find Dacton made her heart beat so fast she could barely catch her breath.

In a flash she was tackled to the ground, a powerful body saving her from a lethal hit. She'd never been happier to feel her Protector and absorb the confidence and strength he offered. From the corner of her eye she saw Dacton's arm extend, and a red beam of light sent another guard to an instant, explosive death.

"Are you all right Regia?" he whispered, one arm clutching her waist.

"I think so." Dacton rolled her over, and when their eyes met, she knew she was safe. She eased her hands up his arms to his shoulders, his flexed muscles hard to her touch beneath his tunic. "What happened to all your clothes?"

"I couldn't function in them." He looked into her eyes. "But I'm glad to see you could. I'm proud of you."

"Why didn't he die, Dacton? I shot him three times!"

Dacton smiled. "I know it was hard for you to shoot, but you were brave. You reacted."

"Answer me, Warrior! Why didn't he die?"

"Because he's an android."

Talina shook her head, and anger roiled in the pit of her stomach. "Do you mean I labored over a decision to shoot a robot? Why didn't you tell me!"

"Easy, Regia, you can't tell an android from a human until you destroy one. I suspected Zotar might have android guards, but I wasn't sure." Dacton brushed stray hairs from her cheek. "I told you to stay in the tunnel. By the gods, woman, you could have been killed."

"Why you arrogant, self-serving..." Dacton halted her insults with a hungry kiss, a kiss she wanted with every ounce of her being. His urgent, but gentle explorations told her he wasn't mad, just worried. Explanations could wait. She needed to taste him and revel in his warmth. The fight she so avidly began dissolved, and she felt herself melt into a pool of desire.

Talina pushed him back. She didn't want him to know how easily he stirred her, at least not yet. "What kind of an answer was that? Do you always take what you want without asking?"

"If you'd like another answer, I'd be happy to give it to you."

"I think not." His satisfied smirk sent a chill down her spine, and his husky, seductive tone revealed more than his words. If she'd had more experience with men, she might have been able to convince him his kiss meant nothing, but they both knew better.

"As you wish." Dacton stood then pulled Talina to her feet. "We have a reactor to disable."

"Is it safe? Did you stop all the androids?"

"I would not put you in danger, Regia. You should know that by now."

When Dacton turned and walked away Talina's heart sank at the sight of a bloody gash across his back. She knew he would not let her doctor his wound now, so she followed in silence. He was proud, too proud for his own good, but she'd tend to his needs later.

Dacton led her through a small hall that opened into a large chamber. She stopped and stared in amazement at the reactor and wondered how something so small could threaten her entire planet. She had envisioned an immense piece of machinery that spilled its lethal contents with great force into the sky. Instead, the fatal chemical was housed in a shiny, round metal cylinder that looked no more than three feet tall and three feet wide, a pipe attached to the top that extended up through the mountain. "It's so little."

He flipped off switches and turned valves connected to gauges beside the unit. "I've stopped the chemical flow." He ran his hand over the housing. "This metal is not from our planet."

Talina reached to touch the reactor, but Dacton grabbed her wrist.

"It's not safe until I run a test. I'm going outside to get the backpacks."

Talina watched Dacton walk from her sight and wondered why she always felt a sense of loss when he left. It was an odd feeling she didn't pretend to understand, a feeling that defied all logic and common-sense. Her attraction to Dacton ran deeper than pure desire. She realized how shallow her lustful feelings for Zotar had been. Dacton had shown her so much more. Dacton had not only saved her life, he'd saved her heart and soul as well. He touched a part of her Zotar never could.

Her feelings for Dacton were special. She felt a mystical bond. His every kiss made her surrender. She knew she'd follow him anywhere he wanted to take her. Was this the thinking of a sane woman, a woman destined to rule her planet? Or were they the musings of a woman in love?

Thoughts of Dacton's masculine physique and searching lips made her temperature rise. His seductive voice and urgent kiss played in her mind. She'd decided to give herself to the warrior, but she knew now that she would be making love to Dacton, the man. Beneath his tough exterior was a tenderness she could not resist. Her decision was right.

Since her people would now view her as a branded woman, she wanted to share a least one moon-cycle of passion with the man responsible. At least she would have the precious memory to sustain her in the difficult sun-cycles to come. It wasn't her reputation, or loss of virginity that scared her, it was losing her heart. She suspected it was already too late.

She stripped off layer after layer of clothing until she reached the original red tunic and pants. The cave was surprisingly warm considering the sub-zero environment outside. She heard the door slam and footsteps on the stairs.

When she looked up, she was face to face with the man of her desire, her indisputable fate. She mentally shook herself. They still had a mission to complete. Finding the reactor was only the beginning. It still had to be destroyed before they could return and help her father fight the vultures that clawed at the throne.

"The storm has gotten worse." Dacton reached in the bag and removed some supplies. "We'll spend the moon-cycle here."

"Thank the stars. I'm sick of being cold."

Dacton chuckled. "I suppose we have Zotar to thank. Without heat for an extended period of time the androids could not function. Their internal circuits would freeze and render them useless."

"Why would anyone use such a robot where the risk is so great?"

"Not anyone. Zotar." Dacton palmed a miniature computer. "He probably doesn't have the proper connections to obtain updated models which have corrections to override such problems. Or he doesn't have the credits. They're very costly."

"I know. Zotar said he could supply us with humanoid robots for a million credits apiece."

Dacton shook his head. "I said they were expensive, not priceless."

"I suspected as much." Talina sighed.

"Ora will need expert guidance to upgrade technology, but The Protectorate will assign an Advisor."

"I see." Talina looked into his eyes. "So you're saying The Protectorate prefers to profit rather than allowing men like Zotar to benefit from our wealth."

"No. The Advisor will command every aspect of Ora's recovery. He will coordinate your technological advancement and assist in any restructuring necessary, including your government."

"So you lied to me. You're not going to help my father regain control, you're here to make sure The Protectorate dictates to us. I don't know why I ever trusted you...you underworld snake!"

"Must you be so stubborn, woman?"

"What more lies could you tell me?" She gritted her teeth before she said something regrettable in anger.

"I have not lied." Dacton grabbed her shoulders and pulled her tight to his body.

Talina's chest tightened painfully. He still provoked her as easily as he stirred her desire.

"Regia, believe in The Protectorate and in me. Your father will remain King. Our only objective is to remove the obstacles currently working against him, and to set safeguards in place that will prevent a future occurrence."

Dacton's reassurance eased the tension in her muscles, and she studied his gaze. He was being patient, which she knew was difficult for him. "I'm sorry, Dacton. I just worry about my father and I..."

In the next moment his lips covered hers and words were no longer necessary. Talina's hands found his cheeks, his hair, his neck. She couldn't control her caresses, wanting to touch and feel all of him at the same time. His tongue searched, his need evident. His hands slid down her back and pressed her womanhood against him. When he groaned at the contact she felt an urgent fire build within her.

Dacton eased back and trailed kisses down her cheek and neck before he lifted his head to stroke her hair. "Come, I have one last area to check." He took her hand in his and headed down another hallway.

"You usually make me stay behind," Talina said, struggling to keep up with his longer stride.

"And you usually don't listen."

The hidden stronghold was larger and more complex than it seemed. They passed through a computer room with at least twenty terminals arranged in a circle in the center, each monitoring something different. Zotar had certainly invested a great deal of thought, not to mention credits. He was cunning and intelligent. She'd never expected anything like this hidden in the Peaks of Venda.

CHAPTER TWENTY FIVE

O

Dacton led Talina to the last door in the hall. He drew his weapon and watched her frown. "This is the only room I have not fully secured, so stay behind me, Regia."

He pushed open the door, astonished to find a room suited for royalty. Zotar. The man had delusions beyond human comprehension. How in the universe had he gotten all these riches here without detection? Well, however he accomplished it, the furnishings would serve them well this moon-cycle.

"Dear stars!" Talina rushed past Dacton. "Where? How?"

"Regia! Don't take another step." Dacton quickly scanned the room then rushed to a doorway in the far corner. He entered to find an empty personal room. He shoved the weapon under his belt and returned to Talina. "Sorry to alarm you, but you were supposed to stay behind me until I secured the area."

"I don't take orders well, do I?"

"Do you want me to answer that?" The smile she gave him warmed his heart. She seemed happy and relaxed, as if she were home without a care. He liked the change in her and hoped her lighthearted mood would last, because she was even more bewitching when she smiled.

"Zotar has excellent taste in furnishings." Talina walked to the canopy pallet.

"Our enemy thinks he's a king. Quite elaborate, don't you think?" He watched her nod. "Of course a king would not steal to satisfy his own personal needs." Dacton strode to the oversized pallet laden with pillows of red, purple, gold and blue. He picked one up and held it toward Talina, pointing to a triangular insignia in the center. "This mark signifies the Royal House of Cardan, ruler of Gravis, one of The Protectorates' newest

Subscribers."

"How did it get here?"

"Zotar plundered their world and took everything of value he could get on his ship. The Cardans survived because loyal followers hid them until The Protectorate stopped Zotar's coup. Gravis is under Advisorship now and doing quite well."

He watched Talina run her hand across the deep-purple satin quilt, then she threw herself face first into its downy softness. She lazily rolled onto her back, her arms and hands still caressing the smooth fabric.

"The Cardans have my sympathy for their misfortune, and my appreciation for their impeccable taste."

Dacton grabbed the bedpost and gripped it tightly. The sight of the seductive princess sprawled in front of him was more than he could bear. His manhood throbbed, and all he could think of was taking her as he'd dreamed of doing for so long. Was she aware of her power to elicit such a sexual response in him? If she were, he doubted she would be so reckless on the pallet in front of him. Her breasts strained against the fabric of Leana's tunic, the outline of her taut nipples begging to be kissed.

The woman drove him crazy! Her every move erotic, every glance sensual. Her soft, sultry voice spurred his masculine cravings into a life of their own. She looked angelic. Watching her was pure joy while controlling himself became pure torture. The beautiful Regia held him spellbound and excited him as much as when her cobalt eyes spit angry fire. His lust sprang to life, and his Protector's instinct yearned to cradle her in his arms and never let go.

He had to keep talking before he showed her what a pallet was really made for. "Gravis closely resembles Ora, which is probably why Zotar chose your planet as his next conquest."

Talina sat up and clasped her hands in her lap. "Explain this Advisorship process you mentioned, or should I call it a dictatorship?"

Dacton maintained his rigid stance. "It is by no means a dictatorship. The Protectorate only insures that your government's freedoms are restored and returned to a state the same, or better than when lost due to a coup d'état. We supervise, offer suggestions, but in general, stay out of your policy."

"In general?"

"There are times intervention is necessary to insure peace. You must understand, your king and his council will be introduced to intergalactic trade and politics, which is a new arena for them. The Protectorate's only function is to maintain peace between all participating planets. To do so often means the Advisor must make some of the ultimate decisions himself."

Talina's gaze locked on the warrior. "What guarantees the Advisor is honest enough to ensure what is best for Ora and not for The Protectorate or his own political gain?"

"Advisors are the highest rank next to our Supreme Council. They're chosen because of their proven ability and are highly rewarded for their service so that monetary gain through corruption is eliminated."

"What about power? They could go crazy and abuse their authority."

Talina stood and faced him as a Legatus performing official duties, and he respected her for her professional abilities. "The position of Advisor carries great power within itself. For all intents and purposes, the Advisor is above the king, or whatever the ruling entity may be called, but safeguards exist to prevent abuse of such power."

"So you're saying our government can function as it always has? That this Advisor, whoever he may be, will only interfere and advise when absolutely necessary? That he, or she, is a person beyond reproach and corruption?"

"Exactly." Dacton was impressed by her stately manner, and extremely proud of her. He'd put her through so much, yet she carried herself with the dignity of her position. It was difficult to suppress his smile, but he did not want her to think he was making fun of her.

"How forceful will The Protectorate be in upgrading our technology?"

"It is necessary to immediately install the proper electronics to communicate with The Protectorate and all your neighboring planets. From there, progress will only be limited by Ora's financial capabilities. Although once you establish intergalactic trade your credits will increase rapidly, enabling your government to choose how and where to invest."

"There appears to be great promise in this plan."

Dacton released his hold on the bedpost to stand in front of Talina, his arms crossed over his chest. "I'm glad you understand and find merit in our collaboration."

Talina stood and paced in a circle around The Protector. "Why wasn't a plan like this offered before?"

"As I previously stated, our policy is non-intervention. We prefer planets progress at their own speed and contact us for assistance willingly. However, that's not always the case. If Zotar had left Ora alone, there was rumor that you, as Legatus, wanted to begin the upgrade process. Am I correct?"

"You are, but how did you know?"

Dacton was amused by Talina's persistent scrutiny, and amazed by her skillful political ability, both spoken and implied. This was the Talina he had waited to see, the woman he knew existed, the part of her she had tried so hard to conceal. He sensed she was a capable leader; compassionate, but demanding; sympathetic, but firm, and always true to her convictions. "We have our sources."

"I hope your sources are as accurate with the rest of their information."

Talina stopped and he gazed deeply into her eyes. "I assure you, Regia, they are." He watched her deep blue eyes soften when he called her Regia, and that gave him pleasure. He was treading in dangerous waters, but he cared deeply for Talina and wanted to see her happy.

"Do you have any more questions?" She shook her head and gave him a smile he wanted to kiss. "Then I suggest," Dacton walked to a door on the other side of the pallet and opened it, "that you take advantage of these facilities while I continue my search."

Talina hurried to his side and gasped when she saw the private room. "Look, Dacton! A tub, shower, sink, mirrors and cosmetics!" She stepped past him and caught a glimpse of herself. "Dear stars!"

He smiled while she touched smudges of dirt on her face. "It's not that bad." Dacton groaned while he stroked a four sun-cycle growth of beard.

"It's not?" She turned and grinned at him.

He joined her at the large, gold-framed mirror and laughed. "I had no idea we looked so bad."

"I had a suspicion, but..."

Dacton ran his hand down the length of her hair and let his hand rest in the small of her back. "You're still beautiful, Regia." He fought the invisible force that pulled them together. When he kissed her again it would be when she was ready. The decision was hers, he reminded himself, but if the eventuality arose, he wanted to bathe and remove his rough whiskers to protect her delicate skin. This mission had offered little time for personal grooming, and he saw how anxious Talina was to get in the tub. "You'll be safe. I'll be close by."

* * * *

The hot spray of the shower worked wonders on her tired, sore body. Memories of a copper tub, bubbles and torchlight played in her mind and an embarrassed shiver coursed down her spine.

How could she have stood before the warrior, naked, trying her best to seduce him? Wine or no wine, her actions were inexcusable. Dacton had not taken what she'd pushed in his face, and for that she respected him. She may not have much experience, but she knew she'd inadvertently tested his willpower as a man, and Dacton passed the test. The protector was made of steel, because she knew he found her attractive. A kiss never lied.

Dacton had done everything in his power to scare her in the beginning, but he'd changed. He wasn't hiding his desire, his concern, or his feelings for her any longer. He may not have told her about his true feelings, but he did not have to—she knew.

Dacton was a passionate man, and if he wanted to keep that a secret, he never would have kissed her. He knew exactly what he was doing as well as she did. Excitement tingled in her stomach. She remembered his hands on her naked body, his urgent kiss that promised pleasure beyond her wildest dreams. Soon those dreams would become reality.

The scented soap and shampoo were the same as she used in Sobrie, but anyone could buy them in the marketplace. Zotar must have entertained lots of women in his chamber to have so many feminine toiletries, she thought as she pressed a gold medallion-like control to stop the flow of water. She stepped out of the enclosure, secured a fluffy towel around her body and wondered what she might find to wear as she walked into the bedchamber.

Talina pulled open the double doors of a tall, polished wood wardrobe and her heart stopped. Translucent gowns of various colors hung neatly inside, all exact duplicates of the ones in her closet in Sobrie. Only one man had ever seen her dressing room, and he had been uninvited.

Zotar. He appeared one afternoon with her servant who was returning her gowns from being cleaned. She remembered the way Zotar had commented on their appearance and how they must look on her. He'd fingered the material and held it up to the light as if he were a professional tailor. Dacton's accusations about Zotar suddenly rang true, and fear settled over her like a heavy cloud, a cloud that also held her father prisoner.

* * * *

Dacton cut power to the main terminal and stared at the screen that faded to black. He scanned the reams of printouts, amazed by the complexity of Zotar's diabolical plan. Ora was only the beginning of his insane scheme to rule the galaxy. Kolere had been wise indeed to send him here first. The information on Zotar's files would prove invaluable to The Protectorate during the trial, if he allowed Zotar to live that long.

His wristpiece confirmed time had slipped away. He placed the microchips in his pocket and headed for the bedchamber. Talina was probably fast asleep, he thought as he opened the door. He stepped inside, barely able to catch his breath at the sight of the woman before him.

Talina stood in front of the table lamp, its light shining through the diaphanous folds of her gown, leaving every sensuous curve starkly outlined with little room for imagination. Blood pounded in his veins and viciously settled in his groin. Half her hair was secured on top her head, but the back spilled wildly in soft curls over her shoulders, with tiny tendrils teasing her forehead and cheeks.

She absolutely glowed, seductive and tempting. "You're stunning, Regia. Where did you find such a gown?" She should be smiling, but she had a distraught look on her face. "What's wrong Talina?"

"I'm scared, Dacton. Look." She pointed to the open wardrobe. "I have the exact same gowns back in Sobrie. I don't mean similar, I mean exact! The only difference is the thickness of the material. You cannot see through the gowns in my closet in Sobrie, but the colors and patterns match perfectly."

He pulled her trembling body to his and held her. She had reason to worry after what he had found in Zotar's files. "I will not let anyone harm you, Regia. You must believe that." He tilted her chin up with his finger.

"I believe you, Dacton, but you're only one man and..."

His fingers stilled her lips then traced their pouty outline. He felt her relax slightly under his touch. "I promise to return you to your father, unharmed. And I will personally see that he is safe on the throne before I leave."

"Thank you. That means a great deal to me."

"I know I've put you through a lot, but I'll make it up to you. Let me shower and change. We'll both like my company better then."

"I like your company now, Warrior."

"Don't tempt me." There was a soft, beguiling quality to her voice he tried to resist, but he found his lips touching hers before he gave it another thought. Her tongue slid into his mouth and he met it lazily, his way of asking how badly she wanted him. The reply confirmed her reluctance had been replaced with a demanding appetite that held him spellbound. Before he could deepen the kiss she pushed away leaving much unfinished.

"Off with you, Warrior," she said as she shoved him toward the private room. "You'll find something to wear on the stool."

As much as he wanted to finish that most promising kiss, he did want a shower. With his gaze locked with hers, he slowly removed his warrior's belt and tossed it on the pallet. He hated to leave her when she looked at him that way, but if her decision was made, she would have that same look when he returned.

Reluctantly he walked into the private room and closed the door. This moon-cycle would belong to them. The new sun-cycle would be time enough to lay a trap to exact his revenge on Zotar, to make his decisions and feel his regrets. Regrets for loving Talina? Never. The only regret he feared was for the future pain Talina would suffer because of their joining.

He was not free to commit to her, but his heart did not understand. While on this mission he had broken every rule in the book, and he would do it again if it meant being with Talina. All he cared about this moon-cycle was loving Talina and proving to her she was safe in his arms. The thought of making love to her on Zotar's pallet irritated him to the core, but he wanted her so much he ached. Zotar may have created this room for Talina and probably spent endless credits on gowns, perfume, and jewels, but silence was expensive.

He had seen Zotar's plans for Princess Talina, and he now had one more reason to take the miserable pirate's life. He would end Zotar's reign of terror, and he would die before he let Zotar's filthy hands ever again touch his precious Regia.

CHAPTER TWENTY SIX

Talina's stomach was in such a tight knot she could barely breathe. The virile warrior would join her soon and she would give him her virginity. How could she please a man with his experience? Where did she start? What if she did not excite him? No, she excited him, she knew it, she felt it, she'd seen it in his eyes.

Stop that, Talina DeAmarant! If she obeyed her inner voice and fulfilled the legend, she had to remain confident. This sacrifice was for her people, for her planet, for...no! She could make no excuses for surrendering her virginity. It was for her, it was for Dacton, it was for love.

The private room door opened, and Talina held her breath. Every muscle tightened when she saw Dacton's powerful presence in the doorway. He entered the room, and her mouth fell agape. Red silk pajama bottoms rode slightly below his trim waist and graced his bronze skin erotically. Her gaze followed the dark streak of hair up until it widened across his broad, bare chest. Her fingers ached to explore the thick masculine matt and feel his hard, warrior's body respond to her touch.

He was the most perfect male she had ever seen. Every time she saw him bare chested she could barely restrain the need to touch the sculpted planes. Dark wet hair clung to his massive shoulders, and she smiled while water dripped from the ends.

"Does this mean you approve, Regia?" He moved closer.

Talina savored his robust aroma, clean, fresh, and lusciously male. His ruggedly refined features were smooth once again, and her hand moved to his cheek. "I had grown accustomed to the beard, but this is nicer to the touch."

He bent and brushed his lips across hers. When she tried to pull him closer, he straightened. "This is not to be rushed, sweet Regia." He slid his arm around her waist. "I want to pleasure you, Talina," he whispered while he combed her hair with his fingers.

"Dacton, I..."

Dacton scooped her into his arms and carried her to the pallet. He laid her in the center and sat next to her. His fingers stroked her hair. "My beautiful Regia, are you sure of your decision?"

"I've never been more sure of anything." She saw tenderness in his eyes, an emotion he usually tried to hide. Right now she saw the real man, tender, caring and very passionate.

He caressed her cheek. "I never want to hurt you."

Talina's stomach quivered as if a thousand butterflies had been released with nowhere to fly. "I know."

"I would never purposely hurt you, but you must know that I..."

Talina's fingers silenced his lips. She was well aware he had come to her with a past he did not want to discuss, a past that included deeds she may never understand, and actions she might never forgive. That could be said for any man. She knew his heart was pure, his touch loving, and his promise for the future of Ora honorable. It was their future that concerned her, but not this moon-cycle. This moon-cycle belonged to them alone.

"Make love to me, warrior." She smiled at the confused expression on his face. "It's a logical request, and you like logic. It's what we both want, so why are you looking at me like that?"

"I want to make love to you, but not because of misplaced obligation, or the need to fulfill some legend. And I don't want any regrets."

"Well, if you're going to regret this..." Talina cut herself off and playfully pushed to a sitting position. Dacton pressed his chest against her and gently forced her back down. His steel gray eyes penetrated through her, and her heart raced when he lowered his head and his lips captured hers.

His hungry mouth moved with yearning, and a serious tenderness excited her. He began a slow, heated search down her neck, nibbling, tasting and seeking until his hot breath teased her breasts. She had never felt so alive, or so much like a woman. A tingly sensation swarmed through her as he eased the gown from her shoulders, his lips caressing each inch of skin he revealed.

Her back arched when his tongue circled the fullness of her breast, drawing closer to the tip each time. She closed her eyes, lost in delightful sensations. She moaned when he closed his mouth over her nipple and flicked his tongue back and forth.

How she had longed for this moment, for him. All those moon-cycles on the trail, their lives in danger, their bodies entwined for warmth. It had brought them close, but not like this. He made her love him, trust him, and want him. She owed him her life, and so much more.

His fingers closed around her breast as he gently moved his oral assault to the other side. She had dreamt what it would feel like to have a man love her, but her dreams did not come close to the sensual awareness Dacton exacted from a body she never knew could be so willing.

One of his hands trailed down her abdomen and he pushed the sheer fabric from her body until it pooled on the floor. Excitement coursed through her when his fingers toyed in her feminine curls. He nudged her legs apart and she felt his touch roam precariously close to the ache that so desperately wanted to accept his manhood. She did not want to wait another second, she wanted him now.

She inhaled sharply when his finger eased into the slick moistness. Dear stars! He said he could pleasure her in ways she never imagined, and as usual, he was a man of his word.

Never would she regret this joining. No matter what happened, loving Dacton was worth any price. She could live as a branded woman as long as she had her Protector by her side.

She felt his finger slide out, painfully slow, to circle above, stimulating a dormant bud of desire. Only his touch could awaken the violent furry that burned white-hot and screamed for release. "Please Dacton, don't make me wait any longer." Her hands raked through his hair, but he ignored her plea. He continued to drive her closer and closer to her moment of awakening.

A tremble began deep within, then one joyous spasm after another gripped the core of her womanhood. The feeling was so profound, so satisfying, she never wanted it to stop. When she moaned her appreciation he took her mouth with a hunger so intense it scared her. Could she ever get enough of this man? He may be her first lover, but she knew in her heart he would be her *only*.

"Now you are ready, Regia." He stroked her cheek. "Don't be afraid, I'll be gentle."

Talina's eyes widened when Dacton stood. His gaze raked her body repeatedly from head to foot, and desire flickered in the depths of his dark, loving gaze. Her heart beat rapidly, and his provocative grin made her wiggle in anticipation against the soft pallet cover. Her body longed for his powerful masculine form, his arousal barely concealed under the silky pants.

He did not have to say a word for her to know he took pleasure in her appearance, but what was he waiting for? To lay helpless under his spell wondering when he would make her a woman was pure torture. "By The Gods, man, what are you waiting for?" She had become desperate and he only smiled at her. "What?"

"You're so beautiful, Talina. So perfect, so loving." Dacton peeled off the only garment that separated him from her.

She stared without pretense at his manhood. She needed him desperately and yearned to seal the bond that would make them one. He was even more magnificent than she had imagined. Could her body actually accept all of him? Somehow she knew everything was perfect and she had no fear.

He lowered himself, an arm on each side of her shoulders, his knee inching her legs wider. She wanted to accept him and all he could give. There would be no more secrets between them, and she knew this act of love would change their lives forever.

His erection pressed against her then slowly slid inside, as if he were claiming her, inch by luxurious inch, moving into a home designed only for him. He felt wonderful inside her, and pride surged. She would now be *his woman* in every sense of the word.

Then he found her barrier and stopped. She was about to lose her maidenhood and become a branded woman. She wanted him, and was ready. Nothing could stop their mating, it *was* destiny.

Dacton hesitated. She placed her hands on his cheeks. "It's all right, I want you to..." Before she could finish, he consumed her completely, leaving only a trace of pain that proclaimed she belonged to him. They were now joined, body to body, soul to soul. It was her turn to give pleasure and bring him to the same heights of ecstasy he had shown her.

His hips began a deliberate, controlled thrust, his mouth tasting hers with a relentless pursuit for absolute possession. With each plunge he picked up the pace, swaying slightly from side to side. She had found heaven.

A melodic hum pierced her senses. Thoughts and feelings that were not her own flooded her consciousness. Their minds began to meld, their emotions collided, then turned into the same joyous thought. The moment was incredible, magical, and deep. So very deep.

Never had she felt such love, or intimacy. They had a sharing so complete that nothing else mattered, not on his world, or hers. A complete union, taking what they alone could give, treasuring the moment of unequaled desire.

Dacton's penetrating lunges built to a frenzy and her body reacted. Sweet pulsations grew and every inner muscle grabbed and pulsed against his manhood. A moan escaped her lips, and Dacton returned the sentiments with a deep groan. Then it happened, he filled her with the liquid heat of his release.

His movements slowed then stopped. He remained perched above her, still inside. She memorized his every feature since this moment may be the only one they shared like this. Then soft as a whisper he brushed her lips with his and planted one last, feathery kiss before he rolled off and onto his back.

Talina wiped tiny beads of sweat from his brow as she turned on her side and rested her head against his damp, heaving chest. He had truly become *her Protector*.

Dacton grasped her left wrist and held it for them both to view. "Your bracelet has turned blue, but it glowed dark pink when we were making love."

"I didn't notice, but I heard a humming sound."

Dacton smiled. "And I thought it was you making my heart sing, Regia."

"You heard it too?" She raised her head to look for his warrior's belt. "Dacton, the yellow stone in your belt has turned green! What does it mean?"

"I'm not sure, but your bracelet and my amulet seemed to have enjoyed our mating as much as we did." He smiled when she blushed, then eased her head back to his chest and stroked her hair. "Sweet Regia. No woman has ever pleasured me so completely, or given me the gift you have. By the Powers of the Universe, I pray you never regret this."

Talina rolled onto his chest and toyed with strands of hair that lay on his bare shoulder. "How could I?" She waited for the cold fingers of guilt to twine around her heart, but she felt only love and satisfaction. When they returned to Sobrie they would have to keep their distance and return to the harsh reality of their lives. But no one could take this moment from her, a moment they would share for all time.

CHAPTER TWENTY SEVEN

Zotar grinned. After a two four time-unit ride, he had finally caught up with Cortain's Royal Guard. They had left tracks a blind man could follow, but they served his purpose. He could not return to Sobrie without witnesses to his claims that the Burly people had killed his men and were allies of The Protectorate, harboring Dacton and Talina.

"Any luck?" he called to the men in the distance. All ten men turned their heads.

"Good afternoon, sir," Gartron greeted. "We have not found Princess Talina, but we did find twelve men from Sobrie—dead. Butchered like animals, not far from here."

"I know, Gartron, I barely escaped with my life. The Burly men caught us by surprise. We fought hard. I was knocked unconscious. They left me for dead when they saw this blood on me." Zotar laughed to himself as he pointed to his chest where the blood of the last Burly man had splattered on him. Cutting a man's throat was messy, but it made his story more convincing. "Have you lost any men?"

"No sir. We are still twenty strong," Gartron reported. "The others are searching along the river."

"Gather all your men. We must make those responsible for murdering Sobrie's soldiers pay with their lives," Zotar commanded the bewildered man.

"Soldiers? When did Sobrie obtain soldiers? We have always been guards. Soldiers are for...war."

"Precisely. You are all soldiers now. And we are at war with anyone who disagrees with Cortain, Regnar, and the council." He studied the man. Gartron was the leader of Cortain's Royal Guard, and he would not be easily fooled. He needed Gartron's devotion and leadership. There were not many men in Sobrie who could give or carry out orders. "The council has ordered me to train an army to protect Sobrie from its aggressors, and I would like you, Gartron, to command at my side."

Gartron saluted Zotar. "If it is our king's desire, I shall serve you."

"Excellent. Now gather your men and follow me." Zotar detected a hesitancy in Gartron's voice. Gartron was loyal to Cortain, but he could deal with that. Manipulating Gartron would require a bit more finesse than the others he had to deal with.

If his plan succeeded, he would find where the Burly people lived and annihilate every last one of them. Whether they harbored Dacton and Talina or not, they were a threat to his success. The Burly men were warriors and were at odds with the government. Any man who defied the government would be killed, because soon he, Zotar, would be the government.

Then and only then would satisfaction be his. Talina would pay as only a woman could, but Dacton would pay with his life, and nothing would please him more than to watch the Protector die slowly, painfully, with Talina watching.

Cortain and the entire government were fools. They all accepted him so easily. He did not even have to work hard to gain their trust. It seemed that all of them were idiots willing to give away their freedom and wealth all too easily—and he was all too willing to take it! He laughed to himself. He enjoyed a good fight once in a while. If these dim-wits refused to fight, he knew Dacton would be happy to battle him.

He and Dacton had a score to settle, and he would be more than happy to make him pay, one drop of blood at a time until the man had none left. Yes, torture was almost too easy a price for Dacton to pay. He would have to think of ways to make him suffer beyond any man's endurance. Yes, this game could prove to be quite fun, and he looked forward the challenge. He could always count on Dacton to make his life interesting.

* * * *

"I never knew such things were possible in a shower."

"There are still many things I can show you, Regia." Dacton noticed her blush and smiled. She had the knowing blush of a woman remembering the feel of her man, a blush he wanted to keep there permanently.

"I wouldn't want you to tire of me, warrior."

"Never. But if this warrior doesn't get some food soon he'll become too weak to ever ravage you again." He took her hand and led her down the hall to a storage area he'd discovered earlier, before the comforts of the pallet chamber distracted them. He found some dried fruit and protein bars, all Protectorate issue. Without a doubt, these were Zotar's stolen supplies.

"What's wrong, Dacton? You look worried."

"It's nothing."

"I know you better than that. Now tell me what's going through that stubborn head of yours."

"I was thinking how pervertedly evil Zotar is, and how much I want to see him...." He caught himself before he said something against his orders. "Brought to justice."

"It scares me to think what he had planned after seeing these."

He led Talina to a small table and chairs in the room outside the storage area. They sat and he watched her touch the nearly transparent lavender fabric she still wore. "I know very well what he planned to do to you. And if he ever tries I *will* kill him. I will hunt him down and..."

"Stop! No matter how evil he is, I do not want killing. How can we return to a peaceful existence if we turn to murder instead of justice?"

"You have a point, but there is only one kind of justice Zotar understands." Dacton handed her the food rations. "It doesn't taste like much, but it is nourishing."

Talina accepted his offering and took a bite.

Dacton laughed when the assault on her taste buds became obvious by the contorted expression on her face. She looked cute squinting and wincing, unable to hide her reaction. He found a bottle of wine, popped the cork, then poured a glass and handed it to her.

"If this wine is like Krow's, we could be in trouble." She took a sip.

"It would be no trouble this time, Regia, because I do not plan to control my urges like before." He watched her blush again. She was so beautiful, and innocent. "I suspect you've learned to like my urges?"

"I may have to test them a few more times to be sure. A Legatus should never make hasty decisions."

"You learn quickly, too quickly I fear."

"Fear? I've never known you to fear anything."

Dacton smiled. How could he tell her his only fear was leaving her? It would happen soon enough, and he would never be ready. But he had to return to The Protectorate. His duty as Chief Protector was real, and so was the marriage ban.

He could come back in ten annual-cycles when his term of duty was complete, but he could not ask Talina to wait that long. She deserved a husband, children, and her rightful place as Legatus. No woman could, or should, put her life on hold for a man who could promise her nothing.

Regret.

He knew it would come. By the Gods, what had he done to his precious Regia? All he did was love her, and now they would both pay. He never should have let his heart dictate the rules, but he'd fallen under her spell.

He watched Talina eat the miserable tasting rations and wondered what was going through her pretty little head. No, he probably did not want to know because he would extinguish her hopes for the future, and the newly found trust they shared.

Talina brushed crumbs from her lap. "What were all those papers you had earlier?"

"Zotar's plans, suppliers, and communications to and from his ship. It's obvious he never expected this place would be found."

"Based on Ora's beliefs, he would have been right. The Peaks of Venda are said to be haunted by the spirits of our enemies. That's why it's believed to be so cold and foreboding, not to mention the Pengores Krow warned you about."

"So this really is considered the forbidden zone to your people?" She nodded at him. "Of course. Zotar plays on weakness and fear." Dacton studied Talina and tried to ignore her cleavage and the faint, dark outline of nipples that begged for attention. There would be time for that later.

"When are you going to destroy the reactor?"

"On our way out. According to The Protectorate's calculations, the mountain should not collapse in the blast, however, if we tried it now, it could be one long, cold moon- cycle."

Talina shrugged her shoulders and tilted her head. "It is getting late, and I'm really tired. Let's go to pallet."

"That is a most interesting idea, Regia." He smiled and reached across the table and took her hand in his. "But I doubt you'll get much rest." He stood and helped her to her feet. She gazed dreamily into his eyes while he led her to the bedchamber. She had been his willing partner twice in pallet and once in the shower, but he craved more, and it was not because of his long stretch of abstinence. He needed her to sustain his spirit and feed the very core of his being which had never before been nourished.

CHAPTER TWENTY EIGHT

O

"Septra, my dear friend." Zotar greeted the man in his private quarters. "Did you have any problems while I was away?"

"Everything went according to plan. The drug you provided worked like a charm. Cortain suffered a heart attack while presiding over the council. I have him sequestered in his quarters with a hand-picked nurse to attend him and make sure he doesn't wake up too soon."

"Good, good. And how is that son of yours doing? Has he convinced the council to remove Cortain from the throne?"

"Regnar is being diplomatic. The request should be granted soon. Our biggest opposition is Kolere and his religious faction. The only priest on our side is Father Makus."

Zotar shrugged his shoulders. "Kolere is old. He could die. It would come as a surprise to no one." He thought for a moment. "Invite Kolere to dinner this moon-cycle and I will serve him just what he needs."

A smile crossed Septra's face. "I like it. You're most clever, Zotar. I knew from the moment I met you that we would have a very profitable friendship."

Septra was as big a fool as everyone else on the planet. If the man had a brain in his head he would surely know how expendable he was, as well as his ignorant son, but for now, they were necessary. "Yes Septra, it is good to have friends you can trust."

"What have you learned of Princess Talina?"

"Not much. As soon as I finish my business here, I'll resume my search. And this time, I will not return without her. It will be glorious, Septra! We'll place her abductor in a cage in the center of the town so everyone can gawk at him. They'll learn not to violate the law by his example. There will be no problems from the populace once they see the fate of our enemies."

Septra nodded. "And what of Princess Talina?"

"I have plans for her as well." Plans he had no intention of sharing with this sniveling fool.

* * * *

"All of our things are at the end of the tunnel." Talina looked up at Dacton. "Are the explosives in place?"

"Yes." Dacton glanced at Talina with a remembering smile. Their moon-cycle of lovemaking had been glorious, but now they had to return to reality and finish the mission. He prayed she would never forget how he loved her, or how their arms had held each other so tightly.

That memory may have to sustain him for the rest of his life. Once Talina knew the truth about the marriage ban for Protectors, she would never forgive him. He was bound to duty or death. Either way, he could not become her life-mate, no matter how appealing the idea had become.

"Okay. Let's go." He took Talina's arm and led her through the arched entrance and secured the heavy metal door behind him. He still hated the rustling sound his flight suit made when it moved, but Talina needed to wear it. She put curves in the metallic fabric that pleased his eye, curves only she could make. He picked up his bag of special tools and led her down the long tunnel to exit the cavern to where they would be safe.

He guided her to where they could hide behind a large rock outcropping about fifty yards from the entrance. "Ready?" Dacton watched her nod, then he pressed the detonator button. They covered their ears against the deafening sound of the blast. Rocks and debris shot from the entrance of the tunnel and repercussions from the blast shook their bodies.

The ground shook and black smoke billowed into the air. He put his arm around Talina and pulled her to him while they waited for the dust to settle. Even though the explosion was over, she still shook in his embrace. "It's all right now, Regia."

Talina looked up into Dacton's eyes and sighed. "I don't know what I was expecting, but that was not it."

He laughed. "No matter how many times I've set off explosives I'm never quite ready for that either. I know it's coming, but it still gets to me. It gets to everyone, so don't feel bad. You're perfectly normal." He tipped her chin up with his finger. "I take that back, you are far superior to normal."

He bent his head and kissed her long and hard, then eased back before he took it too far. There was work to do. He ended the kiss, but she looked at him with the same need in her eyes that he felt in his body. "If only we had more time, my sweet Regia. But right now, we must move."

Dacton led her back to what remained of the reactor room. He held the luna-stone up. Rubble was strewn everywhere and wires hung haphazardly from the ceiling, a spark noticeable every now and then. The secret room behind the reactor had been completely gutted, all weapons inside destroyed.

He inspected the mangled cremare-ray guns, pleased by the total destruction. The he saw it and he felt his eyes widen. It was not possible, yet there it was, the reactor. It stood unscathed, as perfect as it was when they found it.

"I thought you said if your explosives didn't destroy it, nothing would."

He saw disbelief written all over her face. All he could do was shake his head since he barely believed what sat before him. He glared at the round cylinder.

"I had a premonition that something like this would happen."

Dacton raked his hand through his hair. "Indeed."

"On our way here I had the strangest feeling we would have a problem. Remember?" She stared at Dacton. "Okay, I thought you were in danger. But I did have a really bad feeling." Talina shook her head. "I never quite expected this."

"Nor did I." Dacton locked gazes with her. "Those explosives were state of the art. There *are* no better." Talina watched him stare at the reactor. "What did Kolere say?"

"What are you talking about, woman?"

"The legend, you stubborn Protector! I'm sure it holds the key to our dilemma. Why else would Kolere insist you bring me into this God forsaken frigid zone?" She touched his belt. "Look at the stone."

"It's still green." He watched as she cleared away the clothes that obstructed her bracelet.

Talina held up her left arm and pulled her bracelet from under the flight suit. "And this is still blue." Talina dropped her arm. "It all means something. The legend says we must become two flames burning as one, and we more than complied with that request."

Her heated blush brought a proud grin to his face. He could tell she tried to hide her reaction, but it was impossible. He shrugged his shoulders. "So we should make love again? Is that what you're saying?"

"You're missing the point here."

"That I am a great lover that satisfied your every need?"

"No, you pompous male! That we somehow accomplished a mystical bond, and that bond has created a chemical change. Possibly in us, but definitely in your stone and my bracelet."

"What do you suggest?"

"Take off the belt and let me look at the stone."

Dacton removed his coat and unbuckled the belt. When he handed it to Talina, the Delareme amulet fell into her hand.

They both stared in shock at the stone. "That was immovable."

"Was."

Together they stared into the endless depths of the mesmerizing green amulet in her palm. She looked at him, then at her crystallinus chain.

"Feel it?"

He touched her bracelet and jerked his hand back. "It's hot! It must be burning your wrist."

"It only feels warm to me."

"Really?" He touched it again. "You're right. It seemed hotter before, not it's just warm." They both stared at each other in an effort to find the words to explain their intense thoughts and feeling. "Something is very different. There seems to be an electric quality in the air. I can feel my body tingling.

"I sensed what you were thinking before you spoke. There's a prickly feeling in my body as well, and the air is volatile."

Dacton touched her cheek. "Kolere is right, *we* hold the key. Do you feel it?"

Talina nodded. "Definitely."

There was a flow of energy between them, an invisible force. He took the stone from her hand and carefully placed it on top of the reactor. Talina reached out and touched the amulet with her fingertips. He watched amazed while crystallinus links grew in size until the bracelet fell from her wrist and landed in a circle around the amulet.

"I never...that bracelet has not been off my wrist since Kolere put it on me over eight annual-cycles ago!"

Dacton slipped his arm around her shoulders and placed his fingertips on the amulet touching hers. She put her arm around his waist. They formed an unbroken circle between themselves, the chain, and the amulet.

A melodic hum invaded the silence and slowly intensified. They held their position firmly and watched in awe while tiny golden strands of light began to dance around them. The air sparked and cracked as it responded to the high-pitched sounds.

The magic of the moment grew even more when a flame rose from each of their hands. The two flames eased toward each other until they merged into one that burned brightly over the center of the amulet. The flame grew until it nearly touched the high ceiling, then sank into the green depths of the stone turning it deep purple. The once clear crystallinus links absorbed the brilliant color.

Musical sounds engulfed them both, and swirling threads of light caressed his body and he saw the same thing happening to her. They were both encased in intense brightness like nothing he had ever experienced before. Sensations of peace and love coursed through his mind and he could hear her thoughts in his head that acknowledged exactly what he was feeling. As the single flame emerged into the air he shared loving thoughts with Talina, and when he sent her love the flame burned brighter. The blaze grew and twisted when she sent him love in return. Nurturing fingers of heavenly light hugged them, as if their existence were dependent solely upon love.

Their minds were completely melded and he could hear her heart beat the same as his, as if their hearts sang the same song. He felt her strength and she acknowledged his in her own way. He silently acknowledged complete understanding, and she sent the same message back to him. While they shared that thought, the metaphysical fibers wrapped themselves around the reactor, and it began to glow white.

He watched and listened while the celestial hum mixed with the crackling luminescent bolts and the reactor began to fade before his eyes. It gradually became transparent until it dissipated into the air. The amulet and chain dropped to the empty floor in front of them.

Talina looked at him with obvious amazement. He wanted to speak but experienced speechlessness for the first time in his life. It was difficult to absorb the rush of emotions that whirled inside his mind. They both stood still and he worked to untangle his identity from hers since they had become so entwined. Slowly he helped her bend down to the floor.

Dacton retrieved his amulet and he handed Talina her chain. She easily slipped it over her hand and watched the purple fade to lavender, then blue. As the colors changed, the crystallinus links adjusted once again to the perfect size around her wrist.

She watched him hold the amulet in its proper place against the center of his belt. The now purple stone affixed itself to the proper place and slowly returned to its former emerald color.

Dacton cleared his throat. "If I hadn't seen it with my own eyes, I never would have believed it."

"I always believed in the legend, but I never imagined this." Talina sighed and hugged Dacton.

"We certainly created magic." Dacton picked up her hand and kissed her fingers. She moved her arms and wrapped them around his neck. He never felt so good or so strong. He kissed her lips and his began to explore every recess of her mouth. There was an urgency within him he was not sure how to quench. Thoughts flew from his mind to hers, and she returned them with her own desperate need.

Their passion was so strong it was tangible. He guided her to the floor and pulled down the zipper of the flight suit. Her breathing became fast, and he could still feel her heart beat along with his. He wanted to tell her how much he loved her, but for the moment, having her like this was all he needed. She completed him in a way he never dreamed possible. They were indeed two flames burning as one.

CHAPTER TWENTY NINE

Zotar returned to his ship three miles outside of Sobrie, the only suitable landing site he'd been able to find since the primitive planet had no docking facilities. He took a seat in front of the vid-screen and began procedures to contact his androids.

While he waited for an answer, he studied the large ring on his finger, unable to believe what he saw. The damned stone indicated the reactor was not functioning, which was not possible! He must have knocked the hidden chip too hard and caused it to malfunction. The stone was lifeless and appeared black instead of glowing red. He ripped it from his finger and flung it against the bulkhead.

He entered the code again and waited. Nothing. What in the universe was wrong? There was no response. Anger roiled in the pit of his stomach. He slammed his fist on the control panel that housed the main computer and felt his blood boil.

Had Dacton found his secret headquarters? The only satisfaction he had was knowing the Protector could not destroy the reactor. He had used almost all of his credits to have it built out of a newly discovered alloy from a remote planet, outside of The Protectorate's Jurisdiction. It was indestructible. Not even the almighty Protectorate had the means to stop him. They may shut down his monitoring system, but the deadly chemicals would still filter into the air.

They could never stop him. He may have to move his timetable up a bit. Cortain would have to be removed from power this sun-cycle, and Regnar installed in his place. He'd waited too long for that eventuality already. Regnar would install him as Legatus, proclaiming him the only choice to lead Ora against The Protectorate.

The people had already been primed to accept him, the off-worlder who had the best interest of Ora at heart. The only man with enough knowledge to defeat The Protectorate when they made their move against Ora. The seeds were well sown. Then, when he blamed Regnar's death on Dacton and The Protectorate, he would assume full power.

Of course he had to find Dacton before he could kill Regnar. Dacton's capture was more important than ever. If his hunch was correct, Dacton would return Talina to Sobrie and fall into his trap by the river where Gartron and his men waited.

Victory was so close he could smell it. Cortain was out of his mind on drugs, and Kolere grew sicker with each meal. Both old men would be out of the picture soon. That was a given. He retrieved the ring and shoved it on his finger. All he had to do now was wait.

* * * *

The icy wasteland was over a time-unit behind them, and Talina could not be happier to be back on her esroth, heading toward Sobrie, with the wind rustling through the pinus trees. She could hear Kiko purr loud and contented while he snoozed in the special pack Dacton had made to hang over the saddle horn so she could keep Kiko in her sight.

Kiko had given them such an exuberant welcome she'd thought he would never settle down enough to travel. There was no way that silly little creature would allow himself to be left behind again. A smile crossed her lips when she thought about how her father would react when she brought Kiko into the palace. He loved animals and had a soft touch with pets.

Dacton led the way and he looked more virile than she had ever seen him. His constant glances at her over his shoulder reminded her of how protective he was. Protector was the right title for him. He was born to be a warrior and would die a warrior. No amount of annual-cycles could take away his gallant fighting spirit, a spirit she truly admired.

Would any human ever understand the special, mystical bond that now tied them? Possibly Kolere, since he understood the legend, but he was a priest. How could he ever understand the relationship she had with Dacton? But, Kolere may be the only person, besides Dacton, who would understand and sympathize with a branded woman. Her father was a kind man, but he had his limitations where she was concerned.

The reality of her new title had yet to sink in, but it did not matter. She had seen the two flames become one, and knew making love to Dacton had not only destroyed the reactor and saved her planet, but saved her heart as well. She needed him. His tenderness, his warmth, and his love.

She would never regret giving herself to the one man in the universe who could touch her soul, the one man who would give his life to protect her. He may not have said the exact words, but he had sent her love. She felt it in her soul. Dacton would never hurt the woman he loved.

"Are you all right?" Dacton called over his shoulder.

"I'm fine." She smiled. From the moment she fell into his arms as an enemy, he had looked after her. She supposed keeping her safe had become a habit he could not break, and one she hoped he never would. "When will we reach Sobrie?"

"If all goes well, we'll be there for lunch tomorrow." Kiko popped his head up and grabbed at her reins. "You're so silly!" She patted his head and eased him back into his private pouch.

"Silly am I?"

Dacton's voice sounded a bit threatening. Talina laughed. "Not you. Kiko. I'd never call you..." A strange sense of danger flooded through her and her heart raced. The esroth stopped dead in his tracks and began to dance nervously.

She saw every muscle in Dacton's body tense as he turned in his saddle. He sniffed the air and listened, then spun his esroth around and rushed to her side. He grabbed the reins of her mount and pulled her toward the trunk of the largest tree he could find.

"Stand on the saddle and pull yourself up. Climb as high as you can. Hurry!"

The urgency in his voice spurred her into action. "What's that rancid smell?" She managed to get her feet on her saddle and worked to keep her balance.

"Climb for your life, woman. Now!"

She jumped to reach the closest limb. When her hands wrapped around the branch the bark bit into her palms. She swung her legs up to grab the thick branch. She missed. Just as desperation shook her, strong hands grasped the bottom of her boots and pushed until her waist cleared the heavy limb and she was able to continue on her own.

When Talina glanced down Dacton pulled his sword from its sheath. He already had the faze-pistol tucked in his belt, and other goodies in his pocket, so why the bulky sword? With that thought, a pungent order assailed her senses, and then she knew. Dear God, no!

"Hurry Dacton. He's close!" Talina watched Dacton jump and grab the limb, easily pulling himself up.

"Go higher," he ordered.

"Dear stars! The esroths are gone...and Kiko is..."

"Climb woman!"

She knew that tone, and he was right, there was nothing they could do for the animals now. She climbed for her life and prayed Dacton was behind her doing the same. She reached the highest branch that could hold her weight and looked for him.

"Dacton! Get up here!" The stubborn warrior remained on the lowest branch. Then it hit her, he planned to battle the Pengore! Her mind may have been clouded that moon-cycle, but she remembered Krow's warning. No man had ever survived a Pengore attack. Leave it to her stubborn Protector to think he could. There was little choice. If they stayed where they were, the Pengore would wait until they fell.

The malodorous air stilled, and the stench hung so heavily Talina could barely catch her breath. It was obviously a defense mechanism to stun its victims, and she fought to maintain her position. She wanted to climb back to Dacton, he would need her help, but it was useless, he would never allow it. She had to stay out of his way so he could fight. If she distracted him he could make a fatal mistake and be killed.

She held out one last hope that the beast would not see them and just keep walking. It was the best hope she had. If what Krow said was true, the Pengore would kill Dacton, then wait for her to fall from the tree for dessert. Dear stars, there had to be something she could do.

In her pocket she fingered the somna, and wondered how many blasts it would take to put a Pengore to sleep. Her instincts said it would be useless on a creature that size. Dacton said it was only effective within a ten foot radius, and if he inhaled any of it, he would also be rendered helpless.

"Regia?"

"Here, above you."

He glanced up. "Whatever you do, do not come down. Promise me."

Damn! The fetid air closed in on her, and she gasped in desperate need of fresh air.

"Regia!"

"I promise." Then she saw it approach from the north, looming tall against the horizon, the ground shaking with each heavy step. Long, dingy white fur covered the immense, almost human like body.

Beady eyes peered through matted shards of hair, and white teeth glistened against the black outline of a hungry mouth. The Pengore raised its arms and let out a blood curdling scream. It showed off long, razor sharp talons at the end of each three fingered hand, but the most outstanding feature rested between its eyes. A thick horn that narrowed to a point, a horn that would easily gore through a man with length to spare.

Fear struck heavy in Talina's pounding heart. She sensed an apprehension that was not all hers. She had never perceived an ounce of reluctance in Dacton, and she could see none now. From the moment of their joining she had been able to discern glimpses of his inner thoughts, and what she perceived now scared her to the bone. He was going to sacrifice himself to save her. She should have known since he had said it enough times.

"Dacton," she called, "climb higher. You're not safe!"

He made no move. He held the sword and crouched on the limb. All she could think of was how many times he vowed to die to keep her safe. By the Powers of the Universe, she could not let that happen. She needed his help, but most of all, she needed his love.

The Pengore was within striking distance, and from the grunts and groans, the nasty beast intended to rip Dacton limb from limb. One huge hairy arm swiped at Dacton's leg, but he pulled himself up on the limb over his head in time to miss the blow that left deep gashes in the wood where his boots had been.

He quickly lowered himself and his sword made contact with the Pengore's arm. The creature looked at the red gash and bellowed his anger and pain to the forest. He jumped up and down several times, then violently shook the tree. She clung tightly and prayed Dacton had done the same.

"Talina! Are you all right?" he demanded.

"I'm fine." Her voice shook as badly as her body. This was no time to be a coward. Branch by branch she eased her way closer to Dacton. There was nothing she could do to help if she did not get closer. When her foot touched the limb next to him she immediately felt his gaze pierce what little confidence she had been able to muster.

"In the name of the Gods, what do you think you're doing?"

"Look out!" she warned, just in time for Dacton to dodge another assault from the enraged creature.

Dacton pulled the faze-pistol from his belt and fired successive rounds at the creature. "Use this on him every chance you get." He shoved the pistol into Talina's hand.

"What if I miss, or hit you?"

"Then we're both in trouble. Just react."

"Dacton, no!" Talina screamed, too late to keep Dacton in the tree. She could not believe he jumped to the ground to battle a deadly creature four times his size. Had he lost his mind? She held the faze-pistol with both hands and watched the crazed animal crouch in an attack position. She fired, her finger frozen on the trigger.

The Pengore shook his head and looked up at her. She fired again and the animal roared. Terror ran up and down her spine as she watched Dacton lunge at the miscreant of nature that had every intention of having the warrior for lunch. Dacton's sword pierced the tough, hairy hide, and blood stained the dirty white pelt as Dacton twisted his weapon to pull it free.

Blood spurted in all directions, and she watched in horror when the Pengore covered the wound with its hand, then licked the blood off his fingers. She fired off several more rounds and the animal stumbled to his knees. Dacton ran full speed and gored the massive monster in the stomach. Before he could retreat the Pengore grabbed Dacton by the arm, knocking the sword from his hand. The hairy monstrosity lifted Dacton's body toward teeth that would surely end the Protector's life.

Dacton pulled the cutter from his boot and thrust the blade into the creature's eye an instant before the monster rendered him powerless. Carefully Talina took aim at the Pengore's head. She had no choice. If she did not shoot, Dacton would die. If she missed...well, she had to take that chance. With every ounce of concentration fixed on her target she fired three consecutive shots, striking the fur covered head, the beam penetrating through flat scaly ears.

The Pengore fell to its back and released Dacton. He scrambled to retrieve his sword. She watched him circle around to the head that moved from side to side on the ground. Every muscle in Dacton's body flexed when he reared back and took a level swing at the base of the horn.

With an agility unmatched in a creature of its size, the Pengore rolled to his stomach and avoided Dacton's sword. It rose to its feet and lunged at Dacton in one fluid movement. She fired at the animal's back, but it had no impact on the attacking monster. The horn ripped through Dacton's vest and leather tunic. She watched in horror when a long, deep red gash appeared across Dacton's chest. He fell motionless to the ground.

"Over here, you smelly creature!" She had to divert his attention long enough to allow Dacton to regain his footing. She prayed he was conscious. The Pengore turned and took several steps in her direction. She fired again and again striking his throat and chest. She pulled the somna from her pocket.

"Dacton, stay back!" she yelled, just in case he decided to rush to her aid. When the Pengore grabbed for her leg she clicked the round cylinder twice and aimed. One claw tore her pant leg and she gasped in pain. Suddenly she knew she'd inhaled the somna. The Pengore, Dacton and the trees whirled before her eyes, her ears rang. She managed to click the cylinder again and release another round of somna before complete darkness consumed her.

* * * *

Leana ran through the long hall of the cave to the conference room where Krow and the Elders were meeting. They were never to be disturbed while conducting official business, but this could not wait. She pushed open the door without a knock and burst into the room, gasping for breath.

"Leana!" Krow bellowed. "What's the meaning of this?"

"I am sorry, my husband, but the news I bear cannot wait. Dacton and Talina's esroths have returned to camp. Without riders. You must find them!"

Krow rushed to his wife's side and hugged her close. "Are you all right?" he whispered so the Elders could not hear. He felt her head nod against his chest. She was upset, and rightfully so. The esroths would never return to their home unless something was desperately wrong.

Still gasping for breath, Leana looked into her husband's eyes. "I have never seen esroths so distraught. They're dancing all over the corral and won't let anyone near them."

Krow turned to the council. "I must leave immediately. It could mean the evil one has returned with more men." He noted the sadness in the eyes of the Elders as they nodded their approval.

Leana grabbed Krow's hand and squeezed tightly. "Be careful, Krow. Their weapons will destroy you. We can't afford to lose our leader, not now. Please, promise me! Our people need you, but I need you more."

The proud warrior locked eyes with his faithful wife. "I'll be back. And if what I suspect is true, you'll need many dilek leaves and bandages ready in their room."

"It will be done, my love."

He rushed from the conference room to assemble a search party. Somehow he had to find his new friend.

* * * *

Talina moaned as she pushed herself up to a sitting position. Dear stars, how long had she been unconscious? Her hand found the lump on her forehead. Pain stabbed viciously at her temples, forehead, and the base of her skull. Her eyes watered and tried to focus. When the rancid air penetrated her memory, she scrambled to her feet. "Dacton?" Where are you?" She blinked several times and wiped tears with her sleeve.

On the ground in front of her lay Dacton in a pool of blood. One hand still held his bloody sword, the other firmly wrapped around the pointed end of the Pengore's horn.

She rushed to his side and knelt. "Dacton? Can you hear me?" She shook his shoulders. "Answer me, warrior!" Nothing. This was no time to panic. The creature lay dead, and she feared Dacton would soon join him.

"Please dear God, don't let him die!" She laid her hand on his forehead, her anguished tears falling on his pallid face. Her fingers trembled as she searched for life along the thick vein along the side of his neck. Yes! She felt a slight pulse, and let out the breath she held. If she did not find help immediately he would die.

Talina ripped open what was left of his clothes. She picked up the cutter that lay by her foot, reached under her parka and cut a strip of cloth from her tunic. She laid the fabric across the deep gash on his chest and applied gentle pressure to stop the bleeding. He had numerous other wounds that were crusted with dried blood, but they were not life threatening.

There were no supplies and no transportation. Dear stars, she hated to leave him, but without help he would bleed to death. "I'll be back, my love." She wiped his forehead with her hand, then kissed lips that had grown cold.

Tears spilled down her cheeks, and she no longer cared. There was no one here to see her weakness, and she could not pretend to be brave when she felt so lost. Pride had kept her from crying in front of The Protector many times, but he could not see her now.

She stroked his hair and remembered how her attempts to convince him he was not invincible had proved futile. All she knew was that she loved the man who had turned her life upside down, and that would never change. "I love you Dacton, you stubborn, arrogant warrior. Don't you dare die on me!"

Talina stood, and with one last glance, left her Protector and ran down the hill. The sun-cycle was fading fast, and she forgot to bring the luna-stone. How would she find her way in the dark? Even if she brought the light with her, she had no idea how far Krow's cave was from here, or if she could actually find it.

A rustling of leaves in the distance caught her attention and she ducked behind an old fallen tree. The air was still sweet to her lungs so it was not a Pengore. She would never forget that putrid smell as long as she lived. She peered over the log to see who approached. Whoever they were, they rode esroths.

"Dacton, Talina!"

Had she really heard her name?

"Dacton, Talina!"

That voice belonged to Krow! Thank the stars. She jumped up and ran toward the riders who did not slow their pace until they were beside her.

Krow jumped from his mount and pulled Talina into a welcoming hug. "I can see you're all right, but where is Dacton?"

"Oh Krow, it was terrible, the Pengore..."

"Dear Gods, Dacton is dead?"

Talina heard real sorrow in Krow's voice. "Not yet, but we have to hurry."

Swiftly mounting the esroth, Krow pulled Talina up behind him and spurred his mount into a cantor up the hill. "I'd know that odor anywhere. We must be close."

They quickly arrived at the small clearing where Dacton and the Pengore lay lifeless. Talina felt her body shake, her nerves taking over once again.

"No man has ever survived a bout with the ferocious beast, but I pray Dacton will be the first." Krow pulled his esroth to a halt. He held Talina's arm while she dismounted and ran to the fallen man. Krow quickly followed.

Talina knelt by Dacton's side and looked deeply into Krow's dark brown eyes. "Help him, Krow. Please." Krow felt for a pulse at the base of Dacton's neck, then he stared at her in disbelief. Her heart sank, afraid of the news he was about to give her. Instead he nodded.

Krow waved at two of his men. "Bring the litter!" He felt Dacton's forehead, then looked at Talina. "What happened?"

"We were on our way back, riding along when Dacton yelled for me to climb the tree. He started fighting the Pengore from the tree, then he jumped to the ground and...I tried to stop him...I yelled..."

"Calm down. We'll take him to our home and do all we can." He shook his head. "He is close to death." Krow looked up at Talina. "I will not lie to you. There is not much we can do except tend his wounds. It will be very difficult for him. I'm not sure he will survive. I want you to know that."

"I understand." Talina looked into Krow's eyes. "I appreciate anything you can do for him." She watched Krow and his men lift Dacton's battered, lifeless body onto the stretcher and fasten the leather straps to hold him secure.

"Come Talina." Krow offered his hand to help her back on the esroth. "We must hurry."

CHAPTER THIRTY

O

Talina was exhausted after the long meeting with Krow and the Elders in the council chambers. They had much to plan, and were as anxious as she was to have Dacton return to consciousness. The sun-cycles blurred together since they'd been here because she had barely slept, and even when she had she barley dozed. Sleeping in a bedside chair was not easy.

She walked down the hall to Dacton's room and when she opened the door she found Leana wiping Dacton's forehead. Krow and Leana were both a God-send and she would never forget how they helped. "How is he?"

Leana nodded. "Your man has been through much. His wound is healing nicely, but he is still delirious with fever, and there's still poison in his system. We never knew the Pengore's horn contained poison. Every man that tried to fight the monster died and was eaten. We had no way to know."

Talina sighed. "If anyone can survive such an attack, it's Dacton." Leana walked closer to her and placed her hand on her shoulder.

"Stay with him. You can pull him from the blackness of his mind, my lady. If he responds to anything or anyone, it would be your presence and your voice. He cares deeply for you, as you do for him. That is a special bond—a bond that can make the difference between life and death."

"Oh Leana," she hugged her new friend. "I hope you're right."

"As do I." Leana leaned back and looked into Talina's eyes. "Your love will make the difference. I'm sure of that."

"I'll hold on to that thought and pray you're right."

"Please, just call me, Talina, if you need anything. Anything at all."

Leana's kind green eyes offered tender solace, and her sweet, olive face, framed by dark hair gave her courage to face the battle before her. "You're a good friend, and a woman who can more than understand what I'm going through."

"Unfortunately that's true. I will say it's not easy loving a warrior."

Talina smiled sadly. "I never dreamed it would be this hard. He's so stubborn, so arrogant, so..."

Leana laughed. "Our men share many qualities, most of which are good. Besides they would not be good warriors if they weren't so stubborn and arrogant. I suppose we would have them no other way."

"I suspect you are right." She and Leana shared a knowing chuckle.

"Will you be all right alone? I really must return to work. We have much to do to prepare for war." Leana opened the door and stepped into the hall.

An ever deeper pain pierced Talina's heart. She did not want to see any more misery come to the Burly people. They had been so good to her and Dacton. What in the stars had been going on in Sobrie since she left? Nothing good to be sure.

"Leana?" Her friend heard her and stopped.

Leana turned. "Yes?"

"I will do everything I can to bring peace between our people. And I want you to know how grateful I am for all that you've done. Especially after you learned who I am."

Leana smiled. "We do not judge a person's worth by their title or physical appearance, only by the soul. That is who you are. You have a good heart, Talina DeAmarant. I trust you will do what is right. If anyone can bring peace between us, it's you."

The woman closed the door behind her when she left, and Talina sank onto the chair by Dacton's bedside, where she had kept vigil for the past twelve sun-cycles. Sleep would not come. How could she sleep when any minute he might wake. She refused to miss the moment his eyes opened.

She picked up the warrior's belt and laid it across the blanket at Dacton's waist. Tracing the outline with her fingers, she remembered every detail of the moon-cycle that had changed the golden stone to green. His mouth on hers, his hands on her breasts, the sweet kisses that caressed her body, and the virile man who made her feel like a queen.

Silently she prayed. She needed him, wanted him, loved him. The mysterious Protector who lay so quiet had changed her life forever. She had fought hard to escape him, now she fought to keep him.

A slight moan came from deep within his chest and her heart raced at the sound. She took the rag from his forehead, rinsed it in the bowl, then placed it at his hairline. She pulled down the blanket, and with another rag sponged his fevered chest.

"Listen to me, warrior." She rubbed the cloth back and forth across the wide expanse of his nicely furred muscles. "You will recover. You have to. I am not finished with you yet!" She gasped when she saw his lips move and bent closer to hear what he was trying to say.

"I love you, Regia. I love you."

She stroked his cheek. Did he know what he was saying? Was it his heart or the fever talking? It did not matter. She had waited to hear him say those words. Asleep or awake, his heart could not lie. The semi-conscious admission was probably more true than any words he filtered through his conscious mind.

"I love you, Dacton. Come back to me. Fight, damn you, fight!" She thought he would wake more, instead he slipped into a deeper sleep. At least she had seen a sign of recovery, and for now, that was enough. She placed a fresh rag on his forehead then sank lower in the chair to rest her head on the high wooden back. She closed her eyes. Memories of passion pulled at her senses, the feel of his hungry kiss on her mouth sent a chill up her spine. Dacton was strong, and he was a fighter. She would have him back in her arms...and in her pallet.

With every ounce of her being she concentrated on Dacton. She sent him love and light, and willed his strength to return. She begged him to fight, and promised never to leave his side. She sent him visions of love, and a life filled with the happiness they had glimpsed. A happiness she was determined to have again.

Talina searched to find the magic they shared, to link with him and become as one once again. Instead she felt alone. The illusive lights would not dance, the music would not sing, and her Protector would not wake.

* * * *

Dacton took a deep breath and felt something slide from his chest. He felt beside him and found his warrior's belt. After several blinks his eyes focused on the sight beside his pallet. His prayers were answered. Talina. Golden locks spilled over her shoulders and caressed the gentle swell of her breasts as she slept. His Regia was beautiful, and he knew she had saved his life.

A quick glance told him he was back in the room they had shared at Krow's. How long had he been here? How had Talina managed to move him? So many questions, but they could wait. His throat was as dry as when he'd been lost in the desert without water. He reached for a glass on the table next to the pallet, but accidentally knocked it over.

Talina's eyes flew open and she jerked upright in the chair. "What in the stars are you doing?"

"I didn't mean to wake you, I only wanted a drink."

"Wake me? I've waited fifteen sun-cycles to hear you speak, to see your eyes. Oh Dacton, I've been so worried."

"Battling the Pengore made me tired." She jumped out of her chair and leaned over him. He reached up and stroked her face. He lifted his head and took the glass of water from her outstretched hand and drank until it was gone. He handed her the glass then laid back. "I'm afraid I'm still a bit weak, but as soon as I gain a little strength, I promise to show you how I missed you, Regia."

"You have just returned from the brink of death, and you speak of making love?" She laughed. "You haven't lost your arrogant ways."

"Nor will I." He smiled. "And you would have it no other way."

"I will not dignify that with an answer."

"Okay. Then do you think you are strong enough to take a bath?"

"If that is your wish." She giggled at him and he saw it written all over her face how happy she was that he had come back to her. "You are right, Regia. Warm water and sweet smelling soap would help me feel better.

"I'll see to the water. And I must tell Krow and Leana that you live."

"It will be good to see them again, but not before I bathe, promise me?"

"Promise. I'll be right back." Talina waved then left the room.

Alone with his thoughts, Dacton thanked the Powers of the Universe for sparing his life, and giving him the love of a woman like Talina. She had fought like a true warrior. His heart nearly stopped when the Pengore touched her after she fell from the tree. Luckily the somna slowed the animal enough for him to finish his attack. He would have to thank Krow for the knowledge of how to kill the beast, and Talina for his life.

There was much to discuss with Krow, but first, he had to make love to Talina. He needed to treasure every last minute they had before returning to Sobrie. Was it so wrong to crave what little precious time remained before reality tore them apart forever? The moment of truth approached rapidly, but he would be *her* Protector until then.

The door opened and boy after boy poured hot water into the familiar copper tub. He had wanted to join Talina once, and now he would see to it that she joined him. He would trick her into thinking him weak, and then...

"Are you ready for your bath?"

Her voice pulled him from a most vivid vision, one he hoped would come to fruition. He watched the last water boy leave then glanced at

Talina. "Can you help me? I feel a bit shaky."

"Of course. I didn't expect you to do it yourself."

He smiled when she slipped her arm around his waist. He put his arm around her shoulders and leaned enough to make her feel helpful. Slowly he shuffled to the tub. The truth did run parallel to the lie. He was shaky. Too much time in pallet, or was it not enough?

"You'll have to undress me, Regia." He tried to sound weak without revealing his true need. Dacton laughed to himself when she hesitated to lift the thin pants over his engorged manhood. He really had tried to control that, but the sight of her at this moment sent him over the edge.

"I see you're recovering nicely." She stripped away his pants and tossed them aside.

All he could do was smile back at her. He lifted one leg and put his foot down in the hot, soapy tub. He put his hand on the other side of the metal tub, then lifted his leg. At least he was now in, so he eased himself down and let the warmth of the scented water sooth his sore muscles.

His body still burned with a fire he had never known, a fire only Talina could extinguish. When she bent over the tub he took her mouth with his and began to search every sweet recess. He tasted what he had missed, then his hands moved to her back. She felt good, and he wanted more. His hand slid lower and circled her buttocks before coming to rest underneath the full softness.

Talina pushed away and looked him in the eye. "I thought you wanted a bath?" She grabbed his arms and put them back into the suds.

He gazed up at her smiling face. "I want to thank you for saving my life."

"You saved your own life. I'm afraid I didn't do a very good job with the somna."

"Good enough." He found a bar of soap on the bottom of the tub. He picked it up and handed the slippery, sweet smelling bar to Talina. "Would you mind washing my back?"

She took the soap and worked it across his back in a circular motion. "Your wounds have healed nicely."

Her touch was soothing and he relaxed while she massaged every aching muscle with the scented lather. She found his shoulders and a moan formed in his chest. "I will give you one time-unit to quit that."

"I bet, but that might wear me out."

"We cannot have that." He turned and pulled her around to face him. "Kiss me, Regia." She bent down and pressed her lips to his and he nearly exploded with the need she sent to every part of his body. He deepened the kiss and tried to send her to the same edge he found himself. He wanted all of her, and fast.

He brought the kiss to an end, pulled back and stroked her face. Her cobalt eyes looked deeper and he could swear he saw love and need looking back at him. "Take off your clothes. I want to look at your body."

Without a word of argument she pulled the tunic over her head and dropped it beside her. Her firm breasts made his mouth water and his fingers itch. She sat on the edge of the tub to remove her boots. He wanted to grab her and pull her in the tub. Slow and easy, he reminded himself. She glanced at him when she stood, her thumbs slipping under the waistband of her pants. Leisurely she pushed, a little at a time. She drove him crazy!

He had taught her well, her torture was deliciously sweet, deliberately controlled. Every movement sensual and erotic. He fought to maintain control. She stirred him close to the point of no return. He reached for her, but she stepped back to evade his grasp.

"Be careful, you're not a well man."

Her sultry voice taunted him. He smiled. "Then it's up to you to cure me." He groaned when she leaned toward him, rested her hands on the edge of the tub with her breasts inches from his lips. They screamed for attention so he grasped her shoulders and sucked one rosy nipple into his mouth. He lavished her softness, her scent and everything she had to offer.

A moan escaped her lips and that was the invitation he needed to pull her into the tub with him, careful not to break their intimate contact. Her skin was so soft, so feminine. He could wait no longer. His hand found her waist. He poised her over his swollen manhood and eased her down every inch of his throbbing need.

Talina tilted her head back and grabbed the curved, copper sides of the tub. She moved forward and back, side to side. He had found heaven. This woman pleased him like no other, and she offered her heart and soul along with her body.

Water sloshed up his neck and over the edge of the tub splashing onto the rock floor. He placed one arm around her back and the other on the tub and stood. She wrapped her legs around his body and he stepped from the bath. She had renewed his strength, at least for the moment, and he carried her the few steps to the pallet.

"You're so beautiful, Regia." He laid her down and ran his hands through her hair. He inhaled deeply and savored the sweet fragrance of flowers in her hair. It reminded him of the first moon-cycle he carried her in his arms. A bittersweet memory he would cherish.

Talina pushed her hands against Dacton's chest. "Are you sure you're up to this?"

"Need you ask?" He pressed his arousal against her and she smiled. She met his lips and tenderly tasted him in way that drove him wild. "You've learned my secrets well, my love."

"As I should." She kissed his neck and moved down his chest to tease his nipples.

Every caress she lavished spoke love. He knew what she had given him, and God help him, he wanted all she could give. How selfish he was to want her the way he did, but he could not help himself. She filled the hole in his heart that had been there for so long—a hole only she could fill.

He may have taught her the ways of the pallet, but loving him had come naturally to her. By the Gods, how he loved her. He grasped her cheeks and pulled her mouth to his. Urgent and demanding, he searched every recess, hungry for her taste.

Feelings flooded his mind, feelings he had tried to suppress since he was forbidden to love Talina. His duty called, but he ignored it. All he wanted was this woman, *his woman*. His lips moved to her feminine curls. Pleasing her brought him happiness, and he could no more stop this joining than he could stop breathing. He loved her.

He tasted her, stroked her, and relished the scent that was hers alone. She moaned and he delved deeper. He needed this memory to last. Memories were all that would sustain him soon, and the thought devastated him. How could he ever leave her when he wanted her so?

Her muscles tightened and she thrust her hips higher. He sampled her essence until she found release. She was all woman. He could wait no longer to have what his body cried for and his heart desired. Kissing his way to her lips he paused to study the satisfaction he found in her blue eyes. How he wished she would always look at him the way she did this moment.

Gently he slipped between her legs and eased inside. To be one with the woman of his dreams was his only thought. Joining had never brought such contentment or delight. As much as he wanted to prolong their union, he found himself moving faster, plunging deeper.

Melodic sounds filled his ears and bright fingers of light twined around him. He closed his eyes, not sure where reality began or ended. Thoughts of happiness and visions of children invaded his consciousness. Were they his fantasies, or hers? They were the same. They were one. Inseparable. Forever.

Her breathing quickened and he panted for breath. He took her solace while she totally consumed him. The melodious symphony declared them one, and he could wait no longer to spill his seed into the only woman he would ever love.

He gasped for breath and reached for the stars. She writhed beneath him and joined him in sweet release. The euphoria of pure joy glowed on her face. He kissed her one last time then rolled to lay beside her.

Pride soared through his every pore when she opened her eyes and searched his face with wonder. He had always dreamed of having a woman look at him the way Talina did, and he silently prayed she would never stop.

"You're so beautiful, Regia."

"And you're so skilled, my handsome warrior." She touched his cheek with the palm of her hand. "I love you, Dacton."

That sultry voice drove him mad. With every moment that passed she became more deeply imbedded in his blood. He could never release this woman from his heart, she would live there forever. Her flame would always burn within him and no one could take that away. No matter what happened, she would be his, and his alone, if only in his mind.

CHAPTER THIRTY ONE

O

"Leana, I must say," Dacton wiped his mouth with a cloth, "that was the best meal I've ever had."

"I wasn't sure we would ever fill you up." Leana laughed then removed the empty plates and bowls.

"Now my friend," Krow cleared his throat, "if you're up to it, we have much to discuss."

Dacton stared at Krow. "Tell me what's wrong."

Talina could barely believe the horrendous losses the Burly people had suffered in the short time she had been gone. Krow recounted four separate massacres, all at the hands of Zotar. Damn him to Diabolus! Krow's people did not deserve this.

"Krow, I offer my sincere condolences for your losses. I do regret what has happened." Dacton shook his head. "What are your plans?"

"My people are prepared to go to war with the evil one, and the government that supports him. It would be better for us to die with honor in battle, than to be senselessly tortured and murdered."

Talina cleared her throat. "How do you know the government supports Zotar?"

Krow shook his head. "Everyone knows. Zotar has made several public announcements and declarations. So has Regnar, his mouthpiece. We have stayed away from Sobrie for many annual-cycles of peace." He looked directly at Talina. "We left you and your government alone, and they left us alone. There has never been love between us, although the hatred has diminished. But now our spies report they plan to kill us all."

Talina stood, walked over to Krow and took his hand. "You are an honorable leader, and you have my sincere condolences for the loss of your people. However, I cannot condone war between our people. There must be a way to solve this without more loss of life."

"I wish it could be so, Princess, but we must avenge our dead and restore our honor. Zotar laughs at our losses. We are warriors, and we will settle this as warriors."

Talina pulled her hand back and sorrow invaded her heart. She had to stop the killing and destruction that Krow was determined to create. "We have had many talks these past sun-cycles while Dacton recovered, and I beg you not to start a war with Sobrie, you're out numbered and..."

"We will die with honor!"

Dacton held up his hand and silence filled the room. He glanced first at Talina, then turned his attention to Krow. "Do you trust me?"

"Yes," Krow stated flatly.

"Good. I ask you and your people to work with me. Together we can accomplish much, separately we will defeat each other."

"What do you purpose?"

"Talina and I will return to Sobrie. She will find out exactly what has happened within the government, and I will take care of Zotar. My mission is to return him to The Protectorate to be prosecuted for his crimes. Would you agree to such a plan?"

"I want him dead!" Krow screamed.

Talina watched Dacton gather every ounce of control he possessed. She knew Dacton shared Krow's sentiments about Zotar and knew how difficult it was for him to remain calm.

"I share your feelings, Krow."

"How could you? Your people were not burned beyond recognition, shot in the back and tortured like mine!"

"Zotar murdered my brother. The memory is as vivid and painful as yours. Zotar tortured him beyond human endurance and sent me a vid-chip to prove it. Yes Krow, I want Zotar dead. I, too, am a warrior who wants revenge, but I must return him to The Protectorate. It is a matter of my honor." Dacton studied Krow for several long, silent moments. "Will you give me your word not to start a war?"

Krow stood, paced behind the table and shook his head.

The silence grated on Talina's nerves. "I will make peace, and restore all rights of commerce between our people." Krow turned his gaze to her and stopped pacing. "It would be of great benefit to your people to be able to live, work, and trade among us. I will even create a council faction with you as the leader to insure your rights."

"Why should I believe you, Princess Talina? Your government could have done this long ago, but preferred to think of us as animals living in caves!"

"My friend," Dacton began, "Talina was about to assume her

rightful position as Legatus when I so rudely took her from Sobrie to escort me on this mission. She has learned much about your people, as you have about her." He glanced at Talina and smiled. "The Protectorate will oversee everything. The government of Sobrie will be restored, Zotar, Regnar, and anyone else involved with the corruption will be punished. You will see great changes. Changes I am sure you will approve. Represent your people. Come on, Krow. What do you say?"

Krow looked toward Leana, who grinned and nodded her approval. "What assurance can you give me that the government will cooperate with this plan?"

"The Protectorate will place an Advisor to do just that."

"You are this Advisor, Dacton?" Krow asked.

"I wish I were, but I assure you, whoever they send will be more than qualified. And if you have any problems you can contact me, and I'll help work them out."

"Fair enough. But my men will watch, from a distance, to insure this all comes to pass. We will not interfere unless there is a need. Agreed?"

Dacton stood, held out his hand and grasped arms with Krow in true warrior tradition. "Agreed."

Leana made her way around the table and hugged Talina. "I'm so happy our people will be friends." Talina looked into Leana's dark brown eyes. "I care deeply for your people, you have done so much for us."

Leana smiled. "When Krow and I first met you, we knew who you were. Word travels fast. I told Krow that if we treated you right, you would come to understand we are not the barbarians we're thought to be."

"You are a woman wise beyond her annual-cycles." Talina lowered her eyes for a moment, then faced Leana proudly. "At first, I thought if you discovered my identity you'd kill me as an enemy. I apologize for being so wrong."

A sheepish grin crossed Leana's face. "I hope you'll forgive me for giving you only one room. But from the look on Dacton's face, he would have it no other way. And from the look on your face, neither would you."

Talina walked Leana to the opposite corner from Dacton and Krow. "I love Dacton, but you must tell no one."

"But a love like yours should not be hidden. If you do, you may lose him."

"I know Leana, and I fear just that. But you're aware of the customs in Sobrie as well as I am. What is acceptable to your people, and to Dacton, will not be tolerated by mine."

"Is there anything I can do?" Leana wiped a tear from Talina's cheek.

"Pray for things to change. Then, and only then, will Dacton and I have a chance."

"Consider it done. And if Krow sits on your council, I will make him propose the necessary changes in the law so that you can life-mate your warrior."

"Well, let's keep that between us for now." Talina smiled at her new friend and hoped they would have the opportunity to meet again. The men turned from their conversation and stepped over to where she stood. Dacton took his place by her side and slipped his arm around her waist. "What have you women been up to?"

"Nothing." She laughed and Leana joined her since they answered in unison.

Krow eyed Dacton. "I fear our women conspire against us."

"Never, Krow. They're too loyal and devoted."

Krow hugged Leana. "Indeed they are."

* * * *

Talina hoped Dacton would take a break soon since they had been riding hard for over two time-units. The further from Krow's territory they were, the rougher the terrain became. Soon they would reach the peaceful valley, the last refuge before the sharp, jagged rocks and the long, treacherous climb that would take them back to Sobrie.

The clear waters of the river sparkled in the bright sun and she thought how beautiful the valley looked. She really had not noticed before since she had been too consumed with escape plans. Deep green grass, vibrant blue waters, majestic trees, and wild-flowers scattered about.

How she wished she and Dacton could build a home in the midst of such perfection, and raise their children in peace and tranquility. The location was ideal; light-cycles from his responsibilities, and far enough from hers that no one would bother them. "Dacton," Talina called. "Can we stop here?" Dacton slid to a halt so fast she nearly ran him over. Her esroth bumped his esroth's hind-quarters.

Dacton turned in the saddle and looked at Talina. "What's wrong?"

"I didn't expect such a quick response." She dismounted, took Kiko from his pouch and held him in her arms. "I never thought Leana would take such good care of him. In fact, after the Pengore incident, I never thought I would see him again."

"Why are we stopping, Regia?"

"Kiko said he was thirsty."

"He speaks to you now?"

"Don't tell me you're jealous?" Dacton laughed at her while he dismounted, tightened the cinch and adjusted his saddle. She watched him pick up the reins and lead his mount to the riverbank for a well-deserved drink. Talina led her esroth to the water and stopped beside the brawny warrior that held her heart.

"You've been quiet since we left Krow's camp." Talina waited for his reply, but he seemed to ignore her. "Dacton? Is something wrong?" He crossed his arms over his chest and stared at the water. Talina sighed. Dacton hadn't been himself since they'd left. What caused his sudden mood change? He feared nothing, so what had his mind so occupied? "Dacton, talk to me."

Instead of an answer he turned a stoic gaze toward her and a chill ran down her spine. His brows were pinched, his jaw firm, and his eyes cold. She knew that look and it frightened her. It was his masterful Protector's look. The one he assumed when he was about to do battle, but there was no one to fight, except her.

She laid her hand on the front of his tunic and slipped it under his vest. "What is your plan, warrior?"

"When we reach the river on the other side of the mountain, you need to go to Sobrie alone."

"I won't go without you."

"You have to. I will be shot on sight, and I cannot guarantee your safety if you're with me. I'm sure that order still stands."

"Dacton, please. Let me help you." She pressed against him, but he made no move to embrace her. "We can sneak in the way we left, through the tunnel and—"

"No! You will ride through the front gate with your head high. You will tell them you escaped from me, and convince them I mistreated you, that you hate me and..."

"I will do no such thing! I'll appeal to my father. I'll tell him what you've done for our people and for me. He'll see to it you're not harmed."

Dacton grabbed her shoulders as if he were going to kiss her. Her heart raced. She wanted his lips on hers, his arms around her, but he immediately dropped his hands to his sides. The brief flash of desire mirrored in his eyes quickly turned to steel.

"This is no time to question my orders." He led his esroth back to the trail and mounted. Talina glanced at him, his gaze set on the horizon as he waited. She fought tears, but one escaped and fell on Kiko's head. The furry little creature looked up at her with his big round eyes, as if he knew her heart was breaking. She bent and picked him up. When she cradled him in her arms his paw touched her cheek and she leaned into him. "Why Kiko, why is Dacton doing this?"

Kiko squeaked and nuzzled his head against her shoulder. She blinked back tears that threatened to flood. Dacton had reverted back to his old stubborn self. Nausea roiled in her stomach when she turned to pick up the reins. She glanced over her shoulder. He waited with all the passion of a stone statue.

She could only hope that he would mellow out and see things her way by the time they reached the next river. He might be right about entering the city separately, but his cold, uncaring attitude hurt.

Talina secured Kiko in his pouch and watched Dacton trot off without a backward glance. Scary thoughts ran through her mind. Had she made a mistake loving the Protector? She had given him her undying love, and that could never be taken back. If memories were all she ever had, they would have to be enough.

Pain stabbed her heart, and she had yet to separate from the only man she would ever love.

CHAPTER THIRTY TWO

O

Dacton's heart felt as if a piece were missing. The pain he hoped to avoid had arrived with a vengeance and it felt more threatening and real than he had imagined. Those damned rules were back to haunt him.

When Talina looked at him he saw disappointment and betrayal in her cobalt eyes. Remorse settled like lead deep within his chest. He knew this would be difficult, but reality was worse than he ever could have imagined. He wanted to tell her he loved her with every ounce of his being. Instead he was forced to make her hate him in their final time-units together. All because of Zotar.

When she encountered Zotar she had to convince him there was nothing between them except hate. Unfortunately, Talina would only be believed if she spoke from the heart. He had to turn her against him completely or she would be in greater danger. Zotar would use her in ways he did not want to consider. It was for her own good, he reasoned, but he would never forgive himself for the pain he must inflict.

He'd tried to warn her there was a price to pay for loving him. Obviously he had failed to make that point clear and kicked himself for not trying harder. Hell, he'd barely tried at all. He'd wanted her, legend or no legend. Kolere had only provided a good excuse to take his pleasure with her, and pleasure they had. Pleasure beyond human comprehension. They had reached the stars and beyond, and he would treasure every sensuous memory.

Dacton caught Talina's beautiful face out the corner of his eye as she caught up to him. He wanted to taste her luscious lips, run his fingers through her golden hair. All he wanted was to make love to her for the rest of his life. Instead he had to plant seeds of hatred he could never to take back.

"Talk to me, warrior."

How he wanted to smile. She called him warrior to coax a response. He could not let her know he wanted to ravish her right here on the trail. He had to play the part of unfeeling Protector.

"What is there to say? You have your duties, and I have mine. We both knew this sun-cycle would come." Dacton touched the green stone in his belt and eyed the blue of her bracelet. He wondered if their color would change again if they remained apart.

Talina stroked her esroth's neck. "Don't be so stubborn. Surely after all we've been through you have something to say to me."

How could he answer that honestly? He loved her more with every breath he took, but if he told her, it would only hurt her more and put her life in grave danger. He had to spare her further heartache. "We did what we had to do to survive. No more."

"Damn you to Diabolus! I gave you everything I had! I saved your life, I nursed you to health when you almost died. I loved you! And this is the thanks I get?"

"If it's thanks you want, then thank you. If it's a life of devotion, I cannot give you that." He spurred his esroth into a cantor, no longer able to watch her devastation. Curse it all! The only thing he wanted to do was love her. As long as he was a Protector, and she was King Cortain's daughter, that would never be possible. If their positions did not keep them apart, Zotar would. There was no hope for such an ill-fated love.

Talina would never forgive him for this act of cruelty, but that would never stop him from loving her with all his heart. The foolish dreams of a life with the beautiful Regia were just that, and now they would both pay for forgetting who they were.

She would never again look at him with love in her eyes. The past sun-cycles had been the happiest of his life, and it was all because of Talina. Now he understood the marriage ban Protectors were sworn to uphold. Love consumed the mind with thoughts of fancy and made men weak. He could not afford to be weak. His battle with Zotar was on the horizon, and he needed a clear head and every ounce of his warrior's instinct to guide him to victory.

If he was not prepared he would not have to make a choice if Zotar lived or died. He would be the one dead. Until he purged Talina from his system he would not be ready. How was that possible when his body ached for her, and his mind begged to meld with hers?

He had seen enough of life to know it could be cruel. He dismounted and led his esroth up the rocky mountainside without as much as a look back. He'd carried Talina over this rough terrain and the feel of her against him was still fresh in his memory.

When the mine shack came into view he groaned. She hated him that moon-cycle, and he did not blame her. They had come full circle. Hate to love to hate. He heard her stumble and turned, but resisted the urge to pull her into his arms. Instead he watched her right herself and brush her hands off on her pants.

Every step toward Sobrie was painful, yet he could do nothing. His mission for The Protectorate, and Talina's safety, came first. He had endured physical and mental pain before, yet Talina affected him like no other challenge ever had.

Dacton took a deep breath and continued up the rocky mountain. He sensed her right behind him so there was no need to look back. He continued down the slope to the river of no return.

* * * *

How could Dacton have changed so quickly? Only a short time ago they shared their bodies and souls in a love so deep, so all-consuming that neither of them had wanted it to end. Or had she been wrong? If he'd been acting, he deserved an award for his convincing performance.

"Fine, he can have his way," she grumbled to Kiko, whose head bobbed from side to side as she led her esroth over the last of the sharp, rugged landscape. She could not help but think how Dacton had carried her when her feet were bleeding, and how she had responded to his embrace. An embrace she desperately wanted.

"I swear by all that is holy, I will never love another man as long as I live!" Kiko simply looked at her as if she'd completely lost her mind. Actually he would be correct.

The trip over the mountain was longer than she remembered, but she'd been distracted the last time. Now she was alone, with nothing but anguishing thoughts of what had been. Could she ever get Dacton back? She swiped at tears that rolled down her cheeks.

At the bottom she mounted her esroth and cantered to where Dacton rested by the river, the last obstacle before home. Her heart raced. She had to talk sense into him before they reached Sobrie.

Leana had told her about the turmoil she would face, and how Talina's father had suffered a heart attack and was not doing well. She knew Krow had told Dacton the same thing, but he'd said nothing. More proof he no longer cared. How could she have been so blind? If this was love she wanted nothing to do with it.

The strenuous hike over the last rocky mountain had taken its toll. Even the esroths were lathered and they had led rather than ridden over the jagged rocks. Thank heaven this time she had boots on her feet instead of thin slippers. So much had changed, and yet, nothing had changed. She was no longer the naive, spoiled, untouched princess that had been taken from her home. She now had a better understanding of what politics did to people after living with the Burly people and learning of their strife. She had also learned the loving touch of a man, and what it meant to share one's body and soul with another.

Love was a bittersweet emotion she might never learn to control. How could she possibly stop caring about Dacton and all they shared? She led her trusty mount to the water's edge and gave him reign to drink. Sobrie was so close. In less than a time-unit she would be with her father, but dreadful fears still assailed her mind.

This last leg of the trip had been exhausting. Probably because Dacton had separated himself from her. Yet her premonitions had nothing to do with Dacton. The deep seated fear went far deeper than her personal emotional battle.

Dacton had not spoken a word since they left the peaceful valley. How she wished they could make love instead of fighting. She missed him, and he was still here. How would she feel when his physical presence was gone as well?

He squatted by the water's edge and she studied the body that had brought her ecstasy beyond her wildest dreams. How could it all be lost so quickly? Her heart still fluttered at the sight of him, her body still responded, and her soul cried for the completeness she felt when they made love. Dacton had warned her, she remembered well. Now he seemed determined to make her pay the price.

The harder she stared, the more he ignored her. The powerful muscles of his thighs strained against the thin leather of his pants, and his chest heaved against his tunic. He looked poised for battle rather than a fond farewell. What had she said to turn him away? He was astute enough to know they had to part when they entered the city. So why was he acting like it had to be forever?

Dear stars he was stubborn! She had to know, once and for all, if he had any feelings for her. While her esroth drank peacefully she walked to his side and laid her hand on his arm.

"Dacton?" Her breath caught in her throat when he turned his icy gaze to her and glared stoically through her, his muscles tense beneath her touch.

"What is it, Princess Talina?"

She had not been prepared for his emotionless, formal response. "What happened to Regia?"

"That is an endearment I no longer choose to use."

Her composure was gone and she jerked her hand back. "I see." Her head spun and she could not comprehend his icy-cold rejection. She began to shake, her legs wobbled, and nausea rose in her stomach. He might as well have used his cutter on her since his words had the same effect. "This is how you want it to be between us?"

"Yes."

Kiko jumped from his pouch to drink next to the esroths. Sweet furry Kiko. At least *he* would never hurt her. Kiko's love was unconditional, which was more than she could say for the cold-hearted Protector. One more try...she had to. "I understand you no longer want, or desire me, but is it necessary to part as enemies?"

Dacton's gaze locked with hers, but he remained silent. She had her answer. "That's answer enough." There was nothing left to say. Talina picked up Kiko, stuffed him in the pouch, pulled the reins over the esroth's head, and mounted. She spun him around, and with a firm kick to the ribs spurred the animal into a run. The more distance she could put between them the better.

"By the Powers of the Universe, I love you Talina! Forgive me, Regia!"

Dacton's words fell on the empty countryside.

CHAPTER THIRTY THREE

Remorse tore at Dacton's heart, as if his very soul had been ripped from his body. Talina was his counterpart, she made him whole. She was his Regia...his love.

Curse it all! Zotar for his cold-blooded crimes, The Protectorate and their damned rules, and Kolere for insisting he embark on this mission knowing all too well what would happen. It was time to make Zotar pay. All he could think about was how good it would feel to plunge his cutter into the evil man's chest.

Talina's agony still played in his mind more than revenge, more than duty. Somehow he had to make it up to her. How, he didn't know, but he would. Talina was right. She had given him everything, her heart, her soul, and her precious body. He would not let her down. Once this mission was over...

His esroth began to dance around in front of him and projected a severe warning of danger. He cursed himself for being so caught up in thoughts of Talina that he had ignored his warrior's instincts. When he looked up a small army of uniformed men converged around him, armed with weapons only Zotar could have provided. There was no choice. He could surrender, or die. He laughed to himself, thinking death a relief to the pain that ripped him apart.

"Take his weapons and place him in shackles!"

He knew that voice. Zotar. When the soldiers dismounted and walked toward him, he saw Zotar, sitting proudly on his esroth with a demonic grin from ear to ear. How he wanted to wipe that expression off his face permanently! He would as soon as the opportunity presented itself.

Six men tackled him to the ground and took his weapons. He

shuddered when cold steel snapped tightly around his wrists. His boots were pulled off and shackles locked around his ankles. The soldiers jerked him up to his feet and secured a chain to link both restraints together.

Zotar rode up to Dacton and dropped a rope on the ground. "Tie this around his waist!"

Dacton did not blame the men that tied and shackled him. It was Zotar and only Zotar he hated. He remembered the ineptness of these guards, now turned soldiers. Zotar had not even properly trained these men, which would work to his advantage. There was a hint of fear in the soldier's eyes that indicated they had not pledged complete loyalty to Zotar.

Zotar laughed. "Humility serves you well, Dacton. Get used to it!" He took the end of the rope from the guard's hand and wrapped it around his saddle horn. "Do try to keep up. We don't want to keep Princess Talina waiting now, do we?"

Dacton cringed at hearing Talina's name roll off Zotar's lips. Zotar kicked his esroth into a cantor and the rope jerked him to the ground. Rocks and branches ripped his tunic and pants while pain jabbed with every bounce. Dacton struggled to gain footing, but the pace was too fast and the shackles prohibited his movement.

Thorns tore his skin and pain wracked his body as rocks inflicted their hits one by one. Zotar laughed and pressed his esroth faster. The bastard enjoyed this torture far too much. He held the rope with his cuffed hands, but there was little he could do to stop the brutal battering.

Dacton closed his eyes and concentrated on the galloping esroth. Never before had he made contact with a moving animal, but his life depended on it. He summoned every ounce of strength and sent the esroth a picture of quiet rest in a lush green field without his rider. He held that thought firmly, adding an urgency to do it now.

The sound of hooves beat the ground and pounded in his ears. Grass and brush scratched his face while he was pulled through the field. Then suddenly all movement ceased and it went strangely quiet. All he heard was the rapid thump of his heart. The rope went slack, the esroth reared and flailed his front legs high in the air. Zotar hit the ground inches from his aching head. Dacton laughed to himself, amazed his message had worked and extremely happy for the reprieve. He mentally thanked the animal who now ran for freedom.

"You'll pay for this, Dacton Rovarn! I know you're responsible." Zotar dusted himself off while he stood. "Nothing escapes me. Including you!" Zotar pulled the closest man to him out of his saddle and took possession of his esroth. He picked up the reins Rovarn held in his hand.

"Stand up, Protector. Or are you too weak?"

With that insult Dacton pulled himself to his feet. He would never show weakness to his arch enemy even when every bone and muscle in his body protested movement. "Free me and fight like a man, you coward!" Zotar pulled his arm back and took a swing. The man really was a coward since he was still tied, and he could not stop Zotar's ring from tearing his flesh when the blow crossed his face.

Zotar smiled. "Our time will come, warrior."

When Zotar jerked the rope he fell to the ground, but when he lifted his leg to kick him he rolled to the side, but a rock prevented further evasion. He caught Zotar's foot on the next try and took great pleasure when Zotar hit the ground. Dacton smiled this time when the smug look on Zotar's face dissipated.

"Grab him you fools!" Zotar yelled at his men. "Hold him!"

Five men grabbed him. One man for each arm and leg, and one grasped him around the waist. Still he struggled with the hope that his superior strength would win.

"There is no escape." Zotar struck Dacton in the face.

"You can kill me, but The Protectorate *will* stop you. You won't win." Dacton licked blood from his lip.

"I will take pleasure in killing you even slower than Baleko."

"You're a coward!" Dacton wanted to kill Zotar with a passion that burned deeper than ever before. No death would be good enough for the wicked man.

"Am I now. We'll see about that."

Zotar slammed his fist into Dacton's stomach repeatedly. He struggled for breath, still unable to protect himself. Zotar was a malicious criminal he could not wait to destroy.

"Your head is not so high now, Protector." He removed the indicator ring from his finger and threw it into the dirt. "You may have destroyed my reactor, but you'll never destroy me!"

"You're still a coward. You can only fight a man if others hold him helpless. Free me. Let's settle this!"

"I'm tempted. However, I have a delightful surprise planned for you, and I would not want you to miss it."

* * * *

"Kolere!" Talina threw her arms around her mentor and hugged him tightly.

"Sweet Talina, it's good to see you safe. I've been so worried."

The door behind her led to her father's bedchamber and she was afraid of what she might find. Her legs shook and she hated to let go of Kolere for fear she might fall. "How is my father? I must see him."

"Easy child."

She worked to regain her composure, but the look on Kolere's face did not reassure her. "Kolere. Tell me, please. You are the only man I trust to be honest."

"You must be prepared for what you will see. Your father lives, but his mind is..."

"That can't be! He was fine when I left. What happened?"

"Come."

Kolere's voice did not encourage her, but she was glad he held her hand when he opened the door and led her inside her father's chamber.

Talina's mouth fell open when she viewed the thin, frail features of her father's pale face, a face that had been full and happy with excitement the last time she had seen him. He lay immobile, helpless as a child, and mumbled incoherently in a weak voice.

"Who did this to him?"

"The doctors say he had a heart attack and that his mind has been damaged. He has received the best care possible, but there still is no improvement."

His hand was cold when she touched him. "This never would have happened if I had been here." She searched Kolere's sympathetic brown eyes. "Why did you send me away with that underworld-snake!"

"I see Dacton has made quite an impression on you, my child." Kolere took her left hand in his and studied it carefully. "When did the crystallinus links change to blue?"

Talina could do nothing to stop the heated blush she felt invade her cheeks, nor could she confess to her priest that the change occurred during the heated passion that claimed her virginity.

Kolere smiled. "You need not explain. And what of the warrior's belt?"

In her mind she saw the wide leather belt with the beautiful stone strapped around Dacton's trim waist and she searched for the proper words. "The yellow amulet turned green." She pushed mental pictures of the handsome Protector from her mind. "You knew all along that we would...that we had to...ah..."

"Yes, my child, I knew."

"By the Gods Kolere! You approve of my becoming a branded woman?"

Kolere smiled. "Your love is not a mistake."

"It has been the worst mistake of my life! My people will never look at me with respect again. want to see that warrior again. He used me, as you did!"

Kolere stared at her in silence and she fought back tears. "Look what's happened. My father lies near death, the government is in shambles, and the man I trusted with my very soul has deserted me."

"The legend has not been fulfilled. You and your warrior will join forces once again. You cannot deny the bond, it is strong, and you will call upon it one last time."

Anger sparked inside Talina. "Whatever happens now will not depend on some mystic link." She touched the blue crystals around her wrist. "Please, leave me alone with my father."

"Of course." Kolere turned and walked toward the door.

Talina watched the priest stop at the door, grab his stomach and double over. She rushed to the priest. "Kolere, you're ill."

"No, my child. I'm fighting the effects of Zotar's drugs. He poisoned my food. I'll get over it. It's your father I'm worried about. I don't know what Zotar has done to him."

She patted Kolere's back. "Forgive my anger. I know you did what you had to."

Kolere smiled. "Remember your destiny. Have faith in the ancient words, and the inner voice that guides you. You must summon every ounce of courage you possess, and you will need the strength of your warrior by your side."

Talina stared at Kolere as he left the room. She could not believe what he had asked her to do any more than she believed she had the strength to accomplish it. Her sun-cycles with the warrior of legend were over for good. She would not make the same mistake twice. The trust she once gave Dacton was gone.

He may have spoken the truth about his mission, but his love for her had been a lie. If he cared as much as he pretended to, he would never have pushed her aside and turned so cold, not after all they had been through. Why had she listened to her heart?

She heard something behind her and turned. Her father opened his eyes and reached for her. "Father!"

"No m...m. ..more m...m...medicine. Z...Zotar..."

"What are you saying? Tell me, what can I do? No, don't go to sleep. Talk to me, please..." Talina's plea went unheard. Her father lapsed into unconsciousness. Kolere had said he mumble incoherently, but she understood perfectly. Zotar was drugging him. Dear stars, she had to stop Zotar, but who could she trust?

Kolere was her only ally. There could be no more mistakes, her father's life depended on her every decision, as did her people. Whether or not they accepted her as Legatus, she had to stop Zotar and restore her father to the throne. Damn Zotar, Dacton and The Protectorate!

* * * *

Zotar pulled the needle from Dacton's arm and smiled while his body went limp, his eyes still focused. "This is a wonderful new drug. It leaves your body paralyzed, but your mind remains alert, even though you cannot speak."

All Dacton could do was silently curse Zotar. No less than six men guarded him at any given time, and his struggle against the shackles had only served to draw more blood. He had been a fool to be captured, but it could have been worse. Talina could have been with him. At least Talina stood a chance of evading Zotar if she went straight to Kolere.

Zotar placed his hands on the arms of his chair and laughed in his face. He wanted to hit the animal in the face, but he had no body function at all. Damn him!

"I will return with Princess Talina. We have an announcement you should hear." He stood and slapped Dacton across the face. "I'm quite sure you've developed feelings for the bitch. She is quite the looker."

Dacton's breathing became as fast as if he had been running. The evil man simply glared at him with a smile that said his torture had just begun and he planned to enjoy every minute of it.

"I can see you're amused by my comment. Good. I'd hate to be disappointed. We're going to have some real fun!" He slapped Dacton across the face then left.

There was nothing worse than being indefensible and completely vulnerable. This was a situation he was not used to and could not tolerate. He was a warrior and he would find a way out.

* * *

Talina paced nervously while she waited for Zotar. He'd caught her in the hall after she'd spoken to Kolere, her hand on her father's door. At least she'd given her instructions to Kolere to keep medication away from her father. He promised he would, but she feared for Kolere's life as well should Zotar even suspect he was helping her. She hoped Kolere was strong enough for the task considering what Zotar's poison had done to him.

Talina stared into the mirror. The gown Zotar insisted she wear was the most obscene garment she'd ever laid eyes on. Even working prostitutes covered more. She gritted her teeth because she suspected what he had in mind.

The halter top barely concealed her breasts with narrow strips of fabric so sheer the outline of her nipples showed through, and the skirt was nothing more than two strips of the same fabric joined at the waistband, but they were not sewn together in the front or the back. The fullness protected a view of her womanhood, but not if she sat, or a breeze blew at the transparent black fabric.

Zotar said he would kill her father if she did not do everything he requested. She knew Zotar desired her, he'd made that clear on many occasions before Dacton arrived. How could she ever have imagined being with Zotar? Now the mere mention of the man brought a nauseous feeling to the pit of her stomach, and she shivered at the thought of his hands on her. Giving her life to save her father would be easier than giving her body to Zotar. How could she ever have found him attractive when he was so evil? She hadn't known then, and would not know now if it had not been for Dacton.

Dacton. Where in Diabolus was he when she needed him? As angry as she was with the arrogant Protector, she could use his services. *He* would know what to do. If he could kill a Pengore, surely Zotar would prove an easier match. However, knowing him the way she did, one look at this dress and it would be all over for them both. He would have her in pallet so fast she...

The door flew open and Zotar strode in, his eyes fixed on her breasts. She could have sworn she saw him drool when his eyes dropped lower. He was dressed in tight brown pants with a shiny gold shirt slightly bloused at the waist, the draw strings open, his blond hairy chest exposed for her benefit. His size may be comparable to Dacton's, but he did not have the same commanding presence of her Protector.

She touched her hair to make sure the small cylinder of somna remained concealed in knots of curls on top of her head. Zotar would think nothing of her hair being up, she usually wore it this way. She prayed he would not want to remove the pins that secured the up-do too soon. Luckily Zotar had never given thought to her having any kind of weapon.

Zotar took Talina's hand and raised it to his lips and planted a light kiss. A sick feeling assailed her, but she willed herself to smile calmly. He lowered her arm, but did not let go.

"That's good. I knew you were smart. Just remember what will happen to your father should you do anything to displease me. And I will not hesitate."

"No, I don't imagine you would." She hoped her voice sounded more pleasant than she felt since she wanted to stab the man in the back with a very big cutter.

Zotar offered his arm. "Come, *Princess*."

She noted the sarcasm in his voice, but decided to play the gracious, willing consort he expected. Nothing could happen to her father, everything depended on the show he demanded from her.

"Did I forget to mention that I have captured your lover?"

"He is not my lover." Hopefully he did not see through her lie.

"Indeed. Well then it won't matter to you if I kill him. Of course if you portray yourself as my whore, then I might let Dacton live a few more sun-cycles."

Talina's heart sank as the realization struck full force. Terror surged through her already shaky body while they walked toward Zotar's bedchamber. She swallowed hard and entered when he opened the door for her. Six guards filed out of the room leaving her alone with Zotar.

Two flowers graced the pillows, their long stems crossed. She was reminded of the pallet in the stronghold, Dacton's body on top of hers, the melodic hum, the beat of his heart, the love, the passion. She pushed the painful memory aside and turned to face the man that would take what was not his.

Talina's jaw dropped, her eyes widened, she gasped deeply then held her breath when she looked at the dimly lit corner. It was Dacton! Ripped, shredded remnants of clothes did little to conceal his bloody, battered body. Her heart ached for him, her soul cried out to his. Every thought of anger and betrayal melted at the sight of him.

"Surprised, my dear?" Zotar smiled. "I knew you would want Dacton to be the first to know about our life-mating." He looked into Talina's eyes then at Dacton. "Yes, warrior, she will belong to me when the next sun-cycle rises."

Talina could not bear to look at Dacton, instead she took her cues from Zotar, and he wanted conformation. By the Gods, she regretted what she had to do, but if she showed her true feelings for Dacton, Zotar would kill him. It was time for the performance of her life.

"I can hardly wait my love." The lie was hard to swallow, but she continued on by placing her hand at the front opening of his shirt, forcing her fingers to caress Zotar's chest. She thought the heat of Dacton's gaze would burn a hole in her back, but she had to focus on Zotar for fear of betraying herself.

Zotar bent and kissed her lips, forcing the nauseous feeling to erupt full blown in her empty stomach. She pulled her head back to end the kiss before she fell sick to the floor. His arm slipped around her waist and he turned her to Dacton's view.

Dacton sat perfectly still, his bloodied hands lay free in his lap, the same stoic expression on his face she'd seen at the river. She prayed he would make a move to save her, but he only watched, as if he were amused by Zotar's advances.

"She is beautiful, isn't she?" Zotar ran his fingers down over her breast then back up again. He pushed at the fabric until only her nipples were covered then stepped aside. "That's a bit better, don't you think?" He shook his head. "Not quite."

With both hands he pushed the flimsy fabric to the outside of each full breast, exposing her to Dacton. Talina searched Dacton's fixed steel gray gaze for a hint of emotion, but found only hatred. She knew he hated Zotar, and now he hated her. If there were an ounce of compassion left in the Protector he would stop this insanity, but he just stared.

Had Zotar done something besides beat him? If Dacton had been drugged like her father, his eyes would not be open and clear. His decision was clear. She took a deep breath. To save her father, and the warrior who wanted nothing to do with her, she had to sacrifice herself.

CHAPTER THIRTY FOUR

By all that was holy he had to stop this! Killing Zotar would be the kindest thing he had in mind. He desperately wanted to save Talina from the degradation Zotar was determined to put her through, but the drug held him firm. All he could do was watch when Zotar moved behind her and placed his hands on her hips, slowly bringing his fingers higher, following her stomach until he cupped the fullness of her breasts in his palms. Zotar had an evil glint in his eyes when he pinched both her nipples at the same time.

He watched in horror when Talina tipped her head back and parted her lips. By the Gods! She was enjoying it. How low would she go? Zotar fondled every inch of her ivory mounds, pushing, jiggling, kneading. How could she stand there, tossing her head erotically on his shoulder when he was making her skin red? S*he* was not paralyzed! Could he be forcing her somehow to perform every perverted act he could think of?

"She has a fine body, doesn't she?" Zotar grinned. "But you already know it well, don't you?" He dropped his hands to the slit of the skirt in front and in one fluid motion pulled both sides away. Holding the fabric in one hand he slid the other around, spreading his fingers across the flat expanse of her abdomen.

Dacton's muscles twitched and he willed them to move. He had to stop the torture of the woman he loved. She would never forgive him. He vowed to always protect her, yet he was helpless as a baby while he watched another man touch what was his and his alone! Rage boiled his blood, and his decision was clear. Zotar would not live to stand trial.

"I know you have explored this." Zotar stared at Dacton while he closed his hand over her womanhood. "I will take such good care of her that all memory of you will be erased forever."

Never! He would *never* let that happen. Revenge, rage, hatred, longing, and love all merged into a barrage of feelings so strong he felt sure he could will himself to move. He concentrated on his muscles, mentally bounding from the chair to strangle the life from Zotar, but the thought was all that moved.

Talina's hand reached for her hair. She was going to let it loose for him, but Zotar stopped her. She looked disappointed. She must have wanted Zotar's fingers to comb the silky strands he remembered so well.

A fierce pounding on the door forced Zotar to remove his fingers from between Talina's legs. He dropped the fabric and stomped away. "This had better be good or I'll have your head!" Zotar pulled the door open.

A moment later Talina smiled when Zotar held out his hand for her to join him. Dacton watched her pull the halter back into place, and join Zotar without as much as a glance at him. Had the loving woman he held in his arms such a short time ago turned traitor? He knew his words at the river hurt her deeply, but he never expected this.

Dacton took several deep breaths. He had to think with his warrior's logic, not his heart. If he knew his enemy as well as he thought, Talina had been forced to endure his little game. Zotar knew all too well how to use a weakness, but this would not be the end. He would stop their life-mating, and free Talina, even if she could never be his.

His thoughts turned to the six guards that burst through the door carrying a stretcher. They picked him up, laid him on the canvas and carried him out of the palace. Where were they taking him? The damned drugs had to wear off soon or he would go insane. Talina needed him!

* * * *

Zotar squeezed Talina's hand so tight pain shot up her arm. They stood in the center of the market place on a high, covered podium reserved for public speeches. She watched while her people assembled in front of her, one small group after another. It did not take long for the empty cobblestone street to become full of murmuring citizens. Then Zotar held his arm up in the air and a hush fell over the crowd.

Zotar smiled. "Citizens of Sobrie. Thank you for coming this moon-cycle on such short notice. I have a very important announcement." He put his arm around Talina's waist and pulled her against him. "At noon tomorrow, Princess Talina and I will be life-mated."

Talina fought nausea and dizziness, but smiled on command when Zotar squeezed her so tight she could barely breathe. At least he had allowed her to change into the appropriate royal gowns for the occasion. He was a monster, and if given the chance, she'd kill him herself.

Never in her twenty-four annual-cycles had she been so humiliated, so ashamed to be a woman. If she only had Dacton's physical strength she could have overpowered Zotar and stopped all this. Dacton had assured her he had an army at his disposal, so where were they? Another one of his lies.

When Zotar molested her inside the palace Dacton had remained so still, and with such deep hatred in his eyes she refused to meet his gaze. Was it hate for her or Zotar? Probably both. She waved to the people of Sobrie like the happy bride to be.

Zotar stilled the crowd. "Tomorrow will be a sun-cycle of great celebration. First, for our Princess's safe return. Second, for our life-mating, and third, for the execution of the man responsible for taking her from us." He glanced at Talina.

Talina's knees buckled, her heart pounded, and she fought against the fog that swirled in her head. If Zotar let go of her she would fall. Had she heard right? Dear stars! She had to find a way to stop Dacton's execution!

Cold chills ran down her spine at the evil glare of Zotar's sick, yellow eyes. Never had eyes been so cold, so horribly wicked. She forced a smile at his insistence, but it would never be the loving smile she had given to Dacton. She would die first.

Zotar waved at his guards. "Bring the prisoner forward!"

The crowd parted and a wagon pulled in front of the podium steps and stopped. Talina caught her breath and thought her heart would jump from her chest. It was Dacton! His body lifeless, his eyes staring blankly at the top of the metal cage that held him prisoner.

"This enemy of Sobrie is a Protector. I told you they would come, and I promised I would save you. As you can see, I'm a man of my word." Zotar bowed to the people.

She desperately wanted to run to Dacton, to kiss his lips, heal his battered body, and tell him she would never betray him. If it meant her life, she would never let Zotar touch her again. She concentrated hard, with every remaining ounce of mental strength, to send Dacton her love. He had to know, and she might never be this close to him again.

"His name is Dacton Rovarn, and he is supposed to be the best warrior The Protectorate has." Zotar laughed. "How can The Protectorate take care of you if this is the best they can provide?"

Talina cringed when the crowd laughed. She knew if Dacton were able, he would pull the bars apart to rip Zotar's head off for what he said. He had to be drugged, the same as her father. Now she was sure of it. If he had been himself he would never have allowed Zotar to touch her. She smiled inwardly when she noticed Dacton still wore the warrior's belt, and prayed he had enough strength to escape if the opportunity presented itself.

The people that listened to Zotar acted pleased when he spoke, but she also noted their half-hearted cheers. They looked at the cage that held Dacton with fear in their eyes. Most likely they wondered if they might end up prisoners with death warrants on their lives.

A voice deep within whispered a plan. Had it come from her own mind, or Dacton's? She didn't care as long as it worked. Dacton had reason for revenge which went far beyond The Protectorate's charges against Zotar. She knew how painfully personal it had become for both of them. She prayed he would have his opportunity.

"Dacton will remain here, for all to see, until his death at the first sign of the morning sun. Study him well, people of Sobrie, and remember what happens to anyone who chooses to violate the law."

The crowd did not cheer. They simply turned their backs and walked to their homes. Talina felt pride for her peoples' obvious rejection of Zotar's power play. Thank the stars they had not succumbed to Zotar's distorted way of thinking.

"Go to your homes now, but return at dawn. All must witness justice!"

Zotar had yelled his order to the rapidly diminishing crowd and Talina rejoiced inside because her people had rejected him in their own way. Zotar jerked her arm and pulled her down the steps. Pain shot through her. When they reached the bottom he pulled her to the cage and threw her against the bars. She grabbed the cold metal to steady herself, and used the opportunity to study Dacton.

The Protector did not even move his head to see her, but his eyes strained in her direction. It was true, he was unable to move! If he could, he would have some choice words for her, but even more for Zotar. She concentrated hard to send him a message of hope and love. All she could do was pray he received it.

Even though he had pushed her away, he was her love, and always would be. No man could fill the place in her heart that belonged to Dacton. If only she could tell him. A new courage surged through her. She would be back this moon-cycle to free her Protector.

Zotar jerked her away from the cage. "What's the matter, my lovely, did you want to join him?" He laughed. "In your dreams, but never again in the flesh. As soon as *I* take your body you will never think of him again."

"I assure you, Zotar, I will never want anyone but you." Talina nearly choked on her words. At the moment she would say anything to save Dacton's life. She forced herself to take Zotar's arm. The sooner they returned to their quarters, the sooner she could free Dacton.

They walked up the long winding path to the palace, and Talina thought of excuses to evade Zotar's pallet this moon-cycle. She had to convince him to hold with their tradition that forbids sexual conduct before the ceremony. Although for a man with no honor, the prospect was dim.

The silent walk ended inside the main hall by her father's room. Talina had to convince Zotar to leave her alone. She took a deep to steady herself. "Would you permit me to spend this last moon-cycle with my father?"

"What are you up to, Princess?" Zotar snapped.

"Nothing. My father is near death, and I want to be by his side." Talina looked deeply into yellow eyes that reflected a true lust for power without a glimmer of compassion. "You can post guards at the door. I will not leave. And if I do, they can escort me to my own room. Surely you know I would do nothing to place his life in jeopardy. Please, Zotar, grant me this one last wish."

"And if I do, what will you give me?"

"Anything you want." It was difficult to conceal the hatred and fear than ran rampant through her body, but she worked at it.

"I have many things to attend to myself. You may have your one last moon-cycle with the doddering old fool. Use your time well. It will be your last." Zotar turned to the guards on each side of the door. "Princess Talina will spend the moon-cycle in this room. She is not to leave under any circumstances. If she escapes, you will both pay with your lives. Do I make myself clear?"

Both men saluted. "Yes sir!"

Zotar opened the door, pushed her inside, then pulled it shut so hard it shook the walls. She slid the heavy bolt securely in position and checked it twice before she rushed to her father's side. He looked up at her, his eyes less clouded than before.

She was surprised to find him awake. "Father? Can you hear me?"

"Yes, my dear."

"You seem better."

"Kolere was able to convince the doctor to forego my last dosage. I'm still weak, but my mind has cleared."

Talina kissed his forehead. "I have so much to tell you, but there is so little time. I must save Dacton."

"And who is this Dacton?"

"He is a Protector, the man who abducted me."

"Then what is your concern for his life?"

A tear dropped to her cheek, and Talina told her father a short version of the long harrowing adventure she had been on. He just nodded his understanding and that unnerved her. "This is not the response I expected."

Cortain smiled. "Kolere filled me in before I was drugged. I should have stopped you, but I wanted to hear the story from your lips." He grasped the edge of the blanket. "However, I didn't expect this." He pulled back the covers, and laughed at Talina's wide-eyed expression.

"Kiko!" The furry creature jumped into her arms and snuggled close. "I'm sorry, baby, I forgot you."

"I can see he hasn't forgotten you, my dear."

"You're not angry?"

"How could I be. I have my daughter by my side and...a new pet...along with a possible son-in-law from another planet. It's all a bit much, but I'll adjust."

"Please do not think of Dacton as a member of this family. We have much to settle first. I don't even know how he feels right now. There are a few things I left out." She sensed her father figured as much, but she could not tell him every detail of her relationship with Dacton. Some things a father should not know, and some things, like Zotar's depravity, he needed to be spared. He was still recovering and she refused to be the cause of a set-back.

"I am still the one who decides who you life-mate. Once I meet this Dacton, I will decide."

Talina wanted to tell him about her ill-fated ceremony with Zotar tomorrow, but if her plan succeeded, it would not come to pass. "I wish we had more time, but I must go, or you will never get to meet Dacton. Just tell me how to open the secret door."

"I understand. Promise me you'll be careful. I couldn't stand to lose you again."

She squeezed his hand. "I promise."

"All right. Help me up, child."

Talina slid her arm under his shoulders and helped him to sit. He swung his legs over the edge of the pallet, but almost fell back. "I'm afraid you're too weak." He gave her his determined grin and she shook her head at him.

"I'll be fine. If I don't close the door and return everything to normal the secret passageway will be discovered. Then it would be useless."

She helped her father across the spacious room to the long wall at the far end of the pallet, watching carefully as he turned a candle sconce sideways, then pushed down on the wall lamp. When he maneuvered the gold light back into position she heard a grating sound.

"Pull that rug towards you," he instructed, "but don't step on it."

A panel in the floor slid open and she glanced into the hole. The dim light of the bedchamber exposed the first three steep, metal steps. When she turned her head she saw her father pull a temp-lite from his desk drawer and hand it to her.

"I'm afraid I should have replaced the source power, but it should guide you safely out." Cortain wiped a lone tear from her eye. "Go. Don't worry about me."

"I *will* be back for you."

"Take care of yourself and Dacton first. I am old and..."

"I don't want to hear such talk." Talina shook her head at him not to continue his statement."

"You must face the facts, my child. Now go, and don't look back. Do what you must. Save yourself, Dacton, and our people." Cortain pointed at the hidden passageway. "Go!"

"I love you, father." He was right. So much depended on her success. The stairs creaked under her feet and she fought webs made by creatures she did not want to think about. At the bottom of the stairs lay a dark earthen tunnel.

The straight passageway soon ended and she knew she had to go to her left. She was now in the same tunnel Dacton had forced her through, the tunnel that would allow her to go to him. Step by step she came closer to freedom. Freedom? That word made her laugh. Zotar had her trapped, and she wondered if she had made the right decision by leaving her father to free Dacton?

Would being under the control of The Protectorate be any better than Zotar? Probably, but she feared a new kind of bondage. What would the Advisor be like? Could she trust him after her ordeal with Dacton? Curse them all! It still felt like she was going from bad to worse, then back again. Where would it all end?

She found the sticker bushes that blocked the way. Dacton did such a good job concealing the way through she barely found it. Thorns jabbed her palms and fingers. Her sleeve tore. Finally, a large clump fell away. A few more pushes was all it took. Talina quickly crawled through and replaced the dead thistle bush.

Dacton had been a good teacher. Too good, she thought, remembering the moon-cycles in his strong arms. He had protected her well and showed her how to love. So why was she so angry with him? He looked so helpless and beaten lying motionless in that cage.

He had made no promises, nor had he technically broken any. His cold demeanor hurt, and that sharp pain still stabbed her heart. Yet she was anxious to see him, to touch him, to free him. She pulled the canister of somna from her hair and held it securely in her right hand. She had planned to use it against Zotar, but unfortunately he stopped her in the middle of her move. It was for the best since she had no idea how many blasts were left.

Dacton never mentioned how long one little canister would last, and she had no memory of how much she used on the Pengore. Hopefully enough of the sleeping mist remained to take care of the guards around Dacton's cage.

She ran to the back of the closest house, her hands resting against the cold stone wall, her heart about to leap from her chest. This warrior stuff was easier with Dacton in the lead, clearing the way. He instinctively knew what to do. She prayed she did.

Ever so slowly she eased her head around the corner to glance at the cobblestone street. It appeared empty so she dashed toward the intersection, careful to stay concealed within the dark shadows.

One more street, one more corner and Dacton would be in sight. She knew the men that guarded Dacton had been part of her father's Royal Guard, but she did not know where their loyalty lay.

A quick glance said the next street was also deserted so she grabbed the bottom of her gown and ran faster than she thought possible toward the man she loved.

CHAPTER THIRTY FIVE

O

Dacton rolled to his side and groaned when his badly bruised ribs protested. He could not tell if the injuries were from being dragged behind the esroth, or from Zotar's fists and boots. At least the pain meant he was still alive. His face burned and he swiped at blood that still oozed from a gash on his cheek. He glanced furtively around the cage, taking careful note of the guards at each corner.

The lighting around the square was poor, but he did not see any more guards roaming the streets or posted close by. Escape was impossible. The cage was made of the same indestructible material as the reactor, and he was sure Zotar had the only key.

In the distance he heard a woman's voice. Not just any woman, he could swear it was Talina! He jerked his head and forged through excruciating pain in order to see her beautiful face once more. She was real and the light of the three moons danced on her golden hair. Her face was illuminated and she looked like an angel from the heavens above.

If she came to free him, she would truly be an angel. He studied the crease in her forehead and noted her lips were pursed in her most determined manner. What in the universe was his Regia doing?

Talina turned. "Guards! Over here!"

Dacton noticed her hands had formed into fists at her side, and he almost smiled when she started to shake. He knew her well enough to realize she had put on her brave face. He knew she was nervous and scared, but from the looks on the guards' faces, she had them fooled. Why didn't she come closer?

"I said, over here, now! I bring a message from Zotar the prisoner is not to hear."

Four uniformed men rushed to stand at attention in front of their princess.

"Come closer, there is something I must show you."

Four guards slumped unconscious to the ground. Adrenaline pumped fast and gave new life to his half-dead body. Just the sight of Talina running toward him quelled the doubts in his mind, and awakened the need that pulsed in his groin. He wanted her now more than ever before. Since he pushed her away he had not felt whole and nothing felt right. All he wanted was for her to be back in his arms, under his protection.

Whether Talina knew it or not she had become a warrior and the determined look on her face said it all. Relief flooded through him with the knowledge she had not deserted him. He smiled when she hiked the skirt of her burgundy gown so she could use the wheel as a step to climb onto the wagon.

"Dacton." Talina took several breaths. "Are you all right? Look what they've done to you!"

Dacton slipped his arm through the bars and placed his hand on her cheek. "Sweet Regia, it's so good to see you. I've missed you." He moved his hand behind her head, guided her closer, then pressed his lips to hers through the bars. She tasted as sweet as she smelled, and he wanted to devour every enticing inch of her, but the restraints would only allow a light kiss.

Talina pulled back. "There is no time for this. Zotar is liable to find me missing. We have to get you out of here." She shook the door. "Dear stars! This cage is of the same metal as the reactor. I don't have a key, and..."

"Remember how we melted the reactor?" He watched her nod. "Think we can do it again?"

"We could disappear right along with it. You're on one side, I'm on the other. We have to link together...I don't know."

"Are you willing to take the risk?" She smiled at him and his heart melted.

"What do we have to lose?"

He laughed. "Only our lives. But I'd rather disappear than give Zotar the satisfaction of killing me without a fight like he did to..." He stopped himself from saying Baleko's name. He unbuckled the belt and handed it to Talina, the stone falling into her hand as it had before.

Talina clasped the Delareme amulet to her heart.

He placed his hand on hers to reassure her. "Trust the legend. Have faith in our love." As difficult as that was for him to admit, it was the truth. The legend had thus far proven true, and he knew he loved Talina more than life itself. If she loved him half as much, he knew it would work.

"What did you say warrior?"

"I said trust in our love." Dacton knew he had never said the words to her. "Yes, woman, I love you! I adore you! I need you, and..."

"But I was sure that after you saw Zotar..."

"Enough! I thought I would die watching what he did to you. I was drugged and couldn't move a muscle to help. I failed you, and for that I will never forgive myself." He squeezed her hand. "I knew Zotar was forcing you to perform for my benefit. Oh Regia, I will kill that man for what he's done. Just get me out of here so I can..."

"No! Do not let hate consume you." She studied Dacton's face. "All I see is bitterness in your eyes. Promise me you'll do as you were ordered. No more."

"You don't know what you're asking. You don't know the whole story, Regia."

"There's no time for discussion. Give me your word."

Dacton looked down at the solid sheet of metal beneath his bare feet and considered Talina's request. It was the same directive he'd sworn to uphold to The Protectorate. How could he choose duty when Zotar had done so much to the people he loved? Still, he could do nothing from the confines of this damned cage. He swallowed hard, and prayed he could live up to his word. "I promise."

"Then let's do it." Talina laid the amulet on the locking mechanism. She placed the fingers of her left hand on the green scarab. The crystallinus chain began to slip toward the amulet.

Dacton eased his arm around her shoulders, and Talina grasped him about the waist. Cold metal pressed against their bodies. They touched fingertips and waited.

Nothing.

"What's wrong Dacton? There's no lights—no magic."

He searched her eyes. She was afraid. "Do you love me, Regia?"

"You know I do."

"How much?"

She met his gaze. "Need you ask?"

"Concentrate, Talina. Don't let fear block your thoughts." He raised her fingers to his lips. "I love you. Now, and forever."

"Oh, Dacton...I love..."

Purple snaps of light burst through the dark and blue collided with green. Streaks of heated energy emanated from their hands, arms and bodies, snapping and crackling in the still moon-cycle. The glow from Ora's three moons enhanced the striations of light that grew higher above their heads reaching for the heavens. The bright lights returned from above to strike the metal roof and send sparks flying through the air. Luminescent beams encompassed one bar after another and worked their way around the cage.

The phosphorescent beams gained intensity until they turned the moons into suns. Blazing shards of sparkling threads spun over and around every inch of the indestructible metal, creating a brilliance so vivid they were both forced to shut their eyes.

Dacton heard her voice in his mind whisper, "I love you," and he sent the same message in return. Talina's emotions crashed into his. Intense feelings weakened his battered body. Complete euphoria captured his heart and his soul and bound him once again to his counterpart. She was the one woman who had the power to save him from himself. He felt a love so strong he knew it could never be broken.

He held her tightly and absorbed her every thought as his own. Hatred did not exist within the swirling vortex of light, only love so complete it soared above worldly explanation.

Dacton felt her body press tightly against his without any intrusion between them. He opened his eyes to see the last impressions of the cage fade into thin air. The hum diminished. He embraced Talina and held her so tight he felt her heart beat match his perfectly. His lips found hers in a hungry kiss. He would never let her go.

"You two are quite a sight!"

The deep voice startled them both, but he knew it was not Zotar's. He turned. Krow's smiling face looked back at him, as well as the thirty warriors behind him who also grinned their approval.

"By the Gods Krow! It's good to see you. Although your timing is a bit off." Dacton jumped from the wagon then lifted Talina down.

"Don't listen to him." Talina gave Krow a hug. "How long have you been standing here?"

Krow laughed. "Long enough to see that you two are magic together."

"That we are." Dacton picked up the amulet, belt, and bracelet from the empty wagon. Talina held out her hand and he slipped the links around her wrist. He replaced the stone, then secured the belt around his waist.

"I don't pretend to understand what just took place here, my friend, but I can tell you Zotar and his men are on their way. Any ideas?"

"Stay hidden in the shadows. I don't want Zotar to get his hands on Talina. She's to be protected at all cost. There's to be no bloodshed unless absolutely necessary."

"Agreed. I have lost enough good men already."

Krow extended his arms to finalize the plan in warrior tradition and he grasped Krow's arms. "You will be rewarded for your loyalty and support, my friend."

"Get ready, he's here," Krow announced.

"Well, what do we have here?"

Zotar's voice sounded like a snaketor's hiss. He walked toward him with an army of fifty men. The man was deplorable to say the least.

"Why didn't you run for your lives like the cowards you are?"

"It's time we settled this once and for all." Dacton grasped the sword Krow held out to him.

"I'll have to kill all of you. You and the Burly men for being enemies of the people. And your whore for being a traitor!"

"The only traitor here is you!" Dacton concentrated on every move his enemy made.

"Killing you will be far more rewarding than your yellow-bellied brother." Zotar drew his sword and turned to Gartron. "Grab the woman."

Gartron scowled, but started toward Talina.

"Krow!" He watched his friend motion his men from the shadows. They formed a line behind Dacton, swords drawn and determination gleamed in the eyes of every muscular warrior.

"Why don't we settle this between the two of us, Zotar. Your men and mine aren't the ones that want revenge, it's us. Always has been." Dacton nodded to Krow, who took Talina's hand and led her to a safe location in the back. This was the moment he had waited for, his opportunity to kill the one man he hated more than anyone.

Could he keep his promise to The Protectorate and Talina? From the look in his enemy's eyes and the hatred in his own heart, it seemed doubtful. His life and Zotar's life were both on the line, and his future depended on the outcome.

CHAPTER THIRTY SIX

O

Talina wiped her sweaty palms against the fabric of her gown. What was Dacton doing? Was he really going to use this opportunity to kill Zotar? If she interfered now it could turn to total bloodshed. Krow's men were outnumbered. The Burly warriors were superior in strength, but the soldiers behind Zotar were armed with cremare-ray guns. She would have to let Dacton do it his way. Zotar deserved to die, but Dacton promised her he wouldn't kill him.

Zotar laughed. "I wish killing you would bring Jana back, but it won't. It was you who killed her!"

"I never laid a hand on your sister."

"If you hadn't picked that moon-cycle to turn me into the chancellor I would have been with her. The accident would never have happened. She'd be alive instead of scattered across the side of that mountain!"

Talina began to shake. Zotar assumed a fighting stance, his eyes crazed, his body taut and ready. Dacton transformed before her eyes and became the consummate warrior in battle-ready position. His sword touched Zotar's while they circled each other. Everyone backed up and gave the warriors space to fight.

Zotar lunged toward Dacton, his sword aimed straight at his chest. The Protector jumped to the side and Zotar pierced empty air. Talina let out the breath she held. She knew Dacton was a capable fighter, but his injuries made him the weaker opponent in the duel. With the Pengore attack barely behind him, and Zotar's torture, it was a wonder he was even standing. Dacton's muscles flexed and she could only pray he was as ready as he looked.

Her legs weakened when the sound of clashing swords cut through the still air. Metal sparked and she detected a metallic odor. This was a senseless fight, she wanted to stop it to save Dacton. When she tried to make a move forward a hand fell on her shoulder.

"No, princess. You must allow Dacton to defeat his enemy. It's the warrior's way."

"But Krow, he could be killed!"

"Have faith. I've fought him myself. He's powerful."

"When he's not wounded. Look at him!"

"He will win."

Krow never even looked at her, he stayed focused on the two men locked in battle. Her heart pounded wildly, her body trembled, and fear encompassed her mind. The moment those thoughts entered her head, Dacton turned his attention toward her. She gasped when Zotar's sword grazed the top of his thigh. She quickly realized she had mentally projected her trepidation to Dacton. They must still be partially mind-linked. He may not be able to read her every thought, but he certainly sensed her apprehension.

With every ounce of courage she could summon she sent him encouragement, then approval. She knew she had been successful when Dacton groaned, gritted his teeth and deflected another vicious parlay. The sound of Zotar's demonic laugh shook her to the core.

"My only regret is that you will die faster than your worthless brother. You, more than Baleko, deserve to suffer for your crimes.

"Killing my brother did not bring your sister back, and blaming me won't either." Zotar slammed his sword against his even harder than before. His resolve for revenge might even flow deeper than his own.

"That may be true, but I will derive great pleasure seeing your blood spill before your men and your princess whore."

Dacton groaned, gathered his strength and attacked Zotar with renewed vigor. He slashed and lunged, meeting every blow with determination. Sweat beaded on his forehead and trickled down his cheek mingling with blood from his earlier skirmish.

Talina could not control the involuntary shaking of her body. She had to get closer, and with Krow still holding her arm, she pushed her way in front of the other men. Her mind called to Dacton to defeat his enemy. Each wave of thought she sent increased in intensity. She knew he needed her support to feed his waning strength. Then with a mighty crash of metal Dacton's only weapon fell to the ground. "No!"

Zotar raised his sword for the kill. Talina's heart raced faster, her mind struggled to repress the fear that threatened to engulf her and steal the courage she needed to encourage him. When Zotar thrust his arms downward, Dacton rolled away and the heavy blade struck in the ground. Dacton jumped to his feet and engaged Zotar in physical combat.

Dacton lost his advantage when Zotar pulled a cutter from his boot. She watched in horror while the two men struggled and fell to the ground. Both warriors rolled body over body with every muscle in their bodies straining. Grunts and groans escaped their throats while they each man fighting for dominance.

"Krow, stop this, save Dacton! Let me go...I have to..." When she looked at Krow's face she knew he was as worried as she was. He frowned at her disapprovingly then returned his attention to the fight. She would never understand warriors and their stupid codes of honor. Dear God, Dacton could die! If he didn't succeed she feared the blood-bath that would ensue. Krow would kill Zotar, and the soldiers would fight the Burly warriors to the death.

Talina's breath caught in her throat when Zotar's body flew over Dacton's back, the shinny blade on the ground between them. They both side-stepped around the weapon, their gazes fiercely locked. Their teeth showed and they snarled like mad dogs. In a blinding flash of speed both men dove for the cutter. She stifled a scream and watched a furry of fists and legs connecting while they continued the ferocious battle.

They engaged in battle as if they had done so many times before, struggling for supremacy, one insisting on control over the other. Would it never end? All she could do was watch the man she loved fight for his life. She sent her strength to bolster his potency against Zotar.

Dacton righted himself. He spun and sent his foot to Zotar's jaw and knocked him to the ground. He landed with a groan. Any other man would have broken his back, yet Zotar simply rose to his feet. Dacton repeated the move again, but this time Zotar did not fall. Dacton threw himself at Zotar and managed to take the cutter from his hand. He held the point at Zotar's throat.

She had never seen such hatred in the Protector's eyes. His instinct to kill evident in every flexed muscle of his body and every crease in his forehead. Talina closed her eyes and screamed in her mind, "Let him live, do your duty my love."

Moments ticked by like centrums while Dacton's hand remained poised for the kill. She knew his inner struggle waged strong inside him. Her inner voice pleaded, "Let him live!"

Zotar tilted his head back. "Do it coward!"

Dacton's hand began to shake and Talina knew the demons he battled and the restraint it took for him not to slit Zotar's throat. The moment of truth was upon him. She whispered to him once again in her mind. He pressed the cutter harder against Zotar's skin and a trickle of blood ran down the blade.

"Krow!" Dacton took a deep breath. "Restrain this man."

Without hesitation Krow and four of his men rushed forward. They grabbed Zotar and tied his wrists behind his back with leather straps. The remaining warriors converged on the soldiers and disarmed them easily. Talina inwardly smiled since her guard did not seem as loyal to Zotar as he thought.

Krow stepped to Dacton's side and gave him a congratulatory slap on the back. "Well done, my friend." He smiled. "You look like you could use a rest. And a bath."

"Indeed. But first I must secure the palace and alert The Protectorate." Dacton walked to Gartron and his men.

"Gartron." Dacton cleared his throat. "You have become Zotar's first in command. As you can see, he is no longer in control."

Gartron saluted Dacton. "I performed my duties only because I was forced to, fearing for Cortain's life if I did not. But you have my word that I remain loyal to King Cortain."

Talina rushed to Dacton's side and slipped her arm around his waist. "I will vouch for Gartron. You can trust him."

"I trust your judgment, Regia."

"As you should."

Dacton kissed the tip of her nose then turned his attention back to Gartron. "I assume you have holding cells?"

"Yes. Very secure ones."

"Good. Take Zotar and lock him up. Then arrest Regnar and Septra. Use Krow's men to assist you. They'll aid you if any resistance occurs."

Gartron saluted. "It will be as you wish."

"And I want you to destroy all the weapons Zotar gave you."

"It will be a pleasure. We never wanted to use them in the first place."

Dacton nodded and watched Gartron and his men leave the area. He pulled Talina to him and kissed the top of her head. "Krow, take Talina to her father, and place your best men outside the door to guard them."

Talina's fists flew to her hips. "Where are you going? I thought we could..."

"Later Regia. Go now, please. We will talk before I leave."

Talina wanted to argue with him, but he shook his head at her. Without further ado she joined Krow and began the trek through the gates of the outside wall and up the long, winding walkway.

* * * *

Kolere smiled. "It's good to see you in uniform again, my son."

Dacton fastened large gold stars to the shoulder over-straps of his black uniform jacket. "I do feel better. A bath, a shave and clean clothes can do wonders."

"I see the doctor has patched you up nicely."

He almost laughed at the look on Kolere's face. The man was full of questions and wonder, but he held back. "Please, bring me up to date."

"I hope you're not angry. I called the ship and requested intervention, but you already knew that since you have a new official uniform to wear."

"You did the right thing, Kolere. It was time. Zotar could not be allowed to escape, whether or not I was the one to stop him."

"Our men have coordinated their efforts with Krow and the Royal Guard. Zotar, Regnar, and Septra have been placed in holding cells on the lower level. The rest of the council members in question are being held in their quarters until further notice."

"Good. I don't think they will be a problem with the leaders removed." Dacton looked at the elderly priest. "You haven't slept anymore than I have."

"My concern for Cortain, you, and Talina have weighed heavily. I knew I was the one who had to call for help, but I also knew the risks if they arrived too soon."

Dacton smiled. "You did well, Kolere. Your timing was impeccable." He brushed his hair, and checked his appearance one last time.

"I hope you're not too angry with me for insisting you take the woman with the chain." Kolere stared at Dacton.

"No, Holy Man. You can relax. I am long over my irritation. But I am worried about Talina. She will not take the news of my departure easily."

"I would have thought your experiences would have taught you to have faith and patience, but I can see I was wrong."

"Talina and I have fulfilled your legend, and the price has been painfully high."

"Have you truly fulfilled the legend?"

"Yes." The doubt in the old man's eyes tore at his heart. "What?"

"Find your faith and you'll understand what I'm saying."

"It is time for me to meet King Cortain." Dacton opened the front door of Kolere's quarters and gestured for him to lead the way.

While they walked in silence Dacton could not quiet his anxiety. He looked forward to meeting Cortain, but his trepidation was because of Talina. The time had come for him to return to The Protectorate, and the ache in his heart was already more painful than any wound he had suffered on Ora. How could he tell Talina that he loved her, but would never see her again?

By the Gods, he did not want to hurt her. He wanted to love her, protect her, have children with her, yet it could never be. He was a Protector, sworn to duty for ten more annual-cycles. Being Chief Protector was an honor, the highest position a Protector could achieve. A position he could not leave in dishonor.

Why did it have to be so difficult? If he had a normal job he could quit, stay on Ora and fulfill the dreams he and Talina secretly shared. Talina should have listened when he warned her becoming involved with him was dangerous. He never should have allowed this to happen, the fault was all his.

As much as they would both suffer, he prayed Talina would understand. He would never regret loving her, only leaving her. The feel of Talina in his arms would remain embedded in his mind until the sun-cycle he died.

Talina had a responsibility to her father, and her people. He owed his loyalty to The Protectorate. Their love should have never been, yet it was written in the stars. How could fate be so cruel? He enticed Talina to make love to him and she gave him her very soul. Now he had to leave her a branded woman. She would never forgive him for having to face her future alone.

Dacton bowed when Kolere introduced him to Cortain, who sat proudly in the center council seat. "It is an honor to meet you, King Cortain."

Cortain stood. "I have much to thank you for, Chief Protector, Dacton Rovarn."

"I only did my job."

"If you hadn't taken Talina from the palace when you did, she would have been destroyed by Zotar, and life as we know it would have come to an end. You alone have given me back my throne...and my daughter." Cortain smiled first at Dacton then at Talina. He nodded and Talina rose from her seat beside him to stand next to Dacton.

"Talina and Kolere have explained everything to me. I have been in communication with The High Council of The Protectorate, thanks to your Captain Falcon, and have expressed my appreciation for sending you on this mission."

Dacton's eyes widened when he heard Cortain call his little brother Captain! Then out of the corner of his eye he saw the door open and his little brother rushed toward him. They grasped arms, hugged, then slapped each other on the back.

Falcon grinned. "It's good to see you brother, but we will have our time to chat later. Right now you need to speak with Talina before we leave."

Talina took Dacton's hand. "Come warrior, we have much to discuss, and very little time. It has been cleared with my father, and Captain Falcon."

Falcon winked at his brother and nodded.

CHAPTER THIRTY SEVEN

Talina locked the door to her quarters then turned to face Dacton. She felt emotion spark between them, and her body ached to be held. "What are you waiting for warrior? Do you not desire me?"

"By the Gods, Regia." He took her into his arms and cradled her head against his chest. "I love you, I want you, but..."

Talina stilled his lips with her fingers. "Before you say anything more I want you to make love to me. I don't know when we will be together again, and I will not let you leave without one last memory to sustain me."

Dacton took her mouth with a fury, his tongue seeking hers with a passion. Her body shook, barely able to contain the need that burned deep within. She searched his mouth and memorized his clean masculine sent. The feel of his lips on hers and the sweet flavor of his kiss would soon be a memory. She fought tears that burned to escape.

She pulled back and took his cheeks in her palms, careful of his bandage. "You know, this is the first time I have ever seen you in your uniform, and I must say, I have never seen a more handsome man in my life."

"Handsome? With all these scars?" He laughed. "I love you."

Talina ran her hands up and down the front of his jacket. She pushed unanswered questions and thoughts of a sorrowful good-bye out of her mind. This moment was for love. She would savor him, even if this memory was all she could keep.

When Dacton placed his hand on her buttocks and pulled her tightly against him, she felt his swollen need press hard against her. He scooped her into his arms, arms that had carried her many times. His embrace never felt more welcome. He kissed her while he laid her on the softness of the pallet. Her head began to spin from the heady essence that belonged only to her Protector.

Dacton eased his body next to hers and removed the pins that held her hair. A round cylinder rolled into his hand. "Did you plan to use this on me?"

"If I thought it would keep you here." She watched him smile. "It was for Zotar if I'd gotten the chance."

"You have indeed become a warrior woman."

"No, just *my warrior's woman*." Talina hung her head. "I despised what he forced me to do, but I had to save your life and..."

Dacton threaded his fingers through her curls. "I almost died when you were with Zotar. When he put his hands on you, I..."

She touched his lips with hers. "Dacton, please understand..."

"Hush Regia, I do. It's in the past and we shall never discuss it again. I love you." Dacton tilted her chin up with his finger. "Did you hear me, woman? I said I love you."

Before she could open her mouth to answer he smothered her with kisses and pulled her to him so he could slip her gown from her shoulders.

She pushed him back. "This is not fair." She made quick work of his jacket, then removed his shirt and threw it to the floor. Her hands slid up his bare chest and savored his muscled contours. She embedded every curve to memory for the lonely moon-cycles to come.

He stood, kicked off his boots and stared in silence, his breathing rapid. His steel-gray eyes softened in the candlelight. She joined him, her fingers threading through the dark mat of hair on his bronze skin. The feel of him sent tingles to her womanhood that ached to be consumed by him.

She traced his scars and thought how he had fought to save her life. He was invincible, and she loved him, every inch of him. Her hand moved to his belt and she stroked the green stone before finding the buckle in the back.

"You won't be needing this." She let the heavy leather fall to the floor.

"I never needed it to love you, Regia. You create enough magic all on your own."

"But not enough to keep you here."

"My sweet princess, I..."

"Don't make promises you can't keep. I understand duty all too well." She unfastened his pants and let them drop. She smiled when he stood before her dressed only in his virile masculinity.

"It's my turn, Regia."

A shiver ran down her spine when he unfastened the back of her gown and the top fell to her waist. His hands caressed her breasts, then his lips embraced them. His warm breath felt like velvet on her skin. Dear stars, how would she ever live without the man she loved? Until the sun-cycle she died, Dacton would be in her heart and soul.

Her burgundy gown lay in a pool on the floor. He cradled her in his arms and carried her to the pallet. She played with his hair, but she knew it was his heart she held in her hands. He covered her body with his and kissed her deeply.

Every emotion, every thought of what was, and what could be, played from her mind to his. She knew he understood, and she knew his heart ached as badly as hers. He felt her pain, she felt his.

She had found ultimate satisfaction in his love. She kissed him with unleashed passion and treasured the moment. She could not bear to think of this as her last time with him.

He slid inside her and she was desperate for him. No excuses, no legend. Only love. Two flames burned as one, and two souls joined for eternity.

* * * *

Dacton fastened the last button of his jacket and joined Talina on the finely upholstered bench at the foot of her pallet. "Sweet Regia, I wish we had more time."

Talina's watery gaze searched his face.

"I must leave within the time-unit, but first I want to thank you." He stroked her cheek, memorizing the feel of her skin.

"I have done nothing."

Dacton pulled her into his embrace. "No, Regia." He smiled and kissed the tip of her nose. "Your love is so strong, so sustaining, your message so clear. You saved me from myself."

"No my dear Protector, you did that yourself. I only acted as your conscience. But I do have one question. What happened to Zotar's sister?"

"It goes back to our sun-cycles in the academy. Zotar and I had just finished taking final exams and were dismissed for the festive sun-cycles. I was waiting for my brother when I saw Zotar return to the administration building. I followed him to the chancellor's office and caught him tampering with his file. His grades weren't the best and he wanted his commission so badly he stooped to cheating."

"We fought." Dacton laughed. "You could say we redecorated the chancellor's office." He took Talina's hand. "We were both young and foolish. Jana. That was a tragedy. I'll admit I hated Zotar, but I had a soft spot for his sister."

"You were involved with Jana?"

"That wasn't allowed. I saw her as the kid sister I never had. We grew up together." He stroked Talina's silky hair. "Jana's death was premature. We all grieved. I had no idea Zotar blamed me."

"How did she die?"

"Jana was impetuous. She came to the academy to pick up Zotar. When he didn't show up, she panicked. She wasn't a bad pilot, but that moon-cycle her emotions made her crazy and she flew into the side of a mountain."

Dacton shook his head. "If I'd have known the outcome of turning Zotar in, I'd have let him go. It was a senseless accident."

She threw her arms around Dacton's neck. "It wasn't your fault. I can't believe Zotar blamed you. If it was anyone's fault, it was his." She kissed his brow. "It's over now."

"For me. But not for Zotar." Dacton took her cheeks in his hands. "Regia, there is one last thing I must tell you. Please don't hate me."

"How could I hate you. I love you. We're going to spend the rest of our lives together as soon as you return from The Protectorate."

He stood and paced the floor in front of her, wrists clasped behind his back, his heart splitting in two. "I will not be back."

"Of course you will, you..."

Dacton knelt in front of Talina and took her hands in his. "I love you with my very soul, and I always will. But we cannot spend the rest of our lives together. As a Protector I am forbidden to life-mate." He shook his head. "There is no way out."

"Don't go back."

He kissed tears from her cheeks and his heart broke. "I have to. Just as you must stay here for your people, I must return to mine. If I don't they will issue a death warrant. Treason is the highest crime. I would gladly die for you, Regia, if that is your wish."

"That would solve nothing! Oh Dacton, can't you do something?"

"Not for ten annual-cycles." He watched her stand, trying to assimilate his words.

"What do you mean?"

"I'll be released as a Protector in ten annual-cycles, at which time the marriage ban will be lifted, and I'll be free to leave The Protectorate. But I cannot ask you to put your life on hold."

"What kind of law denies two people their fate? Neither you, nor I, can live without our love for that long. We need each other. She grabbed his arm. "Or was everything we shared a lie?"

"No, my love, it was not a lie." Dacton pulled her into his arms and kissed her firmly. His desperation and hers shredded his already broken heart. "By all that is holy, I swear I will come back to you, Regia."

"You will not remember my name in ten annual-cycles!"

"Please Regia, try to understand. I was bound by oaths I took long before finding you."

"This isn't fair. We survived every obstacle on the face of this planet, but cannot overcome one useless rule?"

Dacton took her face in his hands. "Have faith, Regia."

"You sound like Kolere."

He laughed. "So I do, but he is wise."

"I'm beginning to have my doubts."

A knock on the door silenced them both. Dacton left Talina to see who was there. "Little brother."

"Please forgive me. The ship is ready to leave. I'll wait in the hall."

He nodded, closed the door and returned to Talina. "Sweet Regia, I shall miss you more than you know." He pulled her to her feet. "Always remember, I love you more than life itself."

Their lips met for one last time. He tasted her salty tears and felt her body tremble. Dacton summoned every ounce of strength he possessed in order to end the kiss and let her go. While he walked to the door her thoughts flooded his mind, and guilt ripped him apart. He *would* return to her, or die trying.

* * * *

Dacton closed the door behind him and Talina fell to the pallet. Uncontrollable sobs wracked her body. This was the end. She would never see her Protector again. He loved her, and she loved him, but it was all in vain. They both crossed the line when they joined forces to fight Zotar's evil, yet now it seemed as if Zotar had won.

They had both known what they were doing when they fell in love, yet it did not ease the soul-wrenching agony. She wanted to hate him, but to do so would only be to hate herself. They both violated rules they knew carried a heavy price. Life would never be the same, and she mourned the loss. The completeness only Dacton could give would be lost forever to forces beyond their control.

CHAPTER THIRTY EIGHT

O

Dacton paced nervously across the marmoreus stone floor, the sound of his boots echoing against the walls. He had been away from Talina for twelve sun-cycles, and his body ached for her in ways he never knew possible. His mind even seemed weak without the link they shared each time their souls touched.

The High Council had met with him every sun-cycle since his arrival on Bronic, but he had made up his mind that this would be the last time. This meeting would end with his resignation as Chief Protector. It had never been done before, and he was not sure exactly what retribution The High Council would take, but it would be worth whatever price he had to pay to return to his love—his life.

Explaining to his mother had been hard, but she understood and supported his choice. Of course, his mother would do almost anything to have a grandchild. With her two oldest sons being Protectors, she feared she would never live to see babies.

Falcon wished him well, but they both knew he was about to bring shame to himself and his family. A Chief Protector did not just *quit*-it had never been done, and it was not allowed. All he knew was that to become whole, he had to have Talina at his side and in his pallet.

Talina DeAmarant belonged to *him*. She always would. That sun-cycle when he claimed her as his to Krow and his men, he had been serious. Something told him then they were destined to be together. The Council may not understand why their Chief Protector would throw away everything he had ever worked for to return to Talina, but he knew, and that was all that mattered.

The page opened the door. "The High Council will see Chief Protector Dacton Rovarn."

He snapped to attention and marched into the formal chamber to stand before the elders. He bowed his respect and readied himself for his request.

The doyen rose and nodded. "Dacton, we have much to discuss. Now I know you requested time for a personal matter, and we will grant you time when we have concluded our business."

"Thank you." Dacton let go of the breath he had held.

"Please be seated, this could take some time."

Dacton did as requested and tried not to show his impatience. The wait was difficult since every moment away from Talina was an eternity.

The doyen sat in the chair across from Dacton. "We have discussed the intricate problems and solutions facing the people and government of Ora. The Advisor we choose will have to be patient and wise. He must have an understanding of their unique problems. They have more to overcome than most of the planets we accept."

"Very true, but King Cortain and Princess Talina seem anxious to work with our Advisor. They realize their weaknesses, especially after Zotar used them the way he did. However, they are very vulnerable, and it's imperative the right Advisor be appointed."

The doyen nodded. "I couldn't agree more."

Dacton shifted nervously in his chair. The doyen seemed determined to drag this out. He wanted to interrupt him and make his plea, but it would not be advisable to anger the council.

The babblings of the doyen droned on. Dacton's mind was on Ora. He had the distinct feeling Talina needed him. Call it a premonition, but he felt as if they were still mind-linked. Whatever the source, the message was clear. He did not detect any physical danger, but he feared the effects of her mental anguish. She had suffered long enough. They had to be reunited.

The doyen paused. "Yes," Dacton answered, barely aware of the plans he had just agreed to. Only Kolere's words kept him calm. Trust his destiny. He may have started out a skeptic, but he had become a believer. Kolere and the legend said they would spend their lives together, and he must hold on to that thought. By the Gods, he had to get out of here.

"Don't you agree?" the doyen repeated.

"I couldn't agree more." He'd only been half listening, but he'd heard Krow's name. "The Burly people deserve every right accorded to the citizens of Sobrie. And I would like to see Krow receive a commendation from The Protectorate. If it hadn't been for him, I wouldn't be here."

"We are aware of how valuable his assistance was to you and Princess Talina."

"I owe Princess Talina my life as well. She was of invaluable help in completing the mission. She. . ."

"Chief Rovarn, we are more than aware of the help Talina DeAmarant provided."

"I take full responsibilities for my actions."

"As you are aware, some very serious rules were broken on this assignment." The doyen stood and paced behind the council members.

"I have no excuse and will accept whatever punishment the council deems proper."

"We have considered your actions, as well as the instructions Kolere provided."

Dacton stared at the doyen then scanned the faces of the other council members seated along the table. They were extremely accomplished at hiding their feelings which made their facial expressions impossible to read.

Talina, his sweet Regia. She deserved better than to wait for him. Ten annual-cycles was a very long time and he could not fault her if she moved on without him. A woman needed a man beside her, to love her, to give her a family. He knew how important an heir to the throne would be. Damn it to the cosmos! He had to return immediately. His love for her would never die, even if he spent the rest of his life in prison for what he was about to do.

"Chief Rovarn?"

Dacton mentally shook himself. "Yes?"

"Glad to see you're back."

"I'm sorry. It's just that the personal matter I want to discuss with the council weighs heavily on my mind."

"As it should if it's important enough to bring before us." The doyen took his seat. "Now if we can get back to our discussion?"

"Of course. My apologies." Dacton bowed his head as a gesture of respect. What he wanted to do was run from this chamber as fast as he could, and return to Ora where he left his heart.

"As I was saying, we were always aware of the instructions Kolere gave. We knew you would be forced to make decisions against your better judgment."

"I became painfully aware of that from the start." Dacton could have sworn he saw a hint of a smile on the doyen's face. "You ordered me to do exactly as Kolere instructed."

The doyen smiled. "Precisely, and we do not fault you for becoming involved with Princess Talina. Those were your instructions."

He shuddered, the doyen had actually smiled! In fact he acted like he was amused by his relationship with the princess. In all his annual-cycles with the council and doyen, he had never seen a smile on anyone's face until this very moment. "And your point?"

"Ah, I see your patience is still a bit short, but we do understand your motivation. We hear Talina is very lovely."

Dacton stood, fists clenched, every muscle flexed. "Dear council members, if we are through with business matters and down to discussing the appearance of Princess Talina, I must insist the council hear my request immediately."

"Before you speak in haste, Chief Rovarn, hear me out. The reason we called you here this sun-cycle is to discuss the new Ora Advisor. We have labored over the decision since your return, and would like your opinion."

"Absolutely. Who is he?" Dacton held his breath. He was about to hear the name of the man who would work side by side with Talina. How he envied the lucky man. Was he jealous? He smiled to himself, of course he was, and he doubted if he hid it very well.

"The Advisor we have chosen is very experienced. He's sympathetic to Ora's causes. Our only fear is that he has yet to acquire the proper patience required of the position."

Dacton gritted his teeth. Would the doyen ever get to the point? He did not care who the man was! All he could think about was resigning.

"However, the new Advisor adapts well. We think he's well qualified in all other aspects. He's still a bit young for such a responsibility. Most Advisors are over fifty annual-cycles."

"Excuse me," Dacton interrupted, "but..." The doyen held up his hand to silence him.

"All I ask is an invitation to your life-mating ceremony Advisor Rovarn."

Dacton's mouth dropped open, and his heart raced. Had he heard the doyen correctly?

"Don't look so shocked. We're not heartless. We've all been in love once in our lives." The doyen laughed.

"I don't know what to say." Dacton was stunned to the tip of his boots.

"You, speechless? That's a first." The doyen smiled along with the other council members. "Dacton, did you think we would desert you and Princess Talina? We knew when we sent you that yours would be a lifetime assignment. The only proof we needed that you deserved the promotion to Advisor was to return Zotar *alive* for prosecution. And you did that, overcoming great personal sacrifice. For this you are rewarded."

"I don't know what to say except, thank you." Dacton could not suppress his smile that he was sure went from ear to ear. "I will do my best, you have my word."

"And your word is good enough for this council. You know what needs to be done. Now, what was that matter you wanted to discuss with us, *Advisor* Rovarn?"

Dacton stood and respectfully bowed. "I thank you for the time, but the matter I wanted to discuss is of no importance."

"As I suspected. When do you plan to leave for Ora?"

Amused by the teasing quality in the doyen's voice Dacton replied, "Immediately, if it pleases the council."

"It does. However, you must wait two sun-cycles for the proper documents. I have made arrangements for your mother, brother, and any friends you want to accompany you."

"That's very generous, sir."

"We look forward to meeting Talina."

"We?"

"Yes, Dacton. The council and I have no intentions of missing your life-mating." The doyen laughed. "Now go—buy yourself something appropriate for the ceremony!"

Dacton clicked his heels and saluted.

The doyen bowed his head then raised it to look at Dacton. "May The Powers of The Universe be with you Advisor Dacton Rovarn."

"I thank you and every council member for my promotion, and the opportunity to serve Bronic and Ora. He gave a brief bow then turned and all but ran toward the door.

Once he was out of the council chamber and the huge official building he headed straight to the clothiers shop. He would buy Talina the finest life-mating gown on any planet.

CHAPTER THIRTY NINE

O

The mirror reflected dark circles beneath red eyes. Talina threw herself on the pallet. She buried her head in the pillow to hide her sobs, the same as she had every moon-cycle since Dacton left. She would have to stop this destructive behavior, but the pain was too fresh and too real.

Her father had experienced a complete recovery and was busy working on peace and trade agreements with Krow, but nothing could be finalized until the Advisor arrived from Bronic. The Protectorate still had warriors all around the city to insure against further uprisings, but the people were very receptive to the peacekeepers and were adjusting quite well.

Leana had moved to the palace to be with Krow, and she was happy to have her here. Leana was the first woman friend she had ever really had, but she wished Leana would stop insisting that Dacton would come back. He would *never* be back. She had to accept that devastating stroke of fate.

There was no more weather threat since the reactor was destroyed, and the government was functioning even better now than before, thanks to Septra and Regnar's arrest. Yet her life had forever changed.

The thrill of being installed as Legatus had been marred by the emptiness in her soul without the man she loved by her side. Every moment without him drained her strength, and with all the added responsibilities of her position she felt exhausted.

Even the blue of her crystallinus chain had faded, a sure sign Dacton was out of her life. From the moment they made love and ignited the fires of passion, she knew she would never be the same. Forever changed, but no longer two flames burning as one. They had separated, and now emptiness replaced joy.

A knock on the door forced Talina from her private hell. She wiped away tears and opened the door to find Leana's smiling face. Leana rushed inside with a large pink box in her arms.

"I've brought you a gift from our new Advisor who arrived only moments ago."

"Why would the Advisor send me a gift?"

"I don't know, why don't you open it. Hurry, I can't wait to see!"

Leana laid the box across her arms and all she could do was stare at the beautiful wrap with the most beautiful bow she had ever seen. In fact the gold bow almost covered the entire top of the pink box. She placed the beautifully wrapped box on the pallet and ran her fingers over the elaborate bow. "I think I should speak to my father and make the acquaintance of this new Advisor. What did you say his name was?"

"I didn't say, because I don't know." Leana smiled. "Come on, open the box!"

"You seem overly happy, Leana." She studied her friend. "Maybe you should open the gift. I really don't want it."

"Well, you should! It's from..." Leana paused, "from the new Advisor. He's very eager to meet you." She giggled. "If he took the time to buy you a gift, the least you could do is open it."

Talina frowned.

"Come on, the suspense is killing me."

"Later." Talina's hand flew to her mouth and she ran into the private room.

Leana followed her. "How long have you been sick?"

"I'm not sure, but I think I've been retching for the past twelve sun-cycles, Mornings are the worst." Talina straightened. "I hope it's not serious, there is so much to do."

"Oh, I think it's serious, and I fear it will last for a while." Leana smiled as she patted Talina's back.

"I'll be better in a sun-cycle or so," Talina replied.

"More like in eight and a half lunar-cycles or so." Leana laughed at her friend's expression. "I see you're beginning to understand."

"Dear stars! I'm pregnant!" Talina buried her face in her hands and burst into sobs.

Leana put her arms around Talina. "A baby is a gift from the Gods, a gift of great joy. It is also a gift from Dacton."

"Please Leana, I must forget him. He'll never come back, I must learn to face life without him. And his child will never know his father." More tears gushed down her face.

"You don't know that, Talina. Dacton loves you, he'll..."

"Stop trying to give me false hope, Leana. I've faced the reality of my life, which will be without Dacton. You seem to think love can conquer all, but it can't."

"From what Krow told me, you and Dacton share more than mere love. He spoke of magic and sharing."

"Well, it seems Dacton shared a bit too much with me." Talina splashed water on her face. "How will I ever explain this pregnancy to my father?"

"Your father is a very understanding man."

"I know, it's just that I have brought such shame to him...and my people."

Leana handed Talina a towel. "Dry your face and be proud. You are Dacton's woman and he would expect no less."

"You're right." Talina forced a smile. "I'm so glad to have you as a friend, Leana." She gave the sweet woman a big hug, then turned quickly and retched once again. To say she was sick of this would be an understatement.

"Then listen to me. You have to pull yourself together, stop your crying, and start eating. Think about your baby."

"I want his child, more than you could know, but so far he does not like food." Talina laughed while she walked back into the bedchamber, Leana on her heels.

"He you say?"

Talina smiled. "I hate to say *it*."

"Then just say my baby." Leana patted Talina's abdomen. "It's okay to say my baby because that is what *it* is."

"I suppose, but this is very new to me—like just now? So I need time to adjust to this new situation." She looked Leana in the eye. "I believe I am hungry. Come with me to the kitchen?" Talina didn't wait for Leana's answer, she grabbed her hand and pulled her from the room.

When she pulled Leana down the hall they both laughed. "I suddenly have a craving for..."

"Just don't get sick!"

* * * *

Dacton paced nervously across the length of Cortain's office. "Are you sure Talina doesn't suspect I'm here?"

Cortain smiled. "Quite sure. Everything is as you asked."

Galina cleared her throat. "I must apologize for my son, he has never had patience."

Falcon shook his head. "I'll second that. And my brother has been even worse since he fell hopelessly in love."

"Don't tease your brother Falcon, he's liable to start a fight." Galina stood and walked toward Cortain. "Talina has made Dacton a happy man, and I am so anxious to meet her." She picked up a picture from the desk and studied the woman with shiny blond hair. "Your daughter is beautiful."

Cortain smiled. "And so are you, Lady Galina."

Dacton did not know his soon to be father-in-law well, but the twinkle in his eye said he was quite taken with his mother. He was glad. She could use a distraction, and Cortain might provide just what she needed.

"Big brother, what do you say we see to the unloading of those computers?"

"Not right now, Falcon. There's plenty of time."

Galina patted Dacton on the back. "You know you should return to the ship so Talina won't find you here." She moved to stand in front of him. "Unless you want to ruin the surprise, you'd better go with Falcon."

"Women," Dacton grumbled as he left the office with Falcon.

Cortain walked to the bar in the corner of his office. "Your sons look very much alike. Would you care for another glass of wine?"

"They do have a strong resemblance." Galina took the goblet from Cortain. "I'm very proud of them both."

"As you should be, Lady Galina."

Galina smiled at Cortain and blinked several times. "I think the union between our children will be a most productive one."

"I should warn you," Cortain began, taking Galina's hand. "Talina will be angry with Dacton for deceiving her with a surprise life-mating ceremony."

"Speaking as a woman, I understand."

"And a beautiful woman you are." Cortain raised the back of her hand to his lips. "We shall both be proud parents."

Galina took a deep breath. "And grandparents, I hope," Galina replied.

"May I show you the royal gardens? It's a lovely evening."

Galina set her goblet on the table. "I would be delighted."

CHAPTER FORTY

Talina finished the last bite on her plate. "I must see my father now."

"All right, but I wish you'd change your mind." Leana pushed away from the table. "You're just as stubborn as Dac..."

"Please Leana, don't say his name. And don't start with your dreams of his returning. I've accepted my destiny, and it doesn't include *him*."

Talina left Leana in the dining room and stomped down the hall to her father's office. He had been working late every evening, and this moon-cycle would be no different. Apprehension roiled in the pit of her stomach. Leana could be right. This might not be the right time to tell him about the baby, but he had a right to know. The child would be heir to the throne, something he had always wanted. She knocked and entered without waiting.

"Talina," Cortain greeted. "What brings my beautiful daughter at this late time-unit?"

"I heard the Advisor arrived and wondered if you had met him yet?" she blurted before she noticed he had a guest.

"Talina, I would like you to meet Lady Galina. She's ah...part of the Ambassador's entourage."

Talina curtsied. "It's a pleasure to meet you, Lady Galina."

"Talina my dear, you are as lovely as your picture. I have heard so much about you I feel I know you." Galina smiled. "We will have time to get better acquainted later. I sense you have important business with your father, so I'll leave you two alone."

"Lady Galina, I look forward to seeing you tomorrow."

Cortain watched Galina leave the room. "Now little one, what is it that you wanted?"

"I asked if you had met the new Advisor?"

"Indeed I have. He seems like a nice gentleman, someone we can both get along with."

"What is his name?" Talina wanted a full description and life history, but she would settle for a name.

"I think it would be best if you waited for the formal introductions tomorrow at the welcoming banquet."

"Father! I'm Legatus now, I have a right to know."

"And you will. All in good time." Cortain smiled. "Actually, my dear, there will be two celebrations tomorrow. One for the Advisor, and one for your life-mating."

"My what?" Talina's knees nearly buckled. To keep from falling she sat on the couch. "Have you lost your mind?"

"I have recovered completely, my daughter, I no longer babble. I said, your life-mating ceremony will be tomorrow."

"How could you! You have not mentioned a word about my life-mating since my return, nor have I even been introduced to a potential candidate. No! Absolutely not!"

Legatus Talina. You know it's my duty to choose your life-mate, and if I left it up to you, with the mood you've been in, the announcement would never come. It is past time for you to mate. My decision is final."

Talina's heart raced. She had never felt this kind of anger toward her father before, and fought against it. She swallowed hard and tilted her chin high. "I never expected this from you. You always said you would allow me to have a say in the man you picked. Now, without a word, you insist the ceremony take place tomorrow?"

"Please forgive me. I'm only doing what's best for our people. This time of rebuilding is crucial, and you are well past the age to life-mate."

"I love you father, you know that, and you know I will honor my duties as required. But don't expect me to be happy in a loveless relationship." Talina stood and began to pace. There was one important argument she could make to persuade him to change his mind. "This man I am to join with should be told that I am carrying Dacton's child."

A shocked expression crossed her father's face, then he managed a smile. "You shouldn't be so surprised. And I'll make no apologies to you, or anyone else, for carrying the child of the man I love. It's all I have left of Dacton."

Talina walked to the door. "You had better tell this man, whoever he is, so he can change his mind about life- mating with me. I'm sure he's already made all the concessions he was able to in order to mate with a branded woman. I'm quite sure he will not accept a bastard child."

"Trust me Talina. The man I have chosen for you will not change his mind." Cortain walked toward his daughter. "Don't you even want to know his name?"

She scowled at him "No. I really don't care. My heart will never belong to him, but I will do my duty." She turned and walked out of the office and slammed the door behind her.

Cortain sighed then walked to the door of his private room. "You can come out now. She's gone."

Dacton stepped into the room. "How did you know I was here?"

"You left too easily, and I knew you'd sneak in the back way. At least that's what I'd do if I wanted to catch a glimpse of the woman I loved."

"I must be forgetting my Protector's skills more rapidly than I thought."

Cortain laughed. "Love can do that to a man."

"I promise, by all that is holy, I will make Talina forget these past sun-cycles of suffering. Our life together will be magic." Dacton knew very well the kind of magic they could make in each other's arms, and he could hardly wait to rekindle that passion. They had both endured much, but that was all in the past. Nothing would stand in their way. Tomorrow she would be his in every sense of the word.

"I believe you, Dacton. If I didn't I would not be putting her through this agony. By the way, did you overhear our conversation?"

Dacton could not stop the happy feeling that surged through him. "Indeed I did."

"By the look on your face, son, I can see you're pleased."

"Ecstatic! I couldn't ask for a greater gift. My fondest dream is to have a child, but I never thought it possible."

"I just hope this surprise of yours won't be too much for her, especially in her condition."

"Talina is strong." Dacton laughed. "She'll be angry, but she will forgive me."

"You know my daughter well, and angry might be an understatement. It's more like having a semita by the tail."

Dacton groaned. "As I well know. I've heard your semitas."

"Yes," Cortain grinned. "I imagine that moon-cycle you took Talina you would have rather battled a semita than her."

"It couldn't have been any worse." Memories flooded his mind. "I have dealt with her anger before. She is a challenge." Dacton smiled. "But I can hardly wait to see the fire in her eyes." Although seeing her was the least of what he wanted to do.

"Not to change the subject, but your mother...she...ah..."

"She what?" Dacton noted the devilish smile on Cortain's face and the unmistakable red in his cheeks.

"I was wondering about...your father."

Dacton suppressed a smile at Cortain's interest. "My father died five annual-cycles ago." He moved closer. "I saw the way she looked at you."

"And?" the king prodded.

"She could sure use some male company...if you have the time, of course."

Cortain sucked in his stomach and puffed out his chest. "With you and Talina running Ora, I suspect I'll have lots of time on my hands." He slapped Dacton on the back. "Would you mind if I told her about the baby?"

"I think it would be most appropriate, but only if you keep her occupied for the rest of the evening."

"It will be my pleasure." Cortain headed for the door then glanced back at Dacton. "I can see we're going to get along just fine...son."

CHAPTER FORTY ONE

"Leana, I can't, I simply can't!" Talina threw the brush down on the dressing table in front of her.

"You can't fix your hair, or you can't face the ceremony?" Leana smiled. "It's a lovely sun-cycle for a life-mating."

"How can you be so happy? I'm about to become joined to a man I don't even know!"

"You trust your father, don't you?"

"What does it matter? I'm a branded woman, walking up the isle to life-mate a man I don't love, carrying another man's child." Talina burst into tears.

Leana slipped her arm around Talina. "How do you feel about the child?" She moved behind Talina and began to brush her hair. "So you are happy?"

Talina smiled. "Of course I'm happy. This child was conceived in love, a love I will never let die."

"Then hold on to that love. You'll see. Everything will be fine."

"I wish I had your faith." Talina brushed a tear from her cheek. "Fate has not been kind."

"Krow and I will be there for you."

"I know, and I appreciate that more than you know. You and Krow have been so..." Talina began to sob.

"Oh Talina, please, don't cry. It breaks my heart to see you like this, and it's not good for the baby."

"It's just that I care about you both, and you're close to Dacton, and you understand how I feel, and no one else does!" She sobbed even harder. "Leana...what. . what...am I going to do!" Tears flowed like rivers and she no longer cared. There was no point even wiping them away because more would follow.

Leana rubbed Talina's shoulders. "Where is that brave little princess I first met, huh? I remember that first moon-cycle in the cave when..."

"Oh Leana! Don't...please."

"Now stop that. I wasn't trying to remind you of Dacton. But I do want you to find the courage that sustained you then. You're strong, but your faith has become weak." Leana continued to style Talina's hair.

"I know you're right." Talina made a feeble attempt to dry her eyes.

"You're Legatus now. You have an example to set for your people."

"My people...yes..." she muttered.

"I can hardly wait to wear that dress you gave me. It's beautiful. I've never had such a fine gown. How can I ever thank you?"

Talina shook her head. "You already have. I would never have made it through these last sun-cycles had it not been for your support." She smiled at her friend, who was twining pale lavender flowers through the curls and around her crown.

"Now where's your dress and veil?"

She laughed long and hard. "I don't have one!"

"You find that funny?" Leana wove more flowers into Talina's hair. "Did you open that box yet?"

"I guess it's never too late for miracles."

"All done." Leana pushed the last pin into place. "Now go get the Advisor's gift."

Talina walked to the bench at the foot of her pallet and stared at the box. "I guess it's never too late for a miracle."

"I couldn't have said it better myself."

Talina ripped off the ribbon and threw open the lid. She gasped, her fingers slowly tracing the bodice. She blinked several time while the glistening sparkle of crystal stones and polished pearls twinkled brightly. She had never seen such a stunning gown. "Where did a gown like this come from?

"I don't even want to know how much that cost." Leana looked over Talina's shoulder. "It didn't come from here, that's for sure. The style, everything about it is so...so..."

Talina sighed. "You're right, words can't do it justice. I don't understand why the new Advisor would send such an expensive gift to a woman he hasn't even met."

"Like I said, miracles do happen."

Leana could reassure her all she wanted, but no miracle could bring Dacton back. She had a planet to rule, and an heir to the throne growing inside her. At least the child would be born in peace, a peace Dacton secured. "All right Leana, get me dressed."

"Do I detect a change of heart?"

"Let's just call it a change of attitude. If the man can spend a fortune on this dress the least I can do is wear it for him."

* * * *

Dacton turned from the mirror and looked at his friend. "What do you think, Krow?"

"I'm not so sure about that belt with such royal looking clothes, but I approve, and I'm sure Talina will."

"That's all I care about. By the Gods, how I've missed that woman. Once she walks down that isle, I will never let her out of my sight."

Krow roared with laughter. "I will remind you of that when you come knocking at my door after your first fight." He smiled at his nervous friend. "But then, you and Talina are matched like no lovers I have ever seen."

"Indeed we are." Dacton brushed his hair for the fourth time. "Are you sure everything is ready?"

"Yes. Leana is with Talina now, helping her dress, and..."

The door opened and Leana entered, a stern look on her face.

"You look beautiful!" Krow moved to his wife's side and slipped his arm around her. "But a smile would be nice."

"How can I smile when Talina is so miserable? She's trying to resign herself to marry a man she doesn't love, and it isn't going over very well. It was next to impossible to get her to quit crying long enough to fix her hair and make-up. We will all have much to answer for when she finds out everyone knew what was going on except her." Leana looked at Dacton and shook her head. "And it is all your fault."

"It will only be a few more minutes." The time spent apart from Talina had been unbearable, but he had the advantage of knowing. What if she never forgave him? Would she run and leave him standing at the altar alone? No. She had their child to think of, but she could be stubborn and mad enough to...

Leana put her hands on her hips. "Dacton? Did you hear me?"

"From the dazed expression on his face, I would say he hasn't heard a word." Krow looked into the eyes of the woman he loved and smiled. "I'll take care of him. You'd better get back to Talina."

CHAPTER FORTY TWO

O

Talina held Kiko in her arms and stroked his long red fur. She took comfort in his dark eyes, eyes that reminded her of Dacton. Dacton could return tomorrow and it would be too late. She forced back tears that burned to escape.

Music and laughter poured from the temple. All that was left now was to walk down the aisle to meet her obligation. The temple held memories of the warrior, of how he carried her to the cellerage. Her head ached. She prayed this sun-cycle would end, but another would dawn and bring the same loneliness and despair. Instead of excitement about starting a new life, she felt hers had just ended.

Suddenly Kiko's floppy ears perked up and his head cocked to one side, as if he recognized someone. Hope beat in her chest. Why did she still think Dacton would walk through the door and save her from a fate worse than death? Leana entered the waiting room where she sat, and she knew it was false hope. Kiko only recognized Leana.

"Talina, you're going to get fur all over that gorgeous gown. Now put him down. It's time. Everyone's ready." Leana took Kiko from her arms and placed him on the floor, then opened the door and called to Cortain who paced in the hall. "We're ready."

Cortain walked to his daughter's side and took her hand. "I've waited my whole life for this sun-cycle. I pray you'll be happy. Trust me. I love you, and I chose a man that loves you even more." Cortain offered his arm. "I'm so proud of you."

Talina could not respond to her father's generous words. She bowed her head and prayed for the strength to make it through the ceremony. She could reassure her father later, after she came to grips with the situation. There would be plenty of time to spend with him, because she planned to be by her mate's side only when necessary.

As they stood at the end of the aisle, she was thankful for the veil. Thin as it may be, it hid watery eyes, and an expression that most would perceive as anything but happy. The music began, the traditional cue to begin her walk. Talina took a deep, steadying breath, and once Leana was well on her way, she stepped lightly on the flower covered walkway. She lifted her head up and forced one foot after another.

Concentrating on the purple and lavender flowers that adorned the end of each pew, she wondered why, of all the colors of flowers available on Ora, had these been chosen? She glanced at the bouquet in her hands, and except for a few tiny white wisps, her flowers matched the others.

A lone tear slid down her face, the memory of lavender threads of light, and feelings of love consumed her. Why did everything remind her of Dacton? Her gaze moved from the flowers to the two men who stood before the altar. The one wearing deep purple was Krow. Leana had bragged how handsome he looked in the royal color. The man next to him appeared slightly taller, and broader in the shoulders, but he was wearing a white hooded robe that concealed his face.

Willing her feet to move, her eyes remained on the mysterious figure of her unknown groom. This had to be the longest walk of her life. She prayed when Dacton heard the news of her life-mating that he would forgive her. How could he understand when she did not understand it herself. Two people who loved each other should be together, not separated because of duty.

Then, above the music, she heard a faint melodic hum. Her gaze was drawn to her wrist, and she almost stopped dead in her tracks when she saw the slightest tint of blue turn darker. She felt warmth radiate from the links. "Quit dreaming Talina," she mumbled, but with each step the hum grew louder, yet blended so well with the music no one noticed.

Kolere stood before her as she walked up the six steps of the alter to stand beside the man who was to be her life-mate. Her father placed her hand in the stranger's, but her gaze remained fixed on Kolere's smiling face, wondering why he looked so happy.

A searing heat ran up her arm when the man squeezed her hand so tightly she thought it would break. It was not possible to have such a feeling. Dacton was the only man that could elicit such a response in her.

Kolere began with a prayer. She bowed her head and stared at the man's feet. The tips of white boots peered from under the hem of his gold trimmed white cape. Her gaze moved to his knees, then higher to his arm where the cape was pushed back. Her heart stopped, her breathing stilled. The warrior's belt! His arm slipped around her waist, and she immediately knew the touch.

Tears spilled beneath the thin fabric of her veil when her eyes met the steel-gray gaze she knew so well. With a gasp she caught her breath. Her heart raced, and a long overdue smile pressed against her cheeks. If this were a dream, she never wanted to wake. Pent-up emotions spun recklessly through her mind. The loneliness of the past sun-cycles, the agony of lost love, and the feelings of desperation all faded into loving admiration.

Why hadn't anyone told her? She should be angry, and it would serve the warrior right if she were to run and never come back! But her legs would not move, and if Dacton's arm were not around her waist she would fall to the floor. His gaze seared through her, and she knew there was nothing but love in his dark eyes that searched her face.

Kolere conducted the ceremony, but she barely heard a word he said through the mental message of love Dacton continually sent. Her mind picked up one vision after another of being held in his arms and joining time after time. She felt a love so deep and so complete the world stood still, and they were the only two people in the galaxy.

One glance at the amulet that glowed more purple than ever before, and she knew they were joined once again, as they were destined to be. Her heart soared when Dacton's deep voice demanded her attention.

"Talina, my love, my life. To you I pledge all that I am, all that I have. I promise to treasure you, and protect you all the sun-cycles of our lives and beyond. For neither time, nor death, can separate us." He lifted her hand to his lips.

Never had words meant so much. She was speechless. His loving gaze pierced hers and she sensed how anxious he had become. She should keep him in suspense, but it was impossible when she wanted him so badly.

"Dacton, my love, my Protector, my life. I give you the gift of love I will give to no other. My heart and my soul join with yours, never to be separated in this life, or in death, for my love knows no bounds. Eternity is not enough time to share our love." The smile he gave her was the happiest she'd ever seen on his handsome face. How she loved him.

"The rings, please," Kolere said.

Soft murmurings and whispers came from the audience. She and Dacton both turned and started to laugh. Kiko ran up the aisle with a lavender bow tied around his neck and a purple pouch grasped tightly in his little hand. He stumbled up the stairs and rolled to a stop between them, his final resting place on Dacton's boot.

Krow picked up Kiko, who pulled a glistening ring from the pouch and dropped it into Dacton's hand.

Dacton took the gold and crystal band from the furry Atew and slipped it on Talina's finger. "This ring represents the never-ending circle of our love. And I hereby declare you *my woman*."

Kiko squeaked and held out his arm toward Talina. When she reached for him he dropped a larger, matching ring onto her outstretched palm. She silently thanked Kiko, then faced Dacton.

Talina slipped the matching band on Dacton's finger. "This symbol of my love declares you to be *my Protector* for life." When she pulled her hand back, her bracelet brushed against his amulet and shimmering sparks engulfed them both, dancing and spinning, weaving threads of light around them, their minds merging and sharing what words alone could not say.

In a bright flash her veil disappeared and Dacton's hungry lips found hers. They became lost in a world that was theirs alone. His arms held tight, their hearts beat to the rhythm of love, and they felt the separate flames of their souls merge and burn with a single passion.

Dacton scooped Talina into his arms and carried her out of the temple, down the steps, not stopping until they reached an elegant, flower adorned carriage. He placed her on the seat, grabbed the reins, and spurred their two trusty esroths into a fast trot, leaving family and friends waving on the steps.

"Dacton! We can't leave, we have to stay for the traditional celebration and..."

"Sweet Regia." Dacton laughed as he swiftly drove the carriage through the gates of the city and into the countryside. "We're starting a new tradition. I have been without you far too long."

Dacton pulled her tightly against him and kissed her deeply and passionately. She savored his scent, his taste and the love they shared. She pulled back. "You arrogant warrior! You obviously could have been with me sooner, but you had to orchestrate this... this...stupid deception. I should. . ."

"Love me?" Dacton cleared his throat. "I wanted to surprise you, and I can see that it worked." He smiled. "You look so beautiful in the gown I sent. It takes my breath away just to look at you, Regia."

"You? You're the Advisor? I thought you said you had to serve another ten annual-cycles or..."

"Don't question destiny, woman."

He covered her mouth with his, but she pushed him back. This would not be easy, however, it could prove most entertaining. "You lived to be a warrior, and I must say, you're the best I have ever seen. I'm just afraid that you won't be happy if you can't fight and..."

"I know from experience you'll give me all the fights I can handle." He caressed her cheek. "I will have a full time job as your Protector. And from what I've seen, you need one."

Talina smiled. "I don't need a full time Protector, but our child might."

Dacton placed his hand on her stomach and grinned from ear to ear. "And a fine young warrior he shall be."

"A fine young princess, she shall be." She knew he kissed her with all the love in his heart, and she responded with a passion so strong it took her breath away. If he didn't stop now they would make love right here in the carriage.

Dacton ended the kiss. "What's wrong, warrior?" Her lips ached for more.

"Unless you want to break more than tradition and include the laws of indecency, I cannot continue to kiss you."

"Rules have never stopped you before."

"Nor shall they now." Dacton pulled the esroths to a halt and lifted her from the carriage, his fingers busy on the back of her gown. In seconds the silky fabric slipped from her shoulders as he laid her on the grass. "Does this mean you forgive me, Regia?"

"Give me an time-unit or two, then I'll decide."

Dacton needed no further invitation to love the woman of his destiny...his counterpart... his *warrior's link*.

ABOUT THE AUTHOR

Born in Michigan and raised in California, Kathleen is now a twenty-nine year resident of Missouri, living in the beautiful Ozarks. She lives with her husband of forty-nine years and her dog, a Boxer named Ginger. Her son, daughter-in-law, and three fantastic grandchildren live close and keep her life busy.

Writing is Kathleen's passion, which she became serious about when she first moved to Missouri in 1987. Always a fan of sci-fi and romance, she loves combining the two elements into stories of *love and adventure in another time and place*.

OTHER PUBLICATIONS BY KATHLEEN GARNSEY

The Alluring Traveler
Hawk's Redemption

Coming Soon:

Secret of the Kiah